About the author

Emily Madden covets books like some women covet shoes and handbags (although she has a decent collection of each of those too!). While she reads anything and everything, stories that touch the heart and uplift the soul are what she loves the most. Emily lives in Sydney with her two girls and husband. She's a coffee lover and can often be found writing at her local haunts.

Also by Emily Madden

Summers With Juliette
Heart of The Cross

The Lost Pearl

EMILY MADDEN

mira

First Published 2018
Second Australian Paperback Edition 2019
ISBN 9781489290274

THE LOST PEARL
© 2018 by Emily Madden
Australian Copyright 2018
New Zealand Copyright 2018

Published by
Mira
An imprint of Harlequin Enterprises (Australia) Pty Ltd (ABN 47 001 180 918), a subsidiary of HarperCollins Publishers Australia Pty Limited (ABN 36 009 913 517)
Level 13, 201 Elizabeth St
SYDNEY NSW 2000
AUSTRALIA

® and TM (apart from those relating to FSC®) are trademarks of Harlequin Enterprises Limited or its corporate affiliates. Trademarks indicated with ® are registered in Australia, New Zealand and in other countries.

A catalogue record for this book is available from the National Library of Australia
www.librariesaustralia.nla.gov.au

Printed and bound in Australia by McPherson's Printing Group

MIX
Paper from responsible sources
FSC
www.fsc.org
FSC® C001695

To Mum and Dad.
*Thank you for all your love and support. I love you both more
than you realise.*

'No Keia La, No Keia Po, A Mau Loa.'
'From this day, from this night, forever more.'

Hawaiian proverb

One

Hau'oli Momona 'Umi Kumaono

Happy Sweet Sixteen

Honolulu, October 1941

If Charlie Florio could relive one moment over and over again, it would be the instant he laid eyes on Kitty McGarrie. If anyone had told him even five minutes before that his life was about to change for good, that he would never be the same again, he would probably have told them to take a hike.

It was the night of her sixteenth birthday party held in the Persian Ballroom of the prestigious Royal Hawaiian Hotel. He'd only scored an invitation because he was Eddie McGarrie's pal. He and Eddie had become fast friends from the moment they'd met, even though they were from the opposite sides of the tracks. Charlie's family was working class, and perhaps even that was a stretch. Charlie was an enlisted officer, Eddie an Annapolis graduate. Eddie's full name was Edward James McGarrie, son of Rear Admiral Conrad James McGarrie. Everyone knew who Eddie's father was – it wasn't a state secret, but his friend had never flaunted his father's rank. Eddie was just one of the guys.

Stepping inside the ballroom of The Royal Hawaiian was like stepping into a different world. One that Charlie didn't belong in. He should've known that when Eddie roped him in to come to the party it would be a fancy shindig. He agreed without thinking it through and he certainly wouldn't have said yes if he'd known where the party was going to be held. The first he'd heard about where they were going was when they'd been picked up in a limousine, of all things! That should've been his cue to get out of Dodge. Everyone in Pearl, hell, everyone on the whole island knew that only those with serious money to burn could afford to throw a party like this one he'd walked in to. Some might say the event was opulent. Charlie wasn't one of them. In his opinion it was a waste of money, such a crying shame.

Charlie needed to leave. He had nothing in common with anyone in this room. It didn't matter that he hadn't even met Catherine, Eddie's sister. He guessed she wouldn't miss his absence — not when she had a whole ballroom at her beck and call. He hadn't any money on him, but that shouldn't be a worry. It would be easy enough to hitch a ride back to Pearl. Charlie was about to make a hasty exit when he felt a firm hand on his shoulder. 'There you are!' Eddie boomed, and at that moment all hope of leaving, at least for now, was dashed. 'Come on, let me introduce you to the birthday girl.'

Charlie followed Eddie through the throngs of people, with everyone decked out to the nines — women in their fancy dresses, civilian men in their suits, military personnel in their uniforms. At least in his navy digs he didn't stick out like a sore thumb. Eddie was wearing them too, but Charlie knew that's where the similarities ended. He would say hello to the girl, wish her all the best on such a momentous occasion, then the first chance he had, he was out of there.

'Some party,' Charlie muttered more to himself, but it seemed that Eddie heard.

'Nothing but the best for Daddy's little girl,' Eddie said proudly, before turning to a group of guys who were circled around a young woman like bees to honey. 'Hey, Kitty Cat!'

She turned, her eyes and face lighting up the moment she saw Eddie. His friend tended to have that effect on the fairer sex, and whoever this broad was, she was no exception. She was a looker – that was for sure.

'Edward, perhaps now that I'm sixteen you should stop calling me Kitty Cat?' she said with a modicum of seriousness. 'After all, I'm no longer a child.'

The realisation of who was standing in front of them was slowly dawning. This young woman was Eddie's sister, and she was nothing like the girl Charlie had been expecting.

'You'll always be Kitty Cat to me, baby sister.' Eddie reached out to ruffle her hair, but she anticipated her brother's action and expertly snagged his wrist.

'Don't you dare,' she said. 'I didn't spend over an hour at Miss Violett's hair salon this afternoon only for you to ruin my hair five minutes into the night.'

'Over an hour?' Eddie scoffed. 'Seems like a total waste of time, if you ask me.'

'I'd say,' Charlie said, although secretly he did think that her hair was quite lovely. It was the colour of roasted chestnuts and shone like expensive silk under the ballroom lights.

She turned to look at him with eyes the colour of the water that lapped the sandy shores of Waikiki Beach. She arched a perfect dark brow and smiled, bemused. 'Oh, you do, do you? And whom may I ask are you?'

Charlie opened his mouth and closed it again, words somehow escaping him.

'Catherine, this is my pal Charlie Florio. Florio, my little sister and woman of the hour, Catherine.' Eddie made the introduction as Charlie cleared his throat and extended his hand.

'Pleasure to meet you, Miss Catherine.'

She snared his gaze and placed her delicate hand in his. The moment her skin touched his a shot of electricity travelled up his arm. He had never been so captivated by a woman in his life. Correction, she was a girl, barely sixteen, and she was Eddie's sister and a Rear Admiral's daughter. Any one of those reasons was enough to heed caution, but put them together and it was a sure-fire death warrant.

'Oh, Eddie!' A rather buxom blonde in a teal number came bounding towards them and literally wrapped herself around his friend. 'You simply *must* ask me to dance!'

'Sure, want to dance, Penny?' Eddie obliged with an easy smile. The blonde squealed her delight and dragged Eddie towards the dance floor as the band played a Glenn Miller number.

It was only after they'd left that it dawned on Charlie that Catherine's hand was still in his. She must have had the same realisation, because she looked down shyly and a lick of pink tattooed her cheeks. 'I'm ... ah, sorry ...' he fumbled and went to pull his hand away, only for Catherine to stop him.

'Wait,' she said quickly. 'Do you think ...' She bit her bottom lip and Charlie had to use all of his willpower not to dip his head and take that full lip between his teeth.

'Do I think what?' he prompted when she stalled.

She drew a deep breath and exhaled slowly. 'Well, since it's my birthday, I would really like for you to ask me to dance.'

He should say no. He should just politely decline and do what he originally planned to do – leave. But somewhere between those eyes, those lips, that hair and that dress, he lost all common sense. It was only one dance and it was her birthday after all. It would be downright cruel to refuse a girl a dance on her sweet sixteenth. Surely, no harm could come of one single dance?

It was the beginning of the end. Later, Charlie would look back on that day, that moment, and know that if he had to do it all again, there wasn't a single thing he would change.

Kitty's heart beat so loudly it was rivalling the bass drum of the band her father had booked after searching low and high. For weeks she had been dreading this night, but now, she didn't hate it as much as she thought she would. In fact, the arrival of a certain sailor had lifted her mood considerably. She had seen him the moment Eddie had called out to her, she had seen the way his eyes drank her in little by little. It wasn't the first time a guy had looked at her, but it was the first time that she had felt something – a tiny fluttering in her stomach, unlike anything she'd felt before, and it both terrified and excited her.

And now, as he led her towards the dance floor, where her guests (only half of whom she actually knew) were cutting the rug, she hoped her hands weren't shaking visibly. Moreover, she hoped her legs were steady enough that they wouldn't give way as they danced.

Kitty was grateful for the buoyant swing beat of the song and that they were dancing the Lindy Hop and not something slower like a waltz. Somehow, her legs didn't fail her and Charlie was a wonderful dancer. He was tall, which was lucky for her because at just under five seven (and that was without heels) she often found it rather awkward when her partner was the same height or shorter than her. But there were no such worries with Charlie. He seemed to be the perfect partner and every time he put his arm around her waist (albeit too briefly) her heart skipped a beat.

When the dance was over, Kitty stood rooted on the spot, her breathing ragged from exertion, her cheeks flushed. Charlie's eyes clapped onto hers and all of a sudden the air was thick with the promise of a thunderstorm. Somehow the whole world around them stilled and it was just the two of them. The moment felt ... magical. That was the only word to describe it. Charlie took a step towards her, reached for her hand and opened his mouth.

What was he about to say? Would he ask her to dance again? Kitty held her breath in anticipation. She inched closer, not liking the distance between them, and then she waited. Charlie seemed to hesitate, as if the thought weighed on his mind and required more thinking. She rather wished he didn't. Kitty wanted him to ask her to dance again. And again. In fact, she wouldn't care if she didn't dance with another man all night. Kitty had never been a khaki wacky kind of girl, but Charlie could change that.

The band launched into a slow waltz and her heart soared. Surely he would ask her now?

'May I have this dance?'

The words came, but not from Charlie's lips. It took her a moment to realise that they came from someone standing to her right. Stunned, Kitty turned to see a man with a beaming smile awaiting her response. She blinked as if that would make him disappear, but to no avail. It took her a moment to place a name to the face.

'Lieutenant Walter,' she finally said.

His smile widened. 'Yes, may I have this dance?' he repeated, his gaze dipping to her hand still clasped with Charlie's. 'Do you mind?' Within seconds Charlie receded, an unreadable expression flickering across his face.

'Not at all,' Charlie said, nodding to Lieutenant Walter before disappearing into the crowd.

After her dance with the lieutenant finished, Kitty's dance card was full for the rest of the party. Seemed that being a Rear Admiral's daughter and the birthday girl would do that. She encountered her fair share of dead hoofers and as the hours passed, she found herself looking around the ballroom, searching for him again, but there was no sign of Charlie. By the end of the night, Kitty deduced that Charlie was long gone. Her heart sank and she instantly berated herself. She was being foolish. Why did she care if he had left? It didn't matter, did it? It wasn't as if she was likely to see him again. With the rumblings and rumours of the United States entering the war sooner rather than later, her father made mention of sending Kitty and her mother to Australia to stay with her mother's sister, Iris. If he followed through with the plan, they would leave in a couple of months, the day after Christmas.

Kitty didn't want to believe that the US would enter the war. And even if they did, surely there was no reason to banish her to *Australia*? Surely they were the safest in Hawaii. Kitty loved it here on the island. Her family was originally from San Diego, but they had moved to Hawaii five and a half years ago. She never wanted to leave. Not to go to Australia, nor did she want to return to San Diego. As far as she was concerned, Hawaii was home.

'Catherine.'

The sound of her full name had Kitty snapping out of her own thoughts. She turned to see a pair of light blue eyes looking at her and immediately her stomach swarmed with butterflies.

Charlie.

He hadn't left. He stayed.

'You're still here,' she gushed and immediately she felt like a fool. She must've sounded like a stupid schoolgirl.

That's because you are a stupid schoolgirl.

And Charlie was a sailor; Charlie was a *man*.

'I couldn't leave, not just yet anyway.' He smiled and her insides turned somersaults. Her brain must've been following suit because all she could utter was a mumbled, 'Why?'

'Because it's close to midnight and it would be awfully rude of me not to wish you a happy birthday.'

Kitty scanned the ballroom till she found the clock and confirmed that the witching hour was upon them. 'That's ... mighty nice of you, and please, call me Kitty – all my friends do,' she managed to say when she untied her tongue.

Charlie took her hand and lifted it to his lips. The moment the kiss touched her skin, Kitty felt as if her whole body was aflame.

'Happy birthday, Kitty,' he whispered.

Kitty would remember that moment for years and years to come. As the clock chimed twelve and the day heralding her sixteenth birthday came to an end, Kitty McGarrie fell in love.

Two

The Fall

Sydney, November 2016

Sunlight intense and bright flooded the room, piercing her head like a sharp knife. Her skull throbbed and pain consumed her. She squinted, turning away from the offensive glare, but it did little to stop the agony.

'She's waking up,' said a voice from somewhere close by and soon she felt a slight squeeze of her hand.

'Gran, can you hear me?'

She opened her mouth, words lodged in the bottom of her throat.

'Gran?' The voice was familiar and yet, so foreign. Why couldn't she talk? Where was she? With the absence of memory, fear gripped her and her heart pounded loudly. The sound thundered in her ears, intensifying the pain on the right side of her head.

She opened her eyes again, slowly this time, and saw the face that belonged to the voice. The girl's eyes were like her own and confusion compounded.

'Where?' she slurred after frantic, repeated attempts.

'You're in hospital. You had a fall. Do you remember?' The words were spoken slowly, carefully, threaded with concern.

And then, it was all coming back to her. Losing her footing, grasping for the rail, missing, tumbling down the stairs. 'The fall,' she managed with effort. Her tongue felt thick against the roof of her mouth. She blinked, once, twice; the room came into focus slowly as did the realisation that the girl holding her hand, somewhat tightly now, was her granddaughter.

'Kit,' she breathed out.

'I'm right here, Gran. You gave us quite a scare.' Kit's voice soothed her, but the girl's eyes shone slightly and immediately a pang of guilt hit.

'I'm ... sorry.'

Kit's brow creased, marring her youthful face. 'Don't be silly, you have nothing to be sorry about. You had a fall, but you're awake now, you'll be on the road to recovery in no time. Dad's just gone to get the doctor.'

Her granddaughter's words were full of hope. She wanted to tell her not to make a fuss, not to concern herself with an old lady.

'You shouldn't be here.' Her voice was croaky, laden with more emotion than she intended.

'Where else would I be?' Kit laughed.

'You should be out there, looking.'

'For what?' Kit asked, puzzled.

'Love.'

'But I don't understand.'

'Did I ever tell you the story about how I met the love of my life?'

Kit knew the answer to this question. It was a rhetorical one, really.

'How you and Grandpa met? Yes, you've told me many times.'

William Bennett was her late husband. A man she had married and bore four sons to. He was, on the whole, a good man but he wasn't the love of her life.

'No, honey, I'm talking about Charlie.' Her eyes were heavy, closing at their own will. 'I met him the day of my sixteenth birthday.'

Catherine had fallen asleep again. Kit Bennett watched her for a while, trying to ignore the anxiety gnawing at her stomach. Never had she seen her grandmother so frail. She may have been ninety-one but no one called Catherine Bennett 'frail'. She was known for being as sharp as a tack and her dry wit made her seem far younger.

But three days ago something had happened. It had been raining for days and the stairs that led to the back porch were slippery. She must've been heading to put her bin out – that was according to Roy, her next-door neighbour who'd found her by a trail of strewn garbage. Catherine had slipped and fallen head first, hitting her head on the concrete. She'd called out for help and it was by sheer luck that Roy had heard her. The torrential rain had caused a leak in his roof and he was going to the back shed to grab his ladder when he'd heard Catherine.

According to Roy, Catherine was still conscious when the ambulance arrived, even telling the paramedics who were trying to get her on to the stretcher that she didn't need any help. Kit had smiled when Roy recounted this – it was so typical of her grandmother. But by the time they reached the hospital, Catherine had lost consciousness.

The prognosis was grim. Because of Catherine's age, operating on her wasn't an option. Tests showed there was bleeding on the brain, doctors were telling them that it could go either way. If she woke up and continued to make progress, then maybe she would recover. Kit's father had called her just before lunch on the day of the fall and two hours later she was on a plane heading to

Sydney. But then, Catherine had woken up – even if it were only briefly. The doctor had told them that while it had been a good sign, not to get their hopes up. 'Catherine still has a long road ahead, and that's provided the swelling goes down. It might be prudent to think that given her age, a full recovery may not be on the cards.'

His frankness annoyed Kit. She wanted to tell him that he didn't know Catherine Bennett, that it would take more than a little slip on the stairs to keep her grandmother down, but then Kit's gaze fell to the dark purple, almost black bruise that covered the right side of her forehead. It not only blemished her grand-mother's beauty, but it reminded her that even Catherine Bennett wasn't invincible.

Anxiety returned, gnawing again, and Kit stood up and felt the ache in her back from sitting down for far too long. She made her way to the window and pulled aside the curtain, watching as dust particles danced in the sunlight. Outside the world was abuzz with the rigmarole that was Monday morning; cars sat bumper to bumper in peak-hour traffic. The sky was almost cloudless save for a few wisps that only added to its beauty. It was a picture-perfect spring day – almost identical to the one six weeks prior when Kit was last in Sydney for Catherine's birthday. The thought of Catherine's birthday reminded Kit of what her grandmother had said earlier.

'I met Charlie on the day of my sixteenth birthday.'

Who the hell was Charlie?

'Is she asleep, again?' The sound of her father's voice inter-rupted Kit's thoughts. She turned to face him and gave him a half-hearted smile as he stifled a yawn.

'You should go home and get some rest,' she said, while bat-tling a yawn herself. He didn't reply, but his expression told her that she should do the same.

'Mum texted a while back and said that she would be in later this morning.'

Her father nodded and rubbed his stubbled cheek. Kit couldn't remember the last time she'd seen her dad without a clean shave. Even when he was on holidays, he shaved without fail. Her uncles, John, Robert and George, were the same as were her two brothers and numerous male cousins. She used to joke with Jeremy that his scruffy, rolled-out-of-bed appearance would be out of place in the Bennett household. Jeremy. She hadn't thought of him in so long. And there was a reason for that. All thoughts about Jeremy automatically were linked to –

'Kit? Hello?'

'Sorry, Dad.' She shook her head, realising she had slipped into her own world. 'What did you say?'

'I was asking if you wanted coffee? Perhaps something to eat?'

Kit knew she wouldn't be able to stomach food, but the thought of coffee sounded good. 'I'd love one, but let me go and get them.' She grabbed her wallet and made the move to leave. 'I need to stretch my legs, and don't you dare think of giving me money,' she said. 'You can get the next round.' He nodded because they both knew they weren't going anywhere – not for a while.

The smell hit her the moment she left her grandmother's room. The sickly combination of antiseptic and food that was unique to hospitals. It was almost as if someone had bottled it and sprayed it liberally, or worse still was pumping it through the air-conditioning vents. She hated it. It didn't help that for the first time in so long her thoughts had drifted to Jeremy. Perhaps it was all the time she was spending in the hospital. After all, this was the same hospital where she'd spent days covering the news story that made her career, but essentially ended her relationship with Jeremy.

Five years ago, the day before Kit and Jeremy were due to fly to Bali, Kit was part of the news team at the daily paper that covered a scandal revealing cancer patients in major Sydney hospitals had received incorrect chemotherapy doses. Kit had been at the paper a little less than a year, but the story had been her opportunity to make a mark. Her boss at the time had been impressed with her work and offered her the chance to write her first by-line.

The timing wasn't ideal, but this was her career. Offers to write breaking news stories didn't come easily to a young journalist. Jeremy seemed fine with her staying. He even managed to rope his mate, Mick Toohey, to go along in Kit's place. But later, Kit knew her absence, her decision to stay and not go, was the reason why it all ended.

As she stepped out of the elevator, Kit took a moment to compose herself and do the exact same thing she did every time she thought of Jeremy. She stored it in the tiny corner of her mind under the 'Ignore and forget' file. Then she walked over to the hospital cafe and hoped the coffee would be slightly more palatable than it was yesterday.

By the time she arrived back to the room, two things were clear. The coffee was somehow worse today and her grandmother was wide awake and just like that, the crap coffee and even crappier memory no longer mattered.

'Is he gone?' Catherine tentatively opened one eye.

'Who?'

'Your father.'

'Gran.' Kit sighed.

'Is he gone?' she repeated.

'Yes, he's gone.' Upon confirmation that Matthew Bennett, her youngest son, had indeed left the room, Catherine opened her eyes to find Kit looking at her with a narrowed gaze.

'You were pretending to be asleep,' Kit accused, making her feel like a petulant child.

Catherine looked away, pretending to flick a piece of non-existent fluff off the hospital blanket. 'Perhaps.'

'Gran.' Kit sighed again, this time with increased exasperation.

'He was annoying me by asking over and over if I were okay.' She defended her actions.

'You do realise that's because we all love you and want to make sure that you are indeed okay?' This time Catherine met Kit's gaze and guilt hit her with force.

'I know you all do, my dear. But, I just don't like all this fuss being made over me.'

'So you've already said.'

'Have I?' she asked. 'When?'

'When you first woke up.'

'I did?' A frizzle of alarm went through Catherine. She remembered the fall, she even remembered calling out to her neighbour Ray and the arrival of the paramedics, but it seemed that once they loaded her in to the ambulance, her mind went blank. And while Catherine had some recollection of waking up, it was mainly of the splitting headache she had. It was to be expected that she'd have some short-term memory loss, and she was reminded that at her age, she'd had a lucky escape.

Kit tilted her head. 'You don't remember, do you?'

'Of course I do,' Catherine bristled. 'I just momentarily forgot, that's all.'

Kit looked at her intently. 'Then you remember everything else you said?'

Catherine narrowed her eyes. Kit may be her favourite grand-child but right now, she was also the most annoying. Her being a journalist and on the whole naturally inquisitive didn't help either. 'Are you asking me because you're trying to establish if I am of sound mind, Kit? Because I assure you, I am.'

Kit smiled. 'You know, your accent becomes more pronounced when you're upset.'

'I am not upset, just ... frustrated at being cooped up in this silly hospital.'

'This *silly* hospital is helping you get better.'

'Well, I just want to go home.'

'You will. When the doctors say you're ready.'

'I'm ready now.'

'Okay then, tell me what else you said when you woke up earlier.'

Catherine sighed heavily.

'You don't remember.'

'Of course I do,' she said.

'So, you remember telling me that I shouldn't be here?'

'Yes,' she lied, but it sounded like something she would've said. 'And I'm right, you shouldn't. You have your own life, a career that needs more attention than an old woman.'

'You said I should be out there looking for love.'

At this Catherine let out a whoop of laughter, before promptly wincing in pain. Along with splitting her head open, she had cracked two ribs. She quietly let out a curse and noticed Kit raising her eyebrows in surprise. 'Now you're pulling my leg. I would never say that to you.' And that was God's honest truth. She had always encouraged her only granddaughter to focus on her career, especially after all she had gone through with Jeremy. Catherine never shared her feelings about it with Kit, but she believed that Jeremy hadn't been the right one for her granddaughter.

'You did indeed say it.'

'If I did, it must've been the drugs talking.'

Kit shifted closer, dropping the volume of her voice. That action on its own should have been an ominous sign. 'You said something else.'

'I did?'

'Or rather, you asked a question. You asked if you'd ever told me about how you met the love of your life.'

'Oh, you know the story about how your grandpa and I met. I must've told you about a hundred times.'

'You have, and when I told you I knew the story, you said ...' Kit trailed off, her face becoming clouded with concern.

'What?' The frizzle of unease from earlier returned with a vengeance. She didn't like not remembering. She didn't like it one bit. It wasn't that Catherine was a control freak – it was that after watching some of her closest friends succumb to Alzheimer's, it was the last thing she wanted for herself, and for her family to deal with, especially this late in the game. Catherine was ninety-one, she had lived a full life and truth be told, she never thought she would reach eighty, let alone ninety. When your social calendar tended to be filled with funerals, denying the inevitable would be plain stupid. Just last week at Dulcie O'Connor's wake, Maggie Moore predicted that it would prob-ably be one of them to go next. Catherine had almost choked on her scone and told her long-time friend that she was being daft.

'You think you're going to live forever, Kitty?' Maggie asked in a matter-of-fact way. She was also the only person allowed to call her Kitty, ever.

'No. I don't,' Catherine answered honestly. 'I just think taking bets on who will be next is a little morbid.'

'Dulcie and I have been doing it for years.'

'Years?' Catherine was mildly surprised at the admission. 'Years?' she repeated.

'Yes, ever since William's funeral.'

'William? As in my husband William?'

Maggie nodded. 'The one and the same.'

Leaving Catherine to ask, 'Why?'

'Because he was the first person we knew that hadn't died from a long, drawn-out illness. No cancer or dementia, or anything ghastly. It was a heart attack. One minute you're here and the next ...' Maggie clicked her freshly manicured fingers. 'Boom! Gone! It's the best way to go.'

Later, after Maggie's grandson had driven Catherine home, her friend's words settled on her skin, seeping through. Maggie had a point. A quick death was the best way to go. Poor Dulcie struggled for the better part of three years with the disease. Catherine had never been a burden on anyone and she wasn't about to become one now.

'What did I say?' she cautiously asked Kit.

'You said that you weren't talking about Grandpa. You said that you were talking about Charlie.'

Catherine felt the air rush out of her lungs. Speechless, she was speechless. It wasn't the response she'd been expecting.

Charlie. Her Charlie. She hadn't uttered his name in over fifty years. She had made a promise, a vow to keep him a secret. She wouldn't tell anyone who he was. Not even Kit, not even now.

'Gran, who's Charlie?'

Catherine wasn't sure how much time passed before she answered, but she did the only way she could. With the truth ... of sorts.

'He was someone I knew a very long time ago.'

A lifetime ago ...

'When you lived in Hawaii?'

'Yes,' she said tersely, willing her mind not to go back to a place she once loved, a place she called Shangri-La.

'Did ... Charlie die at Pearl –'

'Kit, please,' she implored. Kit knew how Catherine felt about talking about that fateful day. She knew it was a painful part of her life that she never, ever spoke about. 'I'm tired. No more questions.' Catherine closed her eyes, she wasn't lying this time. A sudden wave of fatigue washed over her. As she drifted off, she heard Kit's voice.

'Okay, Gran. No more questions.'

But Catherine barely registered Kit's response. She was already slipping back in time, back to when Charlie was still alive, and as always, any thoughts of Charlie were automatically linked to Pearl. 'My lost pearl ...'

Kit watched as her grandmother fell back into sleep and for the second time that day, she was left wondering.

'My lost pearl ...'

What was her grandmother talking about? As she mulled over Catherine's words, Kit fiddled with the pearl necklace, a gift from her grandmother for her eighteenth, no it was her sixteenth birthday. For each of her significant birthdays – sixteen, eighteen, twenty-one – her grandmother had given her jewellery, pearl jewellery to be specific. Surely her grandmother wasn't referring to that? Still her mind swirled, her thoughts twisting this way and that, bending back in time ...

Kit looked at the beautiful necklace that was far prettier than anything she'd ever seen in her life. 'It's so gorgeous,' she whispered.

'And precious,' Catherine added with misty eyes. 'Keep it safe and close to your heart.'

'Oh, Gran, I will. I promise.'

'I know you will, honey.' She patted Kit's hand. *'I had a beautiful pearl once,'* she added wistfully.

'What happened? Did you lose it?'

'It was taken away,' Gran said with a sad smile.

Catherine mumbled something in her sleep, pulling Kit back to the present. She waited and listened for a while and then it became apparent she was saying the same thing.

'My lost pearl.'

The mystery of what it all meant was eating at Kit. She let the memories consume her once more. This time her mind drifted back to the day of her eighteenth birthday, a bitterly cold July day when the rain had been so bad it had forced Kit and Catherine to abandon their plans for their birthday tradition of lunch – just the two of them. It had always been a special thing to spend her birthday morning with her gran. Each year, Catherine would take her somewhere new and extravagant – high tea at the Queen Victoria Building, lunch at a beachside cafe, or as was the case on her eighteenth birthday, lunch at their local pub so that her grandmother could buy Kit her first legal drink.

Catherine doted on her only granddaughter, a fact that became more apparent as Kit grew older. Her parents were not all that thrilled with it – saying that all the attention would spoil her, despite the fact that out of all her family – her brothers and cousins – Kit was the least demanding. While the boys were always after the newest gadget, video game or latest fad, Kit was forever content with a new book. Her mother admonished that she'd never seen a girl so disinterested in clothes, make-up and boys. Catherine would laugh and say that there was nothing wrong with Kit's interest – that their family was blessed to have a girl in their midst at last. Her grandfather would mumble how Kit's birth took them all by surprise. That it was somehow inconceivable there was a girl amongst the Bennett boys. Apparently they were all convinced she would be a boy because all the others had been boys.

Her grandfather was also someone who had never been pleased with the attention Catherine gave her, especially over the years when she received her pearl gifts. Kit remembered hearing raised voices from the kitchen as she waited for her grandmother on her eighteenth birthday.

'Pearls again, Catherine? I know what you're doing.'

'I have no idea what you're talking about. I bought our granddaughter, our only granddaughter, a pearl bracelet. What is wrong with that?'

'For goodness sake, Catherine, when will you let it go?'

'Let it go? Never. You couldn't possibly understand what it's like.' She could hear the slight wobble in her grandmother's voice, the American accent that was ever so faint slipping in a little more pronounced. A sure sign she was upset. It wasn't often that her grandparents fought and even less often that her grandmother was so upset.

'Oh, I don't know what it's like, do I?' Her grandfather sneered. 'Do you know what it's like to watch your wife pine over a ghost? Waiting year after year for her to get over it.'

'You promised me, William. You promised me you would help me and every time I tried to start, you stopped me.'

'And you promised me you had told me everything, but you didn't, did you?' Her grandfather was really angry now, his voice reaching a level of rage that Kit had never heard before.

'What is that supposed to mean?' Catherine asked, clearly confused.

There was a pause, a long, heavy, drawn-out pause. Kit remembered the pause because the silence was so deafening her ears rang. When her grandfather finally answered, he sounded so sad that despite not knowing what the argument was about, her heart broke for him. 'Never mind.' He sighed heavily. 'I'm going for a walk.'

At the sound of footsteps, Kit slid away from the door and into the living room where the television was on. She heard her grandfather storm

out and a few moments later, out of her peripheral vision, she spied her
grandmother watching her.

To this day, Kit had no idea what the argument was about. Truth was, she had forgotten about it, but Gran's mention of a lost pearl had stirred her curiosity.

Who was the ghost her grandfather had mentioned? Could it be Charlie? And what was his link to the lost pearl?'

'Ah, she's still asleep.'

Kit turned as her father walked back in. He'd gone to move his car from the two-hour parking spot and into the hospital car park.

'Yes, she drifted off about five minutes ago.'

'Five minutes?' Her father frowned and Kit remembered Catherine's ruse.

'I hope you moved the car in time before the parking inspectors came around,' Kit said by way of dodging more questions.

'Just.' Her father wiped his brow.

Kit knew all too well the tenacity of the parking inspectors around the hospital. On their last day of coverage five years ago, she was walking back to her car wondering if she could manage to organise a surprise visit to Bali. Jeremy wasn't due to come home for a few days and she knew that if she worked on her latest piece quickly, she could get it in and be on a plane first thing in the morning. By the time she rounded the street where her car was, she had it all planned. She should've realised the moment she spotted that yellow envelope on her windscreen that it was an omen. She grabbed the infringement notice from underneath the wiper, causing the rubber to grate against the glass like nails against a chalkboard.

Shoving it into her glove box, she drove home, wrote and submitted her piece, and then booked herself on the next flight to Bali. She didn't tell Jeremy she was on her way, and in hindsight that was a bad idea, because what she was greeted with in Bali was her own breaking news story.

Kit shook her head as if she were trying to shake away the memory. Thinking about Jeremy twice in one day. She couldn't recall the last time that had happened.

But something she couldn't shake was the thought of the lost pearl. Every instinct was telling her there were things about the past that were hidden – secrets Catherine didn't want anyone to know. She wouldn't press the issue now, but once her gran was better, she would sit down with her and ask.

Yes, she thought later that night as she slid into her childhood bed, in her parents' house, her feet dangling over the edge of the single-bed mattress. She would let Catherine get better and then ask her about Charlie and the lost pearl again. Whatever it was, she was sure it would not be as big as her overactive mind was making it out to be. For all she knew Charlie was a boy from high school that Catherine had a crush on who probably never knew she existed. And the lost pearl was something she left behind when she fled Hawaii after the attack. Significant losses at the time – but now they were probably not as life altering, as wounding as they had seemed back then. After all, wasn't time meant to heal everything?

Three

Daydream Believer

Honolulu, October 1941

Charlie's lips were soft against hers, just like she imagined they would be. She lifted her hand, pressed it flush against his chest, feeling the thump of his racing heart reverberating against her palm ...

'Kitty ... Kitty ...'

Kitty was daydreaming, or rather, considering it was just on dusk, stargazing might be more appropriate, or as her mother would often say, she was 'off with the pixies'. It was an Australian saying meaning she was in her own little world. It wasn't often that Kitty was reminded that June McGarrie was Australian by birth. Certainly there were no traces of the strange accent, not like her Aunt Iris had. Her aunt had come over and spent six months with them last year, and it had taken Kitty a good few weeks to be able to understand her. Her father had confessed after Iris had left that most of the time he had no idea what she was talking about, it was all gobbledygook to him, which made Kitty wonder for two reasons. First, they had all been speaking English, and secondly, did that mean that when her father had met her mother, he had no idea what she was saying?

'Catherine!'

Her mother's high-pitched voice pulled her out of her reverie. Kitty blinked as June McGarrie's face complete with thin lips pulled into a thin line, so thin that they were literally non-existent, came into focus.

'I'm so sorry.' Kitty shrugged and reached for her glass of water. 'I was –'

'Off with the pixies,' her mother said, with equal parts exasperation and sarcasm. Kitty fought the urge to roll her eyes. 'Yes, you're often in your own little world. Please enlighten us, what was the source of your ... daydreaming this time?'

'My ... um ... math test,' she blurted. Her mother would be clutching at her pearls if she knew the real reason.

'That was today, wasn't it?' Her father, Rear Admiral Conrad McGarrie, peered at her from over his pre-dinner drink. It wasn't often that her father was home for dinner of late, but when he was, he was as interested and attentive as ever. He always knew what was happening in her and Eddie's lives, despite all he had on his plate – which was a large part of the US Navy.

'Yes, it was.'

'How did you go?'

'I got an A.'

'Atta girl.' He winked and Kitty felt a surge of pride.

From across the dinner table, June McGarrie expelled an audible huff. 'A lot of good that will do her when she needs to run a household.'

Kitty's eye roll was noticed by her brother, who suppressed a smirk.

Here we go, thought Kitty. It wasn't uncommon for her mother to voice her opinion that Kitty's schooling was hardly important.

Well, with the exception of housekeeping and dressmaking. Kitty suspected that if it were up to her mother, she would be doing those two classes only.

'Kitty's a bright girl,' her father said, with more than a hint of pride. 'I don't think there is any harm in her being able to run the household finances as well as the actual household.' She knew her father was humouring her mother, while at the same time having a little dig at her. 'Besides, she doesn't need to worry about running a household for a while yet. With her grades, she might even want to go to college.'

Kitty's spirits soared. In her heart of hearts, she always hoped that she could become a teacher. She loved children, loved their raw innocence, and thought nothing could be more rewarding than shaping the minds of tomorrow. Maybe if she worked at keeping her grades up her father would decide that the idea of sending her to college would be more than just a throwaway line.

Eddie snorted and their mother looked like she was about to have an aneurism, or at the very least, blow her top. Poor Pauline, one of their maids, made a hasty retreat after placing the last of the dishes for their evening meal on the table. Kitty's mother could, at best, be described as traditional. In her eyes, a mother's success could be measured by how well she could marry off her daughter. Her father thankfully thought this was rather ridiculous.

'Conrad, please do not fill her mind with such nonsense. Catherine is *not* going to go to college. Everyone knows that women who go to college are likely to never marry. We need to concern ourselves with planning her debut. Of course if we were at home, the Coronado would be the place, but since we are not,' June sighed the most heavy of sighs, before continuing, 'the Royal will have to do.'

Kitty suppressed a groan. Even after more than five years in Hawaii, her mother still could not bring herself to call it home.

For Kitty, nowhere on earth would be home except for Hawaii. If she had it her way, she would never leave. Of course, sooner or later, they would have to as her father's job always dictated a move, but perhaps that wouldn't happen for a long time, well at least not till Kitty had finished high school and was ready for college. But in her heart and mind, she would return to Hawaii and teach, maybe at St Andrew's, where she went to school. It was a girls school, the oldest in Hawaii, established by Queen Emma to provide girls with the same education that was traditionally offered to boys.

'Kitty has just turned sixteen and this is hardly the time to be considering such extravagant frivolity. Especially with war on our doorstep.'

Her father's words had Kitty straightening in her chair, a sick feeling pooling in her stomach.

'You know as well as I do that all this talk of war is nonsense, Conrad.' Her mother huffed. 'It's bound to die down sooner or later. It always does.'

Kitty thought this slightly hypocritical considering her mother was a member of one of the volunteer committee groups that took part in the preparations for the US to go to war and the possible attack on Hawaii.

In the spring of 1940, the Red Cross Honolulu Chapter began organising committees and readying supplies. Kitty was sitting in on tea with Mrs Eleanor Bush, wife of a prominent businessman on the island, when she asked her mother to become a member of a Red Cross committee. Of course, anything Eleanor Bush was part of June McGarrie was ever so keen to join too. Her mother worshipped the ground Eleanor walked on.

Then, over the past summer, Eleanor started the Women's Motor Corps as part of the civilian preparedness activities. June McGarrie, despite being a military wife, had offered her support.

The Motor Corps had several offshoot committees – a general production corps, knitting corps, sewing corps, and the surgical-dressing corps, for which her mother volunteered. Just a week ago her mother was boasting how their stockpiles were coming along nicely. Did her mother truly believe they were doing it all for nothing? Kitty didn't know what to think. The idea of war in Hawaii was inconceivable, but on the other hand ...

Her father furrowed his brows. 'That's just the thing, Junie.' He stared into his whisky tumbler and swirled the amber liquid for a moment before looking up and continuing. 'The talk isn't dying down.' There was a heaviness in his tone that alarmed Kitty.

There had been talk of war before. Everyone knew that America was at peace, but it was an unsteady peace. Kitty flicked a glance at her brother to see if he was concerned with their father's words, but Eddie seemed more concerned with lining his stomach.

'What does Hugh say about all this?' Her mother expertly moved her food around her plate and Kitty didn't miss the look of annoyance that spread across her father's face. Admiral Hugh Ramsey was the Commander-in-Chief, United States Fleet as well as Commander-in-Chief, Pacific Fleet.

Kitty didn't think much of the Admiral – he was just another rotund man with a chrome dome who was too loud and smoked like a chimney. His wife, Lillian, was rail thin and forever sounded as if someone was pinching her nose, had nothing but complaints, and looked down on everything and everyone. Kitty once heard that Lillian Ramsey had seen the posting to Hawaii as an insult. Of course, her mother embraced Lillian and Hugh Ramsey with welcoming grace. She argued that it was simply the Christian thing to do, and she was the first to host a dinner party in their honour. Kitty suspected it had more to do with the fact that the Ramseys had a nineteen-year-old daughter, Margot, who June thought would make a suitable wife for Eddie; a view Kitty was almost certain was not shared by Mrs Ramsey.

'He thinks the Japs don't have the capacity, and it seems that Washington agree.' But it seemed, by the undercurrent that Kitty was detecting, her father didn't share that view.

'Well then ...' her mother raised her eyebrows and trailed off, but Kitty knew the silence spoke volumes. June McGarrie was leaning towards the opinion of Admiral Ramsey and Washington, but undermining her husband's opinion would not be wise.

'It might be best if Kitty and yourself went to stay with Iris in Sydney.'

Kitty froze as her mother dropped her fork in exasperation. 'But, Conrad, it was just announced that the Christmas-tree ship will be arriving on December sixteenth, surely we could wait till after Christmas to make a decision and even then –'

'Enough, June!' her father boomed and Kitty jumped. She had heard the threat before, only this time it held a certain amount of authority – authority that couldn't be questioned. Although Kitty agreed with her mother, a rarity in itself, it was for different reasons. If it were up to June McGarrie, they would be heading home to San Diego by way of San Francisco, but Kitty just didn't want to leave. Full stop.

Silence fell on the table, with the scraping of sterling silver cutlery against fine bone china the only sound. Somewhere outside lightning flashed and Kitty counted.

One Mississippi, two Mississippi, three Mississippi, four –

The crack of thunder followed, signalling that it was at least four miles away and probably over the water. Tropical storms were a way of life on the island, and tonight it seemed that the storm's timing was rather apt – it matched the mood in the McGarrie dining room.

'I have a liberty day coming up and I was thinking of taking Kitty out to Kailua.' Eddie broke the silence with his blasé tone. Her brother had the uncanny ability to swing conversations and moods. Most of the time Kitty was sure it wasn't deliberate – that it was coincidental – but it was always done with impeccable timing.

'What a wonderful treat that would be.' Her mother beamed at Eddie. 'But please, I think we need to call her Catherine now that she's older.'

Her mother's continued attempt to have everyone refer to her as Catherine had her rolling her eyes for the umpteenth time that evening, only this time, her action was caught out by the Rear Admiral, but instead of busting her chops, he winked. Kitty bit down a smile and dropped her gaze. Her mother would snap her cap if she discovered they were in cahoots.

'Yeah, I'm hoping that ...' Eddie blushed and darted his eyes briefly towards Kitty before glancing back to his near empty plate.

Oh boy, here goes ...

Kitty knew exactly what was coming. Her seemingly confident brother was lost for words and there was only one thing, or more importantly one *person* that caused that. Penny Miller. It was no word of a lie that Eddie was carrying a torch for her. She knew it, the Rear Admiral knew it, and by the disapproving thin line that her mother's lips had formed, she knew it too. Her mother didn't disapprove of much when it came to Eddie – her first born rarely could do wrong in June's eyes. But when it came to potential wives for her one and only son, Kitty wasn't sure that anyone would ever be good enough in her mother's opinion, Margot Ramsey aside, that was.

'I was hoping that Kitty would ask if Penny wanted to come along with us.'

And there it was.

Kitty met her brother's eyes and smirked. Edward McGarrie was six foot four, had a mean left hook but he still needed his little sister to come on dates with him.

June McGarrie frowned but it was her father who voiced concern. 'I'm not sure it's wise to be getting sweet on a girl with war on our doorstep.'

'Aww, Dad, it's not like that. Penny's just a swell gal, and I know that Kitty loves spending time with her.'

At the risk of another eye roll, Kitty kept her gaze firmly on the meal in front of her. Cook's mahi mahi was as always wonderful. Oven cooked just the way her father liked it and without bones, just as her mother liked it. Yes, she enjoyed seeing Penny, but why did Eddie have to pretend he was doing it all for her?

'Yes ...' her mother echoed, halting on her words, and Kitty could only guess it was because she too was reluctant for Eddie to be seeing Penny. June McGarrie didn't think the Millers were of the same social standing as they were, and she certainly wasn't impressed with Penny working at the bakery at the Alexander Hotel. But it was the rumours about Annie Miller, Penny's older sister, that bothered her mother the most.

Last fall, Annie was said to have fallen pregnant by an army officer she had been seeing. It turned out the officer was also a married man. As far as Kitty could tell, the pregnancy didn't eventuate past the early stage, which at the time Penny said was the best thing that could've happened. Kitty remembered feeling rather annoyed for two reasons. First, why was Annie copping all the heat? Kitty hadn't come down in the last shower – she knew how babies were made. It took two people to make it happen and while Annie was rather silly to have got into such a predicament, surely the officer in question should've shouldered most of the blame? Secondly, he was the one who was married – cheating on his wife, breaking vows of marriage, and yet, poor Annie was the one branded with the scarlet letter.

Kitty was saddened that even in 1941, it was the woman who copped it all, and she knew it was because of Annie that her mother had qualms about Eddie and Penny spending time alone, and she wasn't the only one. Mr and Mrs Miller would only allow Penny to see Eddie if Kitty was in tow. For months now she'd been playing chaperone as if they were in the nineteenth century. What the parents on both sides failed to understand was that it didn't take long for Eddie and Penny to ditch her and head off alone, leaving Kitty to twiddle her thumbs. She soon learnt that taking a book with her to pass the time was more than a good idea. She had just started re-reading *Gone With The Wind*. Perhaps she should take it with her to Kailua?

Her brother owed her big time. She would need to think long and hard how he could make it up to her. And that's what Kitty did. By the time dinner had ended and Eddie was due to head back to his ship, she had her fix and the best thing about it was – Eddie would have no idea it was self-serving. He was so hell bent on being able to spend the day with his steady that he wouldn't see through her plotting.

'Eddie, hold up!' she called after him as he slipped on his hat.

'What's up?'

'About Kailua ...' She watched as panic flared in her brother's eyes.

'You're not going to leave me in the lurch, are you?'

'No, nothing like that, except, you might want to think about how bored I get on your little dates.'

'They're not –'

'Oh, cut the crap, Eddie, we all know that's exactly what they are. But don't worry – I won't rat you out.' Kitty smiled sweetly and waited a beat for the penny to drop.

Eddie narrowed his gaze. 'How much do you want?'

'Oh, I don't want a dime.' She blinked innocuously.

'Then what *do* you want? I know that look, Kitty Cat.'

'I want someone to talk to. Someone who can carry a conversation and not that bore Jimmy Kerr.'

'Kitty, are you asking me to set you up?'

Kitty forced a chuckled. 'Eddie.' She swatted his arm good-naturedly. 'You know I'm not interested in boys, books have my heart.' And until a few weeks ago that was God's honest truth. 'But I can't take a book with me all the time – Mother saw that I had a book with me when we went to Waimea and asked when did I think I would have time to read when we were supposed to be viewing some of the most majestic waterfalls on the island.'

Kitty watched and waited for the panic to return. It didn't take long. Eddie shifted nervously and swallowed hard. 'I guess it probably wouldn't hurt to ask one of the guys to come along.'

Hook ...

'Now remember, I'm not interested in anyone for anything other than conversation.'

Eddie nodded. 'Yes, you're a book girl, not a khaki crazy girl.'

Line ...

'So make sure whoever you choose fits the bill – in fact, it's probably best you choose someone that is totally unsuitable. Someone that Mother would die if I were to want to date, which, of course would never happen, because I am not interested in boys,' she added hastily.

'Hmm.' Eddie seemed to be considering her request seriously before his face lit up. 'Leave it with me, Kitty Cat. I have just the man that fits the bill.'

Sinker ...

'Thanks, Eddie Bear, I knew I could count on you.' Kitty smiled broadly, crossing her fingers behind her back and hoping her daring plan would come off without a hitch. And she only had to wait a torturous forty-eight hours.

Four

Just Like Vivien Leigh

Charlie looked up in the cloudless October sky like so many he had seen since coming to Honolulu. He found the islands a strange and distant place from his native New York. Before his arrival, the Navy had given all enlisted men a pocket book explaining how different Hawaii was from the mainland, and boy, they weren't wrong.

When he left New York, the snow was knee deep, the air so cold it chilled him to the marrow. February was a bitterly icy beast, the days leading to his departure were inclement with sleet and grey angry skies, as if the sun and its warmth were banished for all of eternity. It had changed on the day he left his childhood home and all he knew. Before then, he hadn't travelled further than Long Island and this fact hadn't hit him until he was sitting aboard the Greyhound bus, his nose pressed against the glass like a ten-year-old boy staring at the cloudless blue sky, a sky that looked somewhat like the one he looked at today, albeit with fifty degrees or so difference in the mercury.

Charlie would never forget the look in his mother's eyes as he packed the last of his measly belongings. He'd been acutely aware of her surveying his every move.

'You're leaving me.' Her tone was even but her gaze said a whole lot more. She was scared and trying to hide it. They were all the family they had – his mother and him. Each other. There was no one else. His mother's family had come over from Italy when she was just a young girl. Even though her memories of the motherland were faint, the Florios from Messina in Sicily made sure, even in a new land with new opportunities, that the family maintained their culture and beliefs. Charlie knew that when his mother married Charles Henry, there were many in the community that thought she was a sell-out. The all-American boy with fair skin and blue eyes and the dark eyed Sicilian girl with olive skin. But it was not only their contrasting looks. They were from very different worlds. He soon enough came to understand that the only reason they married was because his mother had fallen pregnant and Charles had done the 'right thing' by marrying her. Charlie wondered how many times his mother had wished he hadn't.

'Aww, Mamma ...' He gave a heavy sigh. His mother was never one to make a situation all about her. Never. She had raised him on her own, and Charlie could never recall Adina ever complaining. Never once drawing attention to the burden she had to carry.

'I know, I know, you have to go, you need to do this for yourself.' She rang her hands in obvious worry before placing them on her lap. 'But I just can't help but feel that you'll walk out that door ...' Adina nodded towards the front door of their tiny apartment, 'and never come back, just like your papa did.'

Abhorrence filled him, a stab of revulsion at the thought of a man he barely remembered. A comparison to Albert Charles Henry was no compliment. Charlie lived his life strikingly differently from that of his father. Where his father was a liar, Charlie was honest, where his father lacked integrity, Charlie lived life with virtue, and where his father walked out on his family, deserting his pregnant wife and young son – Charlie swore he would never do the same. Never would he desert the woman he loved, never in a million years. If his father's desertion hadn't broken his mother, the loss of her daughter days after childbirth did. He'd been born Charles Florio Henry, but when he was old enough, Charlie dropped his father's surname. He knew that taking on a Sicilian name would only make his life harder, but he didn't care. He'd rather the prejudice and name calling than being known as a Henry for the rest of his life. It was like a noose around his neck and the moment he'd rid himself of it, he'd felt as if a weight had been lifted off his shoulders.

'Mamma, you know that there is only one way I will not return, and that's if ...' He didn't finish, he didn't need to – they both knew the words. The only way Charlie would not be returning was if he were killed. His father was very much still alive, or at least that's what they assumed. Charlie had only seen him once in the last eighteen years – it was on the street outside of St Patrick's on Fifth. It was ironic really, a man who was nowhere near as holy as he purported, walking out of the grand cathedral with his young wife on his arm while holding the hand of a small child.

His father looked at him, his own son, with eyes like his own, and Charlie knew he *knew* who he was. It was Charlie that looked away first – he had to, waves of nausea rode through him and he dashed off into the nearest laneway to blow his lunch. When he recovered, his father was gone. From that day on, every time he looked in the mirror, he made a promise that he would never look at his child the way his father had – with shame and contempt.

'The sun's out,' his mother said. 'I was sure it would rain today.'

Charlie had thought the same. When he hugged her goodbye, he tried not to hold her too tight, tried not to look into her dark eyes for fear she would see right through him. If she saw him wavering, she would clutch onto him and hold him for dear life. Charlie couldn't have it. He needed to do this. He needed to go.

Charlie knew that as an enlisted officer he was going to be at the bottom of the barrel. The pay, at twenty-one dollars a month, wasn't a king's ransom, but it came with three hots and a cot, and it was better than staying in the city. The Great Depression still had a vice grip on America so, for Charlie the Navy was a financial toehold.

'They say that Pearl Harbor means "Waters of Pearl", because of the abundance of pearls there used to be in the water. If I find a pearl, I'll bring one back for you.'

His mother's eyes glistened. 'I don't want any pearl, I just need my boy.'

And then he left. Walking on to the street where, despite the sun, the bitter cold hit him. He pulled at his coat collar, and passed a couple of kids from the brownstone across the road tossing snow in the air then catching snowflakes with their tongues. Their giggling caught his attention, but it was their innocence that kept it.

'Hey, Charlie Florio!' the boy – Leroy – called out, waving his arms.

'Hey, Leroy.'

'Is it true you're heading off to war?' The boy's voice was equal parts awe and terror.

'We're not in the war yet, Leroy.'

No, they weren't. That was February, but now it was October, and the chatter about war was only getting louder.

Charlie had spent two weeks at boot camp before he rode a supply ship across the Pacific, arriving at Ford Island quay Fox 8. Assigned to the USS *West Virginia*, Charlie was awestruck the very first time he walked onto the ship's gangway. So captivated at the grandeur and majesty of the thirty-thousand ton dreadnought that he almost forgot to salute the flag at the stern. Most days he still felt that way, even though his tasks of chipping paint, polishing brass, swabbing and holystoning (an assignment many sailors didn't care for), were labour intensive. He relished in the hard work.

'Hold up, Florio!' A voice from behind brought him back to the present. Charlie was on his way to Chang's, a popular breakfast and diner just off base. He turned to see Eddie McGarrie walking his way, sporting a grin that stretched from ear to ear. Now McGarrie was always a happy go lucky kind of a guy, but when he sought you out first thing in the morning, before he'd made it to the mess for breakfast, before he'd had a chance to have coffee, you could bet your bottom dollar something was up.

'Morning, Lieutenant McGarrie.'

As Eddie drew near, Charlie could see the scowl on his face. 'Now, you know how I feel about you calling me that.'

Charlie shook his head. Edward McGarrie sure was a strange one. 'It's your rank, McGarrie, that's why.'

Charlie was under no illusions that as an enlisted soldier, and one of Italian heritage, his rank was never going to be along the lines of someone like McGarrie who was an Annapolis graduate. Hawaii was unlike anywhere he had been. Life was a helluva lot more liberal than back home. He guessed it was all those palm trees and mai tais, and certainly when he arrived it had the feel that in some ways they were all on an extended vacation. But at the end of the day, they were in the US Navy and the Navy had ranks – ranks that needed to be obeyed and respected. It didn't matter that they were in the Pacific, closer to Japan than New York.

The restaurant was near empty. It was mid-morning and it was not unusual for trade to be on the slow side, which was why Charlie liked going there at that time of day. They took a table towards the back, sitting opposite each other as they did. Dory, Chang's Hawaiian wife, came over to take their order. 'The usual, boys?'

'Yes, ma'am,' they answered in unison.

When Dory shuffled off, McGarrie leaned in and spoke in a conspiratorial whisper. 'Listen, I need a solid.'

Charlie suppressed a sigh. His instincts were right on the money. 'What do you need, McGarrie?' Charlie asked, even though it was a forgone conclusion that whatever his friend was about to ask, he would more than likely do. Eddie was a swell guy. Truth be told, he was a bit of a goofball, but a goofball with a powerful father, and as he'd discovered a few weeks back, a doll of a sister.

'You have liberty day Saturday, right?'

'Yeah, I do. We're still on to head to Wo Fat's in the evening?'

Wo Fat in Chinatown was famous for its chop suey, but it was also on the corner of Maunakea and Hotel. Hotel Street started at the YMCA and ended at River Street and was widely known on the island as 'serviceman's domain' because it was where the military men came to let off steam. Hotel Street and the alleyways that led off it were filled with pool halls, bars and brothels, and on any given night, especially Saturdays, this area of Downtown was a river of sailor whites and army greens.

'You bet your bottom dollar we are. It's going to be some night. Kerr, Roberts and Walter are in too.'

Charlie didn't mind Kerr and Roberts. Like him, they were enlisted. Both guys were easy going, even if Roberts was a bit of a ditz when he had a few too many, but Walter was another kettle of fish. Like McGarrie, Walter was a junior grade lieutenant, but unlike McGarrie, who didn't flaunt his rank and family connections, Walter had no trouble reminding others of who he was and where he came from.

But that wasn't the beef Charlie had with the schmuck. Walter was an angry drunk. Last time they were at The Bungalow, a bar off Hotel Street, he ended up getting into a scrap with some army dudes. McGarrie stepped in to break it up, and somehow Kerr and

Roberts and, inevitably, Charlie got pulled into it too and they were all a hair's breadth away from getting hauled off in a squad car. If it weren't for McGarrie's pull, they would've all spent the night in the pokey.

'It's sure to be a real gas.'

'Yeah, yeah, it always is. Listen, before we head off that night, I'm planning on taking Penny to Kailua Beach for the day.'

'It's a nice spot.' The very first time Charlie saw Kailua Beach, he thought he'd reached heaven. The water was cobalt blue, the white sand so powdery soft between his toes – he'd never seen a place on earth like it.

'I would like you to come too.'

Charlie looked at his friend in surprise. 'Me? You want me to come on your date?'

'Aww, look it's not a date. Why does everyone keep calling it that?'

Charlie didn't know who 'everyone' was, but he did know that whoever it was they were calling it a date because it *was* a date. Eddie was sweet on Penny, only it seemed that he was hell bent on denying it.

Eddie lit a Tailormade and turned his gaze towards the window. 'I need you to come because if you don't, Kitty won't and the only way I'm allowed to see Penny is if Kitty chaperones.'

Charlie felt the air whoosh out of his lungs. 'Kitty asked for *me* to come?'

Charlie had thought about that night many times, that dance, the way Kitty felt in his arms and how he had no business feeling that way. He knew that letting his mind wander back to that night was dangerous. After the party, as he drifted off to sleep, it was the sweet scent of Kitty McGarrie that lulled him and sent him into slumber, but what he dreamt of was nothing short of sweet. His dreams were a cocktail of heady eroticism that was better placed at The Service or New Senator, or any of the many whorehouses in the serviceman's domain.

In his dreams, he'd done more to Kitty McGarrie than hold her gently for the few minutes of a slow dance. In his dreams there was nothing slow or gentle. It was hard and fast. He woke the next morning with a sore head and badly needing the hair of the dog. Charlie concluded that too much drink had led to the dreams and that he'd better lay off the booze for a while. He wasn't sure if he could handle dreams like that. The other thing was to stay away from Kitty McGarrie. That was also a sure-fire way to ward off those kinds of dreams. Now he had to find a way to tell Eddie that he couldn't see his sister. He had to admit, though, he didn't think that Eddie, as nice enough as he was, would take too kindly to anyone, let alone Charlie, seeing his sixteen-year-old sister. She was pretty much still a child – even if the curves she was sporting were all woman.

'She didn't ask for you, not specifically at least. She just made it clear that she was bored with just Penny and me and needed someone to talk to.'

'And why me? Why not Roberts or Kerr or ... Walter.'

Eddie grimaced as he stubbed out his cigarette. 'She told me that I needed to find someone she could speak to, someone with half a brain.'

Charlie nodded. 'That excludes Roberts and Kerr.'

'Yeah, they're a sandwich short of a picnic, those two.' Eddie chuckled. 'And if I'm completely honest, I wouldn't trust Walter not to try and put the moves on Kitty, if you catch my drift.'

Charlie caught his drift and caught it clearly. Walter had a reputation as a bit of a playboy. To him a woman was fair game – and not even the Rear Admiral's daughter would be off limits. There was talk he had a fiancée back on the mainland and if that were true, Charlie wouldn't be the least bit surprised.

'So that leaves me.'

Dory slid their order of bacon and eggs with biscuits and gravy in front of them.

'Coffee won't be a minute, boys,' she called over her shoulder as she walked away.

Eddie grabbed the saltshaker. 'That leaves you.' He placed the salt down and his gaze flickered towards Charlie for only a moment, but it was what he didn't say that had the greatest impact.

McGarrie was asking him to come along not only because he thought he could hold a more intelligent conversation than the other bozos, but he also trusted him because he was sure that Charlie would respect him enough, respect the Rear Admiral enough and Kitty, to not make any moves on her. 'All right.' He nodded sagely before tucking into his own food. 'I'll come along.'

Eddie's face lit up like a kid's at Christmas. 'Atta boy. It'll be a blast of a day. You and Kitty will get along like a house on fire.'

And that was exactly what Charlie was afraid of.

Kitty awoke early on Saturday morning with her stomach full of fluttering butterflies. She threw off her covers and ran to the window, peeling back the curtains to reveal a picture-perfect day. Since suggesting to Eddie that she needed someone to keep her company while she chaperoned, Kitty was not sure if her comments would lead her brother to ask Charlie to come along.

She was clear that it couldn't be Albert Miller or Jimmy Kerr. As much as she loved those goofballs, they both bored her to tears and she knew her brother would rather cut off his right arm than ask Richie Walter. While he thought he was the cat's meow, everyone knew Richie was just a creep. That left only one option – Charlie.

Still, Kitty couldn't be sure that it was a foregone conclusion. She took extra care with her appearance, deciding that her sailor moku two-piece bathers were the go. She changed her dress about ten times before settling on a red and white hibiscus and ukulele print halter-neck dress. The neckline was modest enough not to draw too much attention to the bust, but the cinched midsection accentuated her tiny waist. She opened the make-up box that her mother had given her just before her birthday and took out the rouge and lipstick. Even though Kitty had worn them both before, she had never worn make-up to the beach. She was applying the last coat of her ruby red lipstick when her mother walked into her room.

'You look lovely, Catherine.'

A compliment from her mother was as rare as hen's teeth, so Kitty grasped it with both hands. 'Thank you.'

'Although, I am surprised,' June McGarrie said as she arched her pencil-thin brows. 'You normally don't so much as run a brush through that unruly mane of yours and here you are looking like Vivien Leigh.'

It wasn't the first time Kitty had been likened to the silver-screen star, and even though she thought *Gone With The Wind* was rather entertaining, she didn't care to be compared to a woman who had left her child to marry someone else. Besides, she preferred the book to the movie. But right now, she needed to get her mother off her case.

'You're always telling me I should put more effort into my appearance,' she said. 'And Penny looks glam even at the beach, so I thought I needed to step it up.'

Kitty noticed her mother's frown deepen at the mention of Penny's name. 'I still don't like your brother associating with that girl.'

Kitty felt her hackles rise. 'Penny is really lovely, Momma, and isn't Mrs Miller part of the Women's Motor Corps? I know that Penny did some work for the sewing corps over the summer.'

'Hmmm,' her mother said as she picked what Kitty was sure to be imaginary lint off her dress.

'I best be going, Eddie is picking me up at any moment.' It was a half-truth. While her brother was due to arrive in five minutes, they both knew he would be at least ten minutes late. Kitty often joked with him that he'd be late to his own funeral.

Her mother made a move to leave, throwing one last parting comment. 'Make sure you wipe that lipstick off your teeth. It's positively ghastly.'

Kitty vigorously rubbed her teeth with her finger, removing all traces of red. Once done, she surveyed her reflection and sighed. Who was her mother kidding? She looked nothing like Vivien Leigh, or any other screen star, for that matter. She looked like a little girl playing dress-up. While all her friends had developed curves, Kitty was miles behind. Sure there had been some definition around her hips, but her bust was still lagging. She wasn't in Penny's league, that was for sure. Was that part of the reason her mother distrusted Penny so much? Because she was lucky enough to be buxom? She tilted her face one way, then the other, wondering if she should try to cover up her freckles. Probably wouldn't make a difference. It was shaping up to be a scorcher out and the make-up would melt, making her look like the fool that she was.

Kitty's despair was quickly forgotten as a car horn sounded, heralding her brother's arrival. With her pulse thumping wildly she raced through the house, almost knocking their poor house-keeper, Fumiyo, out cold. She skidded to a halt and opened the front door calmly, and the sight that was waiting for her on the other side made her heart soar.

Five

Kailua Kiss

This is a bad idea. A very bad idea.

Charlie had told himself this many times over the past few days and last night he'd had yet another dream about Kitty, which was the last straw. And this time he couldn't blame the drink. He was stone cold sober. Charlie wasn't a fourteen-year-old boy discovering girls for the first time. One of the first things that Kerr and Miller had told him, by way of initiation, was how there was no shortage of babes to take care of any of his needs, and then they went so far as to take him to Miss Pricilla's where the dames were as cheap as you could want them to be. But the thought of Kitty made him feel like a love-struck teen and he knew that no good could come of it.

That morning, in no mood for the mud and North Dakota rice or dog sandwich and beans that was on offer for breakfast on board, Charlie headed to Chang's. As he downed his breakfast, Dory had commented that he looked like he needed more coffee, and promptly filled his cup and he'd promptly sculled it, and for a while it seemed to take off the edge. The only thing that would've bettered it was if the mug was filled to the brim with whisky, any old whisky. Hell, he would've taken jungle juice right now – he wasn't picky. But it didn't take long for the caffeine to make his brain go slightly haywire and for the blood to start pumping through him a little faster. By the time he met Eddie back on board, Charlie was sure he was going to hurl and when he told him so, Eddie stared at him, cigarette precariously perched on the side of his bottom lip, and told him he had five minutes to do what he needed to do and then they were off.

Charlie didn't hurl. He walked back through the bunks where most of his crewmates were still sleeping and into the bathroom to splash cold water over his face. He looked up to see Walter staring at him from behind, wearing a look that he couldn't quite decipher. 'Heard you are babysitting Kitty McGarrie today.'

Annoyance rankled. 'I wouldn't say it's babysitting. But yeah, Eddie asked me to go along so she had someone to talk to and I'm sure Eddie would've asked you, but ...' Charlie wasn't usually a smart ass, especially with Richie Walter, but in some ways the guy was asking for it.

Walter's jaw set and a vein in the side of his neck popped. 'Like I said, babysitting.'

And then it hit him. The guy was jealous. Did Walter have a thing for Kitty? The more he thought about it, the more it made sense. The way Walter was looking at him now was the exact same way he'd looked at him the night of Kitty's birthday when he cut in to ask Kitty to dance.

'If you'll excuse me, Dick, I best be making tracks,' Charlie said, flashing his foe a broad grin. Poor old Richie was as red as a beetroot. He hated to be called Dick and Charlie knew it. 'I wouldn't want to be late for my babysitting duties now, would I?'

Richie moved lightning fast, rounding a right hook, but Charlie was faster. In a flash the punch flew past Charlie's ear as he sidestepped to the left. If the fist had connected with its intended target, his nose, he would have been a mess, but he was lucky. The same couldn't be said for Richie. The sickening sound of flesh and bones crashing into glass was a sure sign of collateral damage. Richie howled in pain as a few of the guys ran in to see what the commotion was all about.

'I'd punch the mirror too if I woke up to that mug,' Charlie said and snickers and guffaws followed.

'You'll pay, Florio!' Richie gritted his teeth as blood streamed down his hands, dripping onto the floor. Then he looked Charlie dead in the eyes and said, 'We're not from the same lot, you and I. You're just a common Wop, you shouldn't be here.'

Charlie should have felt angry. Walter's jibes were nothing different to what he'd been hearing for years. Tony, Wop, Dago, Spaghetti-bender – various names but the slurs all meant the same. Richie Walter came from a blue-blood family – private schools, Annapolis educated, trust funds and country clubs. Everything, *everything* that Charlie was not. But anger wasn't what ran through Charlie at that moment. It was pity. 'You're right, Walter. We're not the same,' and then with a pointed nod he added, 'but we sure do bleed the same.'

When he walked outside, Eddie was waiting with his brand spanking new Cadillac Series 61. 'What the hell took you so long?'

Charlie slipped into the passenger seat and debated not telling him about what had just gone down, but decided against it. The crew of the USS *West Virginia*, or the 'Wee Vee' as she was fondly called, weren't known as the 'Gossiping Grannies' for nothing. 'I got into a bit of a scrap with Walter.'

Eddie side-glanced him and shot a brow up. 'I'm guessing by your preppy look that you weren't the one left with a black eye.'

Charlie nodded and Eddie let out a low whistle. 'You know he can be a powerful ally but he can also be one hell of an enemy, my friend. What the heck was the fight over anyways?'

Charlie paused before answering. He could be straight with Eddie. Tell him the fight was over his sister and how there were two guys – one filthy rich, one stinking poor (amongst other things) – that seemed to be sweet on her, but he wasn't. Instead he shrugged, pulled out his fags and offered one to Eddie because he knew he wouldn't refuse (Eddie never refused a cigarette). 'He was just being a shmuck.'

Eddie lit his cigarette before offering the light to Charlie. 'Shmuck or not, I'll say it again. The Walters have a lot of pull out there, and in here too. Little Dickie could make life difficult for you if he wanted, so play nice. Hopefully by the time we get to Hotel Street he will be liquored up with a nice hula girl on his lap and he won't want to duke it out for round two.'

Charlie suppressed a groan. Tonight. He'd forgotten about tonight because he'd been so damn wound up about seeing Kitty today. He inhaled deeply and slowly blew the smoke out the open window. 'Yeah, let's hope.' But Charlie knew that with the way Walter was when he was on the drink there was Buckley's chance of that happening. If anything, this morning was just a preview. Suddenly Charlie was unsure about which part of today he was dreading the most. And when they rolled up to the McGarrie house and Kitty walked out looking all sorts of fine, he had his answer.

Kitty tried so hard not to smile like a fool as she stared at the back of Charlie's head. Penny had already caught her daydreaming once, enquiring why she looked like the cat that got the cream. She had managed to dodge her way out of it by fibbing that she had convinced her mother to take her to Violett's to have her hair done next week. She felt bad for doing so, and she was a little surprised Penny had fallen for it. Her friend knew that Kitty was not one to care about her hair being done. Well not before today that was. Kitty suddenly felt the urge to make a standing appointment at Violett's if it meant Charlie would look at her the way he did when they arrived this morning. His eyes seemed like they were about to pop out of his head and while Eddie scowled at her for taking too long to come to the car, Charlie had done the chivalrous thing and opened the door for her and as he did, their eyes locked and a heat that had nothing to do with the weather spread through her.

'I thought we might swing into Kailua Town first for a bite to eat before we head to the beach.' Her brother's voice broke her daydreaming. Penny was the only one who answered, probably because they all knew Penny's response was the only one that Eddie was interested in. She bounced excitedly next to Kitty and giggled as if Eddie had said something that was a total hoot. 'Sounds fantabulous to me.'

Kitty was pretty sure that there was no such thing as fantabulous. Penny was always using made up words. She thought it made her friend sound like a bit of a yuck.

'Can we have some shave ice too?' Penny asked in a cutesy voice that made Kitty want to throw up. But it had its desired effect on her brother. Even from the back seat she could see his grin stretch from ear to ear. 'We sure can, sugar.'

Oh why had she allowed Penny to make her scoot over so she was sitting directly behind Charlie? She would much rather be looking at his handsome profile than her brother's.

Kailua was a far piece from Downtown Honolulu and as they headed by way of Pali Road, up and over the Nau'uanu Pali, Charlie was quiet. It wasn't like Eddie and Penny were giving anyone else a chance to talk, though, with their conversation and not so subtle flirtatious banter. Accepting that it would be the

Eddie and Penny show for a while, Kitty turned her attention to the passing view towards the windward side of the island. She always liked coming this way, loved the panoramic view of the emerald green hills and ridges that were divided by sapphire-blue lakes and streams, and the lush foliage, all against the backdrop of white-crested waves dancing across the majestic Pacific.

'Oh, we're near the lookout!' Penny gushed and Kitty knew what would happen next. They would stop. Sure enough, Eddie slowed the car, angling it off to the side of the road. 'Are we stopping?' Penny asked, in genuine surprise. Kitty wanted to laugh, but bit back her chuckle and followed Penny, who was already out of the car and heading to the vantage point. The strong winds from the pass whipped her hair across her face and blew at her skirt. Kitty's hands went straight down to tame her wayward skirt, but when she looked up and caught Charlie glancing at her a few paces ahead, her legs turned to jelly. He quickly diverted his gaze and hurried to join Penny and Eddie. By the time Kitty reached them, Charlie was standing next to Eddie, leaving her no choice but to stand on the other side of Penny. Before them was a breathtaking view of Kane'ohe, Kailua and Mokoli'i. Kitty must've seen it close to a hundred times and it still made her heart swell and today, it was making her a little light headed too. Although Kitty wasn't sure if that was because they were over a thousand feet above sea level, or if it was the presence of a certain heart-stoppingly handsome sailor. She suspected it was probably the latter.

Kitty tuned in to hear her brother telling Penny that *Pali* meant 'cliff' in Hawaiian. Kitty was sure that Penny, who'd been living in Hawaii longer than both Eddie and Kitty, already knew this, but she *oohed* and *ahhed* enthusiastically. 'I love learning new things about this wonderful island.'

'This site has deep historical significance.'

Eddie and Penny stopped their chattering and turned their attention to Charlie. Kitty's attention was already square on him.

'The battle of Nau'uanu was won by King Kamehameha and resulted in him being able to unite the whole of Oahu.'

'Well someone's been doing some extracurricular reading,' Eddie said, ribbing Charlie.

Unperturbed, Charlie serenely stared straight ahead and continued. 'The battle was fierce and claimed many soldiers; some of them were forced off the cliff.'

'Oh, golly!' Penny gasped as if she were imagining it happening here and now.

'And when was this battle supposed to have taken place?' Eddie was a swell guy but Kitty knew that when it came to Penny, he needed to come up trumps each and every time. She decided it would be highly likely that Charlie would know the answer, but she couldn't help herself.

'1795,' she blurted at lightning speed. Out of the corner of her eye, she could feel Charlie's gaze on her and she felt her cheeks flame and then cool against the roaring winds. 'And it wasn't a *supposed* battle, Eddie, but a real one, with real soldiers.'

'She's right,' Penny said and Eddie visibly stiffened. 'It was in 1795.'

Eddie relaxed and exhaled. Her poor brother. There was no doubt that for a moment he thought Penny was going to rib him about not taking it seriously.

'Come on, I'm about to waste away standing here.' Eddie held out his arm for Penny to slip into, which she did automatically. 'What do you say we get that lunch?'

Kitty glanced expectantly at Charlie, hoping he would do the same or at least walk with her, but he virtually ignored her and walked ahead. Disappointment washed over her. Had she upset him by stealing his thunder? She hadn't thought he was the type of guy to get offended easily. Maybe she was wrong. She told herself that she was reading too much into it. That by the time they reached Kailua, things would get better. They didn't.

They drove down the main drag lined with coconut trees. In the blink of an eye you could miss the town of Kailua, Kitty thought. On the left side of the road stood a movie theatre, smaller than the one on Kalakaua Avenue. A small Flying A gas station was perched on the right next to the Bishop Bank and Hughes Drug Store. The Kailua Tavern stood on the corner of Oneawa and Kuulei. Despite their mother deeming the establishment to be scurrilous, Eddie and Kitty would gladly drive there from Honolulu and often did. Kitty loved the tavern and saw a rather genteel side to it – after all, there was a restaurant and dance floor.

When her brother took a turn at the big banyan tree and bypassed the tavern, Kitty was rather surprised. Instead, he turned the corner onto a small, paved two-lane road, slowing down as they approached a tiny restaurant.

'This place does the best chop suey outside of China,' Eddie declared. Kitty didn't want to burst her brother's bubble by setting him straight. Chop suey was an American-Chinese invention and she doubted that it would be considered a national dish in China. Besides, she'd heard Eddie claim the same about a certain establishment in Downtown Honolulu.

The day was warm and as they walked to the hole in the wall restaurant, Kitty took a deep breath. Surely she could find a way to have a conversation with Charlie. After all, wasn't he here to keep her company? So far, besides the history lesson at Pali, his presence was ... well practically non-existent, and it continued to be that way throughout lunch.

Eddie and Penny were totally oblivious to anyone and anything but themselves. It was like Charlie wasn't even there.

Disappointment filled the pit of her stomach, and annoyance too. She may have only met Charlie once before, but in the short time they'd spent together she thought they had shared a certain something. Her girlfriends had often commented that when they developed feelings for someone, their tummy felt like it was full of butterflies taking flight. Kitty had had that exact feeling the moment Charlie had slid his arm around the small of her back on the night of her birthday. Afterwards, that same feeling returned every time he had come into her thoughts, which was often. Charlie had made an otherwise dreaded night a wonderful memory and when he found her, before the stroke of midnight, just to wish her a happy birthday, she thought she was about to die and go to heaven. He made her heart stop that night, and as she snuck a glance at him today, she could easily say he still could.

But the Charlie of that night was nowhere to be seen. What was different now? Surely in a more casual and private atmosphere, he would be more relaxed. The glumness of his face screamed boredom, so why was he here? The more Kitty mulled it over in her mind, the more her hackles rose.

When they'd finished their meals, Penny declared that she no longer wanted shave ice but a Boston cream bun from Jean's Bakery back on Oneawa. Kitty protested, saying the day was much too hot and shave ice would go down like a treat. Penny pouted and Eddie looked at her with puppy-dog eyes. 'I could go a cream pie, and the ones from Jean's Bakery are rather swell.'

Kitty couldn't help but huff. Of course Eddie would side with Penny. Charlie was her only hope. If she could get him to side with her, then it would be a tie and since shave ice was their original plan, it would be the go. 'What do you think, Charlie?' Kitty directed the question straight to him and he looked up at her, somewhat surprised she was speaking to him.

'What do I think of what?'

'Boston cream bun or shave ice? The plan *was* to go shave ice, but Penny here now wants a cream bun from Jean's *way* back on Oneawa.'

Charlie gave a non-committal shrug before mumbling, 'It really don't bother me.'

A small ounce of victory surged through her. She was about to declare that if Charlie wasn't worried either way, they should go shave ice, but before she could speak, Penny pounced.

'Have you ever had a cream pie, Charlie?'

'No, I can't say I have.'

'Well then, it's settled.' Penny clasped her hands victoriously. 'We *must* go to Jean's. Charlie needs to try her to die for pie!'

'Penny's right,' Eddie said. 'Jean's Boston creams are something else.'

'Sure, why not?' Charlie said, lacking enthusiasm.

Kitty looked at him, her mouth agape. She was still sitting when everyone was heading back to the automobile. 'Come on, Kitty, we haven't got all day,' Penny said to her as if she were a child. Kitty bit down her fury. Her friend was lucky they were in a public place otherwise she could find herself in harm's way.

By the time they got to Jean's, Kitty had settled down some and as they walked into the bakery and the smell that could only be described as heavenly hit her, she had to admit that a cream bun would go down nicely. Besides, she was sure that if she mentioned shave ice on the way home, Penny would jump at the chance and Eddie would gladly oblige.

Penny and Kitty took their buns and slid into a booth. Kitty deliberately made Penny sit by the window, knowing that when the guys arrived, Eddie would slide in first, leaving Charlie no choice but to sit directly across from her. Next to them was a bunch of sailors and Eddie and Charlie stopped to chat. When she saw Charlie laugh easily with them and overheard how he thought

Kailua looked like a 'neat little town', and how he 'couldn't wait to go swimming at the beach', she felt her brows arch in surprise.

'Could've fooled me,' she mumbled.

'What did you say?' Penny asked between mouthfuls of pie.

'I said, only a fool wouldn't like Jean's.'

'Hmm,' Penny muttered.

Kitty strained her ears to hear the goings on at the other table. Her mother often told her that it wasn't ladylike to listen in on other people's conversation, but this was the same woman who actively listened in to the talk at other tables around her whenever she went to lunch, to get a 'handle on what's going on'. Kitty heard one of the officers asking Eddie and Charlie to join them at the Kailua Tavern that night. Even heard him offer to find them female company if they wanted it. At this Kitty choked on her mouthful of pie.

'Thanks for the offer, but we need to get these lovely ladies back to Honolulu by sunset.' This was from Eddie.

'What? Will they turn into pumpkins if you don't?' one of the sailors asked and elicited a rumble of laughter all round.

'Nah, it's more that we have plans to hit the Hotel Street with some buddies tonight,' Charlie said.

'Hotel Street, huh? I hear them girls have some moves there.' Cue more raucous laughter from all around, including, to her dismay, Charlie.

'They sure do.'

'Eddie!' Penny called.

'Duty calls, gentlemen, she doesn't like being left alone,' Eddie said by way of apology. Except, Penny wasn't alone. Kitty was sitting right next to her.

Eddie and Charlie took their seats while talking about the increased naval presence in the area since the opening of the Kaneohe Bay Naval Field earlier that year.

'No way,' Penny wiggled her finger at them both. 'No more shop talk.'

'Sorry, Penny.' Eddie looked sheepishly at her while Charlie just had eyes for his Boston cream.

'So, Charlie.' Kitty smiled and took charge. She had just witnessed Charlie be sociable, jovial and basically all the things she thought he would be. She knew he was capable of stringing a sentence or two together, so if he wasn't going to make conversation with her, she was going to make it with *him*. 'I'm guessing since you've never had Jean's Boston cream pie, you've not been to Kailua before.'

'No, I can't say I have, Catherine.'

'When did you arrive on the island?'

'February.'

'I'm sure the heat would've been a bit of a surprise. I'm detecting an East Coast accent, am I right?'

'Yes, Miss Catherine, I'm from New York. As for the heat, I can tell you sunshine and sand trumps snow and sleet any day.'

So polite. But at least they were talking.

'It would be cooling down in New York right about now, wouldn't it? I bet fall in New York would be a beautiful sight.' Kitty looked up to find Charlie gazing at her intently.

'Indeed it is, Catherine, but I've seen plenty of beauty right here on Oahu.'

Kitty felt her face flame. She held his gaze, relishing the moment until her bothersome brother ruined it all.

'Like those dolls at The Bungalow.' He ribbed Charlie. 'I sure hope Leilani is on tonight,' Eddie said and guffawed.

Next to her, she could feel Penny fuming. With a not so subtle kick under the table, Eddie promptly stopped his carrying on.

'For Charlie, not for me!' Eddie clarified to placate Penny, but it deflated Kitty. Charlie went back to his pie, eating it slowly and methodically. Kitty sighed. So much for taking charge.

Once the group had finished, they headed to Kailua Beach where even for October the sun's heat packed a punch. Kitty remembered when she first arrived in Hawaii how she marvelled that there were only two seasons – summer and winter. Her mother tolerated it, just, saying the humidity in the height of summer rivalled that in Sydney, and apparently that was saying something.

'My parents' beach house is not far from here.' Eddie nodded southward as they reached the coral white sand. 'Just a way down from the Kalama Beach Club.'

The Kalama Beach Club was a small, private club in Pine Grove, along Kailua Beach. It was a haven for well-to-do families getting away from Honolulu for the weekend. Her mother had insisted that if they were to become members, they needed to have a humble abode nearby. What was the point of spending the day at the beach if, in the evening, all they were going to do was drive back across to the other side of the island. That was her mother's theory at least, although Kitty didn't mind the drive. Her mother claimed she got carsick on long journeys (Kitty wasn't entirely convinced of this though), so her father caved in and bought a modest beach cottage that her mother spent close to twelve months having remodelled and refurbished. Alas, now it was modest no more. It was nearing completion, her mother was sure they would be able to have full use of it within the next month or so.

Kitty knew her mother was unhappy with the naval housing assigned to them at Ford Island. She had fumed when her father told her he'd been offered a home in a well-to-do neighbourhood terraced into hills just outside of Pearl Harbor but said he'd prefer to be close to his command centre. June McGarrie made it clear she thought Ford Island was isolated, but Kitty loved their house. She loved it being so close to the USS *Arizona* because when movies were projected on her deck, Kitty could sit in the front yard and watch them.

'I would love to see the house sometime,' Penny gushed and Eddie flashed her a grin that read 'Anytime, sugar'.

Walking ahead of the pack, Kitty decided it was obvious that Charlie had absolutely no interest in her and she just needed to be a big girl and not dwell on it.

Did Charlie already have a girlfriend? The thought made her green with envy. Or perhaps he simply just didn't want a girlfriend. Had he only been nice to her that night at The Royal Hawaiian because it was her birthday? Maybe there had been more to Eddie's ribbing than she would've liked. Perhaps Charlie liked hula girls, or God forbid, did he prefer the girls who worked in the brothels of Hotel Street?

Whatever the reason, it would be a shame to spend the afternoon sulking, especially when she was in her own little Shangri-La. Before her, the ocean sparkled like a field of diamonds against the many different shades of blue. Azure near the shallow, deep indigo, almost sapphire in the deeper water near the Mokes.

'Come on, Kitty!' Penny called from behind her. 'Race you to the water.' In a flash Penny was undressing to her swimming trunks and heading in. Kitty followed suit and they swam in the cool waters of Kailua for what seemed like forever. The boys had found a shady spot next to some coconut palms. Kitty tried not to let her gaze drift back ashore but she swore that each time she did, Charlie was looking right at her. She was obviously imagining it though – he was probably looking at the vast and beautiful ocean, not her.

'I think I spotted a turtle, I'm going to get closer for a look,' Penny said, swimming further out, but Kitty was happy to stay where she was. Turning onto her back, she closed her eyes and felt the sun kiss her cheeks.

Now this is heavenly, my beautiful Shangri-La.

Her peace was broken by nearby splashing. With a start she opened her eyes to find Eddie and Charlie swimming past her.

'Do you mind?' she said, annoyed by the interruption. 'There is more than enough water without you two invading my space.'

Eddie either didn't hear or chose to ignore her, but Charlie stopped swimming and, treading water, gave her a rueful smile. 'Sorry, Catherine, you are absolutely right. Please forgive me.'

He was truly infuriating her. One minute he was smiling at her, the next ignoring her. Kitty had had enough. She didn't say a word but swam away from him and headed back to the spot where they had left their things. The coolness of the trade winds hit her skin, causing her body to break into goose bumps. She dried off and decided to stretch out in the sun to warm up. She needed to be careful not to stay out too long though, or she would burn. She had her mother's Irish skin, which was sometimes more a curse than a blessing, but years of living in paradise had trained her skin to have a hint of colour. Not like Charlie's skin; he looked like he could spend all day in the sun and appear positively sun-kissed by the end of it.

Kitty scowled. She really needed to stop thinking about Charlie. How she wished she had brought a book with her. At least then she would've had an interesting way to pass the time and she wouldn't be –

'A penny for your thoughts.'

For the second time in a matter of moments, Kitty opened her eyes to a smiling Charlie. Her silly tummy promptly filled with a swarm of butterflies.

'They're not interesting,' she said rather indignantly, her cheeks flaming from the half-truth. Kitty wasn't about to let Charlie know her thoughts had been about him. 'I was thinking that … oh, never mind,' she sighed, not having the energy to conjure up a believable lie.

Charlie didn't push her to finish. Instead he rolled his towel out next to her and they sat in silence for a while, watching two people who were clearly in love frolic in the water.

'According to Eddie, they are not an item.'

Kitty scoffed. 'It's been like that for months between those two. I don't know why they pretend they are not an item because they most clearly are.'

'Maybe it's not that simple. Maybe he's being cautious.'

'What, Eddie? Cautious?' Kitty laughed as if that were the funniest thing in the world. Her brother could be described as many things but cautious most certainly wasn't one of them.

'I wasn't talking about Eddie.' Charlie caught her eyes and Kitty swore she felt her heart come to a screeching halt.

'Who ... what ...' She stumbled, tripping over her words.

Charlie slowly smiled. The sun glistened against his damp skin and as he reached for her hand Kitty thought she might die from the anticipation of touching him. 'I was talking about me, Catherine,' he said softly, his hand cool against her own but it only flamed the fire that was spreading within. 'I have feelings for you.'

Kitty felt her heart somersault. 'What sort of feelings?'

Charlie's laugh rumbled through her as he tucked a loose strand of hair behind her ear. 'The sort of feelings I have no business in having, Catherine McGarrie. You make me feel all sorts of things that dollars to doughnuts would not be appropriate to discuss around a girl like you.'

'I am not a girl, and perhaps I would like to know what exactly these feelings are?' she said and it only made him smile again.

'You should go home and pretend you never met me, Catherine. You need a man that can treat you right, not some ...' He shook his head and sighed. 'You need someone that is worthy of you.'

Kitty felt her face flame. While her heart rejoiced that Charlie had feelings for her, she was also annoyed. Annoyed that he was taking it upon himself to tell her what she needed and deserved. All her life she'd had someone – her mother, her father, Eddie – telling her what she needed, what she should do, all because she was young. Well damn it, Kitty wasn't about to add Charlie to the list too.

'I don't want to go home and forget about you, Charlie!' She realised that she sounded like an insolent child, but she didn't care. 'I have feelings for you too and I may ... I may even love you,' Kitty blurted out. She wasn't sure where the words came from, but once they were out there, she wasn't sorry she had said them.

'We've only just met, Catherine. You couldn't possibly ...'

'Don't tell me how I feel, Charlie,' she said.

Charlie cupped her cheek, his face only inches from hers, his breathing laboured. 'No good can come out of this, Catherine. I'm no good for you.'

'How about you let me be the judge of that and for goodness sake, call me Kitty, and if you don't kiss me this very second I think I might just die.'

She didn't think he would do it. She thought for sure he would pull away, but soft lips captured hers in a heady mix of salt and sand. Her body tingled from the electricity passing between them. When he pulled away, Kitty almost protested. Charlie opened his mouth to say something, but the moment was broken with Penny and Eddie running up to them.

Kitty had what she wanted and she hoped the day would never end. Her very first kiss, her Kailua kiss, but most of all, Charlie had feelings for her and till the day she died she didn't think there would be a single moment that could top the feeling she had when Charlie first kissed her. It was like heaven on earth. Shangri-La.

Six

Ghosts and Pearls

Sydney, 2016

Catherine was going home in the morning. Thank goodness. She had been counting the days till she could get out of the dreaded hospital bed and she only had to endure one more sleep. The excitement made her slightly giddy and a little hyper active, or perhaps it was the second piece of cake that she had Kit sneak in for her when no one else was watching. The sugar rush was causing havoc with her sleep now.

The only downside to leaving was that she was going home to a not so empty house. Bev, her daughter-in-law, was staying with her for a while. Catherine would never say it to anyone, but she relished living alone. After William's death, she thought that going home to an empty house would be lonely. Her family had asked if she wanted to sell the house and find something smaller, perhaps a townhouse or villa closer to one of them, or even a retirement village. Catherine couldn't think of anything more suffocating than a retirement village and as much as she loved her family, she loved that she was close enough, yet not too close in terms of distance. The first night after William's funeral, she had woken up with a strange feeling. Yes, she was sad – she and William had been married for the better part of sixty years and before that, she had always lived with someone – her parents, and then when she first came to Australia there was her Aunt Iris, and of course her mother. But it occurred to Catherine that it had taken her more than eighty years to be living alone and the surprising thing was, she wasn't lonely. Well, at first she was. After all, she had loved her husband, even if he wasn't her first love. That honour had gone to Charlie.

Oh, Charlie!

Even thinking about him after all these years made her heart ache. Her mind drifted to the conversation with Kit about Charlie. At the time, shocked that in her confused state she had mentioned him, Catherine had cut Kit off, but now she wondered if perhaps it might be a good idea to tell her granddaughter all about Charlie. Of course she wouldn't reveal *everything*, but enough to sate Kit's curious mind, and then Kit would know that Catherine had also lost her first love, not quite in the same way though. She would swear Kit to absolute secrecy first. Oh, the thought of her sons knowing about Charlie! She couldn't bear to think how they would react. They thought they knew everything there was to know about their mother.

Yes, tomorrow when Kit took her home, she would send her annoying daughter-in-law on an errand and tell her granddaughter the tale she had promised to tell. How she met and fell in love with Charlie Florio. Catherine felt a smile form on her lips. It was about time the secret was revealed. She had carried Charlie in her heart for too long without anyone else knowing. And she wasn't getting any younger – her little spill was proof of that.

With her decision made, Catherine felt at ease. She was relaxed, enough so that she thought she might be able to fall asleep. Her heavy lids slowly closed like curtains falling at the end of a performance. A small part of her realised what was happening; she didn't fight the feeling – she let her eyes close on life, knowing that once they opened again, she would see her love, she would see her Charlie after all these years. She had so much to tell him.

On the day that Catherine was due to be released from hospital, Kit slept in. Her dad was heading to the hospital early and her mum was preparing for Catherine's return home – shopping and cleaning her house before her arrival. Kit's father had insisted her gran was to stay with them till she was up on her feet again. In fact, he had subtly hinted that it might be a good idea for Catherine to move in with them permanently. Her gran, of course, responded to these suggestions in true Catherine style.

'Over my dead body,' she had admonished and her youngest son's face blanched.

Kit felt for her dad, but he did have it coming to him. He should've known that relying on him would be the last thing Catherine would agree to. It was bad enough, in her gran's opinion, that her daughter-in-law was going to spend a few days 'babysitting' her and that they had hired a nurse to keep an eye on her progress.

Catherine had fought them on that one, but in the end, with the doctor's persistent urging, she relented, agreeing to the whole set up to be reviewed after a few days. Kit already knew that her parents had hired the nurse for at least a month, but no one dared disclose this fact to Catherine. Kit certainly wasn't about to spill the beans because she agreed with her parents – the more care and monitoring her gran had, the better her chance of a quick recovery.

Catherine was one of the strongest people she knew. Kit was certain that it was her gran who'd got her through the whole Jeremy matter. There was something about the way Catherine had gathered her and guided her through the ordeal. It was as if her gran knew the excruciating pain she was dealing with. Her mother tried to help her, even her closest girlfriends, but she felt that no one other than her gran could truly understand her agony.

After showering, Kit dressed and went downstairs in search of food. The kitchen was oddly untidy. Her mother was normally fastidious in cleaning up the chaos that was breakfast in the Bennett household. When they all lived at home, her brothers were like bottomless pits from the moment they woke till when they went to bed – and even then it wasn't unusual for them to sneak downstairs at night and raid the fridge, leaving a trail of destruction. Her mother would often lose it in the morning – telling them that if they were going to make a mess, they ought to clean it up. It never worked. Both boys would merely shrug and say the last thing they wanted to do in the middle of the night was clean up. Her mother would sigh and spend the morning running after everyone before making sure the kitchen was pristine before they all left for the day. Kit looked around the kitchen and took it as a sign that perhaps after almost a decade of an empty nest, her mother was relaxing.

After making some breakfast – toast with butter and vegemite and a strong coffee – Kit took out her laptop and trawled through her emails. She had been avoiding work for the better part of a week and while she hadn't any immediate deadlines, there were a few requests from some of her regular contacts. She replied to each of them, letting them know she was back on board and would be home in a few days. Kit loved the freedom that came with freelancing.

On more than one occasion her mother had argued that because Kit was a freelancer who could work from anywhere, it would be easy for her to move back to Sydney. Her mother was technically correct – Kit could work out of any pocket of the globe, but she had moved to Melbourne not long after the Jeremy ordeal and quickly landed a job at *The Age*. After a couple of boom years, she was made redundant and found herself in a bit of a conundrum. She could move back to Sydney where she was offered a role, slightly more senior than her previous one, at a local community paper, or she could try her hand at freelancing. At the time, Kit wasn't sure which one was the scarier option. The first required her to move back in with her parents because unlike Melbourne, Sydney's house prices were ridiculous, but the second screamed uncertainty. In the end it had been Catherine who had given her the nudge to go for the latter option. Catherine reminded her that life, even when carefully organised and planned, was always unpredictable. 'You thought your life with Jeremy would take a certain path, a path that was dead straight with no bumps or surprises, but life had other ideas. Life can change in an instant, Kit, and of all people, you know that more than others.'

Her grandmother was right. She and Jeremy had been high-school sweethearts; together from the moment Jeremy had asked her to dance at the Year Ten formal. She had been crushing on him all year and when he finally noticed her he told her that she was the classiest chick in the room. Kit remembered laughing like the schoolgirl she was and asked what made him think that. She remembered how he gently ran his thumb over her earlobe and told her that while the rest of the girls were wearing cheap cubic zirconia or diamanté earrings, she was wearing pearls. Real pearls. 'You're the real thing, Kit, you know that?'

That was it – she was hooked. That night she allowed Jeremy to kiss her, her very first kiss, and the first person she told was not

Cherie Taylor, her best friend at the time, nor was it her mother. It was her gran, who smiled serenely as Kit retold the tale. 'Those pearls seem to be your good-luck charm,' Catherine had said.

Absently, Kit's hands moved to the very same pearl earrings and a wave of sadness consumed her. She had been thinking about Jeremy a lot lately. Maybe it was a sign. Maybe she should visit him while she was still here. As the thought entered her mind, Kit shuddered. Bad idea. The last time she had done so she had been a wreck. She couldn't put herself through that experience again. To take her mind off it for the moment she focused on booking a flight back to Melbourne for the coming Friday night. It would give her a few days to see that her gran was settled and doing well and just enough time to reassure her it was a good thing all these people were making a fuss over her and helping her to get better.

With breakfast done, Kit downed the last of the coffee and made another cup, knowing that she couldn't get a decent one at the hospital. Then she stacked the dishwasher as she consumed her second caffeine hit.

She was halfway to the hospital when she realised her phone was still on the bedside table where she left it to charge last night. Deciding she couldn't be bothered backtracking, she drove on. She knew where everyone was and her gran was expecting her anyway. It was planned. She would meet her father and help him with Gran. But like Catherine had said before – life, even when well planned, could change in an instant.

After driving around the hospital car park and discovering it was completely full, Kit eventually found a park miles away in one of the back streets. At least it was a two-hour spot. She checked her watch and estimated it would take her a good fifteen minutes to walk to the hospital, so she should allow plenty of time to get back to the car later. It would be close to discharge time for Gran by then. She could maybe leave earlier and meet her mum at her grandmother's. Kit made a note to call her mum from her father's phone when she reached the room.

After fetching her gran and dad a coffee each, she headed towards the lifts only to see massive queues. Two out of the four were out of order so she waited impatiently till she reached the front of the line and squeezed into the elevator with about twenty other people, like sardines. The lady next to her decided it was the perfect time to rummage in her bag for something and bumped into her, sloshing the coffees to-and-fro. By the time she stepped out on her gran's floor, Kit not only had coffee all over her hand but her shirt too. Annoyed, she headed down the corridor to the last room. The door was closed, which wasn't alarming, but once she nudged it open, what she found inside certainly was.

'Uncle John, what a surprise.' Her eldest uncle had come the day of Gran's fall but needed to leave soon after. Her Uncle Robert was in New Guinea at the time, but he'd flown home to see his mother and he was here now, with his wife Karen.

'What are you all doing here?' she asked, but no one answered. They were all just standing around Gran's bed looking solemnly at Kitty. And that's when it hit her.

Gran's bed is empty.

Panic flared.

'What's going on?'

'Honey, we tried calling you ...' Her mother stepped to her side, grim and red eyed, and the panic turned to dread.

'No ...' It was barely a whisper, but her own voice screamed as loud as a freight train in her ears.

'It happened at some point last night.' Her father flanked her on the other side, gently rubbing her arm.

It was a rhetorical question, in her heart of hearts Kit knew the answer, but she was in denial – it could not be true, and yet, she asked it anyway. 'What happened? Tell me what happened.' Her father's eyes were brimming with grief. He took his time answering and every second that passed Kit felt her heart beating faster and faster.

'Gran had an aneurism last night. I'm sorry, Kit ... she's gone.'

Kit's hands gave way and the next sound to be heard was two very ordinary coffees hitting the linoleum hospital floor.

On a sunny spring morning, Kit walked between her brothers into St Patrick's church. She wasn't sure how she had managed to get through the past few days. Mostly it had been a blur. The shock of it all – of Catherine being fine one moment, hours from being discharged to ... gone ... it had been inconceivable.

According to the doctor, as unfortunate as it was, it wasn't uncommon for these things to happen, especially in geriatric patients. Kit hated how he had lumped Catherine in with everyone else – she wasn't your average 'old' person. She was witty, she was interested in the world, and she was sharp as a tack.

Was.

Thinking about her gran in the past tense saddened her. They took their seats in the second-row pew behind her parents and uncles and aunts, and Kit got a flash of déjà vu. The last time she was at St Patrick's was for her Grandpa William's funeral. Only difference was that back then, she'd sat next to Gran, squeezing her hand as she sat stoically.

'They were married here, you know,' she murmured to no one in particular.

'Who?' asked her eldest brother Cameron, who was sitting to her right.

'Grandpa and Grandma.'

'Ha. What do you know,' he said almost philosophically, 'they were wed here and they both got their send off from this world from the same place as well. True soulmates, right?'

'Yes,' Kit answered automatically, but the talk of soulmates made her think of Charlie. Maybe she should have pushed her grandmother a little harder to find out more. All she knew was that Charlie was someone Catherine had known when she lived in Hawaii before the war. A man she met at her sixteenth birthday.

But how did she know him? What happened to Charlie?

Maybe Kit was thinking way too much about it, but she wouldn't be giving it so much thought if Gran hadn't said that Charlie was the love of her life, a love that she had obviously lost. Losing love was something that Kit knew all about.

'She's here,' Ben, her other brother, whispered in her ear and the sound of the congregation standing broke her reverie. Cameron and Ben each grabbed Kit's hand in support as Catherine's coffin was carried to the front of the church.

She listened to the minister wax lyrically about the wonderful life of Catherine Grace Bennett, starting from her early days in San Diego, California, as the young daughter of Rear Admiral Conrad James McGarrie, to her formative years in Hawaii. The minister continued, saying how after the attack on Pearl Harbor, Catherine and her mother came to live with her Aunt Iris in Sydney, where she went on to complete her schooling and enrol in teachers' college. The plan had always been to return to the US after the War, but in early 1945 at a dance, Catherine met a young doctor by the name of William Bennett. William and Catherine married in September 1945, four months after the war ended, and so Catherine McGarrie became Catherine Bennett and in the same month, she became an Australian citizen and she never returned to America.

Kit knew all this. Catherine often said the reason why she never returned to the US was because she met and fell in love with Kit's grandpa. Her father, the Rear Admiral, even came to Australia for the wedding and apparently was over the moon for the young couple. But Kit now wondered why Catherine and William had never made the trip to see her family in San Diego. It was easy to forget Catherine's American heritage because she never spoke about her parents and the trace of an accent was barely there. Kit remembered how she once needed to do a family tree and she asked her father for information about her great-grandparents – all the usual details, names, dates of birth, death, place of birth, that sort of thing – and she was puzzled when her dad struggled to recall Conrad and June McGarrie's names. He had no problem with Grandpa William's side of the family, but Catherine's was another matter. When she mentioned she would just ask Gran, her father frowned and warned against doing so, muttering something about how she didn't like talking about her parents or really any time of her life before she came to Australia. Up till now, Kit had never given it another thought, she just presumed it was all to do with going through the horrible attack, but she had to wonder – why?

She tuned in to the minister's eulogy just as he was wrapping up. 'Catherine was adored by her family, she is survived by her four sons, nine grandsons and a granddaughter, Kit.'

Her gran's long-time friend Maggie Moore was up next, and Kit's heart went out to her as she watched the older woman take the podium and exhale deeply. 'I first met Catherine, Kitty as she was known then, in 1943, so out of everyone here today, I have ... had known Catherine the longest amount of time ...' Maggie's voice was threaded with emotion and Kit felt a lump form in her throat. She had shed buckets of tears already, since the moment she realised Gran was gone. Her head still hurt from it all – the dull ache that could not be erased no matter how much pain medication she pumped herself with. Nothing gave her any relief.

'One of the things I loved most about my friend is she never beat around the bush,' Maggie said when she'd regained her composure, 'often telling it like it was. Catherine was like an open book, what you saw was what you got with Catherine, no secrets.'

No secrets.

Maggie's words echoed in Kit's mind. Here was a woman who out of everyone here today had known her gran the longest, that was true, but did Maggie know anything about Charlie? Kit wondered if she should talk to her to see if she knew anything. She immediately dismissed the idea. It was pointless chasing ghosts. Whoever Charlie was, he was probably long gone and she would never find out who he had been. No – she knew who he was. He was Catherine's love of her life, but as for what happened between Catherine and Charlie, that was a secret that her gran was about to carry to her grave.

Seven

The Letter

The day after the funeral, Kit told her parents over breakfast that she planned to head back to Melbourne.

'So soon?' Her mother frowned.

'I don't see the point in staying, Mum, and the house is kind of getting a little crowded.'

As much as she loved her family, her brothers were both sticking around for a few days and the five of them being under the same roof again was doing her head in. Kit had lived on her own for a number of years and had come to enjoy her solitary lifestyle. Right now, her grief was being crowded by chaos. Ben had flown in from Singapore the night before the funeral, saying he couldn't come all that way for less than forty-eight hours, and Cam had driven on his own from Canberra; his wife Julia and their clan had stayed home. Julia had apparently thought that the kids were too young to attend the funeral and Cam and Julia both agreed that it would be best for them to remember their great-gran, or GG as they called her, as they last saw her.

'At least stay for the reading of your gran's will,' her father suggested as he placed a mug of English Breakfast tea in front of her.

Kit wrapped her hands around the steaming mug and blew on it before taking a sip. 'I don't think I can. I've ignored my work long enough. I really need to get back to it.'

'I still don't see why you couldn't just stay here and work,' her mother said.

Kit sighed and pinched the bridge of her nose. She didn't sleep well last night – actually she hadn't slept well since Gran's fall – and the constant fatigue was starting to wear her down. She needed to get back to Melbourne, back to her own apartment, her own life.

'I mean, you can't keep running away –'

Kit's head whipped up at the same moment that her father delivered a terse warning to his wife. 'That's enough, Bev.'

Her mother exhaled and sipped her tea in silence, and Kit took a moment to process her mother's words.

Running away. Is that what her mother really thought she was doing by going back to Melbourne? Kit was about to defend herself, tell her that she was wrong, when Ben came bounding into the kitchen. 'Morning, all.'

Despite his sunny disposition, Ben looked like he could've done with another few hours' sleep. 'What's happening?' he asked as he made himself a coffee.

'I was telling Mum and Dad that I need to be getting home.'

'Why so soon?' Ben sat down next to her and swiped the half-eaten croissant on her plate. She turned and gave him a pointed glare.

'For starters, I've been here almost two weeks already, since Gran had the fall and secondly ...' Kit paused as Ben licked his forefinger and thumb of the remnants of the pastry. 'It's getting a little crowded around here.'

'You should stick around,' Ben said. 'I'm probably going to be here a while.'

'How much longer?' their mother asked eagerly.

'Well ...' Ben smiled slyly. 'I wasn't going to say anything yet, but Vanessa and I are moving back to Sydney.'

'Oh, Benny!' Her mother squeezed his hand. 'That's great news.'

It was. It was even better news that Ben's return home would take the heat off Kit. She knew that Ben's long-time girlfriend, Vanessa, had been thinking about returning home – they were both teachers at an international school.

'I'm gathering that you both got jobs in Sydney then?' Kit asked.

'Yep,' Ben said. 'Ness is going to be at Queenwood next year and I'm at Newington.'

'Wow.' Kit was impressed. Both were considered to be excellent private schools. For one of them to get a job in any decent school in Sydney would be a mean feat but both of them could only be considered a coup.

'But they are so far away from each other,' their mother pointed out. 'Where will you live?'

Ben shrugged. 'Not sure yet, that's why I'm going to stay a little longer and scope out some possibilities. It might work out better if we're on the Lower North Shore. We'll just have to wait and see.'

'I think the Lower North Shore sounds like a smart plan.' Bev had perked up considerably and Kit could almost predict what her mother was about to say next. 'Now all you have to do is set a date for the wedding and give me some more grand babies – lord knows, Cameron doesn't bring his children home enough. Every time I see them they've grown so much!'

'Hey, are you complaining about me?' Cam appeared out of nowhere looking fresh as a daisy. Kit took after their gran; Ben was all Matthew, their father; and Bev liked to claim that Cam took after her side of the family, the Scotts. Gran always disputed this, and on the couple of rare occasions when her grandmother spoke of her family, she said that Cameron was the spitting image of her brother Eddie.

'Never.' Bev Bennett grabbed her first-born son's hand and gave it a squeeze. 'Ben and Vanessa are moving back home and –'

'Ah, let me guess,' Cam said as he scraped back his chair and sat on the other side of Kit. 'You want them to get married and have babies because I don't bring my rug rats to see you enough.'

Kit smiled into her tea and next to her Ben chuckled while Bev squirmed in her seat. 'Well, it is the natural progression, after all. They've been together for years now, what's the point of being engaged if you never marry?'

Technically her mother was right and wrong. Ben and Ness had been together a long time. If Kit's memory served her right, they'd started dating not long after she and Jeremy had. She painfully remembered how they'd gone on a double date at one point. It all felt like another lifetime. But Bev was wrong about their engagement. Ben had joked at her engagement that perhaps they should do a double wedding and Ness had baulked at the idea, not because she didn't want to share the limelight with Kit, she simply never wanted to get married. Her mother almost choked on her champagne but Ben just gave his trademark shrug and said, 'Fair enough, as long as you know you're stuck with me forever, though.' And that was it.

'Mum, you *know* we're never getting married. We meant it the first time we said it at Kit and Jer–' Ben stopped short of finishing his sentence and the table fell silent. Kit knew what he was about to say – they all knew. She hated that it was so painful even after all these years. It was why she needed to leave, why she needed to get back to Melbourne. Here there were constant reminders about the life she'd lost. In Melbourne no one knew about Jeremy.

'So where are you going to be teaching?' Cam broke the awkwardness. His timing was always impeccable. At six foot four he was forever sticking out like a sore thumb but he also had the uncanny ability to make you laugh and to keep the conversation going. If there ever was a party, Cam was the life of it; if there was ever tension in the air that needed to be broken, Cam was the man to do it.

Ben filled Cam in on his plans and Cam nodded attentively, giving Ben advice on some good suburbs to check out real estate wise. Their mother stood up and made Cam a coffee without asking him and of course, her brother took it dutifully. She then went about cleaning up the breakfast dishes. Her father's phone rang and he excused himself to answer it. The boys chattered over her head, leaving Kit alone in her thoughts.

'You know, I think Grandpa went to Newington,' Cam said. 'Maybe you'll be able to find some old photos of him there.'

'Yes, that's right,' their father concurred as he walked back into the room, 'and your gran did her leaving certificate at Queenwood. What a coincidence.'

'Did she?' Kit was genuinely surprised. 'I never knew that.'

'Kit, I'm sure there are a lot of things you don't know about Gran.' Her father chuckled. How right he was, but it did make her wonder. How much more was there to know?

'I have to admit, I never knew until I spoke to Aunt Maggie that your gran, my grandmother June and her sister Iris had moved from the Eastern Suburbs to over the Bridge and to the North Shore in 1943. I had just presumed that when Mum and her mother were sent here from the States they moved to Mosman right away.'

'Why did they move?' Kit asked, more to herself than anyone else. As much as it seemed that it wasn't a big deal, something told her that maybe it was. Her grandmother always referred to the house in Mosman as the home where she first lived when she came to Australia. Why would she do that if it were not true? What was it about the house in the Eastern Suburbs?

'Maggie wasn't sure. It was such a long time ago. Anyway, speaking of your gran, that was John on the phone. They are reading her will this afternoon at her house. He wants all of us to be there.'

'Okay. If the will's done and dusted today, I can fly home tomorrow.' And before her mother could object Kit added, 'After all, there won't be anything else I'll need to do in Sydney then so I should go home.'

By the time they were ready to go to her gran's house, Kit had packed and booked her ticket on the first flight out the next morning. She was sleeping so poorly that she was sure she wouldn't have any trouble rising before dawn, and she'd already refused her father's offer of a lift to the airport and booked a taxi.

Her brothers had convinced her to do a dinner, just the three of them, after they were done with the will, so their parents took one car and they packed into Cam's SUV. Wading through the throng of toys, books, food wrappers and half-full water bottles, Kit squeezed in between the two child-safety seats.

'Sorry 'bout the mess.' Cam gave her an apologetic smile in the rear-view mirror.

'The mess I can handle, but what is that God awful smell?' Kit blocked her nose and poked around gingerly for the source of the offensive pong. Cam turned and breathed in deeply as if he could barely smell it, and considered it for a long while before answering. 'Must be my sneakers at the back. I've been meaning to take them out.'

Kit rolled her eyes. Typical Cam.

By the time they arrived at her gran's, Kit's head was pounding thanks to the lack of air from the broken air-con and Cameron's smelly shoes. The solicitor, her uncles, aunts and cousins were all seated in the living room. Kit knew that if she didn't take something for her head soon it would only become worse. Excusing herself, she headed to her gran's bedroom, as her grandmother had kept headache tablets in the chest of drawers next to the bed. She'd told Kit that it was easier than dragging herself to the kitchen in the middle of the night if she needed medication.

Kit steeled herself – walking into her gran's bedroom for the first time after her passing was going to be hard.

'Just get in and get out,' she mumbled as she took a deep breath and opened the door.

And then she just stood rooted to the spot, looking at the neat as a pin room that had her grandmother's nightie still laid out on the bed. It was a routine she had followed for as long as Kit could remember. Her gran would make her bed as soon as she woke up and place her nightclothes on top.

'Kit,' her mother called, 'where are you?'

'Coming.' She pulled the top drawer but it was stuck. It was only as she yanked once more did Kit realise something was jammed. Crouching down, she could see a white piece of paper lodged in the back. Carefully, she slid her hand and pulled it free. It was an envelope, the timeworn paper yellowed and marked. On the front in beautiful cursive writing was the name *Kitty*. She flipped it over, her hands curiously fingering the back flap. The folds and creases told her that the envelope had been opened and closed many times.

Who was the letter from?

Should she open it?

Before she could properly consider these questions, her mother called out to her again.

'We're all waiting for you, Kit!' The impatience was obvious.

'Coming.' Impulsively, Kit slipped the letter into her handbag, grabbed the headache tablets and headed out.

As soon as Kit sat down, the solicitor – whose name escaped her – began to read out the particulars of her grandmother's will, but her attention wasn't on what he was saying, it was on the envelope burning a hole in her handbag. Her gaze was glued to the bag and she didn't realise the solicitor was talking to her until she looked up to find her entire family staring at her.

'Kit, did you just hear what Jim said?' her father asked.

Jim. She thought. The solicitor. The whole room was looking at her. 'No, sorry, I missed it. Was it important?'

'Was it important!' her mother scoffed.

'Kit,' her father said, 'your grandmother left you her house.'

'Oh, okay. I thought she would've left it to her children not her grandkids ...' she trailed off when her mother baulked further and on the other side of the room Cam shook his head and said, 'Kit, she left it to *you* and only you.'

'What?'

'Congratulations, Kit,' her cousin Ryan said dryly.

'Yes, you are the sole benefactor of this house,' Jim confirmed.

'Gran left me the house?' She was astounded and that was putting it mildly.

Afterwards, when they were all leaving, Ryan was the only one who didn't say goodbye to her. In fact, if Kit was not mistaken, he deliberately gave her the cold shoulder.

'Don't worry about him,' her Uncle John said when he noticed her staring at a sulky Ryan. 'No one was surprised that Mum left you the house.'

Kit gave a rueful laugh. 'I was.'

'Kit, we all knew how special you were to Mum. When you were born, you lit up something inside her. It was like she was waiting for you all her life, or at least she found something she had lost.'

'She found something she had lost.'

Her Uncle John's words played over in her mind as they drove to the restaurant. Kit had made Ben squeeze into the back seat instead of her, despite Cam offloading the offending sneakers with their mother. Maybe it was the distraction of the letter, or maybe it was just that the medication worked, but her headache had gone and she wasn't going to risk any residual smell reigniting it. Cam drove them to a pizza place in Hunters Hill that they had been to many times when they all lived in Sydney. Kit was surprised to see that Pino, the long-time owner, was still at the helm and what's more, he remembered them all.

'Hey, look, it's the Bennetts!' He greeted the boys with hearty handshakes and drew Kit in to place three quick pecks on her cheeks.

'How are you, Pino?' Cam asked. 'How's the family?'

'They are all *molto bene*,' he said, and proceeded to give them way too many details on each and every member of his family, switching between English and Italian. Kit tried her utmost to pay attention but she was eager to start and finish the dinner so she could get back to the house and read the letter in privacy. 'I was so sorry to hear about Catherine, she was a wonderful woman.'

'She was indeed, Pino.' Cam slapped the older man on the shoulder. 'Now, please lead us to our table. The sooner I get your legendary pizza in my belly, the better.'

Pino did as he was asked, yelling out instructions to a passing waitress in Italian, and within minutes of them sliding into the booth the waitress had deposited a bottle of water as well as Pino's own red wine as a condolence gift.

'So that was something, huh?' Ben said. 'I mean it wasn't a surprise to anyone that Gran left you her house. You were her favourite, after all.' Unlike Ryan's comments earlier, Ben's words were not loaded with malice.

'It was a surprise to me,' Kit said as she poured them each a glass of water.

'You didn't look very surprised,' Cam noted.

'It was the headache.' It wasn't entirely untrue, just not the main cause for her lack of concentration.

'I suppose that counts you out of wine then?'

Kit deliberated briefly before caving. 'Go on, one glass should be okay, I'm not sleeping all that great and it might help.'

'So I guess this means that you'll be spending more time in Sydney, Kit,' said Ben.

Kit tilted her head and looked at him. 'What do you mean?'

'You have the house now, right?'

'Yes, but I don't see why that means I need to spend more time in Sydney.'

'But you have to decide what to do with it. Are you going to keep it? Sell it? Rent it out?' Ben quizzed.

Kit shook her head. 'It's all so unexpected, I haven't had time to really give it too much thought.'

'Are you still going home tomorrow?' Cam asked.

'Yes. I can always come back if I need to, once I decide what I'm going to do.'

'Either way, someone will need to clear out Gran's stuff,' said Ben. 'God, I think some of Grandpa's things are still there too. You could save yourself a trip and ask Mum to do it.'

A prickle of fear hit Kit. She'd stumbled across the letter by accident. What if there were more? She wasn't even sure what the letter contained, but the fact that it had been hidden could only mean one thing – it was a secret.

'No!' Kit blurted, a little too quickly, and elicited raised eyebrows from her brothers. 'What I mean is, as great as Mum is, I think I should be the one to go through her things. It's what Gran would've wanted.' While it was the truth, Kit also didn't want her mother to find anything that might raise questions.

Ben nodded. 'You're right. It should be you. If you decide to rent the place out, let me know. If I can't find a place that suits Ness and me – Gran's might be the perfect compromise.'

Kit considered her brother's words. She had no idea what she wanted to do, but if she did keep it, letting Ben and Ness live there would make sense. Having total strangers living in her gran's home didn't sit well with her.

'I'll let you know. At least I know you'll keep the place fairly respectable, unlike this guy here,' she said and jerked her thumb in Cam's direction.

'Watch it,' he mock warned. 'Just remember who's the designated driver tonight.'

'Pipe down, children,' Ben said, pulling his classic middle-child move by playing the moderator. He refilled their glasses and raised his. 'Let's make a toast to Gran.'

All three Bennetts clinked glasses. 'To Gran,' they said in unison as Kit felt her eyes water.

'And to Kit's last night in old Sydney town,' Cam added.

A couple of hours later, when Kit was finally alone, she pulled out the envelope from her bag and sat cross legged on the bed, her heart thumping as she slid out the pages and discovered there were actually two letters.

She read them both. Then read them again. What they contained raised more questions than answers, but two things Kit knew for sure.

First, she definitely needed to be the one to go through her grandmother's things, and secondly, she needed to cancel her flight to Melbourne because the only place she was going in the morning was back to her gran's house.

Eight

Gloomy Sunday

Honolulu, November 1941

While it wasn't rare for it to rain in Honolulu, especially coming into winter, it was unusual for it to last more than a day, so when rain shrouded the island for the better part of three days, Kitty felt that it had been an age since she'd seen the sun. Her mood reflected the thick grey clouds and her mother likened her to a caged animal.

'One would think that you had never needed to live through a rainy day in your life,' June said as Kitty scowled and stared glumly at her breakfast. 'I remember a terrible winter when it rained for almost all of July.'

Kitty was sure her mother was confused. July was the height of summer and she was about to remind her of this when June continued. 'When the sun did eventually return it took almost a week to thaw out. Sydney can be bitterly cold sometimes.'

It wasn't often that her mother spoke of her hometown and Kitty could only guess that Sydney was weighing on her mind because the talk of America entering the war was only getting stronger. Just the other day her father had all but confirmed that after the new year, Kitty and her mother were to set sail for Sydney.

And that was the other reason for her mood. If she hadn't liked the idea of Sydney when her father had first broached the subject, she surely detested it now, and for good reason. Leaving Hawaii would mean leaving Charlie, and that was the last thing she wanted to do.

Since the magical day at Kailua a little over three weeks ago, the day that ended with their first kiss, *her* first kiss, she had seen Charlie another couple of times. Eddie had noticed how pleased she had been after that day and had presumed Charlie did a satisfactory job of keeping her company, so the next time Eddie had wanted to see Penny, Charlie came along. And then the next time too, and today they were due to go back to Kailua, but it was not to be. Rain beat rhythmically against the windowpane, each drop shattering her heart. The plan was to visit the Kalama Beach Club as her father and Eddie were members and Eddie was going to treat them to a day there, followed by dinner at Chez Paris where her mother and father had a usual table. But of course, the rain had washed away all her hopes for a day with Charlie. Her stomach dropped at the thought of not seeing him. They hadn't kissed since Kailua, and Kitty was sure it had nothing to do with Charlie not wanting to kiss her, but because they hadn't spent any more time alone.

She had planned to talk to Charlie about meeting at her parents' beach cottage. Kitty had overheard her mother saying the renovation was near completion. She also overheard her mother telling a tradesman where the spare key was hidden. She hadn't figured out how she would meet Charlie there. An insignificant detail as far as she was concerned. She knew her parents would never approve of her relationship with Charlie ... not that she would consider what they had was a proper relationship, but what they had was *real*.

Kitty loved Charlie and she was almost certain that he loved her. He wouldn't have kissed her otherwise, would he?

'Oh, I almost forgot,' her mother cut into her thoughts. 'Eddie telephoned earlier. Plans have changed because of the inclement weather, you'll no longer be making the trip to Kailua.'

'Yes, I thought as much,' she grumbled.

'There are plans for you all to go to the movie theatre instead.'

'A movie?' Kitty's mood lifted considerably.

'Yes. Eddie said those hairpin turns are too dangerous on a day like today. He'll pick you up in an hour, that is, if you are amenable to spending the day in Waikiki.'

Kitty was amenable to anything if it involved Charlie; she would see him on the moon if she had to. She gave a nonchalant shrug. 'I guess that will have to do.'

'Catherine,' her mother said as she stood up from the breakfast table.

Kitty looked at her, trying damn hard not to break into a grin. 'Yes, Mother.'

'Please keep an eye on your brother. Promise me you won't let him do something that he will regret. As much as it pains me to say this, you are my only hope that he won't throw away his future and ruin his life.'

'I promise, Mother. I won't let Eddie do anything I wouldn't.'

Later, Kitty would wonder if this one moment, this one little lie, was the reason why everything would unravel around her with such brutal force.

'Babysitting again, Florio?'

Charlie didn't need to look up from polishing his shoes to see the expression on Richie Walter's face, the scorn in his voice said it all. 'If you're asking if I'm accompanying Eddie today to provide company for Kitty, then yes I am.' Charlie finished buffing his boots and stood so he could look at Richie eye to eye.

'Company is it?' Walter sneered and Charlie didn't like it one bit. Fire pumped through his veins but he kept his cool. Ever since their altercation a few weeks back, Walter was subtly but surely pushing his buttons. A sly comment here, a dirty look there. Charlie just didn't bite back but he had to admit – it wasn't easy. It seemed the more he pretended the jabs didn't bother him, the harder Richie Walter tried.

'You know, if you're in need of company, the cuties in Pearl City or at Hotel Street will stroke your ego for the price of a steak dinner.'

Charlie looked at him. Even without Walter spelling it out, he was sending the message loud and clear. He thought Charlie was way out of his depth spending time with someone like Kitty McGarrie. The annoying thing was, Walter was right. He had no business even agreeing to be in her company. Kitty came from status – her family background was more aligned to that of Walter's. More than once, Charlie had wondered what the hell he was doing, but he told himself over and over again that what he had with Kitty was special. He knew they could never be together, but was there any harm in enjoying her company? She was funny and smart and it sure as hell didn't hurt that she was beautiful, but most of all – he just loved being around her.

Did it surprise him when Kitty told him she was falling in love with him that day in Kailua? Yes, he was taken aback but he would be lying if he didn't admit that his feelings were growing too. Every time he saw her, he liked her more and more. Was he in love? Charlie didn't know – all he knew was that he had never felt like this about a girl before – ever, even ones that he had slept with.

'You got any girls that you'd recommend?' Charlie looked Walter straight in the eye. 'I know you're a regular at The Modern and The Pacific, or are the girls at The Bronx more your style?' While the girls at The Modern and The Pacific were all white, The Bronx was known for having women of mixed race and it seemed that Walter didn't like what he was hearing. His eyes narrowed as he stepped closer. Charlie shifted his feet and readied for a fight. It was a long time coming. Richie knew it and he knew it. 'Why you–'

'Hey, Florio!' Eddie McGarrie strode in at the exact moment that Richie was raising his fist. Charlie saw Walter registering Eddie's voice and watched as he quickly dropped his fist and slung his arm around Charlie's shoulders.

'McGarrie, we were just talking about you,' Richie said smoothly. Eddie looked from Walter to him and back again to Walter.

'You were?' There was an element of disbelief in Eddie's voice and with good reason. Eddie was well aware there was no love lost between the two men, and that they would be standing in front of him with one man's arm over the other's shoulder was inconceivable. Charlie let Walter do the talking. After all, he was the one that was about to slug him.

'Yeah, yeah,' Walker said a little too enthusiastically, 'we were just firming the details for tonight. You know, Wo Fat's then The Bungalow Room? Like we talked about the other day? You, me, Roberts, Kerr and this *swell* guy here. We're *Goombare*.' Charlie detested the way Walter used the word that back home, people would use to indicate that someone was like family. They were far from that.

There were no such plans and Eddie knew it, but to his credit, he played along. 'I'm keen to go to The Bungalow Room, but only if you promise no trouble. I don't want to pull you out of a fight like last time.'

'You don't have to worry about me,' Walter crooned, turning his attention towards Charlie. 'But we need to keep an eye on this dark horse.' He nodded in his direction. 'Later, gentlemen.'

'What was that all about?' Eddie asked as soon as Walter was out of the room.

Charlie shrugged. 'Same ol' thing. Keeps riling me up hoping I'll snap. Don't worry, I know better than that.'

Eddie shook his head. 'Jeez, anyone would think you were both sweet on the same girl.'

Charlie froze. Did Eddie suspect something?

'But we know that can't be the case,' Eddie said.

'Why's that?'

Eddie looked at him and blinked. 'Even on an island where we outnumber the dames by far, you, my pal, don't need to go on skirt patrol – they all come to you. I see the way girls flock to you when we're out on the town. The only ones Walter can get are the ones you have to pay for.'

'Yeah, ain't that the truth, he's a real Gavoon,' Charlie muttered, thinking that calling Walter a knucklehead was far too polite.

Eddie was wrong. The one girl that he wanted he couldn't have – even if she loved him and he loved her. He loved Kitty. It was pointless to pretend otherwise, and yet Walter was better suited to Kitty than Charlie would ever be. Richie Walter could give her everything that he could not – a comfortable life, a life she was accustomed to. But there was one thing Charlie had that Walter did not – Kitty's heart – and he would rather be dead than let a man like Richie Walter take that away from him.

They were late to the theatre on Bethel Street; the rain had slowed them down so by the time they arrived it was a packed house.

'Looks like everyone in Oahu had the same idea,' Charlie said. Kitty scanned the theatre, craning her neck, but all she saw was a sea of heads.

'I can't see any empty seats,' Penny whispered.

'Maybe we should leave,' Eddie said and Kitty's stomach dropped. But before anyone could answer Eddie, the usher appeared.

'Follow me, folks.' He led them halfway down the rows and shone his flashlight to some empty seats on the aisle.

'But there are only two seats,' Eddie said.

'I have two more up the top to the right. One couple can sit here, the other can follow me.'

One couple? Kitty's face flamed. The usher mistook them for being on a double date.

Charlie cleared his throat. 'Pardon me, sir, but we're not–' The lights in the theatre dimmed and the screen illuminated. The movie was starting.

'Look, folks, I haven't got all day,' the usher said. 'Two here, the other two follow me. Figure it out.'

'Charlie and Kitty can sit here,' Penny said, literally pushing them towards the seats. 'Eddie and I will sit elsewhere.'

'Hey, hurry up and sit down!' someone yelled from the crowd and Kitty and Charlie had no choice but to take their seats.

Once they were settled, Kitty looked around for Penny and Eddie but she couldn't see them. Her heart was beating erratically in her chest. This was the first time she and Charlie had been alone since the moment on the beach at Kailua.

'Can you see them?' Charlie's breath was warm against her ear but it sent shivers down her spine. Kitty turned to see his eyes glowing against the darkness and for a moment she was mesmerised by them.

'No,' she said finally.

'Good,' he said, simply turning his attention towards the screen but even in the dimness of the theatre she could make out the smile on his lips.

She could tell he was glad they were alone. Well, they weren't *alone*, but as far as everyone else around them was concerned they were just another sailor and his girl on a date. The thought of being Charlie's girl unfurled warmth deep in her abdomen. It spread from inside to out and heated her whole body. She removed her cardigan and folded it on her lap.

Suddenly the volume of the music increased several decibels and Kitty nearly jumped out of her skin.

'Did that scare you?' Charlie leaned over, concern threading his voice. 'The movie isn't too scary for you, is it?'

'Scary? Goodness no! I love horror movies.' Kitty was glad when she realised they were seeing *Dr Jekyll and Mr Hyde*. She loved Spencer Tracy and Ingrid Bergman and *The Strange Case of Dr Jekyll and Mr Hyde* by Robert Louis Stevenson was one of her favourite books.

'That's too bad ...' Charlie said. 'I was going to offer to hold your hand.'

Kitty smiled. 'I would like it very much if you would hold my hand anyway, but only if you want to.'

'Actually, I have a better idea.' Charlie reached his arm around her shoulder and pulled her in close. The move was daring, but Kitty didn't care. She relished being close to him and she was sure the grin on her face went from ear to ear. When Charlie's fingertips lightly skittled down her bare shoulder, Kitty didn't want the movie to end. She could sit there all day. Every now and then, she would sneak a glance at Charlie and every time he would be watching her and not the movie. They were so close and yet, Kitty knew that despite the relative anonymity, Charlie wouldn't risk kissing her, so the moment she got the opportunity Kitty leaned over and kissed him. The move caught Charlie by surprise, but it wasn't long before he was kissing her back and with such passion that it made Kitty's head spin.

'We shouldn't have done that,' he whispered when the kiss finally ended, but his smile betrayed his words.

'I don't care,' she whispered back. It had been too long since his lips had been on hers. Three weeks too long. It had been like a drought. She was sure that one more kiss would ease the ache and longing, but their second kiss only made her want him more.

When the movie finished and Charlie removed his arm from around her, disappointment flooded through Kitty. The lights came on, and she stood to look for Eddie and Penny in the crowd. She spotted her friend waving madly at her then gesturing to the exit of the theatre. 'Come on,' she said to Charlie. 'Let's meet them outside.'

As they made their way towards the exit, someone stopped her. 'Miss McGarrie.'

Kitty blinked at the man before realising it was Richie Walter. 'Richie, hello, what a surprise.'

'A pleasant one I hope.' Richie gave Kitty a smile that made her uncomfortable. He had a reputation of being a bit of a ladies' man and Kitty couldn't help but feel that every time he looked at her, it was as if he were leering. She thought that when he had danced with her the night of her birthday. He held her too close and his gaze dipped more often than not to her chest.

'Florio, who would've thought you'd be here?' Richie may have been smiling but his tone was bone dry as he addressed Charlie.

'Yes, who would've?' Charlie's response was just as sarcastic, letting Kitty know there was something less than friendly between the two men. They glared at each other for a moment, each one unblinking. She'd never seen Charlie look so angry.

'Did you enjoy the movie?' Kitty asked politely, to stop the staring. It worked. Richie turned his attention towards her.

'I did indeed. You know, Kitty, next time you want to see a movie, let me take you. I can assure you I'm a much better date than Florio here.'

'Oh, we're not on a –'

'You don't have to explain yourself to him, Kitty,' Charlie said before gently placing his hand on the small of her back to lead her away. 'Come on, Eddie and Penny will be waiting for us.'

Kitty bid Richie farewell because at the end of the day, she was Rear Admiral McGarrie's daughter and she'd had years of her mother's drilling about acting with decorum. But she did not have to turn around to know that Richie Walter would be watching them till they were out of his line of sight.

'What was that all about?' Kitty asked when they were far enough away.

'Nothing,' Charlie said abruptly and Kitty stiffened. He must've felt it because he sighed. 'Richie Walter is a creep. He goes out of his way to make trouble and lately he seems to be directing that trouble towards me.'

Kitty wanted to ask why, but she spotted Penny and Eddie and knew Charlie probably wouldn't give her a straight answer.

'We're going to the Black Cat,' Penny declared by way of greeting and no one complained. Kitty's mother would be horrified if she knew that her daughter was frequenting such a lowbrow establishment, well, lowbrow according to June McGarrie.

The rain had turned into a light drizzle and the group dodged puddles as they dashed from the theatre to the nearby Black Cat, and were lucky to score the last free booth. The cafe was loud and busy; someone had selected 'Chattanooga Choo Choo' by Glenn Miller and a couple of sailors and their girls were dancing up a storm. A waitress took their order and soon talk settled on the movie.

'I spent more time buried in Eddie's chest than watching the screen,' Penny declared. 'Spencer Tracy was a positively ghastly character,' she added with a shudder.

'Lucky I was there to protect you,' Eddie said with a smug smile, and Penny promptly blushed.

'Were you not jumping out of your skin, Kitty?' Penny asked.

'I've read the book so I knew what was coming,' Kitty said nonchalantly, hoping that her face wasn't as red as Penny's. She hazarded a look in Charlie's direction. He was focused on stirring sugar into the coffee in front of him, but there was no mistaking the hint of a smile.

Penny looked at her in awe.

'I don't scare easily.'

'That's the truth,' Eddie said. 'Except when it comes to Thanksgiving. Don't show Kitty Cat here a raw turkey. She'll be screaming for the hills.'

'Is that so?' Charlie asked, amused.

Kitty frowned at her brother. 'To be fair, I was five –'

'Seven,' Eddie interjected.

'Regardless, I was a little girl –'

'You still are,' Eddie interrupted again and her hackles rose.

'As I was saying, when I was *younger*, sometime during my childhood, I stumbled across Cook stuffing the festive bird. She was bent over and all I could see was this giant ... white thing –'

'And Kitty thought that our cook had turned into some sort of half-woman half-bird monster!' Eddie kindly finished the story and the whole table, minus Kitty, erupted, but it wasn't long before she joined in.

'I love Thanksgiving,' Penny said when the chuckling subsided. 'It's my favourite holiday.'

'Mine too,' Charlie said with a hint of sadness, and Kitty realised that it would be his first Thanksgiving away from home.

'It must be hard for you sailors, being away from your families,' Kitty mused. Even though her statement was general she was thinking about Charlie more than anyone else.

'Sure is. Thinking about the holidays makes me miss home.'

'Do you have a large family, Charlie?' Penny asked and Kitty realised that she knew virtually nothing about him. His accent was definitely East Coast, if she had to take a stab at it she would say New York, but that's about it.

'I have a lot of cousins and aunts, uncles, my grandma is still alive, but as for immediate family, it's just Mom and I.'

Charlie had no siblings? What happened to his father? Kitty so desperately wanted to ask but there was something in his tone that warned her against prying.

'Where will your mom be for Thanksgiving?' Kitty said. 'Not on her own, I hope.'

'Probably at my Aunt Doris'. She has eight kids and three grandchildren already so I'm sure if Mom goes there she won't be lonely.'

But Charlie will be, Kitty thought sadly.

'Eight kids!' said Penny. 'That's sure to ensure chaos! It's bad enough when my family are all together and there are only six of us.'

'Four at our house, and that's if Dad and Eddie are home, otherwise it's been known to be just Mother and me.'

'Not this year, Kitty Cat, Dad and I will be there. Hey, Charlie, you're on liberty, right? You should join us.'

Charlie flicked Kitty a glance before shifting in his seat. 'I am on leave, Eddie, but it seems like an awful imposition on your family.'

'Nonsense! My mother lives for entertaining. Besides, we can't have you eating a paltry turkey dinner all alone on your first

Thanksgiving away from home. God knows how long this war will go on and when you'll get to go back to the Big Apple.'

'Hush with the war talk,' Penny chided. 'I'm not liking it one bit.'

Eddie shook his head. 'Whether you like it or not is beside the point, the talk is only getting louder that the Japs are planning something. Hell, my dad is shipping my mom and Kitty off to Australia in the new year, that's how serious the talk is.'

'We don't know that for sure, Eddie,' Kitty said quietly, even though she knew her father had all but made up his mind. She felt Charlie's eyes on hers but avoided his gaze.

'Australia?' Penny said it as if it were Mars.

It might as well be Mars. Kitty knew that it was far away, further than what the West Coast of the United States was.

'Why Australia?' Penny asked. 'Surely it's safer here? We are so far from Japan and we have more than half the US Navy here.'

'That's what I thought,' Kitty said with a sigh. She didn't want the US to enter the war. She didn't want to go to Australia. She wanted to stay exactly where she was, in Hawaii. She wanted to stay where Charlie was.

Billie Holiday's 'Gloomy Sunday' filled the cafe and just like that, Kitty's mood turned to match the song. She looked outside at the seemingly relentless rain and thought that there couldn't be a gloomier Sunday than today.

She was wrong.

Nine

Thanksgiving

Charlie sipped his drink under the weight of June McGarrie's stare. He was sure that from the moment she had laid eyes on him the McGarrie matriarch could see right through him. She was polite enough, but her questions were always tinged with suspicion.

'Eddie tells me that you lived with your mother.'

'Yes, ma'am,' he said a little too enthusiastically and flashed her a smile that was not returned. 'Although most of the time I was alone at home, with my mom working and all.'

'Oh? Your mother works?' To her credit, June McGarrie did appear to try to sound non-judgemental, but the look on her face said otherwise. It was clear that the Rear Admiral's wife didn't think highly of women who worked. Charlie thought it best not to point out that some women – no, a lot of women – had no choice but to enter the workforce to support their families. Women like his mother had no choice. Her hopes and dreams of staying at home and raising a family were broken when the man she loved, the very man she counted on to support her, walked out not only on her but on Charlie too. Overnight they went from

living in Midwood, Brooklyn, a relatively middle-class neighbourhood, to sharing an apartment with his Nonno Vincenzo
and Nonna Maria in East Harlem. His mother thought Charlie
was too young to remember, but he had some residual memories
from when he was as young as five. Even to a child who knew no
better, the difference between Brooklyn and Harlem was striking.
His grandmother was affectionate and boisterous, his grandfather
was more reserved, Charlie recalled. One of his earliest memories
of his Nonno Vincenzo was the way he would stare at Charlie for
hours on end as if he were angry with him, and not say a word.
He was the same with Charlie's mother, and it was only after his
mother gave birth to his sister, a child who died the same day as
she was born, that his demeanour to his own daughter began to
change.

His father's desertion had implications deeper than the obvious financial ones. Charlie was sure his mother never got over
losing his sister Antonia. Not that she often spoke about her, and
if she did, she never mentioned her by name – she would refer to
her as 'the child', 'the baby', 'la bambina'. The only reason Charlie remembered his sister's name was she was buried in the same
cemetery as his nonno.

By the time Charlie started school, he and Nonno Vincenzo
were inseparable. It was Vincenzo who taught him Italian and
who took him to school on his first day because his mother had to
go to work. Charlie would never forget holding Vincenzo's timeworn hand tightly as they approached the school gates. 'But what
if none of the other children want to play with me? What happens
if nobody likes me?' Charlie remembered the turmoil that rumbled within. The concerns were very real for a five-year-old. His
nonno had crouched down and looked him straight in the eyes.

'Listen, *ascoltami*, Carlo.' Vincenzo would often call him Carlo,
the Italian version of his name, and he would also often say the

same thing twice – once in English and then in his native tongue. Charlie was sure this was why he was able to grasp Italian so easily. 'There will be times in your life when there will be people that don't like a you for whatever reason. Maybe they don't like the look of you, sometimes for no a reason at all, nothing that you can do. You cannot a make be your friend, *amico*, *capisce*? Just be a yourself, and no worry, *non preoccupati*.'

The words were slightly confronting but they were raw and honest, and for years after Charlie would heed his grandfather's advice and the present situation was no exception. He knew that June McGarrie didn't like him and he knew why. Never in his life had Charlie cared for people's opinions, but for some reason, he wanted Kitty's mother to not dislike him. So Charlie did what he swore he would never do – he lied to gain approval.

'My mother is a kindergarten teacher.' The lie was so smooth he almost believed it himself. It could've been true; his mother was certainly a smart woman, she was also patient and kind, key qualities that were required for a good teacher. He told himself it wasn't an outright lie, but a stretch of the truth. His mother worked as a cleaner at the local school.

'Oh, I want to be a teacher!' Kitty said, her eyes brimming with excitement. One glance at her had Charlie immediately feeling ashamed. He never wanted to lie to Kitty, and yet, hadn't he effectively just done so?

'Nonsense, Catherine,' her mother chided. 'You know that will never happen.'

Kitty looked crestfallen at June McGarrie's bluntness. Charlie wanted to say something – he wanted to tell Kitty that she should ignore her mother's harsh barb because she would make a wonderful teacher.

'What grade does your mother teach?' June turned her attention back to Charlie.

'Preschoolers,' he replied without skipping a beat. 'She adores children.'

'And yet, you are an only child.'

'I had a sister ... she died not long after birth.' There was an audible gasp from Kitty while Mrs McGarrie merely blinked.

'That would've been hard on your mother and father.'

It was subtle, but the question was loaded in the weight of the words. She wanted to know about his father.

'It was hard, especially since my father was ... departed not long before we lost my sister.' It wasn't a lie, not entirely. His father had left when his mother was pregnant, but Charlie knew that the way his words came out it seemed as if his father was dead. In a way he was – he was certainly no longer part of his life and Charlie doubted he ever would be again.

'That's enough of the interrogation, don't you think, June?' The Rear Admiral clapped Charlie good naturedly on the shoulder. 'The poor boy came here to eat and speaking of which, we should do so soon. I need to meet Hugh in a couple of hours.'

Charlie looked into his drink, swirled it and took a measured sip. It was cognac, he had never had it before today and he doubted that he would again. He was more a bourbon or whisky kind of guy, but when the Rear Admiral offers you his top-shelf cognac, you don't say no. He had met Rear Admiral McGarrie in passing once before and Charlie was sure that he wouldn't remember him, but to Charlie's surprise, he not only recalled his name, but remembered their conversation.

'Charlie and I need to eat and go too,' Eddie said as they made their way into the most fancy dining room Charlie had ever seen. It certainly was nothing like the Thanksgiving dinners they had back home. It wasn't a holiday that Italians traditionally celebrated, but Nonna Maria took any opportunity to cook for

her family. They would all squeeze into their apartment; the few
pieces that furnished the living room were moved out to make
space for a long trestle table and spindle-backed wooden chairs.
Nonna would be yelling directions from the kitchen where she
had been holed up for the better part of the day preparing for the
meal. The amount of food was astounding. It was one of the few
days in the year, along with Christmas and Easter, when the table
was laden, and the white tablecloth was covered with plates and
platters. Antipasto – mushrooms, artichokes, anchovies, capers
and his nonno's handmade prosciutto and salami. More recently,
Nonna Maria replaced the pasta that would follow with a turkey
stuffed with beef, pork, rice, chopped celery and of course accompanied by *insalata* and baked vegetables.

The McGarrie Thanksgiving table bore little resemblance to
that of his extended family's back home. Charlie would bet his life
that the plates were all fine bone china, the silverware sterling and
the glassware the finest crystal money could buy. The only com-
monality was the turkey and some of the side dishes. That was it.

Charlie pulled out Kitty's chair for her, before doing the same
for Mrs McGarrie. 'Thank you, Charlie,' Kitty said warmly while
Mrs McGarrie raised her brows at her daughter.

'Kitty, please do not allow yourself to be overly familiar with
Edward's friends. Refer to him as Seaman or Mr Florio, thank you.'

'Actually, Charlie's practically ready for promotion, right,
Dad?' Eddie said. 'Won't be long before you're moved on from
Seaman. Bet you can't wait to stop holystoning.'

The Rear Admiral considered Charlie and nodded slowly. 'I've
been hearing some stellar reports about you, young Florio. A man
like you will be an asset in war.'

'Oh, Conrad, please no talk of war tonight,' June said. 'Thanksgiving is no time to be talking about war.'

'Thanksgiving or not, it's inevitable that the US will be in this war – sooner rather than later.'

'I heard that they've stepped up the training over at Kaneohe,' Eddie added.

'Edward!' his mother admonished, and he sent her a sheepish look.

'Sorry.'

Charlie glanced at Kitty, who was sporting the same petrified look as she had that day at the Black Cat when Eddie was talking about Kitty and her mother being sent to Australia. His heart broke for her.

'Your mother's right, Eddie. Thanksgiving isn't the day we should be focusing on war. It's a day all about being thankful for what we have here and now. I, for one, am thankful to Rear Admiral and Mrs McGarrie for opening their home to me and inviting me to share this meal. It's my first Thanksgiving away from home, and in some ways considering how warm it is out, it's hard to fathom that it is the holiday I love so much, so for that I'm thankful.'

A small spark of surprise flashed across June McGarrie's face but it was the Rear Admiral who spoke up. 'Well said, young man. Perhaps we should go around the table and say our individual thanks, and then if you are comfortable doing so, Florio, you can lead us in saying grace.'

Out of the corner of his eye Charlie noticed the very different expressions on the faces of the two McGarrie women when they heard the Rear Admiral's suggestion. He knew that his response would anger one of them – and for the first time since arriving at the McGarrie house, he didn't care. Winning over Kitty's mother was a lost cause.

'I would be honoured to do so, Rear Admiral McGarrie.'

It was positively delightful watching her mother squirm while Charlie held her hand and led grace. Thankfully Kitty was sitting on the other side of Charlie and was able to hold his hand and was sure his face reddened slightly when she gave his hand a squeeze. The dinner was delicious – Cook had prepared a scrumptious meal and Kitty, elated to have Charlie in their company, had even managed to forget her turkey woes. That was, until Eddie had reminded everyone of the incident. It was one of the rare times her mother had leapt to her defence and chided her brother.

Thanksgiving was also a rare occasion when her parents allowed her to have a glass of wine or two. By the time Kitty had finished the second glass, her lips tingled and she felt slightly light headed. Her mother usually kept an eagle eye on her to ensure she was behaving appropriately but tonight she seemed preoccupied, scowling at Charlie as if he were some stray that Eddie had found on the sidewalk. At least her father seemed to like him, and she'd been pleasantly surprised when he'd invited Charlie to say grace.

Her heart soared at the thought of her father approving of Charlie. It would certainly make it easier to have her father on side, and Eddie too. He and Charlie were friends and she was certain that he would support her. Her mother was another matter, but that was something that she would worry about when the time came. Kitty slipped into her own dream world imagining her father walking her down the aisle and Charlie waiting for her at the end, dressed in his Navy uniform and looking all sorts of handsome. Next to him, Eddie would be beaming at her as Penny, her maid of honour, stood on the other side.

'Catherine, Catherine!' Her mother's shrill voice pulled her out of her reverie. 'Did you hear what I asked?'

'I'm sorry, Mother, I didn't hear what you said.'

'Your father and brother are both about to leave. I was asking if you'd like to accompany me to call on Lillian and Margot Ramsey.'

Her stomach dropped. Charlie was leaving so soon? Her brother was already standing, declaring that their pals had arrived and were waiting for them outside, the honk of an automobile horn heralding their departure.

The thought of spending the rest of the evening watching her mother kotow to Lillian Ramsey, while being subjected to Margaret's dullness was enough to put her to sleep. 'Actually, if it's all right with you, Mother, I would like to be excused. I am feeling tired and might go to bed early.'

Her mother considered her before nodding. 'Yes, you do look a little peaked. Head on up and I'll have Fumiyo bring you something in an hour or so.'

'Oh, don't bother Fumiyo for anything. I'm sure I will be asleep by then.'

Kitty bid farewell to everyone, ensuring that her gaze didn't linger on Charlie as she said her goodbyes. Then she headed up to her room, but had no intention of going to bed. Instead, as soon as she heard her mother leave, she snuck out and called Penny. She had a plan, and she was sure her friend would agree to it with little or no convincing.

'Oh, Penny, I'm not too sure about this.' Kitty nervously nibbled on her bottom lip, her heart thumping wildly.

'Don't you dare chicken out on me now,' Penny warned. 'After all, this was your idea, remember?'

Yes, she did. But two hours ago, fuelled by wine, Kitty suspected, sneaking out and driving Downtown to The Beachcomber Club seemed like a great idea. Daring yes, but a great idea all the same. But now, as they sat in Penny's car, a way down and across the street from the club where she knew for sure Eddie and Charlie would be, the adrenaline had worn off and anxiety had taken its place. They were in an alley off Hotel Street. There were girls aplenty on the street, but they were working girls, certainly not young women like Penny and Kitty.

'Come on, we can't sit here all night.' Penny made a move to get out and Kitty's panic heightened.

'Wait!' In the darkness, Kitty met her friend's gaze. 'Maybe I haven't thought this through properly. I mean, what if they see us?'

Penny narrowed her gaze. 'I thought the whole point *was* to find them.'

'I know ... I mean ...'

'Look, Kitty,' Penny said, shifting her body so she was facing her. 'We can do this, and I know that you're scared that you're about to walk in there and see some other girl sitting on Charlie's lap –'

'I'm not –' Kitty protested and Penny held her hand up to stop her.

'Kitty, honey, we both know you're sweet on Charlie.'

Kitty looked up and searched Penny's eyes, but there was no judgement. 'Is it that obvious?' she asked nervously.

'Only to a blind man,' Penny said dryly, causing Kitty to gasp and cover her face with her hands.

'Relax.' Penny chuckled. 'I only had my suspicions when you called me tonight. I mean, why else would you be calling me to go after Eddie tonight of all nights? And don't give me some bull-dust story about how you know I would want to see him on Thanksgiving. I love you, Kitty, but we've been friends long enough for me to know how your mind works. In fact, I wouldn't be at all surprised if you had manipulated Eddie in bringing Charlie along to our dates.'

Kitty dropped her gaze to her lap. Penny was right – they had known each other a long while. Penny was one of the first friends she had made when they moved to the island. Her father was a civilian contractor and they had moved to Hawaii a year before the McGarries. They'd met on Kitty's first day at St Andrew's and became fast friends. That afternoon Eddie was waiting for her, and as she walked out of the school gates with her new friend, Kitty was sure that Eddie had fallen in love with Penny on the spot.

'I don't have much time left, Penny. My dad is still hell bent on sending my mother and me to Australia.' Kitty shook her head as if it were all so unbelievable.

'Do you love him?' Penny asked gently.

Kitty stared straight ahead and breathed slowly. Even though she had professed her love to Charlie already, and perhaps foolishly prematurely, she had yet to say it out loud to anyone else. 'I do, Penny. I love him so much.'

'Well then,' Penny said without skipping a beat. 'What are we doing here? The night isn't getting any younger and neither are we.'

The club was loud, dark and smoky. With her hand firmly in Penny's, Kitty allowed her friend to lead her through the crowd. The Beachcomber was a well-known haunt for army and navy personnel, a place where the men could go to let off some of the steam from the stresses that came with their military duties. Kitty knew the establishment was run by a husband and wife team who had come over from Hollywood some five years ago, and according to her mother, anyone who came from Hollywood possessed loose morals. Mrs McGarrie abhorred Eddie visiting The

Beachcomber and had no qualms in making her feelings known, so Kitty could only imagine the disdain if she were to discover her daughter in such shady company too. Kitty couldn't help but giggle at the thought and it eased her nerves some.

A woman was singing on stage. Her hair was bright copper and her dress was emerald green. It clung to her curves like a second skin, shimmering against the light, making it look as if it were made of precious jewels. Her voice was as beautiful as she was and the audience was captivated. Kitty noticed that every time the singer leaned forward, a chorus of cheers and wolf whistles would erupt as the crowd, mainly men, were treated to a glimpse of her ample assets. Kitty wasn't sure why, but the men's responses annoyed her. Here was a woman with a clear talent and yet all these men could care about was how much of her breasts they could see.

When she said this to Penny, her friend merely shrugged. 'It's her choice.'

'But she probably gets peanuts.'

'I heard there are girls who work here who can be hired to provide private company, if you know what I mean. They are the ones that earn the big bucks. But they can't have boyfriends or husbands, or even their own bank account.'

Kitty's eyes widened like saucers. 'How'd you know that?'

'I overheard someone talking at Miss Violett's a couple of weeks ago. They bring them in from the mainland, San Francisco mainly.'

Kitty was about to ask more but the crowd erupted again as the singer gave them more than a glimpse this time. The noise was deafening and it seemed to take an age for it to subside. She scanned the crowd for any sign of Charlie or Eddie, but it was a hard task between the smoke and the darkness and so many men in uniform looking the same. 'I don't see them,' Kitty yelled over the noise.

'Neither do I, oh, wait! I think I saw Richie Walter. They would be with him, right?'

Kitty felt a shiver scuttle down her spine as she remembered the way Richie looked at her that day at the theatre. 'Yeah, they probably are.'

'Yes!' Penny yelled excitedly. 'I see Eddie.'

Kitty followed Penny's line of sight and spotted her brother, standing out above the men around him. Her heart beating fast, a fresh wave of anxiety washed over her.

'Penny.' She tugged her friend's hand a little too hard, causing her to turn and scowl. 'What if he's with another girl?'

Penny's face softened. 'Aww, honey! Remember what you said to me outside in the car? How you love him and how you don't have much time left? You hold on to that and if there's a girl sitting there – you remember that. Besides, there probably won't be.'

Kitty swallowed the lump in her throat and nodded. 'You're right. I'm probably letting my imagination take over.' But when Charlie and Eddie and their gang came into full view, Kitty could see that her worst fears were realised. There were two girls sitting amongst them. One of them looked quite cosy with Richie Walter, the other was clearly with Charlie. There was no mistaking it – she was sitting on his lap. Her long blonde hair fell like waves down her back and her head was tipped back while she was laughing at something Charlie had said. The action not only revealed her creamy neck but placed her chest practically in Charlie's face.

Kitty was rooted to the spot. In that instant, the world around her slowed to a screeching halt. All she could see was Charlie with another woman, being far more intimate than she had ever been with him, and all she could hear was the sound of her heart beating so fast she was sure it was about to break.

She didn't know who spoke first, whether it was Penny calling out to Eddie or if Eddie had spotted them. Either way, her brother was surprised and angry. He hadn't seemed to notice her, all his rage was directed at Penny, demanding to know why she had come. Later Penny would tell Kitty that she'd made some lame excuse about being out with her sister and left stranded when Annie ditched her for a man. In his slightly intoxicated state Eddie had accepted the story.

Charlie was shocked as well. The moment his eyes connected with Kitty's the guilt was clear. He opened his mouth to say something, but Kitty turned and ran. Away from where Penny and Eddie were yelling at each other and away from Charlie.

She pushed through the crowds, not caring one bit if she was knocking into anyone.

'Kitty, wait!' She heard Charlie's voice behind her. She couldn't stop – she wouldn't stop until she was out of the damn club. The thought of Charlie on her tail only made her go faster. She bumped into a table, and then had a boozy army guy step on her foot, but Kitty didn't let it slow her down. She held her breath till she was outside in the clear and safe.

Oh, Kitty, you stupid, stupid girl!

Her eyes stung, her vision blurred but she finally allowed herself to stop and breathe. She glanced behind her and was both relieved and heartbroken there was no sign of Charlie. He had probably given up chasing her and was back in the arms of the blonde. She hobbled towards Penny's car, her foot throbbing with pain. It hurt almost as much as the pain in her shattered heart.

She had been a fool. What had she been thinking? Sneaking into what was essentially a gentlemen's club? Just what exactly had she hoped to achieve?

This is what happens when you listen to your heart. You end up with heartbreak, Kitty thought. Indeed. And all the nonsense about love stopped immediately. It would be better this way. Now she had to hope that Penny wouldn't take too long. Her foot was really starting to hurt.

It had all happened so suddenly and out of the blue. In a flash, Walter had pushed some blonde broad onto his lap and while he politely tried to explain he would like her to get up, she had simply laughed it off and snuggled closer, thrusting her chest in his face and wiggling her toosh not so subtly against his crotch.

'You remember me, don't you, honey?' she asked with more than a hint of suggestion. 'We had a good time last time you were here.'

He did remember her, and for more than one reason. He remembered because Walter had tried to get her to pay attention to him, even though she clearly preferred Charlie. He remembered her because Walter then tried to buy her, telling her he would pay her double what Charlie was offering. Dolly – he remembered that was her name – grinned at Walter, telling him she would rather sleep with Charlie for free than accept his offer. Then, without saying a word, she took Charlie's hand and led him to one of the private rooms. Charlie remembered her because her breasts were full and firm and pressed into his face as she mounted him and expertly rode him. He remembered her because she had been the first woman he'd had in a long time, a very long time. Afterwards he tried to pay her – the exact sum that Walter had offered – and she looked somewhat offended.

'It's not often that I get to really enjoy what I do, and I really enjoyed you,' she said and shrugged casually. 'So let that be payment enough.'

Charlie had walked out of that room grinning. But this, all this was before he had met Kitty.

When Dolly had landed on his lap and rubbed herself against him, he knew she was vying for a repeat performance. She was certainly beautiful and almost irresistible.

But Dolly wasn't Kitty, and the fact that this woman sitting on his lap would more than likely be willing to offer her services for free and he wasn't the slightest bit interested should've scared him. But it didn't – he didn't want anyone but Kitty, and the thought made him grin like a fool. The problem was – Charlie couldn't make it obvious that he was rejecting her, not straight away. Walter would become suspicious. He had become even more of a thorn in Charlie's side since they'd run into him at the theatre and especially so tonight because he knew that Charlie had spent Thanksgiving at the McGarries'. He needed an excuse to get himself out of it diplomatically, and the way Eddie had been downing the booze, he was sure it wouldn't be long before his friend was close to passing out and he'd need to take him back to the ship.

'It's not going to happen tonight, sweetheart.' Charlie wanted to add that it would never happen again, but he stopped himself.

Dolly merely tipped her head back and laughed, wiggling with increased enthusiasm. 'Oh, and why not?'

Charlie didn't get a chance to answer – the next thing he knew was Eddie calling out to Penny and looking up to see Kitty staring at him as if he were a ghost.

The moment their eyes connected, she was off in a flash, and before Charlie could think through his actions, he was after her. She was fast – at one stage, he thought he had lost her, but spotted her red top darting in and out of the crowd towards the exit.

Once outside the club, he scanned the street, certain she would be there and she was. When he reached her, she was leaning against a car, rubbing her right foot.

He stood a few feet away, suddenly unsure what to say to her. 'Are you hurt?' he finally asked, his breath still laboured from the chase. Kitty visibly stiffened at the sound of his voice and it sent a barb through his heart. She hadn't expected to see him. Did she really think he wouldn't follow her?

'Kitty, are you hurt?' he repeated, taking a step forward, towards her.

'Don't talk to me,' she said and turned away. It was clear by the wobble of her voice that she was crying. The barb in his heart twisted. Of course she was hurt – *he* had hurt her.

'Kitty –'

'I said don't talk to me!' she yelled, this time looking straight at him with tears running down her beautiful face.

'Kitty, I need to talk to you, because I need to explain what you saw.'

'What is there to explain, Charlie? You had some ... strumpet on your lap. I may be young and naïve, but I am not completely stupid. I know what that all leads to and it's not board games.'

Charlie couldn't help himself. It was the most inappropriate reaction, but he burst out laughing. This, of course, only increased Kitty's anger.

'You think this is funny?'

'No, it's not, it's serious ... but, Kitty, I am pretty sure I haven't heard anyone use the word "strumpet" since I studied Shakespeare in high school.'

'Well ...' Kitty dropped her gaze and went back to rubbing her foot. 'It was the only word I could think of. I'm *so* angry.'

'I know you are, baby ...' Charlie closed the gap between them and gingerly placed a hand on her shoulder. 'But I would really like it if you'd let me explain. Can you give me the chance to do that?'

Kitty nodded and put her foot down. 'Okay.'

'Come on.' Charlie offered her his hand. 'Let's get off the road before one of us gets run over.'

Kitty took it and gave him a tentative smile. A second later she was howling in pain. 'Aww! My foot!'

Charlie swept her into his arms and carefully placed her on the trunk of the car.

'I was trodden on as I was leaving.'

'You mean as you tried to run away from me.' He gave her a rueful smile and he carefully removed her shoe.

Kitty huffed. 'You would've run too if you caught another woman sitting on your boyfriend's lap.'

'Is that what I am, your boyfriend?' Charlie grinned and watched as Kitty straightened her back.

'Well you don't have to laugh at that too. Is it so funny?'

She was so adorable when she was mad that Charlie couldn't help but chuckle. 'I'm not laughing at you, Kitty. I'm grinning like a fool at you calling me your boyfriend.'

'Is it okay that I called you my boyfriend?'

'Kitty, I am honoured that you would consider me so.'

'You make it sound like it's a chore!'

'It's nothing of the sort,' he said softly. 'Any man would be lucky to be your guy, Kitty. Now, let's have a look at this foot of yours.' Charlie gingerly lifted her foot, causing Kitty to yelp in pain.

'It's already swollen,' he observed. 'Make sure you put some ice on it as soon as you get home.'

'It hurts so bad.' Kitty sniffed and Charlie reached into his pocket and pulled out a handkerchief.

'I know, honey,' he crooned and placed a gentle kiss on the tender area. 'A bit of ice and you'll be dancing again in no time.'

'Charlie ... who is she? The girl, I mean.'

'No one that you need to worry about, Kitty.'

'But she was sitting on your lap. I saw that clearly.'

'Yes, she was. And if you had arrived seconds before you would've seen Richie Walter throw the poor girl onto me.'

'That *poor girl* looked like she wasn't too distressed.'

Without adding to Kitty's woes, Charlie did his best to downplay the whole thing. 'It's her job, Kitty.'

'A pretty crappy one, if you ask me.'

'And I was in the process of letting her down gently when you arrived.'

'You were?' There was genuine surprise.

'Yes, and for a very good reason ...'

Kitty opened her mouth and he knew what she was about to ask. She was going to ask him what the reason was, but before she could, Charlie leaned forward and crushed his lips against hers. She tasted as sweet and as heavenly as he remembered.

Kitty slid her hands around the nape of his neck and pulled him closer. A moan escaped her and it heightened his need to gather her into his arms and whisk her away.

'I love you,' he murmured against her lips.

'Oh, I love you so much, Charlie.'

'I wish I could take you away somewhere. I feel like we are always on borrowed time.'

Kitty gasped. 'I might have the answer to that.'

'You do?'

'My parents have a house in Kailua.'

'Yes ... I remember Eddie saying so when we were there.'

'It's been renovated, but I heard my mother say it's been completed ahead of schedule.' She grinned coyly.

'Kitty, what are you suggesting?' It was a rhetorical question really. Charlie knew exactly what she was alluding to.

'We could meet there, Charlie, away from everyone and everything. Say yes, say you'll meet me there!'

It was sure as hell risky, if they got caught ... 'Kitty I —'

'Don't you dare say no, Charlie. I'm all but certain to be shipped off to Timbuktu soon. I am running out of time with you!'

Charlie sighed. She had a point. Time was not on their side. 'Australia is a long way away from Timbuktu, Kitty.'

'It's also a long way from you,' she countered.

'It's risky ...'

'One day, Charlie. Surely you can give me one day of memories.'

He could give her that – one day. One day to last a lifetime, because at the end of it all, Kitty was worth the risk.

'Yes, Kitty. I can give you one day.'

Ten

The Invitation

Sydney, October 2016

'I don't understand why you will not let me help you.'

Kit was glad she had her back to her mother so she didn't have to hide the eye roll. Despite Kit insisting she could handle going through her grandmother's things on her own, her mother had a hard time accepting that her assistance was not needed. 'I've told you, Mum, it's something that I feel I need to do on my own.' Kit finished making her coffee and joined her mother at the breakfast table.

'Have you at least given some more thought about what you're going to do with the house?'

'Mum, it's barely been twenty-four hours. Until late last night I was sure that I was flying home this morning.'

Bev patted her hand. 'I am glad you're still here, you know that *this* is home.'

Here we go ... Kit inwardly groaned. It was the same old story every time she referred to Melbourne as 'home'.

'I still don't understand why you didn't just move back when you lost your job.'

'You know why, Mum,' Kit said gently. 'And before you say it – no it's not about running away, it's about a fresh start, a new lease on life.'

Her mother considered her for a moment. 'And you don't think that would've been possible here?'

'What, here in my childhood home? Mum, you know I love you and Dad but there is no way I would ever consider moving in with you.'

'I will try and not be grossly offended with that, but no – I meant getting another place in Sydney after ... well, after you know what.' Her mother shifted uncomfortably on her chair. Even after all these years it was still hard talking about what had happened with Jeremy. 'Your lease had expired and it was the perfect opportunity to get a new place.'

Their lease expiring had been a coincidence when she landed the job at *The Age*. 'And that's exactly what I did, Mum, I got a new place.'

'In a different city.'

'Yes, because I got a job there.'

'You could've found a job here.'

Kit's patience was running thin. It seemed that every time she saw her mother, her decision not to live in Sydney was all they talked about. 'I'm not even going to rehash what we've gone through almost a hundred times already.' She downed her coffee and slid back her chair. She was anxious to get to her grandmother's early and start going through her things. After stacking her cup in the dishwasher, she headed to the fruit bowl, which seemed to house more car keys than fruit, in search of the keys for her old car.

'Ben's taken your car,' her mother said when she saw Kit rummaging.

Her annoyance kicked up a notch. 'Mongrel,' she muttered before seeing her mother's displeasure.

'Sorry,' she said, feeling like a petulant child. 'I wish he'd checked with me first.'

'He was meeting some real estate agents and until this morning, we thought you were leaving.'

Kit sighed and knew her mother was right. 'Yeah, I know.'

'I can take you,' Bev offered. 'I need to go to the church to finalise a few things after the funeral.'

'That would be great, thanks.'

The drive to her grandmother's was quiet, with the only sound being the music on the car radio.

'You can change the station if you want,' her mother said, breaking the silence. 'I know you don't like my kind of music.' It wasn't a dig, there was no malice behind her words. Usually it was the first thing Kit did when she got into her mother's car, because Bev was spot on, she didn't share her mother's love of easy listening music. But not today – today, Kit couldn't care less about what station was on.

'Nah, it's okay, I don't mind it.'

Kit noticed her mother turn towards her for a second with a surprised glance. They lapsed into silence for a while when an old Carpenter's hit came on. Kit listened to the lyrics – it was a song she knew her mother loved and it wasn't long before her mother was singing along. Bev Bennett had a beautiful voice. Kit's father often joked that she could've been a star. Her mother would always blush and tell him that she didn't need fame or fortune – she had him. They were the real deal, her parents, a love that lasted. Kit couldn't sing if her life depended on it. She had the Bennett gene when it came to all things musical. In fact, they all did. She wondered if her mother was a little disappointed with that?

'You have a great voice, have I ever told you that, Mum?' Kit couldn't recall ever actually saying that her mother could sing or praising her for it. She never thought she needed too – her father often complimented her. She remembered her gran doing so too. In fact, Gran once told Bev that the only woman she'd heard with a better singing voice was a buxom performer in a gentlemen's club in Hawaii. Kit remembered it because the revelation shocked her on two levels. One, her grandmother rarely mentioned Hawaii; and two, what on earth was her grandmother doing in a gentlemen's club? Thinking about it now made Kit wonder, had her gran been there with Charlie?

'Thank you, Kit ... I don't think you've ever said that.' Her mother sounded surprised and pleased.

'Well, you do and I'm sorry I haven't said it before. I'm kind of jealous of it, to be honest.'

Her mother gave a girlish laugh and her face turned a lovely shade of crimson. 'You jealous of me?'

Kit chuckled. 'It's not that funny, Mum.' But for some reason, it made them both laugh out loud till tears streamed down her face. Kit pulled out a couple of tissues and handed one to her mother before wiping her own cheeks. She had to admit – it felt good not to be crying out of sadness. The laughing had lifted some of the heaviness that she'd been carrying in her heart for the past couple of weeks.

'I know you think I'm annoying, but –' her mother said soberly and quickly the light-hearted mood dissipated.

'Mum.' Kit groaned.

'No, let me finish. I know I hurt you when I said that you ran away after what happened with Jeremy, and I'm sorry. I never meant for it to come out so harshly, I guess I was acting out of frustration.'

'I know, I get it – you didn't want me to move to Melbourne.' Kit appreciated her mother's apology.

Bev shook her head. 'It's not about me not wanting you to move to Melbourne, Kit. I know that you're an adult, you have a career and you need to take opportunities that come your way. I knew that job at *The Age* was going to be great for you.'

Kit was baffled. Had she not just had a completely different conversation with her mother earlier that morning? 'Umm ...'

'I've confused you.'

'Yeah, you kind of have.'

'Kit, my reservations about you moving was that if you were in Melbourne, I couldn't help you. I saw how fragile you were after Jeremy and I so desperately wanted to help, but you were drawn to Catherine, and well ... I guess I felt a little left out. I guess you can say I was a little jealous.'

Whoa. Kit had not expected that to come out of her mother's mouth.

'You and Catherine always had such an amazing bond, and don't get me wrong, I loved it. I loved watching you with her, but in my heart I always thought that when the day came that you really needed me, that as your mother *I* could be there for you.'

Kit felt a stab of shame that she had never considered how her mother would feel having her daughter be so close to her grandmother. 'Wow, Mum ... I'm so sorry, I didn't realise you felt that way. I never meant to push you away, I mean, I didn't consciously choose to do so.'

'Honey, it wasn't your fault. I know you went to your gran because it felt like the natural thing to do. I don't want you to feel bad about that. I saw how much Catherine helped you, and I always thought that once you got a little better ... once you got over that first few months, that by then I might be ready to help you. But then ...'

'I went to Melbourne ...'

Her mother nodded. 'I was so angry at myself for not being there for you when you needed me and I took it out on you and on Melbourne. That's why I never came down to visit you and why I keep harping on about you moving back.'

'Mum, I really think you're being too hard on yourself. The truth is ... yes, Gran did help me through those early days and weeks, but what helped me the most was that move to Melbourne.'

'I know,' Bev said, and sighed. 'I keep telling myself that, I mean, you seem ... better and maybe you're right, maybe the fresh start was exactly what you needed to put it all behind you and for your heart to heal.'

Kit didn't like the way her heart twisted with doubt. She didn't want to tell her mother that she didn't think her heart would ever be whole again, that every day she was riddled with guilt and filled with loss. How could it? But they were close to her gran's place and Kit was saved from further discussion.

Bev slowed the car down as they approached the house. For years the sight of her grandmother's house brought Kit joy and now that joy was tainted. It was not only the loss of her gran, but the potential secrets that lay hidden inside. The letter was proof of that and Kit had a gut feeling there was more.

'I can come and pick you up when you're ready. After the church, I need to shop for some groceries for dinner, but other than that, I'll be around.'

'Thanks, Mum. I might call Ben and see where he's at later. I'm not sure how long I'll be or how much I'll get done, but I'm hoping to go through and sort her bedroom at least.'

'Don't be surprised if there are still your grandpa's things in there. Catherine was a bit of a hoarder. Just a couple of months ago I found one of those old Arnott's biscuit tins in the kitchen. She almost chopped my head off when I suggested she could throw it out.'

'Please don't tell me there were actual biscuits from God knows when in it.' Kit screwed her nose up at the thought of fifty-year-old scotch fingers and milk arrowroots.

'I never got to see inside. Catherine grabbed the tin out of my hands as if it contained gold bullion. Then she threatened that if I ever tried to throw it out again she would murder me. It was very odd. It was the first and last time she ever spoke to me like that.'

'Yes, how strange,' Kit mused while her mind worked over-time. Now that her mother mentioned it, she remembered that biscuit tin. After her grandpa passed away she was in her gran's kitchen looking for a recipe her gran had written out years ago and had misplaced. The tin was high up on the shelf above the fridge and when Kit suggested they look inside to see if the recipe was there, Catherine said with absolute certainty that it wasn't.

Kit needed to find that biscuit tin.

She said goodbye to her mother, let herself inside and made a beeline for the shelf above the fridge. Disappointment flooded her when there was no sign of the red Arnott's tin. After her mother discovered it, her gran would surely have hidden it somewhere else. The most logical place would be her bedroom.

The same melancholy feeling that had engulfed Kit yester-day returned as soon as she stepped foot in Catherine's bedroom. While her first instinct when she arrived was to rip the room apart in her search for the box, the solemn act of methodically packing away her grandmother's belongings seemed more respectful.

She opened the first of the wardrobes and almost instantly emotion clogged her throat as her gran's scent engulfed her. Tears welled, spilling freely down her cheeks. She missed her gran and the sense of loss was overwhelming. She also felt ashamed that her quest to look for clues about Charlie had seemed more important than the task at hand.

People often say how the funeral was the hardest part about someone passing. Kit disagreed. Until this moment she'd underestimated how difficult the task of packing her gran's things would be. It was a hundred times worse than the funeral. How on earth was she going to get through this? She was a basket case and she hadn't even started. Kit paused, allowing a moment to cry, and strangely enough, it gave her the strength to continue, partly because she knew Catherine would want her to get on with it. She could almost hear her gran urging her to dry her eyes and make a start.

'I can do this,' Kit said out loud.

Carefully she took out all the clothes, placing them in piles on the bed. Her grandmother had always been a woman of impeccable taste and her love for fine fashion continued way into her later years, but it wasn't until collection upon collection of designer suits were laid out before her that Kit realised just how vast and undoubtedly expensive the collection was. She had only gone through a quarter of her grandmother's clothing and Kit was sure that what she had before her was worth well into the thousands. She removed the hangers and neatly folded each item with the aim that she would donate them all to a local charity. She knew that Catherine wouldn't have it any other way.

Kit had been working for close to a couple of hours when a knock on the front door startled her. She popped her head out to see Maggie Moore on the doorstep.

'Mrs Moore, what a nice surprise.' Kit opened the front screen door and invited the older lady to come in.

'I hope you don't mind me stopping by unannounced,' Maggie said as she pulled Kit in for a hearty hug. 'I ran into your mother and she told me you were here.'

'Would you like a cup of tea? I could do with a break.' Kit turned and walked down the hallway towards the kitchen, and Maggie followed.

'I'd love one, dear,' Maggie replied, then stopped in front of Catherine's bedroom. 'I can't believe that she's gone.' Emotion threaded her voice.

'I know.' Kit gave her shoulder a squeeze. 'I'm still having a hard time with it all.'

'Come on,' Maggie said. 'Let's have that cuppa.'

Kit led her into the kitchen where Maggie made the move to make the tea. 'No, you sit down,' Kit instructed, and pulled out a chair at the table.

'You're as bossy as your gran,' Maggie said. 'She never let me make a pot of tea, even in my own home. I remember when she first moved down the road from me and I had her over one day, she made my mother sit down at her own kitchen table and made the tea.' The older lady chuckled at the memory. 'Can you believe that?'

'I can.' Kit smiled as she placed the kettle on the stove to boil. She took out the teapot, filled it with tealeaves then placed cups and saucers, sugar and milk in the middle of the table and noticed that Maggie seemed to have drifted down memory lane. Once the kettle boiled, she made the tea and carried it to the table.

'Mrs Moore,' Kit said as she sat down, 'there was something that you said at Gran's service that surprised me.'

'What was that, dear?'

'Something about how Gran lived somewhere else, then moved to the house in Mosman?'

'You didn't know that?'

'No.'

'Oh, well when your gran first came here after Pearl Harbor, they rented a house in the Eastern Suburbs. I guess when the lease expired they moved over the Bridge.' Nothing in Maggie's tone indicated there was anything unusual in the story. Perhaps it really was as simple as that.

'Did she talk much about Pearl Harbor to you? Or her life in Hawaii?'

'Goodness, no!' Maggie exclaimed. 'Catherine made it clear that Hawaii and everything that happened there was off limits early on. I guess losing her brother would do that. It affected the whole family. Her mother, June, was a hard woman, hard on your poor Gran, but anyone could see she was devastated by her loss. The war was a terrible time, Kit, a terrible time. We did what we could to get through it, and in the end there were happy endings for some. Your grandpa and gran were a happy story. William swept your gran off her feet. She was a sad sack before him. Even sour faced June McGarrie smiled more when he was around. He saved your gran. Soulmates they were.'

'Yes.' Kitty dropped her gaze. The letters she discovered yesterday would indicate that her gran had more than one soulmate in her life.

When Maggie had finished her cup of tea, Kit offered her a refill. 'One's plenty, thank you, dear. I should be getting on before it's too hot out there.'

'I don't have a car here otherwise I'd offer to take you home. I'm sorry about that.'

'Nonsense.' Maggie waved her hand and picked up her bag to leave. 'I am perfectly capable of walking home.'

They were almost at the front door when Maggie stopped suddenly. 'Oh, I almost forgot.' She opened her handbag and fished out a wad of mail. 'The postie was coming past as I arrived. I got to talking to him and put these in my bag. Glad I remembered to give them to you; they are probably bills and stuff. I haven't had anything exciting sent to me in years.' She chuckled.

'Thanks. I probably need to redirect the mail to my place or Mum and Dad's. Not sure what I want to do with this place. Feels wrong to sell it, but it's kind of big for me.'

'I'm sure whatever you decide to do, Catherine would approve.'

Kit bid Maggie farewell, placed the letters on the hallway console and went back to work. It took her another hour or so, but she managed to go through all of her gran's clothes.

Deciding she needed some lunch before she could continue, she scoured the cupboards and managed to find a couple of cans of tuna, Vita-Weats and some cheese she was fairly sure was safe. Not in the mood for watching television while she ate, Kit decided to go through her gran's mail. As Maggie predicted, it was mostly bills, letters from charities Catherine supported, a couple of generic letters from local real estate agents, but it was the last letter that caught her attention. It was addressed to Catherine McGarrie, which wasn't all that unusual, but what made it stand out was the postmark. It was from San Diego.

Kit slid her finger under the back flap and paused. Should she be doing this? Shouldn't she give Gran's mail to her dad or one of her uncles who were handling all of Gran's finances? She felt conflicted. On one hand, she thought she didn't have the right to do so, but on the other hand, someone had to. Also, considering she had already read what she was sure was the most intimate letter her grandmother had ever received, she decided she should keep going.

Without giving it another thought, Kit ripped open the envelope and pulled out the contents. There were three sheets of paper: one looked like an invitation, one was a printed booklet or program, and the other was a letter. She read the letter first.

October 2nd, 2016

Dear Catherine,

My name is Chuck Wallis and I am part of a special organising committee for the 75th commemoration of the Pearl Harbor attack. I am writing this letter to you because as I understand it, you are the daughter of the late Admiral Conrad McGarrie and sister of Lieutenant Edward McGarrie, one of the many lives lost that tragic day. I know that we have invited you to commemoration ceremonies in the past without success and we also sent you a letter earlier this year about the special ceremonies planned for this coming December with no response. I do understand that at present, your age or some other reason may prohibit you from traveling to Hawaii. If this is the case, we would very much appreciate it if some other member of your immediate family would consider attending some of the special commemoration ceremonies we have scheduled for the two weeks from December 1st to December 14th. Your family was very well known, especially because of Admiral McGarrie's illustrious career with the US Navy.

I have enclosed a program detailing the schedule of events as well as an invitation for the official 75th commemoration ceremony that will be attended only by veterans and their immediate families. With every passing year, fewer and fewer veterans are with us, but in saying this, we have had a very positive response with many survivors and their families planning to make the trip, including some former sailors who may have known your brother.

Should you or a member of your family decide to make the trip, please RSVP to the details on the invitation. A member of our committee will contact you and be on hand to answer any questions and or queries.

Looking forward to hearing from you.

Sincerely,

Chuck Wallis

Kit folded the letter. She desperately wanted to go – she needed to represent her family – but she knew that her parents would never agree. They would remind her that there was a reason why her grandmother never went back and why she wouldn't want anyone to go. Sighing, she folded the letter and left it on the kitchen table. She went into the bedroom again and moved on to clearing out the bedside drawers. To her disappointment, there was no sign of the Arnott's tin there or under the bed.

Perhaps her grandmother had got rid of it after all, but considering her reaction to Kit's mother, that seemed highly unlikely. It had to be in another room, but where to begin looking? A quick search of the other rooms including her grandfather's study, which seemed untouched since his passing, came up with nothing. Deciding that she'd had enough for the day, she called Ben to see if he was around to pick her up. By sheer luck he was only a few minutes away.

Kit was closing the windows when she heard Ben walking up the front steps. 'I won't be long,' she called out as she pulled plastic bags of clothes into the hallway.

'Wow, is that all Gran's stuff?'

'Yep, well, all her clothes at least. I haven't gone through the linen cupboard – that's going to have to wait for another day.'

'Do you want me to load these in the car now?' Ben asked.

'I'm not sure where's best to take them. I was originally think-ing Barnardo's but the style of Gran's clothes might not be right for them. Did you have any luck today?' She headed towards the kitchen to clean up her lunch dishes.

'Nope,' Ben said as he followed her. 'Everything was either way over our budget or in such bad shape that it was nowhere near worth what they were asking. At this rate, I might have to beg you to rent this out to me. That's only if you decide not to sell.'

'Sure.' She filled the sink with hot soapy water. 'The more I think about it, the less I want strangers in here, at least for now.'

'You know I'll be hitting you up for mate's rates, don't you? After all, I *am* your favourite brother.'

Kit chuckled. She had her back to her brother, but she could tell by his tone he was grinning. 'I'll take that into consideration.'

'Hey, what's this?'

'What?' she asked as she wiped her hands dry.

'This letter.'

Kit whipped around to find Ben reading the letter about the 75th anniversary commemoration. She opened her mouth to say it was nothing, but it was too late. He had read it.

'Obviously we can't go, right?' Ben said as he read the program and invitation.

Kit remained silent, debating whether she should say some-thing. It was killing her knowing something that could be explo-sive and not being able to talk to anyone about it.

When she didn't respond, Ben looked up and narrowed his gaze. 'What?'

'Nothing. You're right. We can't go.'

Ben cocked his head, suspicion clear in his eyes. 'No, there is something there. Why would you of all people consider going to Hawaii knowing how Gran felt about the whole thing?'

Kit expelled a long, drawn-out breath as she plucked the invitation from Ben's fingers. 'Okay, so there may be a reason to go.' If she was going to talk to anyone in her family about the letter, about Charlie, Ben was the one.

'What is this reason? It had better be good.'

'Oh, yeah.' Kit gave a rueful laugh. 'You could say that.'

'Well then, spill.'

'You'll need to be sitting down when I tell you. And we're going to need wine for this one.'

Ben twirled the car keys on his pointer finger and motioned towards the door. 'Right then, to the pub we go.'

Half an hour later Kit nervously sipped her wine as Ben read through the letters. His brow was furrowed in concentration, not giving away any reaction. She wished he would hurry up and read the damn things and tell her what he thought – the suspense was killing her. But knowing that the pages were time worn and the writing was of an older cursive style, she understood why it was taking Ben a while to get through them.

When he finished, he carefully placed them on the table and took a sip of his drink. Then he shook his head and looked as if he were lost for words. 'Wow,' he finally said. 'Wow, wow, wow.'

'I know, right?'

'And you found this in her room yesterday?'

'Yep.' Kit nodded. 'When I went in looking for the Panadol, it was stuck at the back of the drawer.'

'I wonder why she kept it hidden?'

'Who knows? But there's more.' Kit told Ben about the Arnott's biscuit tin and what their mother had said.

'You think there could be more letters in the tin?'

'Maybe. But considering the content in those,' she said, nodding to the letters on the table, 'maybe not. I mean it's obvious, considering the dates and circumstances, that Charlie's letter was written first and then Gran wrote a letter back to him that she never got a chance to give to him because –'

'The attack happened,' Ben completed her sentence.

'Exactly.'

They were both silent for a while before Ben spoke. 'How old was Gran in 1941?'

'Sixteen.'

Her brother's eyebrows shot up. 'Jesus! My grandmother was younger than I was when she lost her virginity.'

Kit almost choked on her wine. 'I can't believe that's your take out from all this!'

'You were right, it warranted wine and a sit down. I wonder if Dad or the others have any idea about it?'

'I don't think so, and I don't want anyone else to know, so you're sworn to secrecy, got it?'

Ben mimed zipping his mouth. 'My lips are sealed.'

'Not even Ness can know, got it?' Kit warned.

Ben rolled his eyes. 'Yeah, got it.'

But they both knew that her threat was a moot point. Her brother would be sure to tell Ness the first chance he got. Too bad she couldn't take Ben with her to Hawaii, but it would raise too many questions. Maybe she could go under the guise of writing a news story.

'You're thinking of going, aren't you?' Ben cut through her thoughts.

'I'm giving it some serious thought, that's for sure.'

'You know Mum and Dad will not be too happy if you go.'

'I know, which is why I'm not telling them.'

'Seriously? I know you're an adult, but I can't be the only one that knows you're out of the country.'

'No, I'll tell them I'm going, just not the actual reason why.'

'Wait, so you just happened to need to go to Hawaii out of the blue? I don't think they'll buy it.'

'They will if it's for a story I'm working on.'

Ben nodded. 'That might work.'

'And by the time I go, you'll be back in Singapore and my cover won't be blown.'

Her brother scowled. 'Hey, I'm not that transparent, am I?'

'No, Benny boy.' She patted his hand affectionately. 'You're too honest. You have way too much integrity. Now be a good brother and go get us another round.'

'Good thing I'm not the journo then,' Ben grumbled as he slid out and headed towards the bar.

In his absence Kit pulled out the program that detailed the events planned for the 75th anniversary. There was a lot going on with events open to the public and selected events and ceremonies that were private – restricted to veterans and their families. Kit decided that ten days should be enough. As soon as she was back at her laptop, she would email her RSVP and start looking at flights and accommodation.

Ben returned armed with a bowl of hot chips smothered with tomato sauce and their drinks. Kit frowned. 'This wasn't what I was drinking.' She pointed to the flute of sparkling wine in front of her. 'I was enjoying a nice pinot grigio and this is ... some pink bubbly thing.'

'It's not from me. It's from the guy at the bar.'

Kit looked up to see a very attractive man smiling at her. Even from this distance she could tell he was way too manicured for her liking. His skin was smooth and tanned and she was sure his eyebrows were in better shape than hers. He lifted his champagne flute and in order not to appear rude, Kit returned the gesture with a fake smile pasted on her face. 'I can't believe you allowed a complete stranger to buy me a drink,' she said with gritted teeth.

'Why not? The guy asked if we were together, I told him I was your brother and he said he wanted to buy you a drink. It's perfectly safe to drink, by the way. I watched the bartender pour it.'

'You could've lied,' Kit hissed.

'Why would I do that?'

Kit rolled her eyes. 'Because I'm not interested.'

'How do you know? You haven't even met the guy!'

'I don't have to, I just know.' She shrugged and took a sip of the drink. It was surprisingly good, and she decided that it was worth finishing.

Across from her, Ben was looking at her intently.

'What is it? Do I have something on my face?'

'When was the last time you went out on a date?'

'What? Where did that come from?' Kit laughed nervously but inside her stomach dropped. She knew immediately why Ben was asking her.

'When was it, Kit? Three weeks ago? Three months ago?'

Kit looked down to her drink.

'Jesus, Kit, don't tell me that there's been no one since Jeremy?'

She didn't like the pity in his tone. 'And what if I said there hasn't?'

'Kit ...' Ben shook his head. 'Don't you think that it's ...'

'Sad? Pathetic? Go on,' she egged, her voice equal parts anger and heartbreak. 'Say it.'

Ben reached over and covered her hand with his. 'I was going to say that maybe it's time you thought about jumping back into the dating game. It's been three years, Kit.'

'Four and a half,' she automatically corrected him as her eyes welled with tears.

Ben opened his mouth to say something, but she cut him off. She didn't want to talk about Jeremy or moving on anymore. She would move on when she was ready to move on. She knew that people didn't think it was normal that she wasn't dating, but on the whole it was no one's business, not even Ben's.

'Anyway,' she said with exaggerated chirpiness. 'Who knows? I might meet someone fabulous in Hawaii.'

Kit could guess the answer to that question already. Chances were slim to none. Ben was the first person in quite a while to bring to her attention how long it had been since she had dated. She had been single for close to five years. Kit had to admit that she never intended for it to be so long ... it sort of happened. But it made her wonder – would she ever meet someone else? She wasn't sure, but she had to admit, it did scare her sometimes.

But what if she *didn't* want to find someone?

Now that scared her even more.

Eleven

One Lovely Day

Hawaii, December 1941

On the day that Kitty and Charlie were due to go to Kailua for their secret sojourn, the sky was picture perfect. It was so clear and blue that it reminded Kitty of the calm Pacific. Her mother was under the impression that Kitty and Penny were going to spend the day at the Kailua Beach Club. Kitty had it all planned, right down to Penny coming to the front door and making it known that they were heading off together. Although Penny Miller was not one of her mother's favourite people, Kitty knew that she would not worry about them spending time together if Eddie wasn't involved.

'Don't forget that I'm going to Una Walker's to play bridge tonight,' her mother said as Kitty ran out the door. 'Fumiyo will prepare a meal for you, so please pay her the courtesy of being home in time for dinner.'

'I will!' Kitty called over her shoulder as she slipped into Penny's car.

'Have a good day, Mrs McGarrie.' Penny smiled.

'I shall,' June replied blandly as she eyed Penny's rather revealing swimsuit. No doubt a myriad of disapproving comments were steamrolling through her mother's mind. Kitty bit back a giggle, only allowing the pleasure of releasing it once they were a safe distance away.

'Don't you dare laugh at me,' Penny chided. 'I'm dressed the way I am because of you.'

'Oh no, don't you shift the blame on me. I did not ask you to wear *that.*'

Penny smiled and shrugged. 'Call me crazy, but I love getting into character.'

'Crazy or not, I really do appreciate you doing this for me. You truly are a great friend.'

'I really hope you've thought this through, Kitty.' Penny's smiled sobered some.

'I have,' Kitty said defiantly. 'I'm to be shipped off in about a month's time and I know I would regret it for the rest of my life if I didn't take this chance. You understand why this is so important. I may never have another chance like this.'

Penny nodded. 'I understand, and I couldn't bear to think how hard it would be to be away from Eddie. I adore him so much.'

'And it's obvious how much he loves you.'

'Really?' Penny's face turned bright red.

'Oh, Penny, don't be daft, you know he does!'

'I guess I do.' She giggled. 'Can you keep a secret?'

Kitty was intrigued. 'You know I can.'

'Eddie and I are thinking of getting married.'

'Oh, Penny!' Kitty couldn't help but imagine her mother's reaction when Eddie told her he was marrying Penny Miller.

'Well, don't get too excited, Eddie thinks we should wait till I've finished school. But I would gladly marry him tomorrow if given the chance.' Penny sighed dreamily.

Kitty felt the same about Charlie. She allowed herself to dream about a double wedding. Eddie and Penny, she and Charlie. It wasn't that far removed from reality, was it? After all, Charlie was Eddie's friend and her father seemed to like him too.

'But you have to promise you'll tell not a soul about this,' Penny said gravely. 'I mean it, Kitty. Eddie would flip his lid if he knew I was telling you about it.'

Kitty did feel a little hurt that Eddie felt he couldn't share this with her. They had always been close, but when it came to him and Penny, he was very secretive. 'Cross my heart.' Kitty did the motions to prove she meant it. 'I cannot wait till we're sisters. I always wanted another girl in the family.'

Penny squealed. 'Oh, let's hope we're both blessed with girls. Girls are fun.'

Kitty agreed. She could picture herself with lots and lots of daughters, and maybe a son.

'Kitty ...' Penny had concern written all over her face. 'You will be careful with Charlie, won't you?'

'What do you mean?' Kitty laughed. 'Charlie is the perfect gentleman. He is nice and sweet and ...' tingles and goose bumps danced over her skin as she said her next words, 'he loves me.'

Penny chewed on her bottom lip. 'Yes, that's exactly what I mean. You know how it is when a guy and a girl love each other, heck sometimes they don't even love each other and they ... you know ...'

Penny's face was bright red. Kitty knew what her friend was trying to say. It wasn't anything that she hadn't already thought about, especially as the day drew closer. After all, she was about to spend a whole day with Charlie. Alone. Would he be expecting her to? Most of all, how did she feel about it? Kitty would be lying if she said she wasn't nervous. She was torn and, truth be told, she didn't know what she wanted to do. 'Are you trying to give me the birds and the bees talk?'

'Well, darn it, someone has to. Has your mother talked to you about this?'

'Goodness no!' Kitty laughed at the thought. Her mother had had a difficult enough time talking to her about getting her periods. What June McGarrie didn't realise was that by the time she got around to talking to her about it, Kitty had been having her period for two years. It was Penny's sister Annie, who was a few years older than them, who had prepared them for how their bodies were going to change. Kitty would never forget the look on eleven-year-old Penny's face; Kitty was about ten at the time. It must have mirrored her own because all the talk about bleeding and cramping and such was nauseating. Later, when it happened to her for the first time, Kitty was grateful for Annie's candour and for Penny's experience before her own.

'I just don't want you to go through what Annie did. I mean, I know that you and Charlie are not the same ...'

'I know that you are worried about me, and I love you for it, but it'll all be fine. Nothing like that is going to happen to me. After today I don't know when I'll see Charlie again, let alone be on my own with him. I just want this one day that I can look back on and say at least we had one day together.'

'You're right.' Penny smiled, but didn't look at all that convinced. Kitty pushed Penny's concern out of her head. In about an hour she and Charlie would be together and alone, and that's all she wanted to think about. It was going to be one lovely day and she couldn't wait.

The trolley snaked through Honolulu to Kaimuki, the noise of metal on metal – the crackling, staccato sounds of *pop, pop, crack,*

crack – filled Charlie's ears as the trolley car turned. He sat by an open window, feeling the jerky stops, hearing the screeching brakes like chalk on a blackboard, and the snapping sounds from the electric cables. Behind him two older gentlemen spoke of impending war and debated how long it would be before America was drawn into battle, but one clear thing they seemed to agree on was that it would be Japan that would draw them in. Neither of them seemed to care that Japan had declared they wouldn't attack.

War. It was all everyone spoke about these days. When Charlie arrived on the island ten months ago he was told to pretty much get used to the fact he would never see battle – not while he was posted on Hawaii. With that in mind, it wasn't long before he adapted to the relaxed pace and the slow way of island life.

But now it felt as if they were all sitting on a ticking time bomb. The words 'it's only a matter of time ...' and 'once we're in battle ...' were thrown around more and more. It was no longer 'if', but 'when'. Rumours of war were rampant. In tea houses in Chinatown and gambling parlours in Honolulu, bets were being taken as to when it would break out and where.

Every day drew them closer to the inevitable, and every day that passed was one less day that Kitty would be here.

In one way he was thankful for the Rear Admiral's foresight and his decision to move Kitty away, as it was for her own safety. Charlie wondered whether, in his decision to send his wife and daughter to Australia, the Rear Admiral knew something no one else did. Did he feel that even the mainland wasn't safe? Either way, in less than a month, Kitty would leave and Charlie was unsure if he would ever see her again.

He told himself that he should be grateful for another reason too. If Kitty wasn't here, the temptation of wanting her in the way he did would dissipate. He would bury himself in his work and force himself to enjoy the company of women like those who worked on Hotel Street. Surely after enough booze he wouldn't care who was on his lap. A warm body with ample bosoms and vixen red lips should be enough to sate his need.

Who am I kidding? he thought.

That night when Kitty had walked into The Beachcomber and found his face in another woman's chest he was miserable. All he could think of was Kitty. She consumed his every thought, and he knew that was dangerous.

He had lied to Eddie this morning about his plans for the day. He had told him that an old pal was in town, staying in Kaimuki, and they were going to catch up.

After a few more stops, Charlie was off the trolley and searching for a jitney ride to Kailua. He almost chickened out. The fact that he and Kitty were sneaking around and going to great lengths to do so meant they both knew how wrong this was.

But it's only one day. If you don't go, she will be heartbroken.

The thought of hurting Kitty nearly killed him. It was bad enough seeing the look on her face that night. In hindsight, the way he'd run after her was extremely risky. But Eddie had been so inebriated and preoccupied with Penny that the next morning he thought the whole thing was a dream. In fact, Eddie seemed to only remember seeing Penny. He didn't mention Kitty and there was no way Charlie was going to tell him. It seemed that none of the other guys, including Walter, realised that Kitty was there, and Charlie knew he had much to be thankful for. Walter was surprisingly civil to him of late, even going so far as to being somewhat nice to him. Not that Charlie cared if they were pals or not. He knew they were never going to be friends, there was nothing in the world that could change his fundamental dislike and mistrust for Richie Walter, but he wasn't going to complain that the snide comments and looks had stopped, for now at least. Still, there was something about the sudden lack of interest or at least the lack of overt animosity that didn't sit well with Charlie. There was almost something malevolent about it all. Could it be possible that Walter was brewing something?

Shaking the thought out of his mind, he focused on scoring a ride. A couple of minutes later, he found a jitney and arrived in Kailua a little after their agreed meeting time. Following Kitty's instructions, he made his way to the McGarrie beach cottage and once he saw it, Charlie skidded to a halt.

'*Maronna mia!* Holy smokes,' he said out loud.

He should've known that when it came to the McGarries even a cottage wouldn't be so modest. It was unlike any cottage he had seen. The outside was freshly painted in a shade of blue that reminded him of the colour of a robin's egg. Charlie was sure the paint would have some fancy name, and he could almost imagine June McGarrie insisting on it being shipped over from the mainland. His grandfather had taken him to The Hamptons as a treat when he was young, and looking at the grandeur that was in front of him, it reminded him of all the imposing holiday homes there. He decided then that their owners must have money to burn, and it was incomprehensible to a young Charlie that such huge homes were only used occasionally. Just like the McGarrie beach cottage.

Walk away, Charlie. Walk away right now. You don't belong here. You will never belong in a house like this.

It was sound advice. He could walk back to the main street and jitney back to Pearl. But before he could consider that idea further, the front door opened and Kitty appeared. She looked beautiful and happy. One look at her and Charlie knew he wasn't going anywhere but inside that house with her. God help him.

'You're here!' Kitty had been waiting for less than half an hour but it felt like hours. Every time a car passed, she would pull the curtains aside to see if it was Charlie. Of course, she had no idea how he was coming, only that he was catching the trolley to Kaimuki and a jitney from there.

They stood on the perfectly manicured lawn looking shyly at each other as if it were their first meeting.

'Do you want –'

'Maybe we should –'

They both started talking at the same time and laughed nervously.

'You go,' Charlie urged.

'I was going to ask if you wanted to come inside for a while or if we should head to the beach?'

She watched while Charlie expelled a breath as if the latter option was what he was hoping for. 'I think going to the beach is a great idea.' He smiled and as always it made her tummy flutter.

'Come on.' She walked up to him and grabbed his hand, threading her fingers through his. For the first time she didn't need to look around to make sure they couldn't be seen. It felt good. It felt right. 'Let's walk through the house. We have a private beach all to ourselves.' She led Charlie up the porch to the front door.

'Private beach?' There was no missing the awe in Charlie's voice. Kitty thought it may also be tinged with sarcasm, but when she looked over her shoulder there was no sign of it.

'Holy smokes!' Behind her Charlie had stopped and was looking around the room in wonderment. 'From the outside it looks huge but from the inside ...' he shook his head.

'My mother's doing,' Kitty said. 'All of it. She drove my father crazy till he allowed her to have free rein. Secretly I think he only agreed to let her renovate the cottage to keep her occupied and out of his hair. He called it her "little project".'

'There's nothing little about this joint,' Charlie drawled. His mouth was still gaping when they made their way down the back porch towards the private beach. Kailua was beautiful at the best of times, but a secluded beach attached to a wondrous piece of real estate ... well, Charlie now knew what a million bucks looked like, but the woman he was with, she was priceless.

'Are you hungry? Fumiyo has prepared a picnic for us.'

'Your cook made us a picnic?' he asked in panic.

Kitty giggled. 'Not exactly for *us*. She made it thinking I was coming here with Penny.'

She spread out the picnic blanket and set down the basket she had earlier put in the shade of a small tree. Fumiyo had filled it to the brim with her famous turkey and cranberry sandwiches, key lime pie and fresh homemade lemonade.

'Wowsers.' Charlie marvelled as Kitty unpacked the basket. 'I'm sorry I don't have something stronger like a beer.' Kitty watched as his gaze dipped to her lips. Suddenly, despite being outdoors, Kitty was finding it hard to breathe.

'I'm fine with lemonade for now. Later, I'm sure I'll find another way to quench my thirst.' He grabbed two bottles and popped their tops, handing her one. 'What should we drink to?'

Kitty considered him for a moment before answering. 'To one lovely day.'

'I like that.' Charlie clinked his bottle against hers. 'To one lovely day.'

Kitty lifted her drink to her lips. But she didn't get to taste a single sip. Instead Charlie took her face in his hands and crushed his mouth against hers, and it was sweeter than any lemonade.

Charlie couldn't help himself. There was something about how the sunlight hit her deep mahogany hair, reflecting shades of gold, that made her look even more beautiful than he'd seen her before. The kiss took Kitty by surprise. She dropped the lemonade in her hand and it went all over her skirt. Charlie felt the cool liquid spill on his trousers only moments before Kitty gasped and pulled away from the kiss.

'Oh no, I'm a total mess!' She inspected the damage and frowned before she looked over at Charlie. 'And I spilt it all over you too. I'm so sorry.'

'I should be the one apologising. If I hadn't kissed you, we wouldn't be in this mess.'

'Don't you dare apologise for kissing me,' Kitty chided before leaning over and drawing him in for a deep kiss. 'But we should get cleaned up. Did you bring your swimming trunks?'

'I sure did.'

'Follow me.' As they made their way inside, Charlie was alarmed to realise they were heading towards the staircase. 'There are some bathrooms upstairs. We can change there.'

He grabbed his bag and silently followed Kitty as she led him into a bedroom that was easily the size of his apartment back home. 'There is an en suite through there.' Kitty pointed to a closed door.

'A what?' Charlie asked blankly.

'It's a bathroom, silly.'

'Inside a bedroom?'

'It's adjoining,' she explained as she opened the door for him. What was inside had to be the fanciest bathroom he'd ever laid eyes on. Charlie was gobsmacked.

'It's smaller than a normal bathroom and it adjoins two rooms. A fault in the design of the house, according to my mother,' Kitty said dryly. 'I'll leave you to it. I'll go and freshen up too.' She closed the door behind her, leaving Charlie to fully take in his surroundings.

Small? There was nothing small about it. He'd never seen a bacchousa, as some Brooklynites called their bathrooms, like it. On one side, huge double-hung windows framed a spectacular view of the ocean and allowed the sunlight to spill into the room. A large clawed bathtub was installed in front of the windows, so you could enjoy the soak and the vista of Kailua Beach. The tiles on the floor were a matt black, but there was nothing dull or dreary about them – they accentuated the white wall tiles and the striking black-and-gold border that was about three quarters of the way up the wall. He shook his head as he stripped out of his uniform and into his swimming gear. Unsure whether he should head downstairs or wait for Kitty where he was, he went into the other adjoining room to discover it was an even bigger bedroom.

Floor-to-ceiling windows lined one wall and on another, tall French doors led onto a wooden veranda. Pulling aside the sheer white curtains in front of the doors, Charlie saw the pièce de résistance – the sparkling Pacific Ocean. He sat down on the bed that was perfectly placed to take in the view.

'There you are.' Kitty appeared in a two-piece swimming out-fit that knocked the air out of his solar plexus. It was the colour of lush ripe strawberries and highlighted all the right curves.

'Wowsers.' Charlie was sure his tongue was hanging out of his mouth. Kitty giggled shyly as she came to stand in front of him.

'I was wondering where you'd got to.'

He swallowed hard as all the blood rushed from his head and down his body.

'I was admiring the view.'

'Sorry to disturb you.'

'You're not.' He smiled, leaning back onto the bed and pulling Kitty down with him. Their lips met – soft and slow. While their kisses to date had been brief and chaste, Charlie took his time to languidly savour Kitty's lush lips. His mouth found her creamy neck, and he made his way down, leaving a trail of kisses in his wake. A moan escaped Kitty's lips and only strengthened his desire for her. He ran his hands down to her waist, desperately needing to feel her bare skin under his fingertips. Without thinking, he took hold of the strap on the back of her swimming costume.

'Charlie ...' she breathed dreamily.

'I know.' He sighed reluctantly. 'We should stop and head to the beach.'

'No,' she said with such clear conviction. 'I don't want to stop.'

Puzzled, Charlie looked up to find her lips swollen and bee stung from his kisses, her gaze full of want and desire. There was no mistaking what was on her mind. It was the same thing that was on his, and yet, he still asked, 'What are you saying, Kitty?'

She bit her bottom lip as her cheeks reddened and Charlie had to hold himself back from ravishing her. 'I'm saying that I want ... Charlie, I want you ... all of you.'

He shook his head. His heart and body were screaming yes, but his mind was trying to be rational. 'Kitty, we shouldn't.'

His response disappointed her. 'Charlie, I love you and after today I don't know when I'll ever see you again. It may be weeks, months, who knows, but one thing I do know is that if we don't make love today, I will regret it for the rest of my life. Can you tell me with absolute certainty that you wouldn't regret it?'

She held his gaze, those sapphire-blue eyes of hers penetrating into his soul, and there was no way he could lie to her. His heart was thundering so fast, so loudly, the sound reverberated in his ears. 'Kitty, I love you so much, and God help me, the way I feel about you shouldn't be legal. If your brother or father were to find out ...' He shook his head and expelled a long shaky breath.

There hadn't been many times in his life when Charlie had acted with his heart and not his head. Logic and reason always ruled, but when it came to Kitty McGarrie, none of that mattered. She was right. One day he would look back and regret not making the most of the moment. 'I promised you one day, and I shall honour that promise.'

Kitty smiled full and bright, and for a small moment in time he allowed himself not to think about impending war, about how he and Kitty were from totally different worlds – worlds where their love would be frowned upon. He allowed himself to be cocooned in the here and now, for today it would only be the two of them and the rest of the world would cease to exist. It was, after all, for one day only. What harm could come of it?

The curtains billowed in the breeze. Outside she heard rolling waves crashing against the shore and the distinct cry of the Hawaiian honeycreeper in the distance. With her head nestled in the crook of Charlie's arm, the only sound she could really hear was that of his beating heart.

This, exactly this, was heaven. With her eyes closed she basked in the afterglow of their coupling as a self-satisfied smile slowly spread on her lips. Charlie was a gentle and attentive lover. He didn't rush, took his time exploring every inch of her body, making sure that all her senses were fully heightened, making sure she was ready before slowly moving on to the act of lovemaking.

And that was exactly what it was. It was even more glorious than she imagined it would be. Annie once spoke about losing her virginity. She described it as messy and excruciatingly painful. Kitty's first time was none of that. When they were one, Kitty felt an indescribable feeling consume her. At that point she truly understood what it meant to have a soulmate. To have that one person in this whole entire earth who was made just for you. For Kitty that was Charlie. He was the right sock to her left. It was as if she had loved him for a thousand years already, and she would love him till she took her last dying breath.

'You know that we cannot stay here all day.'

Charlie's voice broke her reverie. Kitty fluttered her eyes open. 'I don't see why not.'

His laugh reverberated against her cheek. 'You're supposedly spending the day in the sun. Shouldn't you have evidence to show for it?'

Kitty sighed and propped herself up on one elbow. 'I suppose you have a point.' She ran her hand over his chest, her fingers toying with the chain of his dog tags. His body was so close to perfection it gave her butterflies.

'You know I do.' He tucked a strand of hair behind her ear then moved his hand to caress her bare backside. Automatically Kitty moved her body closer, hooking her leg over his hip. 'I know what you're trying to do,' he said, but he didn't move her away.

Kitty pouted. 'Is it so wrong that I want to stay here with you all day?'

Charlie chuckled as he dropped a kiss on her shoulder. 'We'll come back in a while, but right now, we should head out to the sun. After all, what's the point in having a private beach if you can't enjoy it?'

Reluctantly, Kitty untangled herself from his warm body and dressed. The sun was high in the sky when they walked out onto the stretch of sand with not another soul around. They lay side by side in companionable silence, letting the rays of the sun kiss their skin. The breeze that had graced them earlier in the day was gone and Kitty felt a sweat pool in between her breasts. When it became unbearable, she sat up and removed the top of her swimming costume.

'Kitty, have you lost your mind?'

'I'm hot and there's no one else around.'

Charlie sat up and shielded his eyes from the sun, his gaze squarely on her breasts as he spoke. 'There are other ways to cool down ... you could go for a swim.'

'Good idea.' She gave him a sly smile as she stood up and peeled off the rest of her swimming costume, dropping the top and bottom strategically on Charlie's lap. He didn't speak immediately; he looked at her toes, then knees, before his gaze lingered between her legs. Then he fisted her swimmers, threw them aside and stood up before peeling off his trunks.

'Come on, let's cool off proper.'

They ran hand in hand into the surf, the water cooling her down immediately and making her body break out in goose bumps.

'Cold enough for you?' Charlie asked as he cupped her breasts underneath the water, languidly running his thumbs against her already pebbled nipples and pressing his lips against the side of her neck. Kitty groaned her response as she wrapped her legs around his waist, letting the buoyancy of the waves rock their bodies together.

'Charlie ...'

'Hmm?'

'I don't think I ever want this day to end.'

He sighed, full and heavy. 'Neither do I, Kitty. Neither do I.'

Later, as they emerged from the water wrapped up in their love, neither one of them felt the sinister wind that whirled past, chilling the air. Neither of them noticed a lone figure standing on the beach. They didn't know that he had been watching them for a while, and they were blissfully unaware of the wrath he was about to unleash.

Twelve

Seeing Ghosts

Honolulu, December 2016

Whoever came up with the term 'cattle class' had the right idea. It wasn't that Kit was a particularly snobbish traveller – she had done the Melbourne to Heathrow flight countless times and that was way longer than Melbourne to Hawaii, but there was something about red-eye flights that messed with her. It didn't help that the plane had run almost two hours late – something about engineering issues.

The first thing that hit her as she disembarked was the heat. Even though she arrived in what was technically winter, it was a whole lot warmer, not to mention more humid, than it had been in Melbourne where it was currently, technically summer.

The second thing was the Hawaiian music. There was actually Hawaiian music playing as she walked through the terminal and women in hula skirts placing leis around people's necks.

The third was the number of Japanese tourists. There were large tour groups everywhere. As preparation for her trip and during the flight, Kit read all she could about the Pearl Harbor attack and the aftermath. She wished that it were something she'd done earlier. Maybe she could have helped her gran sort out her feelings about it all. It was obvious that the attack had scarred her for life, but over the years, her family had all taken the same approach to it – you don't talk to Gran about her childhood unless she mentions it. You don't ask about Pearl Harbor. And for goodness sake, you never, *ever* mention Hawaii.

But now, knowing all she did, Kit wondered if they had done her grandmother a disservice by tiptoeing around it?

And then there was Charlie ...

In the lead-up to her arrival, she'd been almost boorish in her ambitions. She was going to come and find Charlie, or at least find someone who knew him.

The problem was, without so much as a last name there was very little to go on. Ben tried to warn her, but she insisted that being a journalist she had all the skills that she would need to know what to do once she arrived.

But now she was here and suddenly it didn't seem all that simple.

Dragging her luggage into the searing midday sun, she scanned the crowd for the driver she had arranged with the hotel. Finally, she spotted a man holding her name chatting to a guy in his early thirties. Even from a distance it was clear they knew each other well, but that was not what bothered her. It was what the driver did next. He glanced at his watch, looked over at the doorway from the arrivals hall ever so briefly before shrugging and opening the car door for the guy.

'He couldn't be,' Kit said aloud and stopped in her tracks, gobsmacked. The guy was stealing her ride, and worse still, the driver was enabling him.

'Hey, hey!' she screamed as she ran as fast as her dodgy suitcase would allow, arriving in the nick of time.

'Can I help you?'

'Yeah, you can tell me what gives you the right to steal my ride.'

'Your ride?' The man looked at her blankly for a moment before realisation seemed to dawn. 'You must be Bennett, Kit and you're an Aussie.'

'*Kit* Bennett and yeah, I'm an Aussie,' she bit out, perhaps a little too sharply. In her defence she was dog tired, and while it would've been relatively easy to step away and join the nearby taxi queue, years of going toe-to-toe with her brothers and cousins was ingrained. Kit had always been stubborn.

'Well, Kit Bennett, Clint here has been waiting for you for over three hours.'

'My flight was late leaving Melbourne and I had no way of communicating.' Despite Clint standing right next to her, Kit directed her tirade at the man squarely in front of her.

'No way?' He cocked a brow. 'Are you telling me that cell phones haven't made their way down under?'

Kit felt her irritation kick up a notch, but by the same token, she begrudgingly had to concede that he had a point. 'Look, yes, maybe I should've called and left a message.' She sighed before turning to the driver and addressing him directly. 'I'm sorry.'

'Ah, that's okay, ma'am.' He gave her a small smile before turning to look to the other man for direction.

'Take Ms Bennett to her hotel,' the man instructed him, while still watching her. He seemed satisfied that she had admitted she was in the wrong. 'I'll catch a cab.'

'If you're sure,' the driver said, making his way to the trunk of the car with the suitcase.

'Yes, Clint, thanks.' He nodded to the driver, before turning towards Kit. 'Enjoy your vacation, Bennett, Kit.'

He was gone before she could reply, the driver holding the door open for her.

'Here you go, miss.'

She climbed in and apologised to the driver, Clint, once again.

'Ah, mistakes happen.' He seemed way less perturbed about the situation than the other guy. Kit considered asking Clint why the man had seemed so annoyed, but decided against it. Chances were she wouldn't see him again and it didn't matter. Her energy was better spent on the task at hand. Finding Charlie.

When Clint put her suitcase down in the lobby of the Hilton Hawaiian Village, Kit tipped him and he smiled and bid her farewell. 'Enjoy your vacation, miss.'

'Thanks,' she replied, not bothering to correct him. Of course it would seem as if she were here for a holiday.

'Aloha, welcome to the Hilton Hawaiian Village.'

Kit looked up and was greeted by a smiling young woman but instead of returning her smile, Kit looked past her and was instantly mesmerised by the view of the beach that was right out of a movie scene.

'It's beautiful,' she murmured, before immediately realising the receptionist must have wondered what she was talking about. 'Sorry, it's just that view ...' Kit motioned to the beach. 'I mean, how do you get any work done?'

The woman, whose nametag told Kit her name was Leilani, chuckled. 'Oh, it's a struggle, that's for sure. Are you checking in today?'

Kit handed over her reservation details and went back to staring at the view. She was a Sydney girl and Kit always believed that her home city had some of the most beautiful beaches she'd ever seen, but this was something else. She wondered if her gran had spent any time down here.

Her research on Waikiki had told her that around the time her gran had been a young girl there had been three main hotels – The Royal Hawaiian, The Moana, now known as the

Moana Surfrider, and The Halekulani. The Niumalu Hotel had stood on the grounds now occupied by the Hilton Hawaiian Village.

'So you're from Melbourne?' Leilani asked.

'Yes, originally from Sydney though.'

'Oh, I love Sydney. I spent some time down under last year. Sydney was amazing. You guys are in summer, right?'

'Yes, we are.' They chatted politely for a few moments more before Leilani handed over the room key.

'Now, we have a very busy week coming up. We are a few days away from the 75th anniversary of Pearl Harbor and the hotel is at near capacity.'

'I know, that's why I'm here.' Leilani looked surprised so Kit elaborated.

'My gran's father and brother were in the Navy. Her brother died in the attack.'

'I'm so sorry for your family's loss.'

'Thank you.' Kit smiled, feeling like a fraud. She barely knew anything about her gran's family. 'My grandmother passed away not long ago, so I'm here in her honour.'

And she'd probably be rolling in her grave right about now.

'That's so sweet of you. You know the hotel is hosting the gala dinner on the eve of the commemoration, right?'

'Yes, I'm going along.'

'You'll meet the veterans and some other families of veterans.'

Yes, Kit thought. That was the plan.

Her room in the Rainbow Tower looked out over Waikiki Beach with panoramic views of the Duke Kahanamoku Lagoon and Diamond Head as well. When Kit mentioned that she'd heard Diamond Head was a popular tourist trap, Leilani advised her to go to the climbing spot early, before the crowds, and then she rattled off a list of other places Kit should see while she was on the island.

Kit realised Waikiki was a holiday paradise, but sightseeing wasn't what she was here for. Her focus was finding Charlie and the first chance she would have would be the Veteran Gala Dinner. Maybe someone would remember Admiral McGarrie and if she were lucky, she would meet someone who knew Eddie McGarrie.

'I'm going to find him, Gran. I'm going to find Charlie and give him this letter.'

Kit only hoped there would be someone to give the letter to, otherwise the whole trip would be a waste.

The next day as Kit got ready for the Veteran Gala Dinner her phone beeped with a message from Ben. It was a single word.

Anything?

Since disclosing the letters to him, her brother had become actively interested in her search for Charlie. They had made the assumption that Charlie would more than likely have been in the Navy and they compiled a list of surviving veterans who could possibly fit the bill. None of them went by the name 'Charlie', though, so their only hope was that out of the remaining seven men named Charles or Chuck, one could be her gran's Charlie.

'What if he's dead already?' Ben had asked.

'Then we leave this alone. I only want to give Gran's letter to him, not to anyone in his family. I mean if the guy is no longer around, I'm not going to drop a bombshell on his family that their grandfather or father or, God forbid, husband had a pretty hot affair with the Admiral's daughter. The letter from Charlie said they could never be together. What if that was because he was already married?'

Kit knew that there was a big risk that her trip would end up being fruitless, but even if that were the case, the one thing she could take from it was the overwhelming admiration and respect Americans had for their veterans and servicemen and women. The whole of Waikiki was buzzing with the vibe of the commemoration and while there was a sombre undertone there was also a celebratory feel. Tomorrow was 7 December and it was a big day. Kit was attending a service early in the morning at Pearl Harbor and spending most of the day there before heading back to Waikiki for the parade down Kalakaua Avenue. Leilani had arranged transport for her and after hearing about the airport debacle, she promised it would be a smoother trip.

Kit replied to her brother's text as she contemplated outfits. Then she snapped her two choices and sent the photos to Ben with the comment:

Ask Ness which one I should wear.

Ben replied with:

Groan. Really????

Just do it, Benji!

Don't call me Benji, you know I hate it. (Angry face emoji)

Show her the damn photos! Please!

Fine.

A few moments later, Ben texted his reply.

Ness says to go with the blue. It'll highlight the red in your hair and it'll also ... shit I can't believe I'm typing this to my sister ... NESS says it'll also help you pick up a sailor (crying emoji, shocked emoji).

Kit laughed at Ben's discomfort.

Doubt there'd be any young sailors there tonight – it's a gala for veterans remember? Besides I'm only looking for one sailor.

Good luck, keep me posted.

Thx

But as Kit walked over to the main lawn where the gala was to be held and saw the number of people attending, she realised that it would take more than luck to find a needle in the haystack.

'Hey there, you're looking a little lost.' Kit turned around to see Leilani holding a near empty tray of drinks.

'Yeah, you could say that. Guess it's all a little daunting.'

'Just relax and mingle. Remember these people all have a lot in common with you – you all have family members who were touched by the attack on Pearl Harbor.'

Kit nodded even though on the inside she was increasingly feeling like a fake. If anyone scratched beneath the surface they would discover that besides knowing their names, Kit knew nothing about Edward and Rear Admiral Conrad McGarrie.

'Why are you serving drinks?'

'Long story.' Leilani sighed. 'Stay here, I'll be back in a moment with a fresh tray and you can have a glass to calm your nerves.'

Bless Leilani, a few minutes later she returned true to her word. 'Beer or wine or champagne?'

'While I'm tempted to have one of each, I'll take a champagne for now.'

'Good choice, although the craft beers are good too. It's a local microbrewery owned by a friend of mine. He's from Kailua, which is where I live.'

Kit picked up a bottle and had a closer look. 'Impressive.'

'It is.' She nodded and then her face lit up. 'I think he may actually be here tonight. I'm pretty sure his pop was in Pearl Harbor. If I see him, I'll tell him to keep a look out for you.' Leilani excused herself to get on with her job and Kit felt a tap on her shoulder.

'Excuse me, miss, hope you don't mind me asking, but who are you here with?'

The older man was a veteran, as Kit could tell because he was wearing a hat that showed he was a survivor from the USS *West Virginia*.

'I'm here on my own,' she said, and smiled.

'You're Australian?'

She knew the accent would raise questions. 'Yes, but my grand-mother was born in America. Both her father and brother were there that day, at Pearl Harbor, I mean.'

'Who were your grandmother's father and brother, if you don't mind me asking?'

'Edward and Conrad McGarrie,' Kit said, expecting him to shake his head and say that he'd never heard of them. But instead, the older gentleman's eyes widened immediately and his face paled. His reaction worried Kit as he looked like he'd seen a ghost.

'Sir? Are you all right?' she asked, concerned.

'Well I'll be damned ...' he said, looking at her intently with his blue eyes. He was silent for a few seconds before asking, 'Kitty? Kitty McGarrie, is that you?'

Thirteen

Road to Infamy

5 December 1941

'Be ready in an hour, Florio.'

Charlie looked up to see Richie Walter standing in front of him. The man was smiling, but there was something about it that sent alarm bells ringing in his mind. Walter had been way too chummy to him, but every now and then, out of the corner of his eye, Charlie swore he could see him glaring at him full of hatred.

'Yeah, I guess.' Charlie went back to shining his shoes and Walter chuckled.

'What? An evening in the company of Pearl's finest ladies of the night not interest you?'

Not in the slightest, Charlie thought. Not after the day he had with Kitty last week at Kailua. It was so perfect it felt like a dream. Holding Kitty in his arms, making love to her while the waves crashed around them. Charlie had never felt something so wrong could feel so right.

'I'm on duty in the morning,' Charlie said by way of excuse. 'Don't have liberty till Sunday.'

'Which is why you need to bury yourself between some honey's legs,' Walter said and slapped his back. 'Trust me, you're not going to want to miss this. It's going to be a night to remember.'

Walter walked off whistling Guy Lombardo's 'It Looks Like Rain in Cherry Blossom Lane'. Only later would the real impact of the song make sense.

That evening, a cab dropped them off in front of the Y at the top of Hotel Street, suitably liquored up thanks to a bottle of rum that Eddie had supplied. Most of the others had the weekend as liberty, and Kerr was hell bent on dragging them all to the football game the next day between University of Hawaii and the Williamette Bearcats.

'I heard it's a sell out.' Roberts lit his cigarette, the tip glowing against the velvet black night as they made their way to China Chop Sui on Maunakea for a feed before heading to a pool hall for a beer or two.

'Nah, I can score us seats, easy,' Kerr boasted. 'Besides, military gets free entry.'

'I'm in,' Walter chimed. 'Those Oregon boys have nothing on ours.'

'Hey, aren't you a New England boy?' Roberts pointed out.

'Ay, wise guy, I'm here now and while I am, I'm as Hawaiian as they come.'

'For a Hawaiian you sure don't like the water. I don't think I've ever seen you swim,' Roberts ribbed, and Charlie's sour mood lifted ever so briefly. Walter likening himself to a local was laughable when they were all *malihinis* – newcomers.

He'd never noticed it before, but Roberts was right, he couldn't recall seeing Walter in the water. Ever.

'Who needs swimming when you're skirt patrolling?' There was something deeper in Richie Walter's overly defensive comment, but Charlie didn't have the energy to scratch beneath the surface.

Eddie passed him the bottle but he waved it away. Charlie didn't have much thirst for Tennessee whisky tonight. He shouldn't have come. Should've made up some crap about feeling unwell, but he knew Eddie would've found a way of making him change his mind.

'Hey, Florio, wanna know a secret?' Eddie jabbed him with his elbow as they walked a few paces behind the others.

'Sure, what's up?'

'I'm going to ask Penny Miller to marry me tomorrow.' Even in the dark night, Charlie could see that Eddie was grinning like a fool. A love-struck fool.

'Well, what da you know?' Charlie slapped his hand in Eddie's. 'Congratulations, pal.' He couldn't help but feel envious of Eddie – he was free to marry whomever he wanted.

'I told her that we should wait till she finished school next June, but then the other day, I got to thinking – what if we're at war by June? I know she's young, but I want a wife to come home to after the war, you know what I'm saying?'

'Yeah,' Charlie muttered, the envy in his gut tightening.

'And tonight, I'm going to treat it like it's my stag night. Booze and a good time, right?'

Charlie nodded without answering.

'I really appreciate you putting up with Kitty these past couple of months, but after tomorrow, you're off the hook.'

'Thanks, good to know.' Charlie hoped the sombre tone in his voice wouldn't be transparent.

'Hey, why so glum? I just told you I'm getting married and you sound like I've invited you to a freaking funeral.'

'Ah, gee, sorry, Eddie. It's great news, really. I'm happy for you and Penny.' He smiled and not because he had to, but because he really was happy for his pal. 'Your families will be thrilled.'

'Well, Penny's are, my dad took a little convincing, I got him on side, but my mom ...' Eddie grimaced. 'She's going to flip her lid.' He laughed and it was so infectious that Charlie joined in too.

'Wait, your mother doesn't know about this?'

'Nope. It was my dad's idea. Kitty doesn't know either.'

'Hey, don't look at me, I'm not about to spill the beans.' Charlie laughed awkwardly.

'Are you two bozos coming?' Walter called out from the door to the restaurant.

'All right, hold your horses,' Eddie replied. 'Come on.' He slung an arm around Charlie's shoulders as they headed in to join the others. 'So you and Walter, you seem friendlier lately.'

'Guess you could say that.' Charlie didn't add that he still didn't trust the guy as far as he could throw him.

'He's not that bad. Glad you guys could work out your differences, whatever they were.'

'Yeah,' Charlie said through gritted teeth. 'Me too.'

In the end it was a great night and by the time they hit the Tropical Bar on the ground floor of Wo Fat's, Charlie's mood had improved. There was talk about where to go after the game on Saturday. Kerr had a pilot pal at Wheeler who had invited him for a round of cards. But Walter was more interested in getting in on a champagne blowout that some of the guys from the *Arizona* had planned at the Halekulani. Roberts had his sights set on going to The Royal Hawaiian for a night of hula and swing.

'Apparently Tootsie Notley is performing,' he told them. A former model and one time 'Matson Girl', Tootsie Notley was probably the most famous hula dancer and nightclub performer in Hawaii. 'Can you think of a better way to spend a Saturday night than fox-trotting and swinging in Waikiki?'

'No can do.' Eddie shook his head. 'My folks said they're going to the Bloch for the Battle of the Music. I promised I'd go and I got to keep them happy, especially my mom.'

'Heard the troupes from the *Pennsylvania*, *Tennessee* and *Argonne* are all playing the elimination round,' Kerr said. 'And there's a dance contest too. Are you planning on entering, twinkle toes?'

'No chance.' Eddie let out a hearty laugh. 'I'll leave the dance floor antics to Kitty. I'm sure there'll be plenty of eligible dance partners for her.'

Jealousy coursed through Charlie's veins at the thought of Kitty dancing with another man. It was eating him alive. He kept his focus on the drink in front of him as beads of condensation ran down the side of his beer glass.

'On second thoughts, heading to the Bloch doesn't seem so bad.' Walter suddenly changed his tune. 'After all, there is a dance contest *and* the Battle of the Music on.'

It was the taunting tone Walter used that made Charlie look up and see the matching glint in his eyes.

'Sure, you should come, you all should,' Eddie said, clearly missing the gibe Walter had directed at Charlie.

'Yeah, what do you say, Florio?' Walter asked innocently.

Charlie shrugged. 'I haven't made up my mind. I was thinking of heading to Pearl City, Bill Tapia's band is playing, or I might go to the Enlisted Officers' Club.' It was a lie. He had no plans for Saturday night and as much as he wanted to see Kitty, being in the same room and not able to be near her the way he wanted would be torture.

'You should really consider coming,' Richie Walter said to him with overenthusiasm that was as transparent as glass. 'The *Arizona* won the last round and they are rumoured to play a few tunes. Are you interested? 'Cause I sure am.'

Charlie narrowed his eyes, wondering what exactly Walter was up to. 'Like I said, I'm yet to decide.'

'Hey, maybe I can play a few rounds!' Roberts's outland-ish suggestion was met with raucous laughter. Everyone on the

Wee Vee knew that Roberts was tone deaf. 'What's so funny?' he asked. 'You don't believe me?' If anyone questioned Ken Roberts's sobriety, his next move left no doubt. Roberts half-stumbled, half-jumped on stage, swiping a ukulele off an unsuspecting young local and proceeding to play the worst rendition of 'Sweet Leilani'.

Charlie had lost count of the number of times he'd heard the Bing Crosby song. It seemed that every band in Honolulu had the tune from the popular movie *Waikiki Wedding* in their repertoire. But admittedly, none of them had heard the song played or sung quite like this. Between his poor music skills and tone-deaf singing, not to mention the cigarette hanging precariously off his bottom lip, Roberts had the whole place in stitches. It helped that the crowd was mostly drunk or almost there. 'It's a good thing you're not in the brass,' Kerr yelled out at one stage. 'Your playing of the colours would be sacrilegious.'

When it was time to call it a night, Walter suggested they head back towards Hotel Street in search of female company.

'I think it's best we pack it in,' Eddie said.

'Aww, come on! You know you want to. I mean, after tonight, you won't get a chance to sample other ... well, you get the picture.' Walker laughed and Charlie could see Eddie's irritation.

'You heard the man, we're packing it in. No girls for us tonight.' Charlie turned towards the Chinatown end of the street where they could catch a cab back to base, but they all were stopped in their tracks by what Richie Walter said next.

'I know why *you* don't want to go, Florio. It's because you have a girl already.'

Charlie turned to see a sneering Walter. The man may've been drunk, but his eyes were clear and focused and suddenly the agenda was crystal clear too. Walter hadn't been nice to him because he suddenly liked him – it was the exact opposite. All the little jibes were now making sense. He had been biding his time, working up to this exact moment. But he couldn't know – there was no way possible.

'I don't know what you're talking about, I have no girl.' He looked Richie Walter straight in the eyes, but he called his bluff.

'Hey, Eddie, ask our friend here where he was last week the same day Kitty was in Kailua.'

Charlie felt the blood drain from his face. He couldn't. He couldn't know.

'What are you talking about, Walter? Kitty was in Kailua with Penny.'

'Oh, is that what they told you?' Walter's voice conveyed equal parts glee and sarcasm. 'Because that's not what I saw, I saw –'

Charlie didn't let him finish. He let his right hook silence him. Walter wobbled briefly before falling to the ground.

'What the fuck, pal?' Kerr yelled as he ran to help Richie, who was out cold.

Charlie looked at Eddie and at the same moment the penny dropped. He watched as shock, then disbelief before finally anger set in. He opened his mouth to explain but no words came. Eddie moved fast, fisting his shirt and getting in his face.

'She's my sister, my sister!' he yelled. 'I trusted you! You of all people!'

Charlie waited for Eddie to hit him. Braced for a pulping. He had betrayed his friend, and for that shame consumed him, but it didn't change one crucial thing.

'Why?' Eddie asked in an enraged whisper.

'Because I love her.'

It was the kind of question asked in the kind of way that no matter the response, it would not make it better. And it didn't. All it did was give Eddie the perfect reason to deck Charlie. And that's exactly what he did.

The next morning, Charlie woke with a splitting headache and as he gingerly moved his hand towards his eye he knew without seeing his face that he had a shiner. He had no recollection of how he got back to base, and as he rose, he wondered if Eddie was around.

Heading to breakfast, he grabbed a dog sandwich and some mud, scanning the room for Eddie, but there was no sign of him, nor could he see Roberts or Kerr and there certainly wasn't any sign of Walter. Charlie didn't care if he never saw that son of a bitch again in his life, but he needed to find Eddie. He needed to make things right. Not that he knew how, he was just hoping that by the time he saw his friend ... Charlie shook his head. After last night, he wasn't sure if Eddie McGarrie would ever see him as anything but a scumbag who'd taken advantage of his little sister. It wasn't like that and if Eddie spoke to Kitty she would tell him the same.

Shit. Kitty.

'What the hell happened to you?' Dorie Miller, mess attendant and Wee Vee's heavyweight boxing champion, gave him a once over.

'Bar fight,' Charlie grumbled, taking a quick survey of the room and making sure there wasn't anyone there who would contradict his story. 'Some army pilot from Wheeler was being a smart ass.'

'So he decked you?' Miller eyed him suspiciously.

'I drew first blood.' Technically, that wasn't a lie. Charlie hit Walter first. Then Eddie hit him. But when Walter showed up, it wouldn't be long before people put two and two together.

'Looks like you didn't do a good enough job if you're sporting that pearler.'

Charlie shrugged. 'What can I say, too much booze, I was off my game.'

'Boozing the night before you have early morning duty? That doesn't sound like you.'

'Yeah,' Charlie said sarcastically as he took a sip of his coffee, burning the roof of his mouth. 'Motherf–' he cut off the curse and shook his head.

'I'll leave you to your misery,' Miller said. 'But come and see me for some pointers some time. They'll save you a lot of pain when you next get into a scrap. You don't want a repeat of last night, do you?'

Charlie didn't want a repeat of last night. But he knew there was nothing Dorie or anyone else could do that would save him from any pain. If anything, there was more pain to come.

Kitty.

Downing his coffee, he scraped his chair back and stood up. Charlie needed to write a letter. It was possibly the hardest thing he'd ever done in his life.

The problem was figuring out how he was going to get it to Kitty. By the time he'd finished his tasks Charlie had an answer. It was risky, a long shot, but it was his only hope. Charlie held his breath and hoped the odds were somehow in his favour.

Fourteen

Eve of Infamy

Alexander Young Hotel, 6 December

Saturdays at the bakery on the ground floor of the Alexander Young Hotel were always busy. But this Saturday would live in Penny's mind for years to come.

Not because of the two lines of customers that snaked outside the door and weaved their way down Bishop or Hotel. Not because of those who flocked to the store for the famous lemon crunch cake, or the sailors and soldiers who came for the doughnuts. But because of the young man who had come battered and bruised and quietly asked for a favour.

Had she not been so busy that she forgot about the letter she had stashed in her work apron; had she insisted to Mr Dwyer, her boss, that she had taken ill and needed to leave early; had she realised the gravity of the letter, the urgency of the matter or the collateral way in which her world, her life, the whole island would change in less than twenty-four hours, then perhaps Penny would have acted sooner.

Instead, the letter from Charlie didn't reach Kitty until much later than he intended. For years this would play on Penny's mind.

The Bloch, 6 December

'Catherine, please do not slouch and at least *pretend* you're enjoying the music.'

Under normal circumstances, her mother would be right. The music that troupes from the *Tennessee*, *Pennsylvania* and *Argonne* were playing usually would be entertaining, but not tonight. Sure they'd played all the hits including 'Take the A Train' and 'I Don't Want to Set the World on Fire', as well as performing swing, ballads and the jitterbug, but Kitty's mood was glum and for the first time in her life, her mother wasn't her least favourite of her parents.

Her father had come home with the news that he had booked Kitty and her mother on the SS *Monterey* to San Francisco two days after Christmas. Kitty gasped. It was even earlier than she had anticipated. Her mind went into meltdown. She knew from Eddie that Charlie was due to have liberty on New Year's Day and she'd banked on seeing him then. She had been a fool to think their one day at Kailua would be enough. Making love to Charlie only strengthened her feelings and she needed to see him again.

It was just plain cruel she'd found her soulmate and it all was about to be ripped apart by her father. He was overreacting. He had to be. She knew there was a war on, but everyone was convinced the Japanese were going to invade the Philippines, not Hawaii.

'But how long are we expected to stay *there*?' Kitty had dared to ask, not being able to bring herself to say 'Australia'.

Her father had given Kitty a look that she had often seen reserved for her mother, a look of annoyance and authority. 'For as long as I tell you, young lady.'

Her mood was made worse by Eddie's absence. He was supposed to be at the Bloch tonight – sharing her pain. Truth was she was hoping that Eddie could talk some sense into her father. He always had her back and despite their five-year age gap, they'd always been close.

'May I have this dance, my Kitty Cat?' Her father's voice cut through Kitty's thoughts. He may've been tall in stature and firm in nature, but Conrad McGarrie's blue eyes were always kind and his tone soft when it came to his only daughter. His lopsided smile told Kitty that her father came with a peace offering.

'Of course, Daddy.' Kitty took her father's hand and let him lead her through the waltz number.

'I know you're upset with me, Kitty,' he said softly as they settled into the dance. Kitty tilted her head to meet her father's gaze and the denial she was planning on never left her lips. It was pointless, the Rear Admiral would have seen right through the untruth.

'Hawaii is my home, Daddy. My school is here, my friends, my ...' She stopped in the nick of time before revealing the true reason for her heavy heart. 'My whole life.'

'I know you love it here, Kitty. I know you want this island to be your home forever.'

'I do, Daddy. Just the other day, Penny and I spent the day at the circus and as we came home to Ford and passed the fleet I thought, Isn't that a beautiful sight? The Queens of Pearl all lined up. Battleship row,' Kitty said wistfully, omitting that she also felt more than a tinge of pride that the man she loved was on one of those dreadnoughts.

'That they are, but those battleships are here for a reason, Kitty. *I'm* here for a reason. Pearl is the heart of the US Pacific Fleet –'

'Rear Admiral Conrad McGarrie,' Kitty interrupted, using her father's full title, something she used to do often as a young child. 'I know all of this.'

'No, Kitty. You don't.' Her father's voice was firm and tinged with a note of warning. For the first time in a long while, the thought of war didn't simply annoy her, it scared her.

'Daddy, do you know ... something?' Rumours were always rampant. It seemed the *Honolulu Advertiser* forever had a new story, a new slant on the war. Just last week their headline had read 'War This Weekend'. Of course the weekend came and went and no such war eventuated. But Kitty had to admit – they were living on borrowed time. All the training exercises, all the manoeuvres, were done for a reason. Since spring the civilian effort had kicked up too, with the blood banks, the Women's Motor Corps and the Red Cross preparing for an attack.

The Rear Admiral shook his head. 'You know I can't share navy intelligence, but no, this is my gut feeling more than anything else.'

There was something to be said for her father's intuition. Twenty years ago, Conrad McGarrie's actions, spurred on by a gut feeling, had led him to receive a Navy Cross. Kitty was well aware of her father's thoughts about the resources, or rather lack of, that were being made available to the military in Hawaii.

Her fear spiked, her body stiffened and her father noticed. 'I didn't mean to scare you, Kitty Cat, but I need you to understand why I'm doing this.'

She didn't like it, but she did realise that her father's decision came from a place of deep concern. 'I understand,' she said, and braved a smile that immediately lit up her father's face.

'Atta girl.' He placed a soft kiss on her forehead and Kitty leaned into his warm embrace. It wasn't only Charlie she was leaving, but Eddie and her father too. They all meant the world to her.

'Well look who the cat's dragged in,' her father drawled.

Kitty turned to see Eddie talking to Jack Evans, a seaman from the USS *Tennessee*, who earlier in the evening had been cajoled into dancing with young Patty Campbell in a jitterbug contest. They were a fabulous pair and it was no surprise to the audience when Jack and Patty were declared winners.

'Eddie!' Kitty bounded towards her brother, pulling him away the moment he was done talking. 'Thank God you came! Mother was driving me insane!'

Normally Kitty's moaning about June was met with much sympathy from her brother, but tonight there was noticeably less camaraderie. Eddie nodded, the sunny disposition he'd displayed while talking to Jack was gone.

'I'm guessing you want to go home then?'

'Oh, that would be fabulous!' Kitty's spirits lifted. 'Do you think you can manage to convince Mom and Dad?'

'Sure, leave it with me,' Eddie said with slightly more enthusiasm. 'I got something I need to talk to you about, anyway.' As Eddie left her side, Kitty couldn't help but feel that something was a little off. What was with him tonight? Why was he in such a mood? And what did he need to talk to her about?

Penny!

Kitty gasped, her hands flying to her mouth. Eddie had asked her to marry him.

It had to be!

As Eddie walked back towards her, Kitty bounced with excitement but contained it the whole way home. Her brother's silence only confirmed her belief. The one thing puzzling her was why he was being so distant and moody about it all. Maybe he was concerned about how their parents would react. Certainly their mother wouldn't take kindly to the news, but Daddy was far more level headed and would surely bring her around. Didn't Eddie realise she was on his side? Maybe he wanted her help to convince Mother. Kitty wasn't sure how much help she could be. After all, their mother wasn't going to start taking advice from her, but for Eddie, Kitty would do anything.

'Come on, Eddie.' Kitty turned to her brother the moment they were in the door. 'I am dying to know! What did you want to talk to me about?' When Eddie faced her, Kitty felt her smile disappear. It was only then she realised how tired Eddie looked. He was in uniform but it was slightly wrinkled and his face stubbly. Kitty couldn't recall ever seeing her brother as anything but clean shaven and his uniform well pressed.

'Eddie?' she asked with concern. 'Is something wrong?' Kitty reached out to him but was horrified when he flinched and moved back.

'Eddie, what's wrong? Is it something to do with Penny?'

'Penny?' he scoffed. 'No.'

'You didn't ask her to marry you?' Kitty's alarm was growing.

Eddie sent her a stare filled with such malice that she felt something stabbing at her heart. 'That was supposed to happen today, but instead I was busy dealing with more pressing issues.'

'More pressing issues?' Kitty echoed, wondering what could be more important to Eddie than proposing to Penny. 'Eddie, you're scaring me, what's going on?'

'How long?' he asked quietly, his voice loaded with bitterness. His bloodshot eyes and stubble made him look years older than his young twenty-one.

'What are you talking about, Eddie? How long *what*?'

'You and Charlie.'

Silence boomed around the room. Kitty swayed, her hand shooting out to grip the staircase. A cold prickle washed over her as she struggled to breathe, a tremor of dread setting in. 'How?' she finally managed to ask before her brother dropped his gaze, shaking his head in disgust.

'Eddie, please!' She grabbed his hand and squeezed it for dear life. 'Please let me explain.'

'There is nothing to explain, Kitty. No words can make this right. It's wrong, Kitty. Wrong! Charlie is ... you're from different worlds.'

'I don't care!' Kitty yelled, surprised and angry her brother expressed such close-minded views. 'I love him, Eddie. I love him with all my heart.' Her voice wobbled, her heart ached but she was not ashamed to say the words.

'You love him?' Eddie sneered. 'Are you insane, Kitty? You're only sixteen. You don't know what love is. I don't know what he said to you to make you think this was okay, but it's not. It is far from acceptable. You're a *child*!'

Her temper surged. 'That's not fair! I'm not a child. I'm less than a year younger than Penny and it's totally acceptable for you to love her. Why shouldn't I decide whom I love? My heart wants Charlie and I don't care what you think, I will never stop loving him!'

Her brother's eyes, a mirror of her own, looked at her with cold disdain. 'This stops now. You hear me? It stops before it gets out of control. If you disobey my order, there will be consequences.'

Never before in her life had Kitty hated her brother, but she did now. Fury flooded her veins, making her blood boil. She dropped the hand that was holding his and raised it, then before she could fully think about her actions, Kitty slapped Eddie across his left cheek.

He flinched in shock. She suspected the sting dancing on her palm was greater than what he felt, but still within seconds there was an imprint of her fingers across his face.

Eddie said nothing. He glowered for what felt like an age before leaving wordlessly; the sound of the front door slamming cut into her heart.

Kitty crumpled in a heap at the bottom of the stairs, sobbing. She and Eddie had never fought like this before. He always was the one to stick up for her – no matter what. His reaction was surprising and heartbreaking. Eddie loved Penny – she knew that without a doubt and she thought her brother would understand her feelings. But at the end of the day, Eddie was no better than their mother. Kitty was still sobbing when Penny arrived a little while later.

'Oh, Penny!' She threw herself into her friend's arms and replayed what had happened with Eddie.

Penny held her, letting her sob before producing a handkerchief from her handbag. 'Here, dry your tears. I have something to give you.'

'What is it?' Kitty hiccupped, her head throbbing from her crying.

'It's a letter ... from Charlie.' Penny handed over an envelope with her name on it. As she ran her fingers across Charlie's penmanship, a rogue tear slid down her cheek, smudging the K of her name.

'Where ... how did you get this?'

Penny sighed. 'He came to see me at work and begged me to give it to you. He was worried that if he came here, he would run into Eddie. They had a pretty nasty blow-up last night. Eddie hit him.'

Kitty gasped. 'Is he okay?'

Penny grimaced and wrapped her arm around Kitty's shoulder. 'He's sporting a black eye, but somehow I think the physical wound will heal a lot quicker than his heart. He looked heartbroken, Kitty. I wish there was something I could do.'

Kitty fingered the envelope, desperate to read the letter.

'I'll leave you in peace to read that,' Penny said. 'I'll fix us something to eat.'

As Penny walked towards the kitchen, Kitty opened the envelope and with a thumping heart and trembling hands, she read Charlie's letter.

When she was done, she folded it carefully, held it against her heart and cried a river.

Hours later, as the moon shone brightly in the velvet night sky, Kitty McGarrie penned a letter back to the love of her life. Tomorrow was Sunday. She and her mother were off to church. Afterwards, she was to accompany her parents to the Walkers for their anniversary party, but Kitty had already decided that she was going to have a headache and would have to go home.

She needed to see Charlie. She needed to give him her letter.

Nothing was going to stop her.

Fifteen

The Sinister Wind

Honolulu, December 2016

'Hey, Pops, don't run off like that, okay?' A man in his early thirties who, Kit gathered, was the older gentleman's grandson, appeared by his side. His tone was equal parts concern and annoyance. 'Sorry if he was bothering you,' he said.

Kit felt her eyes widen in recognition. Right in front of her was the guy from the airport, and by the look he was giving her, he had recognised her too.

'Bennett, Kit.' He smiled as if it were the funniest joke in the world.

'This is Kitty, Adam,' the older man said. 'Kitty McGarrie.'

'Sir, Kitty McGarrie was my grandmother,' she said gently. Maggie had often told Kit that she looked like her grandmother when Catherine was young. She wanted to ask how he knew her but she didn't get the chance. Adam's cocky grin was gone, replaced by a scowl.

'Come on, Pops.' He all but dragged his grandfather away. 'Let's go and find our seats.'

'But, Adam ...' The older man stared back at her with the saddest expression on his face, and Kit had to fight the urge to go and rescue him from his wretched grandson.

At that moment there was an announcement for everyone to be seated. Kit had checked her table number upon arrival so she walked over to her allocated spot.

'Hello,' she said to those already at the table.

'Well, hello there, dear,' said an older woman who probably was her gran's age.

The age that Gran was when she passed away. A stab of sadness hit her.

'Why don't you come and sit next to me,' she said warmly. 'I do believe we're the only girls on the table tonight and, God knows, I could use a little shielding from all this testosterone.'

Her comments elicited a chuckle from the man sitting next to her, presumably her husband. Kitty liked her already.

'I'm Penelope Kerr, but please call me Penny, all my friends do.'

'Your friends are a dying breed,' piped her husband.

'Oh, shush now.' She gave him a friendly swat on the arm. 'This scallywag is my husband, Jimmy Kerr. Now, he would probably like to make it known that he's *Commander* Jimmy Kerr, but let's not let him get too much of a big head, shall we?'

Kit smiled. There was no mistaking the pride in Mrs Kerr's voice. 'Nice to meet you both, Captain and Mrs Kerr, my name is Kit Bennett.'

The Commander looked thoughtful for a moment. 'Bennett did you say? I can't remember any Bennetts, can you, my love?' he asked his wife.

'No, I can't say I do either. Who are you here for, dear?'

'My grandmother's brother and father ... her brother died at Pearl Harbor. Her father was Rear Admiral Conrad McGarrie. I believe he was later promoted to Admiral?'

The smile on the Kerrs' faces vanished and just like Adam's pop, they looked as if they'd seen a ghost. Which could only mean one thing.

'Did you know my gran?'

'Are you going to tell her?' Penny knew exactly what her husband was referring to. She shook her head and looked at the young woman who was at another table talking to the head of the 75th Commemoration Organising Committee. She certainly looked like her grandmother, especially from the side profile. 'Too many years have passed and I'm sure that it wouldn't make any difference if she knew.' And then she added, 'Besides. I made a promise.'

Jim scoffed. 'We both know that the woman you made the promise to asked you out of self-preservation.'

'That's true.'

'And you told me.'

'I told you in 1945!'

'Still, you have broken that promise once, perhaps it's time to consider doing so again.'

Penny was silent as she considered Jim's words. 'She may know already.'

'Or she may not.'

'I'll be opening a Pandora's box.'

'Or you'll be giving a young woman some answers. If she doesn't know, there are two missing pieces and you can give her both. Time is running out, Penny. Next year one of those pieces might no longer be here and perhaps neither may you.'

Penny had to admit Jim was right. As she watched Kit walking back towards the table, Penny was reminded of another secret she held in her hands on this very night seventy-five years ago. Penny knew many survivors of that day held more vivid and precise memories, not so much of the day itself, but of the night before, 6 December.

Penny Kerr had been coming to commemoration ceremonies long enough that she'd heard many survivor stories about the eve of infamy.

The group from the *Arizona* who had spent the night drinking at the Halekulani and were too drunk to make it back to base; those who had spent the night at Lau Yee Chai, Honolulu's most famous Chinese restaurant at the time, celebrating the festival of the harvest moon; the pilot from Wheeler Field who had spent the night playing cards and then had a drag race with a fellow pilot on the Kamehameha Highway on his way home.

There were parties and dances being held in the glittering hotels and ballrooms of glamorous Waikiki, while on the beach, flames of torches lit up the night for ukulele bands and dancing hula girls on the sand. No matter where people were that evening, they all remembered that Saturday night as their last night of normal.

For Penny, the moment she delivered Charlie's letter and realised the enormity of it, her normal had already begun to fade away. She remembered walking home, the night clear with a bright moon, a gentle salty breeze licking at her bare legs. She remembered passing the dreadnoughts of Pearl Harbor twinkling in the yellow light of the sodium-vapour lamps. She remembered how the wind picked up suddenly, how her body broke out in goose bumps, and she remembered the unease that crept through her as that sinister wind followed her all the way home.

Even now, decades later, the memory made her shiver.

'Tomorrow,' she said. 'I will tell her tomorrow.'

Sixteen
The Angry Sky

Honolulu, 7 December 1941

Charlie lay awake in his bunk listening to the sounds of the ship and the other men around him. It was a Sunday, a slow start for many. Those who were up sat around the cabin in their PJs, some in robes or their skivvies; he spotted someone walking past in a kimono. One guy was wrapping presents and telling everyone who cared that there were only seventeen shopping days left till Christmas, while another was writing a letter and by the wistful look on his face, it was probably to his girl back home.

It was still early, but as far as he was concerned, it may as well be midday or early afternoon. He hadn't slept a wink last night, and barely anything the night of the fight.

He kept playing that night on rewind in his mind. Maybe if he hadn't provoked Walter he wouldn't be in this mess. He hadn't seen Eddie since he threw the punch that had knocked Charlie out cold. Roberts told him that he, Kerr and another guy they had run into from the *Arizona*, Milton Cook, had brought him back to Pearl. He'd come to by the time they had dragged him to his cot. He slept that night, in fits though. The dull thumping pain

183

that started at his right eye and spread into his forehead and deep inside his head was nothing compared to how his heart felt.

Kitty.

Knowing that Eddie had most likely gone to see his sister on Saturday fed Charlie with all sorts of anxiety. Would Eddie tell the Rear Admiral? Kitty still had a few weeks before she was due to be shipped out, but Charlie knew that with their relationship blown wide open it was likely he would never see her again.

He wrote the letter and then in a daring move, he walked to the bakery where he knew Penny worked more often than not on a Saturday and begged her to pass it on to Kitty. Penny promised she would and Charlie sure hoped so. He didn't know what his next move was going to be only that –

'What the Dickens?'

His reverie was shattered by what sounded like planes flying over. Was the Army conducting a training exercise they weren't aware of? It was strange on many levels. It was too early on a Sunday morning for one, and even though there were planes scheduled to arrive from the mainland, they weren't due till later in the day. What the hell was happening?

A moment later, Charlie got his answer.

Over the horn, the commanding officer was yelling, 'This is not a drill! We are under attack. Repeat, this is not a drill!'

Charlie wasn't sure why, but the very first thing he did was check the time.

7:55 am.

The exact time America came under attack and was dragged into the war.

Charlie raced up the ladder, making his way up to topside, rushing to the open side of the deck. The sight that greeted him was the most shocking he'd seen in his whole entire life. The sky was littered with planes flying at various degrees of altitude. Low-level planes buzzed directly overhead and above them were smaller planes – bombers. As one whizzed by he noticed the big red insignia on the wingtips, and that's when it hit him – the Japanese were attacking them.

The bombers were like dragonflies skimming the surface of the water. He spotted two objects fall from a passing craft, saw two wakes heading for the ship. It took two seconds to surmise they were torpedoes, but before he could yell out and warn others, they hit and exploded with a thunderous bang.

The first explosion was monstrous and was quickly followed with another five or six equally tremendous blows in rapid succession. Moments later the *West Virginia* began to list. Behind him, he heard a popping noise. Charlie stared up to see a Japanese fighter plane coming in ahead of the torpedo plane, strafing the decks. He dived for cover, his eyes darting frantically, searching for a safer spot as bullets peppered all around him. He was getting ready to move, to dodge the rain of terror, when he looked up and saw an angry sky and fear snaked through him, gripping him with an iron fist. But it wasn't the time for cowardice, to hunch in a corner and wait it out.

His country was under attack. America – land of the free, home of the brave. He came here to be ready to fight, and that was what he was going to do. He stood, the steep incline of the ship making it hard to move, and at that exact moment, the forward magazines of the USS *Arizona* blew up, shooting wide sheets of flames skyward. The *Arizona* was raining sailors – her men were thrown into pools of fiery fuel, oil covering the sea, turning them into matchsticks.

Fire swept from the *Arizona* down the port side of the *West Virginia*.

The list on the ship increased rapidly. Sailors slid by him, somewhere he heard commands for counter flooding to stop the ship from turning turtle, but before he could act on the order, they were bombed. The rumble of the first bang had barely subsided when the second bomb fell. Charlie heard the horrific sound as it pierced through the top layers of the ship. Unlike the first bomb, it didn't explode upon impact, but did so a few seconds later with catastrophic results. The blast caused the entire bow of the ship to be lifted up out of the water and slammed back down. Charlie felt like a ragdoll being flung around. A tidal wave of water engulfed him, hurling him into the air; the torpedo had created a geyser, continuous jets of white foam flashing by as seamen were tossed into the water.

His vision blurred by the oil- and fuel-covered water, Charlie knew he had to swim to the top. Even in the depths of the harbour he could hear the explosions and the sounds of death and destruction from the chaos above. When his head broke the surface, and he filled his lungs with precious oxygen, bullets rained down. The Japanese were attacking them in the water from two directions.

The smoke from the burning oil created a black fog that floated ten feet over the surface, but it wasn't enough to hide the hundreds of sailors hats floating in the salty brine; black stencilled names standing out on the white cloth.

The *West Virginia* sank on an even keel, but for one of the shining stars of the Pacific Fleet, the *Arizona*, there was no saving grace. Her teakwood decks, once holystoned into a rich glow, were now a bone yard strewn with body parts by the hundreds.

For Charlie, who had never seen a dead body outside a funeral parlour before, it was a sight that would haunt his dreams for years to come.

The sheer number of corpses surrounding him was astounding. Most of the faces were so blood soaked or disfigured that he wasn't able to identify anyone he knew, and Charlie thought it was better this way. Then, as if they weren't against insurmountable odds for survival already, the water itself was on fire.

Hell had been unleashed.

Directly in his line of sight, a chunk of metal as large as a locomotive went spiralling towards the sky; by the time it started on its way down, it was obscured by smoke. Through the cacophony of desolation he heard a plea for help. It was coming from his left, some thirty yards away. Charlie dived under and swam to the man who was slipping below the surface and taking in water. It was only when he was a few feet away that he recognised who it was.

'Walter?' he finally managed to say, sure that his eyes were deceiving him. The man was covered in oil, but when he spoke, there was no mistaking that it was Richie.

'I can't ... can't ...' he gasped, hands frantically flailing. 'Help me!' he begged, his eyes consumed by fear.

As Charlie tread water, the realisation sunk in. Richie Walter couldn't swim. He moved closer as Richie slipped below, but when he failed to come back up, Charlie darted under. He struggled to keep the man in his line of sight with the chaos around them, but then he saw him. Charlie dived, frantically swimming to reach Walter before he sunk to the depths. He caught him just in time. Hooking his arms under Richie's armpits, he made his way up to the surface. Fatigue consumed him, every muscle in his body ached as he pulled Richie along with him. Charlie wasn't even sure if he was conscious or not. He wasn't moving and that wasn't a great sign. His own movements seemed minuscule, progress was inch by inch, and time seemed to drag. The thought of giving up briefly crossed his mind. It seemed easier to let Richie go, to allow them both to fall to the bottom of the harbour to a sure death, a watery grave. Charlie closed his eyes and saw his mother's face. The look in her eyes the morning he left her last February flashed clear as day. He couldn't do this to her. She had already lost one child, a child that had no hope of survival. There was no way, when he could save himself, and save the life of another man, that he would give up.

But there was another reason to fight for survival. Kitty. He had promised her that he would find a way for them to be together. He'd promised her that he would love her till the day he died. But today wasn't that day.

Adrenaline pumped through his veins as he surged upwards, breaking through the oily surface and gasping for air. Richie's face was as white as a sheet. 'Don't you dare die on me now, Walter,' he muttered as he swam towards the beach, losing count of the floating bodies he passed. At one stage, he saw a man floating on his back, blood gushing from his neck. He was screaming in pain, screaming for someone to help him. Charlie considered leaving Walter, or at least trying to help the guy who was still conscious. But within seconds his pleading and screaming stopped and he disappeared underwater. Charlie knew he was dead. His task now was to get Richie to land and see if he could be saved.

When he got to the beach, he slumped on the sand for a moment, knowing he needed to perform CPR as soon as possible if there were any chance to save Richie.

'Charlie!' Jimmy Kerr came running down. He was still in his civvies from the morning, the right side of his body covered in cuts. 'Jesus, is that Walter?'

'Yeah,' Charlie managed to say as a fresh wave of gunfire danced around them.

'The mess hall,' Kerr shouted. The two men grabbed Richie and dragged him in the direction of relative shelter. Charlie prayed they got there before one or all three of them were shot dead or blown up, and somehow they did. The hall was teeming with injured sailors and soldiers. A makeshift triage area was being set up in one corner with a couple of nurses assessing the scores of injured. There was no delineation between living and dead — there was just desperation and determination.

Charlie checked Richie's pulse — it was faint and dropping. 'Shit,' he swore. Knowing they were running out of time, Charlie looked at Jimmy and he nodded. If they left Richie here, he may not make it. They needed to act fast.

Scanning the room, they found a free spot in a corner and they all but dumped Walter's body and started working on him. Kerr managed compressions while Charlie monitored breathing. His gaze alternated between Jimmy labouring over compressions and Richie's lifeless face. How long they had been going at it, Charlie couldn't tell. He checked the pulse again. 'Pulse is improving!' he yelled to Kerr who seemed buoyed by the news and quickened his compressions. A moment later, Richie's body jerked and he started coughing up water.

Charlie was filled with relief. Slowly they helped him sit up, leaning him against the wall of the mess hall. Richie's eyes widened as he took in their surroundings.

'Don't talk,' Charlie instructed, and for a while he obeyed until it seemed he remembered something and became highly anxious and agitated.

'Stay put, Richie. We need to get someone to look at you,' Kerr said.

Richie shook his head and gripped Charlie's arm, opening and closing his mouth as he tried in vain to communicate. 'Eddie,' he finally whispered hoarsely and a fresh wave of fear seemed to consume him.

'What did he say?' Kerr asked.

'Eddie. He's trying to say something about Eddie. Where is he, Walter? Did you see Eddie?'

Richie nodded frantically. 'On deck ... bomb ... overboard ... we hit the water ...'

'Alive or dead?' Charlie asked.

Walter shook his head. 'Can't tell.'

Eddie was somewhere in the water. He needed to find him. 'I'm going back out to look for him.'

'What? Are you crazy?' Kerr yelled. 'You heard Richie, we don't even know if he's alive. From where I was standing on shore, I couldn't even tell if the *Arizona* was still there, let alone the Wee Vee.'

Both ships were gone, but he didn't tell Kerr that. It didn't matter.

'I don't care if he's alive or dead, I need to find him.'

He sighed and Charlie knew Kerr had resigned himself to the fact that he couldn't change his mind.

'Get Walter looked over, okay?' he said to Kerr as he stood. He was about to walk away when Richie called out to him.

'Florio.'

Charlie turned and saw something in Walter's eyes. A man that as little as an hour ago he considered an enemy.

'Thank you,' he said simply, but the words were filled with humble gratitude and humility. Charlie nodded in return, knowing that this man before him was now a friend and the real enemy was outside.

Running out of the mess hall, he dodged the raining bullets. The angry sky now stretched down to the land, bringing with it death and destruction. Scores of sailors were coming out of the water, oil slicked and horribly burnt. The smell of scorched flesh filled his nostrils. Charlie could see the skin peeling off their faces and their bodies as they stumbled ashore. The sight was sickening and for the first time since the attack, the sheer enormity of it hit him.

Could there be a more ignominious death for a sailor than to be bombed and torpedoed while in port?

'Eddie! Eddie!' he called as he passed the walking wounded. None of them answered. Many didn't even look at him – they were dazed, in a state of shock.

Oil slicks had turned Battleship Row into a sea of flames. Fuel tanks gushed, ammunition stores exploded. He looked to where the *Arizona* once stood proudly and his stomach sank, a sick, giddy feeling overtook him. Along with the *West Virginia* sinking on an even keel, the *Utah* was nowhere to be seen and the *Oklahoma* looked like a great beached whale.

A plane flew by so low that Charlie could almost make eye contact with the enemy. Behind him, machine-gun fire rang out and a moment later the plane was in smithereens. In the distance he could hear cheers and whoops celebrating the decimation of the Japanese bomber. They may have caught them by surprise, but America was fighting back.

He waded into the water, ready to dive in and search for Eddie. But he didn't make it far. About ten feet in front of him he saw a man he swore looked like his pal. His face was covered in black soot and he was bleeding from the side of his head, but he was alive.

'Eddie!' he yelled furiously over the noise.

The man looked around, searching for the voice that called his name.

It's him, Charlie thought with immense relief. *I've found him.*

'Eddie!' Charlie yelled again, but his voice was drowned out. High above in the angry sky a bomber pilot was doing his duty for his nation. He dropped a bomb that exploded a few feet away from Charlie.

First came the explosion, then the sensation of being propelled through the air and dumped on the shore. Pain, excruciating and debilitating, consumed his body. Charlie opened his eyes but he only lasted a second before his whole world faded to black.

Seventeen

Not My Hawaii Anymore

Downtown Honolulu, 9 am, 7 December 1941

The wait for the church service to commence seemed longer this morning, or perhaps it was all in Kitty's imagination, after all, Father Joseph always started mass at St Andrew's at exactly nine o'clock each and every Sunday. Sometimes her father and Eddie joined them, but more often than not it was just the two of them as it was today.

It was balmy, not unusual for the time of the year, but all the same, the heat was stifling and she could feel the back of her skirt sticking to her legs. As she shifted in her seat, her mother threw her a disapproving look.

'You are not a six-year-old, Catherine, so stop squirming like one.'

'Sorry, Mother,' she said, trying her hardest not to move about even more. Whenever her mother told her not to do something, Kitty's knee-jerk reaction was generally to do the opposite. 'But the heat is really bothering me today ... I fear I feel a headache coming on.'

June McGarrie's frown deepened as she raised the back of her wrist to Kitty's forehead and held it there a few seconds. 'Hmm, not warm. Still if you think Hawaii has heat and humidity, wait till we get to Sydney.' Her mother gave her freshly curled hair a gentle pat. 'It'll wreak havoc with your hair, I tell you.'

Kitty's heart sank to her knees. She didn't care about her hair or how it would look in Sydney, all she cared about was being away from Charlie. Her hand moved to the letter in her purse.

'Where is Father Joseph?' her mother asked impatiently as she flicked a glance at her wristwatch. 'He never starts this late.'

Outside the sound of planes could be heard. Kitty always thought they sounded like a swarm of bees, and it wasn't particularly alarming. The Army and Navy often held training exercises, but it was unusual that they would be flying so close to St Andrew's. Usually they flew over Hickam or Ford Island near Pearl Harbor.

A moment later, Father Joseph burst into the church, rushing towards the altar as fast as his rotund physique would allow. His face was bright red and he almost looked like the lobsters that swam in the tanks in the Chinese restaurants. Kitty stifled a giggle at the thought, but the words that came out of Father Joseph's mouth were enough to wipe the smile off her face and chill her to the bone.

'We're under attack! The Japanese are bombing us!'

The entire congregation gasped before cries and shrieks erupted.

'Where are they attacking?' a man in the front pew shouted.

Father Joseph shook his head. 'I'm not sure. I was told there are unconfirmed reports of Hickam Air Base being hit as well as bombing in Pearl Harbor.'

Charlie! Kitty thought in a panic as her mother clutched at her hand.

'Edward,' June whispered, and Kitty's panic doubled.

'Where's Daddy?' Kitty asked as fear gripped at her heart.

'He's golfing with Admiral Ramsey, I dare say they are no longer there.'

'What should we do?'

'I was assigned to head to the Naval Hospital in an event of an attack. Sit here, I'm going to try to find out all I can, then we'll figure out our next move.'

Her mother rushed off. There was a crowd at least five deep who had surrounded Father Joseph, no doubt all with the same goal as her mother – the search for more information. Some church goers had already fled. Kitty stood and looked around; sometimes the Millers came to St Andrew's, but she couldn't spot them today.

The longer her mother was away, the more apprehensive Kitty became. When she finally returned, her face was pale. 'It is as expected, Pearl Harbor has been hit. There are casualties, nothing is known at this stage. We don't even know if the attack is still going, but one thing is clear – the hospitals are bound to be full. We need to head over, probably to the Naval Hospital, and help out as best we can.'

Kitty stared blankly at her mother. Her voice was deathly calm.

How can she sound so calm when the whole world has turned upside down?

As her mother drove towards the hospital they could see black smoke billowing over Pearl Harbor, shrouding it like a cloak of mourning. In the distance she could see Ford Island burning furiously.

'Don't look,' her mother instructed, 'look straight ahead.' But how could she not? How could she not look and think of

Charlie or her brother and wonder if they were lying there alive or dead?

Even from the outside of the hospital, the chaos was evident. Injured men were being carried in, some of them unconscious, some of them moaning and screaming with pain. The scene before them could have been lifted from the Atlanta hospital scene in *Gone With The Wind*. Her mother parked the car on the side of the road and rushed inside with Kitty following.

If the scene outside was disturbing, inside was pure hell. Men were lying on the floor in the corridor begging for help. The one closest to her was missing a leg and was bleeding so heavily the blood was pooling around him. For Kitty, who had never seen such pain and suffering, it was terrifying and confronting. Nausea rolled through her as the smell of antiseptic hit her nose and she clutched at her stomach.

'Excuse me, miss.' Her mother grabbed one of the young nurses nearby. 'I'm June McGarrie, Rear Admiral McGarrie's wife. My daughter and I are here to help.'

'We could sure use it, ma'am. Let me find Matron Riley and see where she needs you.'

As the nurse rushed off, Kitty turned to her mother. 'I think I'm going to be sick.'

June McGarrie flicked her a look of annoyance. 'Find a bedpan or a bucket and make it quick,' she hissed. 'Once we're in the wards and helping there'll be no time for that.'

Kitty grabbed a bedpan, not even checking if it was empty or clean, and dashed outside in the nick of time. Her skin began to flush hot and cold as her mind swirled. The breeze carried the smoke from Pearl Harbor, the smell putrid and overwhelming.

'Kitty?' A familiar voice then a touch on her shoulder and she turned to see Penny's red-rimmed eyes and pale face.

The two friends held each other for a moment before Penny pulled back. 'Any news?'

Kitty silently shook her head. 'I'm here with Mother, we're going to help out any way we can.'

'That's why I came as soon as I heard. Come on.' Penny grabbed her hand tightly. 'Let's get inside.'

'It's awful,' Kitty whispered tearfully.

'I know, I couldn't believe my eyes as I drove here and saw all the damage and what they've done to all those ships ...' Penny shook her head. 'It's not my Hawaii anymore.'

Kitty felt an intense melancholy consume her. It shrouded her like the black smoke coming from Pearl. 'They are okay, aren't they, Penny? I mean Eddie and Charlie are so strong ... and ... and they've trained for this sort of thing.'

Penny looked at her with a weak smile but didn't say anything because they both knew war was a different beast altogether. Death in battle came to those who were weak and those who were strong. It didn't discriminate. War was fair that way.

They were put on runner duties, assisting nursing staff with fetching supplies and materials needed to treat the wounded. The hospital was full and the overflow was lying all over the hallways and even outside on the lawn. The horseshoe driveway was packed, bumper to bumper, with trucks and ambulances all carrying the dead and wounded.

The tide of gruesomely injured men kept coming. At one stage, Kitty saw a young doctor and nurse run outside telling ambulances and cars filled with the wounded, dying and dead not to unload, that the hospital was full to capacity and more.

They worked tirelessly, with no pause for a break or food or even water. After a few hours, Kitty's shoes started to pinch. When she chose them this morning, she hadn't thought she would be in them for more than a couple of hours, let alone running in them through the Naval Hospital. Blood stains covered her dress, but she didn't care. For the past three hours she and Penny had been assisting a nurse called Millie, who was attending to those with more minor injuries. Kitty knew there had been many who were far worse, and those who didn't make it at all. She saw dead bodies being wheeled or carried down the corridor towards the morgue. Each and every time she wondered if one of those men was Eddie or Charlie.

Little or nothing could be done to help the scores who were severely wounded. Kitty spotted a nurse walking around marking some of the men with a capital 'M' on their foreheads with red lipstick. When she asked Millie what it meant, the nurse soberly explained, 'The M is for morphine. They have little or no hope for survival, so the least we can do is keep them as comfortable as we can.'

Kitty had no time to be horrified. It seemed that every time something shocked her, there was quickly something else even more horrific to claim her disbelief.

No one could have predicted the level of atrocities, and despite the Women's Motor Corps effort in preparing for attack, the small hospital didn't have enough equipment, doctors or nurses to handle the flood. Nor did they have enough supplies. Beds were stripped to make roll bandages out of the sheets and alcohol was used to cleanse wounds – and to wash off the sticky oil from burnt skin.

Many of the men coming in were near naked, their clothes burnt or so badly damaged by the oil, and in some cases they were as naked as a newborn child. Under normal circumstances, Kitty would've been embarrassed, but this wasn't the time for modesty. The Red Cross had given all the volunteers, mostly women, armbands and instructed them to hand out clothes that had been knitted and sewed by the various corps. Many of the men started calling them angels of mercy. Kitty didn't think that what she was doing was heroic, unlike the nurses and doctors.

Millie turned her attention to a young sailor from the USS *Tennessee* who had been in the mess hall when the first of the bombs hit. He looked like he was in great pain, but was being stoic as Millie carefully threaded stitch after stitch.

'I just thank my lucky stars that I was ashore,' he drawled. 'Those poor bastards on the ships didn't stand a chance. The *Arizona* is gone, pretty sure the *Utah*, *Oklahoma* and *West Virginia* too.'

Penny wobbled and Kitty grabbed her arm just before she collapsed in a heap; the tray of instruments she was holding crashed and scattered on the floor. She was so pale that Kitty was sure she was about to faint.

'I'm so sorry,' Penny apologised as they collected the debris. 'My boy and Kitty's were on the *West Virginia*. We have no idea if they are okay.'

Under normal circumstances, Kitty would've baulked at Penny calling Charlie her boy in public, but these were not normal circumstances. It was far from that.

Millie gave Penny a sympathetic glance before returning to her stitching. 'You girls should take a break.'

'No, I'm fine,' Penny said, even though she looked nothing of the sort.

'Maybe I'll go and fetch us some water,' Kitty said and Millie nodded.

'Good idea.'

She was returning with two cups of water when she heard her name being called by a man who was stretchered on a trolley in the corridor.

'Jimmy?' She stepped closer and saw that he had bandages on close to half his body. 'You should be in a room, not here!' she admonished but at the same time she knew that everyone was doing their best. The dedication of the physicians and the nurses in particular astounded her.

'Believe me, I am fine.'

'Have you any news on Eddie or Charlie?' she asked desperately.

'I was with Charlie – he rescued Richie Walter and we performed CPR on him in the mess hall of all places.'

Thank God! Kitty thought silently, her fear abated.

'But then Charlie went back out.'

'What do you mean? Why would he go back out if you were all safe?' Suddenly she was angry with Charlie.

Jimmy looked at her for the longest time before answering. 'He went back for Eddie. He went back to look for your brother.'

'Did ... did he find him?' Kitty asked on tenterhooks. She desperately wanted Jimmy to say that he did, that they were both safe and unharmed and in the mess hall.

'I don't know, Kitty. Not long after Charlie left there was a series of pretty big blasts. One blew the side out of the mess hall and they started moving us out. I was sent here because of my shrapnel wounds. Richie was sent to the USS *Argonne* because he seemed okay, thanks to Charlie. He was a hero out there today. When he found out Eddie was still out there, he didn't blink an eye, he went right back out into that hellfire.'

Kitty should've felt proud that Charlie had saved a man, and that he was selfless enough to search for Eddie, but right now, she was wondering what good being a hero was if it meant that he or Eddie or both were dead? 'Are there other hospitals that Eddie or Charlie would've been sent to?'

'The USS *Solace* is one. The *Argonne* is more of a clearing station and I heard that a makeshift field hospital was set up near the Officers' Club in the Navy Yard.'

'Tripler?' Kitty asked.

Jimmy shrugged. 'Not sure, it's a bit out of the way for our guys, and it might be overwhelmed with casualties from Schofield.'

'Schofield was hit too?' Kitty wasn't sure why that was hard to believe. At this point nothing should come as a shock, but it did.

'Pearl, Hickam, Schofield,' Jimmy confirmed grimly.

'Kitty, where did you get to?' Penny appeared in the doorway, her face showing some relief when she saw Jimmy.

'Jimmy!' She rushed to his side. 'At least one of you is safe! Now we have to find the others.'

Kitty and Jimmy exchanged looks. As Jimmy went on to explain to Penny what he knew, Kitty excused herself. She was going back to continue helping Millie when she spotted her father walking down to the end of the corridor.

'Daddy!' she yelled. Her father paused and turned as she ran towards him. When he left the house he was dressed in his golf whites and in good spirits, whistling the tune to Glenn Miller's 'Sunrise Serenade' and declaring he was going to have a good day. By that Kitty knew he was confident that he was going to beat Admiral Ramsey. Now, only hours later, he looked like a completely different man. Kitty always thought her father's uniform made him look younger. But not today. Today he looked a decade older than he had this morning, his face as white as the uniform he wore.

'What are you doing here?' Kitty asked before her gaze flickered to a sign to the right of his head.

'Go find your mother, Kitty ...' he said grimly and she knew exactly what he was about to say next, 'and meet me in the morgue.'

Eighteen

Aloha Forever

'What is it, Kitty?' her mother asked impatiently and at that moment Kitty froze. How was she going to do this? How was she to tell her mother that Eddie was gone?

'Dad is here,' she managed to say after a pregnant pause. 'He asked me ... he wants you to meet him in the morgue.'

Her mother stared at her with puzzled annoyance before she read between the lines. The look on her face when she realised her son, her only son, was dead was something Kitty was certain she would never forget. She never knew how they made it to the morgue.

Once they were inside, she saw her father standing next to one of the corpses, and at first it was hard to comprehend that the charred and disfigured body before her was her brother. Even as her mother broke down and sobbed while clutching his hand, Kitty clung to the possibility that it wasn't Eddie. Whatever slim hope there was, it was dashed by the hospital pathologist and the navy dentist who carried out the mandatory identification checks. Kitty didn't shed a tear but her mother sobbed inconsolably.

They buried Edward James McGarrie two days later in Oahu Cemetery. Father Joseph conducted the service, an abridged and rather rushed one due to the number of burials yet to be conducted. As they lowered the coffin, a full military salute discharged their volley shots, making Kitty jump with every bang.

At the conclusion of the service, her father supported her mother while Kitty gently guided Penny to the cars that would drive them back to the house. There would be a wake. Her mother insisted that she would not let the death of her only son pass without him being honoured with a wake. As they drove, the once lively streets looked desolate. Within hours of the attack, martial law had been declared throughout Hawaii. Strict curfews were enforced and orders were issued for streets to be cleared with all civilians confined to their homes between the hours of 9 pm and 6 am.

Schools, theatres and saloons were closed. Basically anywhere there might be a concentration of people was shut down. Businesses were tightly controlled – goods on shelves were being monitored, liquor sales were banned, and even gasoline was being rationed.

Life as Kitty had known it had changed in the blink of an eye. The night of 7 December, just shy of midnight, Kitty was staring out of her bedroom window and saw that there was a lunar rainbow, a moonbow, a Hawaiian omen of victory. But whose victory was it? It seemed a cruel taunt. Kitty's whole world had been ripped apart. Lives lost, families broken, an island shattered seemingly beyond repair.

She was unsure what would come with the break of dawn, but one thing she did know was that her island paradise, her carefree life, her Shangri-La was gone. Disappearing in the roiling black clouds of smoke still burning over the carnage that was Battleship Row.

Two days ago, when she woke up the hardest decision she had to make was what threads she would wear to match the shoes she wanted to wear to church. And of course, how she was going to fake a headache to sneak out and get her letter to Charlie.

Charlie.

There was still no sign of Charlie dead or alive, and the not knowing was tormenting her. Penny had been moved to another Red Cross station yesterday and Kitty sent over to Schofield, and there was no sign of him in either location. Penny had discovered that, sadly, Ken Roberts had died in hospital in the early hours of the next morning after the attack. His funeral had been scheduled for the following day. It seemed that Eddie's funeral wouldn't be the only one Kitty would be going to in the coming days.

The driver turned into Nauuanu Avenue and the sight pierced her heart. She had been here just last week. She and Penny had walked down the popular shopping strip admiring the Christmas lights and decorations that lined the street. Now, the lights and any sign of Christmas had been erased.

When they arrived at the house, Penny and her family were already there. Her mother sighed at the sight of the Millers' car. Her father looked straight ahead as if he didn't even know where they were. The driver opened the door on her mother's side but she made no move to get out. Neither did her father. Kitty reached over and took each of their hands in hers.

'I know you are hurting. I am too. Eddie ... Eddie was my brother and I will miss him dearly.' An age passed and neither one of them moved. 'Come on,' she said and nudged them gently. 'Our guests are waiting.'

Her father let go of her hand and got out and Kitty was poised to follow, but her mother yanked her back inside. She held her hand so tightly that Kitty yelped in pain.

'I loved my son. I *loved* him. All I could think of as they lowered him into the ground was the first moment I held my little boy. I thought my heart would burst from love and today he was taken from me forever and my heart will never be the same.' Her mother's voice was so melancholy. Kitty was unsure if she'd ever heard such emotion from her before.

Then June McGarrie's voice hardened. 'Pray that you will never know the pain of losing your first-born child.'

Kitty had always known that Eddie had been her mother's favourite. Even in death he would continue to be so. But instead of being mad at her mother, she was mad at herself. The last time she had seen her brother, they'd fought. He left the house not talking to her and Kitty had decided she wouldn't care if she didn't see him again.

She hadn't meant forever.

It was then that she shed her first tears over her brother and they wouldn't be the last. She knew that the guilt she felt would never subside. She would carry that guilt, the remorse, for the rest of her life.

When she finally made it inside, Jimmy Kerr and Richie Walter sat flanking Penny.

'Kitty.' Richie stood first and took her hand. 'I want to offer my deepest condolences, but I'm not sure that would be enough.'

'Thank you, Richie.' She squeezed his hand and turned to accept a hug from Jimmy.

'Sit down.' Penny moved over to make room for her and Kitty sat down. She was drained and fatigued and hadn't slept properly since the attack. She wasn't sure there had been anyone on the island who had.

'Can I get you a drink?' Jimmy offered and Kitty noticed they all were holding scotch tumblers. Under martial law, the sale of all liquor had been banned, but her father had an extensive wine and liquor collection. 'Something strong, perhaps?'

Kitty shook her head. The thought of scotch or even wine made her stomach turn. 'Just a soda would be fine, perhaps a cola.'

Jimmy returned promptly with her soda.

'To Eddie,' Jimmy toasted quietly, and without a word they all sipped their drinks. Kitty savoured the icy coldness as it trickled down her throat. Next to her she heard Penny starting to cry again, cradling her tumbler of scotch like a baby.

'Hey, now ...' Jimmy reached over and rubbed her shoulder as Kitty snaked a hand around her waist and drew Penny's head to her shoulder. 'He died serving his country. I know that may be cold comfort to you right now, but Eddie will never be forgotten. What happened to Hawaii, what happened to the United States last Sunday ... well as President Roosevelt said in his speech, *"It will be a day that will go down in infamy"'.*

'Jimmy's right,' Richie said. 'As grateful as I am to come out of that day, I won't let Eddie be forgotten. I'm awaiting my service orders, I know that Jimmy is too, and I promise you that wherever I go to serve our nation, Eddie, and Charlie too, will be on my mind. I owe my life to that man, to Charlie Florio. He is the reason why I am still alive and standing here today.'

Kitty had to compose herself so as not to fall into a heap. 'Have you heard anything?' she asked Richie and then watched as the two men exchanged a glance.

'Nothing,' he said, dropping his gaze to the floor. 'I can't find his name on any casualty list and he's not at the Naval Hospital. I know the lists are not complete and they are constantly changing and there are conflicting reports about the number of ... about how many men we've lost.'

Later, Kitty would discover the number was in excess of two thousand, but in the days immediately after, no one knew for sure. It seemed that death was vast and endless. The morgues were overflowing, and basements of old hospital laboratories and vacant nurses' quarters were being used as temporary morgues.

Kitty thought of Millie and all the nurses and physicians working to save lives. After discovering her brother had passed, Kitty had returned to where she had been assisting Millie, tasked with telling Penny. Millie had taken one look at her and immediately knew. She will never forget the look the nurse gave her before insisting that Penny and Kitty were no longer needed. 'I've got this, girls. You go on home.'

'Do you think the Rear Admiral may be able to find out what happened to Charlie?' Penny said.

Kitty looked over to the other side of the room where her father and Admiral Ramsey stood. Dressed in their full uniforms, both sporting grave expressions, the scene was more apt for a strategy meeting than a wake. Kitty knew that her father and the Admiral would leave soon. The head of the Pacific Fleet seemed rather impatient to do so. In the thirty seconds or so that Kitty had been watching them, he had checked his wristwatch twice. His behaviour annoyed her.

'Perhaps,' Kitty said and sighed sadly, 'but he is hurting more than I have ever seen him before. I'm not sure that my request would be well received.' Kitty was almost one hundred per cent sure it wouldn't, not from her at least.

'Maybe Jimmy or I can ask?' Richie offered. 'After all, he was our crewmate, and the man that saved my life.'

Kitty's spirits lifted a touch. 'That would be lovely.' She smiled her thanks. 'It would mean so much to me.'

But Richie never got the chance. Less than a minute later, he and Jimmy were summoned by the Admiral. They were to ship out at dawn the next day; they were heading to battle. Kitty never saw either of them again and she would never get to know if they made it through the war alive.

Later that day, her father told them they were due to leave Hawaii in a fortnight. Kitty discovered the Miller family would also be leaving the same day. Two weeks passed at a snail's pace. Normally this time of the year flew by in a blink of an eye with parties and festivities and all the excitement and joy that led to Christmas. It wasn't easy for Kitty to sneak out – not just because of the curfews but because her mother insisted she accompany her to assist the Women's Motor Corps as often as they could in the time they had left on the island. Not knowing what happened to Charlie was making her slowly go mad. Penny had gone back to the Naval Hospital but had no luck finding anything out. Kitty made a pact with herself that if she hadn't heard anything by the time they were to leave, she would ask her father. After all, she had nothing to lose.

With the assistance of the staff, Kitty and her mother packed up most of the house, and much of the furniture was put into storage. They didn't know when they would come back. One small grace in all of it was that her father had rescinded on his decision to send her mother and herself to Australia. Considering the battles that were flaring up in the Pacific, he thought it best for them to sail to San Francisco then head home to San Diego.

'What about the cottage in Kailua?' Kitty had asked.

Her mother sighed and looked at her as if she were a nuisance. 'I don't have the time or inclination. I'll send one of the staff to close it up securely.'

But to the best of Kitty's knowledge, she never did.

On 25 December 1941, Kitty woke to a bright, warm and sunny Christmas Day. They made their way to the docks. The Aloha Tower, the tallest building in Honolulu, had been painted grey. Kitty had seen the SS *Lurline* docked on the harbour plenty of times, but never like this. Normally the mood was jubilant – people were either heading off on a voyage or returning home from spending time abroad.

But not today.

There was no band playing 'Aloha Oie', no leis to throw overboard, no local boys diving to collect coins that passengers threw into the water.

Her father stood on the dock as they said their farewells. Kitty waited for her mother to say goodbye before she did. She held him tight before letting go.

'Take care of your mother, Kitty Cat,' he whispered as he stroked her hair. He hadn't done so since she was a child and the gesture made her eyes sting with tears.

'I will,' she promised, although she firmly believed that her mother would be just fine. She was already planning renovations of their San Diego home. Kitty had wanted to point out that perhaps wartime was not the best time to be doing so, but decided against it. She knew her mother was in the depths of grief and perhaps renovation and redecoration were the best ways for June McGarrie to channel her sadness.

Her father stood back and blinked furiously. He was close to tears. Kitty had never seen her father cry. Never. Not even when they buried Eddie. He was waiting for her to board. Her mother had already made her way towards the ramp to embark.

Ask him now, she thought. *It's your last chance.*

Her skin prickled with nervous anxiety.

'Daddy ... I need to ask you a question.'

'What is it, my Kitty Cat?'

'I ... I was wondering if you knew what happened to Eddie's friend Charlie? After the attack that is?'

She watched her father's eyes change from confusion to clear understanding as to why she was asking. His expression and demeanour seemed to shift slightly.

'He's gone, Catherine.' His tone was quiet but absolute. 'You're best to forget him. Go now,' he urged. 'Your mother is waiting.'

Kitty wasn't sure how she made it to the deck of the ship, but thankfully she found Penny and sought comfort in her arms as the SS *Lurline* pulled away from Honolulu.

Kitty vowed there and then she would never return to the place that had claimed her soulmate. Charlie was out there somewhere, he probably had been buried in the very same cemetery where they had laid Eddie to rest, but for her, paradise was lost.

This was her last *Aloha*.

Aloha forever.

The once luxurious SS *Lurline* was a shell of her former self. Before leaving San Francisco, she had been converted into a troop ship. Cabins were two rows of canvas bunks, three tiers high. She left Honolulu Harbor accompanied by a destroyer escort for the two-week long journey.

The majority of the passengers were women and children, and they were constantly warned not to let anything fall overboard for fear that a Japanese submarine would spot it and sink the ship. Once, a ping-pong ball flew into the sea and the poor child responsible cried for two days, convinced the ship would be hit. Kitty was grateful that Penny was on the same journey. Mrs Miller, Annie and Penny were heading to San Francisco to stay with Mrs Miller's sister for a while. They were originally from Oregon, but had sold their home when they moved to Hawaii.

Kitty had never been seasick in her life; on every other journey she'd made she had been fine, but this time she could barely lift her head off the pillow. A few times she had felt well enough to

venture onto the deck or into the dining room, but the longer
they were at sea, the worse she became. Kitty attributed it to
a broken heart. June McGarrie couldn't understand it, and Mrs
Miller gently suggested that the seas seemed rougher than usual.
She apparently had overheard a number of passengers comment so.

'Is anything else bothering you?' Penny asked one day as she
placed a cold flannel on Kitty's forehead. Penny herself didn't look
the best, she had lost a lot of weight since the attack, which wasn't
unusual, but Kitty had heard Annie and Mrs Miller chide her
because she wasn't eating.

'No, it's just this constant nausea. The doctor saw me again this
morning. He is sure that it'll all subside once we reach San Francisco.' Kitty saw a look flicker across Penny's face, almost as if she
wanted to say something, but then she changed her mind and gave
Kitty a smile that didn't quite reach her eyes.

'Yes, you're right. It probably will. Once we are settled in San
Francisco I'll ask my mother if I can come down and visit you.'

'That'll be lovely.' Kitty attempted to smile.

'At least we'll be in the same state. That's better than you being
in Australia, right?'

Penny never got to visit Kitty in San Diego. Two days after they
docked in San Francisco, Kitty wasn't any better and she certainly
was in no shape to travel. When Penny called on her friend to bid
her farewell, she arrived at the exact moment a doctor was leaving. Inside she found a distraught Kitty and ropable Mrs McGarrie. It didn't take long to figure out what was going on. While
she had suspected as much during their journey, Penny had hoped
that she was wrong.

June McGarrie looked Penny straight in the eyes and made her swear she would never tell another soul what she had just witnessed. 'If you ever loved Eddie, you will take this secret to your grave.'

Penny knew she was about to make a pact with the devil, and yet she did it anyway. 'I promise, Mrs McGarrie. This secret shall die with me.'

Nineteen

Commemoration

Hawaii, 7 December 2016

Kit left the hotel a little before dawn and made her way to the commemoration site in the dark. By some kind of coincidence it was Clint, the driver from the airport, who collected her.

'I was expecting you to write a complaint to my boss, which would've been kind of funny,' he said as they pulled away from the Hilton.

Kit was confused. 'And why is that?'

'Because Adam, the guy who needed a lift, is my boss.' Clint gave a little chuckle and Kit sighed. Figures. It explained why Clint did as he was told the other day.

Adam. His name was Adam.

'He was in from LA and had just flown back home,' Clint continued. 'He was over there for a fancy beer symposium. Some of his craft beers won some awards.' The sense of pride in Clint's voice was unmistakable.

'So he's a beer man as well as a car guy.'

Beer and cars. Typical male.

'To be fair, the beer is his thing. The cars he took over when his grandfather, Charlie, retired. Adam has a microbrewery in Kailua. It's doing very well. Fastest growing beer brand on the island and on the mainland too. Hey, think he might even be negotiating an export deal with you Aussies!'

'That's ... great.' Kit was doing her best to be polite and listen to Clint but her mind was working overtime.

She remembered Leilani talking about her friend the beer maker and how he was there at the dinner.

Adam's pop was called Charlie.

Yesterday, his grandfather called her Kitty, mistaking her for her gran.

What were the chances?

'Hey, Miss Bennett, you okay back there? You look like you're about to hurl.'

'I'm sorry, Clint. It's just really early and I'm struggling without my morning coffee.' It was a lie. She'd bought one from a cafe in the hotel run by a coffee chain, but taken only a few sips before depositing the disposable cup in the nearest bin. Just her luck – an elderly couple had been walking by and saw her screw up her face in disgust as she muttered, 'This is the shittiest coffee ever,' before the near full, double-shot, skinny cappuccino landed in the trash with a *thunk*.

'You want me to swing past a diner on the way? I know a place near Pearl that does a decent cup of joe.'

'No, I'll wait till later, thanks, Clint. Hey, do you know if Adam will be there today?'

'You want me to put in a good word for you?'

'What? No! What would make you think that?'

Clint shrugged. 'I dunno, I guess you're a good-looking gal, he's a handsome guy ... not inconceivable, you know?'

'Ha. Hadn't noticed.' Kit was lying. She had noticed Adam was good looking. Too good looking.

'Well, he certainly noticed you.'

'He did?' Kit wasn't sure why it gave her a thrill.

'Yep. Called you the pretty, irritating Aussie.'

And just like that, the thrill shrivelled up. 'I think you misunderstood what he was saying,' Kit grumbled, annoyed at herself for thinking that Adam was anything but what she first thought him to be – an arrogant male.

'To answer your original question, I do think that the older Mr Florio, Charlie, will be there. Even though he's been living on the island for decades, he hasn't attended the commemoration ceremony often. A lot of folks just find it too hard to be in the place where they lost so much, saw so much pain, you know?'

Kit did. In more ways than one she knew exactly what Clint was saying.

The ceremony was to be held on the USS *Arizona* memorial. As the ferry took them across the still harbour, the first rays of sun coloured the dark sky. Shades of burnt orange interlaced with inky grey as the last of the twinkling night sky was fast disappearing. From all the reading she had done, Kit knew that on a bright sunny Sunday, on 7 December 1941, at precisely five minutes to eight, the Japanese attacked Pearl Harbor. The entire attack lasted a little more than an hour and a half. It resulted in over two thousand, four hundred deaths and another seventeen hundred or so wounded.

Two battleships were completely destroyed, and another six were damaged as well as a number of cruisers, destroyers and auxiliaries. By far, the battleship with the greatest damage and the one that had sustained the greatest loss of life was the USS *Arizona*. Close to twelve hundred men were killed on the *Arizona* alone. To this day, the *Arizona* still leaked oil. Many of the men were entombed on the ship and some survivors chose to have the *Arizona* as their final resting place.

No amount of reading and research prepared Kit for the way she felt when she saw the memorial of the USS *Arizona* with her bare eyes. She knew that just below the surface of the waters of Pearl Harbor lay a ruin and a tomb as well.

The sun was rising in a cloudless sky, and from what she'd read, this day seventy-five years ago had been picture perfect too.

As she sat and listened to the sombre ceremony, Kit was struck by how emotional it was, even so many decades later. The attack was a surprise, not unlike what the Diggers experienced in Gallipoli. They were sitting ducks. When they asked the Pearl Harbor survivors to come on stage, Kit almost lost it. Listening to their stories gave her goose bumps, but when they introduced Charlie Florio, it was the last straw. Tears rolled down her cheeks and she couldn't stop them. Charlie told of the story of how he was on the deck of the USS *West Virginia* when he saw a torpedo hit the *Arizona* and how only moments later, as he was propelled up in the air and thrown into the water, a bomb hit.

'My memory is a bit hazy after that. But I'm told that I rescued Richie Walter, you all know him as Commander Walter. I don't think Richie will mind me saying that we didn't care much for each other before that day. We had mutual friends, but we weren't friends ourselves. I think it may've been something to do with a girl.' Charlie's words elicited a ripple of chuckles from the crowd, and from behind, Kit felt a gentle tap on her shoulder. Jimmy Kerr offered her a handkerchief and she smiled her thanks.

At the conclusion of the service, Kit turned and greeted Commander and Mrs Kerr. 'Thank you for this.' She held up the now not so clean handkerchief. 'I'd offer to give it back, but I'm not sure you'd want it.'

'I'd be careful if I were you,' Mrs Kerr said. 'The last time Jim gave a girl a hankie, he ended up marrying her.'

'And as I recall, she never gave me that hankie back,' Jimmy Kerr said with a smile. He excused himself, leaving Kit with Mrs Kerr.

'Come and sit a while,' the older lady said, and as she moved to do so Kit couldn't help but look around for Charlie. She needed to talk to him and she was all but convinced that he was *the* Charlie she was looking for.

'Are you looking for someone?' Penny Kerr asked.

'No ... I mean yes ...' Kit wasn't sure how to answer, her eyes still scanning the crowd. 'This is going to sound crazy, and I know that last night you said that you didn't know my gran all that well but she said a couple of things before she passed and well ... it's kind of why I'm here today.'

'What sort of things?'

It wasn't the question itself, it was the way in which Mrs Kerr asked it that made Kit look at her. There was something in Mrs Kerr's eyes that startled her. It was a look of fear mixed with slight panic, as if she was almost afraid of what Kit was about to say.

'She told me about a man she met on the night of her sixteenth birthday.' Kit watched Penny's eyes closely as she spoke, watched as her pupils dilated with every word she said. 'She told me that this man was the love of her life and I'm wondering, Mrs Kerr ... I am wondering if that man is here today.'

Kit watched as the fear was replaced by resigned sadness. Mrs Kerr grabbed both her hands and held them tightly.

'My dear girl. The answer to that is yes.' Kit was about to stand but Mrs Kerr seemed to anticipate this and tightened her hold. 'But before you go looking for him, and I do think you have worked out who he is, there is something else you need to know ...'

Kit waited eagerly for Penny to continue but the older woman sighed. 'Have dinner with me tonight. I'll book a table at Fresco Italian Restaurant. Is six o'clock good for you?'

Kit was stunned. One minute they were talking about Charlie, she was sure of it, the next Mrs Kerr was arranging a dinner date?

'I promise I will give you all your answers then, Kit.'

'Okay.' Kit couldn't help but feel disappointed.

'Don't worry, dear,' Mrs Kerr patted her hand. 'What I have to tell you I've carried around for seventy-five years, another few hours isn't going to kill me.'

But it may kill me, Kit thought.

After the ceremony, Kit returned to the harbor area by navy boat and headed to the USS *Missouri* battleship where the treaty that ended World War II was signed. There was so much history here, history that was entwined in her family, that was part of her, and tonight, more of that history would be uncovered.

As soon as Kit was back at the hotel she called Ben in Singapore and relayed everything she had discovered, including the part where Mrs Kerr had said there was something else she needed to know.

'What do you think it is?' Ben asked.

'I have no idea. I mean, Charlie did say that he and some other guy had been fighting over a girl, which could've been Gran, but I can't see how that might be it.'

'Who knew Gran was such a hussy?' Ben's voice became muffed all of a sudden.

'What the hell are you doing?'

'Packing. I'm heading to Sydney tonight. Ness has another week and then she'll join me.'

'At Mum and Dad's? Have fun with that.'

'Well if someone allows us to move in early ...'

Kit laughed. 'Okay, you've twisted my arm, you can move into the house earlier. My flight back is via Sydney anyway, so I might stop in for a couple of days and catch up with Ness.'

'Hey, what am I? Chopped liver?'

'I just saw you, Ness I haven't seen in ages.'

'Fine. Keep me posted on what you find out tonight.'

'I will.'

Kit said goodbye to her brother and then changed before heading to Fort DeRussy to watch the opening ceremony of the veteran's parade honouring the remaining Pearl Harbor survivors. The parade ran from Fort DeRussy, continuing along Kalakaua Avenue, and ending at Kapiolani Park. Kit spotted some of the veterans who had spoken at the commemoration ceremony.

'There are fewer and fewer that march each year,' Kit heard a woman behind her comment.

For the second time that day, Kit thought of Anzac Day. When she was little, she went to an Anzac Day parade with her grandparents. Her gran was so upset that she refused to ever go again. Being here, seeing this parade, she fully understood why.

Flicking a glance at her watch, Kit left before the parade began to meet Penny Kerr. Even though it was less than a ten-minute walk back to the Hilton Hawaiian, it took Kit a while to wade through the crowd. When she reached Fresco, she was told that one of the party had already arrived.

'Mrs Kerr has reserved the private dining room,' the hostess informed her. Kit followed her through the restaurant, which boasted a fusion of Italian cuisine and local influence. She was glad that Penny had the foresight to book the private dining room it would give them a chance to –

Her thoughts were interrupted when she spotted a man sitting alone at what obviously was her table, but it soon became clear that there was no mistake. Three places were set and her assumption that she was dining alone with Penny Kerr was obviously wrong, and it was clear the moment he saw her that this man was thinking the exact same thing.

'Oh good,' Penny Kerr said behind her. 'We're all here.'

Adam leapt up to pull out Mrs Kerr's seat and then did the same for Kit.

'Thanks,' she mumbled.

'You're welcome,' came his reply, and as her eyes met his, a strange warm buzz danced on her skin.

Their host, who introduced herself as Ainsley, gave them a rather detailed rundown of Fresco's drinks menu, including their vast collection of vintage wines and an emphasis on their local beer selection.

'Now, Kit, are you fine with having a wine to begin with?' Penny asked.

'Yes ... that'll be lovely, thank you.'

'Adam? Wine for you or would you rather drink your own brew? I see that it's on the menu here.'

'It certainly is.' Ainsley giggled and looked at Adam.

Oh, God, Kit thought. His damn beer must be everywhere on the island.

'I'll join you both for a wine,' Adam said, sending Kit a look that said he was just as surprised as she was with the whole dinner arrangement.

While Mrs Kerr chatted with Ainsley about wine, Adam and Kit sat awkwardly and rather impatiently. Or that's how she felt. For all she knew Adam could be sitting there thinking how annoyed he was, and when he began drumming his fingers on the white linen tablecloth she knew her guess was correct.

'I know you are both wondering why I called you here.'

Kit exchanged a look with Adam before clearing her throat. 'I gather it has something to do with my gran and ...'

'And my pop,' Adam finished.

'Adam, how much has Charlie told you about the attack and the months leading up to it?'

'Until recently, nothing. He hadn't spoken about it in years – not to me and as far as I can remember ... he never spoke about it to my dad or to Grandma Rose.'

Kit wasn't sure why the mention of Charlie's wife and child startled her. After all, Adam had to come from somewhere.

'And, Kit.' Penny turned to address her. 'You told me that your grandmother never mentioned Charlie or indeed anything to do with Hawaii until the days before she passed?'

'Kitty's dead?' Adam seemed shocked at the news. Kit was confused.

'How do you know about my gran if Charlie never spoke about her?' Kit narrowed her eyes.

'If you were listening carefully, you would've caught the part where I said that Charlie only recently has begun talking about her. For goodness sake, some days it's all he can talk about.'

Kit was shocked by his tone and certainly didn't like the way he referred to her gran as 'her'.

'Firstly, her name was Catherine, or Kitty as she was called by those who knew her as a young lady, and secondly, why now – why after seventy-five years has Charlie decided to talk about Kitty?'

She thought about the letters; thought about the words that Charlie had written; the promises he made. She wanted to ask why he hadn't acted on his promise, but she would save the question for later.

Adam was silent. His cold look turned to anguish. 'Charlie has Alzheimer's,' he said quietly. The news knocked the wind out of her and suddenly she felt extremely sad. It also explained why Charlie had called her Kitty McGarrie the other day. He didn't just think she looked like her gran, he thought she *was* her gran.

'I'm sorry ... it must be very hard on him ... and your family.' Kit hoped her earlier words hadn't come across as insensitive, but Adam flicked her a look that screamed he didn't want her pity.

'It is hard ... It's just Charlie and me. I am all he has left, which is why I firmly believe that he can't ever see you again. It's too hard – it confuses him. The other night he got so worked up after seeing you that I needed to take him back to the room and have the nurse give him something to calm him down.'

'I'm sorry.' Kit apologised not because she thought Adam needed her to, but because she was genuinely sorry that she had caused Charlie some distress.

She thought about her gran's letter that was in her hotel room. She had promised herself that if she did find Charlie, she would give it to him. He was its rightful owner. But now all that seemed highly unlikely. 'And I don't want to cause Charlie any more stress, so if you don't want me to see him, then that's fine. I'm leaving in a few days and after that, you'll never need to worry about me again.'

'I'm glad,' Adam said curtly.

What the hell is his problem? He could've at least been a touch more polite about it, Kit thought.

'Well then ...' Mrs Kerr picked up her glass of wine and skolled it. Kit was surprised and somewhat impressed. Penny Kerr was a remarkable woman for her age. Maggie and her gran were both exceptional too, but Penny seemed far younger than her ninety-two years. Kit was also stunned that the wine had been delivered and poured and it seemed that neither of them had noticed. They'd been too busy fighting.

'What I'm about to say might come as a bit of a shock, to both of you.'

'Trust me, Mrs Kerr,' Adam said, 'after discovering that my grandfather had a sordid affair with the daughter of a navy Admiral, nothing you could tell me could shock me.'

And there it was again – the blatant disrespect for her gran. It was really starting to rankle her.

'Oh, I suspect that it might ...' Mrs Kerr topped up their glasses, refilling her own too. 'To do this story justice, I need to start at the beginning, the night of Kitty McGarrie's sixteenth birthday. It was held not far from here, you know. In the ballroom of The Royal Hawaiian, affectionately known today as the Pink Palace. I was dancing with Eddie McGarrie – he was my beau at the time and if things had gone differently I would've married him and you and I, dear,' she patted Kit's hand, 'would've been family.'

Mrs Kerr sighed and paused a while before continuing. 'As I was saying, I was dancing with Eddie when I spotted Charlie and Kitty dancing. I could tell there and then there was something special between them, but of course, Kitty was the daughter of a Rear Admiral as he was then and Charlie was an enlisted sailor. They came from very different worlds, the McGarries and the Florios.'

'That's putting it mildly,' Adam said wryly and Kit frowned.

'It wasn't so simple.' Penny shook her head. 'Times were different back then. Class, status and where you came from, many things that you young folk don't need to worry about so much these days, that all mattered. Even my relationship with Eddie wasn't all that welcomed, so we did what he had to do to see each other.'

Kit listened to Mrs Kerr relay the story of how Kitty and Charlie fell in love. With every passing moment, she began to understand just how important Charlie had been to her gran. When it came to the point where she had to talk about the day of the Pearl Harbor attack, Penny's voice wobbled.

'It's okay, Mrs Kerr.' Kit squeezed her hand. 'You don't have to go into it if it's too painful.'

'No, I'm fine, and I need to tell you how this all ends ... or at least give you as much of the puzzle as I know.'

The puzzle? Was this the secret that Penny had referred to earlier?

A few minutes later, Kit had her answer.

Her heart was beating so loudly in her chest that it reverberated in her ears. Her head was spinning and all she could think of was to call Ben and ask him to go straight from the airport to her gran's house and find the red Arnott's biscuit tin, because she was fairly sure she knew what it contained. If the letters she had found uncovered Kitty's secret love, then the box would certainly uncover or hold clues to a secret child.

'Don't even think about it,' Adam warned as soon as they bid farewell to Mrs Kerr. 'We are not going to look for this ... child.'

'Are you insane? You cannot sit there and say that. Besides, it's not your call to make. This child, whoever he or she may be, was born in Australia. I don't know if you caught the part about me heading home by the end of the week, but I can tell you this – as soon as I land, I'm looking for Charlie and Kitty's child.'

'She may've miscarried. Mrs Kerr already confirmed that after she saw your grandmother in San Francisco, she never heard from her again. And even if the child was born, they would be over seventy now. What if they are unwell like Charlie? What if they don't want to be found? Did you think of that?'

'Of course I did,' Kit snapped back. 'It might shock you to discover that I'm a journalist.'

'Really?' His eyebrows shot up in genuine surprise. 'Now that I would've never have guessed.'

'You know, I really don't get it.'

'Get what?' Adam refilled their glasses with a new bottle that Ainsley had just delivered.

'My gran was a woman of impeccable taste – in all things.'

'Good for her,' he drawled sarcastically. She ignored the barb and continued.

'After all I have heard about Charlie, he sounds like a wonderful man. He must've been, my gran loved him dearly, it seems. So how is it that his grandson is such an arsehole?'

Adam paused mid-sip but he didn't seem as annoyed or offended as Kit thought he might be. Maybe he was used to being called names. Or maybe he knew he was an arsehole.

'I never get you Aussies changing things to suit your little country.'

God! He really was infuriating. 'Okay, you're an *asshole*, Adam.'

'That's better.' He gave her a smile and, damn it – it made him look all sorts of handsome when he did. 'When it comes to Charlie, I'm an asshole.'

Now Kit felt like the asshole. 'Look, I'm sorry, that was uncalled for.'

'No, you're right.' Adam gave her a wry smile and Kit felt a deep glow in her belly. 'A year ago there were little signs that things were not quite right. Nothing too obvious at first, little things here and there, and I just put it down to old age. But one day he didn't recognise me and that's when he started talking about Kitty. About the time they had snuck to Kailua and let me tell you, I heard things come out of my pop's mouth that shocked me. It was clear that what he and Kitty had was very steamy. But I guess what concerned me the most was that I was losing him and fast. I have hired full-time care because he refuses to leave the house. It centres him and I don't want to take that away from him. He's happier when he's back in the past, and that should comfort me, but it annoys me. It's like his whole life after Pearl Harbor meant nothing. Like my gran and my dad meant nothing.'

Kit felt his pain, because she shared it too. 'Do you really feel that is true?' she asked quietly. 'Because in the short time that I've known you, all I've seen is how much you care for Charlie. You wouldn't care that much if you didn't believe in him. Clint told me how you took over Charlie's business.'

Anger flashed in his eyes, but not the type of anger that came with annoyance; it was the protective kind. 'Clint had no business talking to you about Charlie.'

'Oh relax, he was trying to talk you up – saying how much you help your pop etcetera, etcetera.'

'Oh.'

They fell into silence and Kit said, 'I guess I should get going.' She stood up, unsure how to leave it all and she was somewhat surprised when Adam did the same. 'Umm, well, nice to meet you, Adam. I really hope that you get as long as possible with Charlie. I lost my gran way too quick and it was heartbreaking.'

'Likewise and ... thanks. I'm sorry that you lost your gran recently. It must've been hard.'

Kit gave a tentative smile. 'It still is. We were very close, and now I'm discovering all these things about her and it makes me wonder ...'

'Wonder what?' Adam probed.

'Who was she? What was her life like back then? Not just her life, but life on this island before Pearl Harbor. So much is written about that day that I feel people forget Hawaii existed before then. I wish I could just jump back in time to 1941, before that day that changed not only the US, but my gran too. God, that sounds stupid.'

'No, it's not stupid at all.' Adam surprised her. Kit was sure he would tell her that jumping back in time was as stupid as it got. 'You don't go for another few days, right?'

'Yes, why?' she asked carefully.

'I think that I could help you with your time travel.' He was smiling at her, and she was finding it hard not to smile back.

'How?'

'If you're game, meet me at reception on Thursday at nine sharp. I need a day or so to line something up.'

'Why are you doing this, Adam? I mean a moment ago we were arguing, you clearly don't like my grandmother and now you want to help me understand what her life would've been like?'

'Because I understand how it is to think you know all there is to know about someone you love and then discover that's not true.'

Even without spelling it out, Kit knew he was talking about Charlie.

'When Charlie first got sick, I researched all I could about the time period. I figured that if Charlie was going to be living in the past, I needed to be there too, or at least know what the hell he was going on about. Honolulu back then was a different place.'

'So you went back to the past to help him in the future?'

'I guess you could say that.'

It was incredibly sweet, and Kit was beginning to wonder if she might have misjudged Adam Florio. Unsure what to do next, Kit awkwardly stuck her hand out. 'Well, goodnight, Adam,' she said a little too brightly, and then promptly cringed.

He took her hand, gave her a lopsided smile that made her all tingly from her head to her toes. 'Sweet dreams, Bennett. See you Thursday morning.'

Twenty

A Wide Brown Land For Me

Sydney, March 1942

When Kitty sailed out of San Francisco on board the SS *Mariposa* on 12 January 1942, she knew two things. Her life was about to irrevocably change – she was carrying Charlie's child, a child he would never meet. The second thing was that she was sure her father would never speak to her again. And these two things were breaking her heart.

When the doctor confirmed her pregnancy, her mother was shockingly calm.

'I have to say, Catherine, I am not in the least bit surprised you have got yourself into this predicament.' Her mother stood in the doorway of the hotel bathroom as Kitty endured a terrible bout of morning sickness. 'Your choice of friends has always been questionable. That Miller girl was a bad influence, I knew that from day one.'

Kitty didn't have the energy to argue, despite knowing how wrong her mother was. The fact that Penny had turned up just as Doctor Lombard was leaving was a small grace. Her mother hadn't liked it – not in the slightest – but it helped to see a friendly face, even if it were only for a few minutes before her mother asked Penny to leave, making her promise to keep what she referred to as 'Catherine's shameful condition' a secret. On her way out, Penny had managed to slip Kitty her address. Kitty had been in such a daze that it was only after her friend had left that she looked at the crumpled paper in her hand and realised what it was. She tucked it in with the few possessions she had, along with the letter she never gave to Charlie.

The journey to Australia was long and arduous, and even more heartbreaking than the one to San Francisco. When they left Hawaii, she had Penny, but now she had no one. Her mother, for the most part, ignored her and that was just fine by Kitty. The ship was mainly carrying troops and supplies; Kitty and her mother were amongst only a few military dependants on board. She lost count of the number of times her mother had relayed the story about how her husband had wanted to send them to Australia and here they were. Kitty could see they were wondering why Commander McGarrie would be sending his wife and daughter to a Pacific nation when war was raging all around them. After all, the US was sending troops there for this exact reason. Of course, the truth was they were heading to Australia to ensure the pregnancy was hidden. Kitty knew her mother would rather banish her to the ends of the earth rather than risk her shameful secret being exposed.

By the time they arrived in Melbourne in February, Kitty's nausea had subsided. She briefly remembered Doctor Lombard saying this would happen at the start of the third month of her pregnancy. Every night she splayed her hands across her belly and drew strength from knowing that she still had a connection to Charlie.

The life that was slowly growing in her belly was her only solace in a world that was crumbling around her. Within weeks of arriving in Melbourne, the Japanese sought to expand their victory at Pearl Harbor and they were successful in the occupation of most of Southeast Asia and large areas of the Pacific. The greatest loss came in Singapore with the fall of an entire Australian division. The same month, hundreds of Australians were killed or injured when the Japanese bombed Darwin. In response to this all Royal Australian Navy ships in the Mediterranean theatre, as well as the 6th and 7th divisions, returned to defend Australia. There was a growing danger to domestic security and it seemed that Kitty had gone from one island under threat to another.

Her Aunt Iris had planned to meet them in Melbourne, where they would stay for a few weeks before catching the train to Sydney. As soon as Kitty walked onto the dock, Aunt Iris enveloped her and Kitty burst into tears.

'Hush now, Kitty Cat,' Iris crooned while stroking her hair, but hearing the moniker that Eddie used to call her only made her sob harder. Her mind had been so consumed with her pregnancy that she hadn't had the time to properly mourn her brother. She missed Eddie fiercely, her grief compounded every time she remembered their last time together. The fight. He was so angry with her and she with him.

'Stop mollycoddling her, Iris,' her mother said, as if her elder sister was a child. 'She made her bed, now she can lie in it.'

Kitty's aunt reluctantly released her but not before giving her hand a reassuring squeeze. 'Come on, I have secured us rooms at a respectable hotel on Collins Street, not far from the Royal Arcade. We can do a spot of shopping once you are rested and refreshed.'

'This is not a vacation, Iris,' her mother said bitterly. 'The sooner we get to Sydney and get this all ... sorted, the better.'

Kitty felt her heart stutter. *Sorted?* What did her mother mean by that? Surely not what she thought it meant!

'You want to wait till we are in Sydney before Kitty is seen by a doctor? I have a friend who can put us in touch with a doctor here. He is in St Kilda, not far from where we went to school, Junie. He'll be discreet.'

Kitty knew her mother and Iris had spent some time living in Melbourne. Their father worked for the government and was moved from Sydney to Melbourne at the turn of the century. It was through her father's line of work that her parents had met. Eddie had told her once that their father had initially fallen for Iris, but as she was already betrothed, he started courting her younger sister, Junie, instead. Kitty had often wondered about this. How would her mother have felt being second choice, living in her older sister's shadow?

Within twelve months her parents were married and a year later, the same year that her Aunt Iris lost her fiancé in World War I, Eddie was born.

June McGarrie's nostrils flared. 'I'll wait till we are in Sydney. I would prefer to have her see someone when we are settled. I am sure whoever you have lined up in Sydney will do.'

Panic ignited. 'I am not letting you take me to some ... butcher! I am having this baby and that is final.'

Sympathy flickered over her Aunt Iris's face, but her mother looked at her with disdain before snagging her wrist. 'Taking you to get rid of it would be the easy way out. While I did consider it, I would easily have made you do it in San Francisco where facilities are years ahead of this country. Rest assured, you *will* have this child. You will endure the discomfort that comes with gestation, and come August, you will suffer the consequence of your promiscuity, you will pay the ultimate price for not keeping your legs closed. You will endure a long, hard and painful labour. And once that child is born, once it leaves your womb, it will be removed from the room without you seeing it or laying a finger on it, and you will never speak or think about that child again for as long as you shall live. Do I make myself clear?' Her mother tightened her hold and Kitty yelped.

She was stunned. Her mother was planning to give her child up for adoption. She couldn't do that – it was her child! 'I ... I want to keep my baby,' she stuttered, her breathing ragged.

June McGarrie stared at her for a moment, blinked, then let out a maniacal laugh. 'You stupid girl, are you that delusional as to think that you will be permitted to keep a bastard child? You are extremely fortunate that your father and I didn't wash our hands of you. It was my first preference, but your father has always had a soft spot for you, God knows why. He insisted on this course of action. If you know what is good for you, you will listen to me, do as you are told and be grateful that we care about your reputation enough that I don't leave you on some street corner penniless and pregnant.'

Kitty looked at the passing traffic on the streets of Melbourne. Everything looked so different here. From what she could see, Melbourne was a bustling city, one that seemed larger than Honolulu. She missed her home, but by the same token, she realised that she would rather be alone wandering the streets of a foreign city than in the company of her mother right now.

When they were settled in their hotel rooms, her mother and aunt went downstairs for lunch and Kitty decided against joining them.

'But you need to eat something, Kitty,' her aunt said. 'You are extremely thin, and the baby –'

'Let her be, Iris,' her mother abruptly interjected. 'She will need to grow accustomed to being out of the public eye for the next six months.'

When she was alone Kitty fell in a heap on the bed and wept herself to sleep. She awoke with a jolt when she heard her mother and aunt returning. Groggy from sleep, she dragged herself to the bathroom and drew the bath. As she undressed she noticed changes in her body. Her breasts were fuller but her aunt was right, she had lost too much weight. Her hipbones jutted out and the outline of her rib cage was prominent. But it was her face that bore the greatest changes. Years of living in Hawaii had ensured her skin was tanned and golden. Since their expulsion from paradise, there hadn't been much sun and Kitty was pale and gaunt with deep dark shadows around her eyes. It was as if she had died along with Eddie and Charlie. Lowering herself into the bath, she surrendered to the warm water and closed her eyes. For a moment she allowed her mind to drift back to that day in Kailua when she was floating in the water and Charlie appeared next to her. Squeezing her eyes shut, she willed herself back to that day – just to have one more moment with Charlie.

But the reality was that she would never see him again and the only part of Charlie that Kitty had left, her mother wanted to take away from her.

She couldn't let that happen. She needed to find a way to keep her baby. She had no idea how, but if it were the last thing she did, she couldn't lose her first-born child. She had lost too much already.

A week later they arrived in Sydney and made their way to her Aunt Iris's house in Rose Bay. Kitty might as well have been in Timbuktu – the people, the strange accents, the whole place, it was as far removed from Hawaii as she could have been. They had driven past a beach and Aunt Iris had said that it was the Pacific Ocean, but it looked nothing like the Pacific she knew. Kitty was not on her own, but at that moment, as she stared at the indigo waves cresting the shore, she had never felt so lonely in her life.

The very next day, accompanied by her mother, her Aunt Iris drove her to a doctor at Crown Street Hospital. It would only be much later that Kitty would come to understand why her mother had chosen Crown Street. It was notorious for carrying out forced adoptions, often intimidating young unwed mothers. Years afterwards, she would wonder why her Aunt Iris didn't warn her.

Kitty held her hands protectively around her belly as they walked down the corridor of the hospital's maternity ward towards the doctor's office.

'Mrs McGarrie, Miss Maison,' the doctor, a man in his late fifties or early sixties, greeted her mother and aunt. 'I'm Doctor Howard, please take a seat.'

Kitty felt alarmed and shocked that the doctor made no effort to acknowledge her. Aunt Iris pulled a spare chair from the corner so she could sit down and Kitty did so, feeling rather out of place even though, ironically, this visit was all about her.

'Now, how can I be of assistance today?' Doctor Howard again looked directly at her mother when he asked the question. Kitty's hackles rose.

'Doctor Howard, I am sure that my sister has adequately explained our ... situation.'

Kitty directed a searing gaze at her mother. She wanted to stand up and scream *Next* to her, her Aunt Iris gave her hand a squeeze. 'We just want to ensure that Kitty is looked after for the duration of her pregnancy.'

'What is paramount is the smooth transition afterwards. It is essential that everything is handled discreetly,' her mother added.

The adoption. Her mother was referring to her giving up her baby.

'Of course, Mrs McGarrie, we are well reputed in handling such matters with the utmost discretion.' Kitty didn't care for the smugness in Doctor Howard's tone, nor did she like the way he smiled with satisfaction. 'I have all the necessary paperwork here.'

'Excellent,' June said and nodded. 'We'll have that sorted out before we leave today.'

'No!' Kitty yelled before she had time to think.

Her mother glared at her, her aunt gave a little yelp, and the doctor looked at her as if it were the very first time he had noticed her.

'I beg your pardon?' He frowned.

'No. I am not letting you take my baby away.' Kitty was livid but her words were spoken with calm certainty. There was no 'we' in this – this was her baby and her decision.

'It would serve you well to keep your mouth closed, Catherine,' her mother hissed. 'And perhaps if you had kept your legs closed as well we wouldn't be in this shameful predicament.'

'And what is exactly shameful, Mother?' she countered. 'Carrying the child of the man I love? Or that he died defending our country?'

'That you chose to lie with a man before marriage, that you were stupid enough to fall pregnant to some ...'

Say it, Kitty silently willed her. *Say it.*

'Now, now ...' Doctor Howard cleared his throat and peered at Kitty with his glasses perched on the bridge of his nose. 'The situation is difficult for everyone. Let's all take a deep breath. Can I have Catherine on the examination table.' He was back to talking about her, not to her.

Without a word, Kitty did as she was instructed, clenching her teeth as the doctor prodded his fingers on either side of her belly, pressing deeply and making her cry out in discomfort. Once he was done, he again turned and spoke to her mother. 'By the size I estimate gestation to be between sixteen and eighteen weeks. Due date middle of August.'

'Thank you, Doctor.' He mother stood and slipped her gloves on. 'I appreciate your time today.' She smiled serenely by way of farewell but the moment they were back out in the corridor the smile faded. 'If you ever pull a stunt like that again, you're heading straight for the unmarried mothers' ward.'

An abrupt feeling of euphoria washed over her. The thought of being away from her mother for even a moment sounded highly appealing. 'Perhaps that's a good idea.' Kitty tilted her chin and looked her mother straight in the eyes.

'Kitty, no –' Iris began but her mother raised her hand to silence her sister's protest.

June narrowed her eyes, trying to call her bluff. Kitty wouldn't be intimidated.

'Perhaps someone will see how ridiculous it is that I am being forced to give up my child. If Charlie had lived we would have married.'

Her words again enraged her mother, Kitty could tell by the wild look in her eyes, but when she spoke, her voice was calm. 'I think you're right, Catherine. It would be a good idea. Wait here with her, Iris. I'll go and inform Doctor Howard of my decision.'

When her mother was out of earshot, Aunt Iris grabbed her hand fearfully. 'This is a terrible idea, Kitty. I beg of you not to stay here.'

'I think it's the best thing, Aunt Iris. No Mother around to hassle me to sign papers to give up my baby, and if I don't sign anything, they can't take the baby, can they?'

Aunt Iris didn't reply. She only shook her head sadly. Moments later, her mother returned with Doctor Howard. 'I hear you'll be joining us for a while.'

It was the first time he had really addressed her.

'Follow me.'

Kitty hastily said her goodbyes and followed Doctor Howard to the end of the corridor then down a set of stairs. She noticed that while some parts of the hospital, including the doctor's examination room, were bathed in sunlight, the area they were heading towards was notably darker.

'Are you leading me to the dungeon?' Kitty asked with a nervous laugh. The doctor turned and glanced at her over his shoulder, throwing her a look that was part pity and part bewilderment. He stopped to open a door and gestured for Kitty to go first. As she did, she noticed he was clutching her file; on the corner of the file was a stamp, BFA. Puzzled, she wondered if it was a code.

'Ah, Matron.'

A tall, rail-thin woman with hair the colour of snow tucked into a low bun on the nape of her neck turned and looked at Kitty from top to toe. 'Another one?' Her words were both condescending and cold – so cold that Kitty felt a shiver scuttle down her spine.

'This is Catherine McGarrie.'

'How do you do?' Kitty said politely, and watched as the woman narrowed her eyes. They were light blue and reminded Kitty of icebergs.

'American,' she sneered and Kitty recoiled.

'It's bad enough your lot are trawling the streets causing all sorts of havoc, but now we have promiscuous teenagers too.'

'I think Catherine would fit in well with Gwen,' Doctor Howard said and this elicited raised brows from the matron. By way of explanation, the doctor handed her Kitty's file and the matron raised her brows even further. Her mouth formed a perfectly round O then she flicked her gaze towards Kitty ever so briefly.

She nodded. 'I see. Right.' She snapped closed the file and slipped it under her arm. 'Follow me.'

Annoyance prickled. They were talking about her as if she wasn't there.

Matron led her past a number of rooms, most with four to six beds in them. They were mainly empty, although there were a few beds with girls sitting on them. One was moaning as if she was in a lot of pain and it alarmed Kitty when Matron made no obvious move to acknowledge the girl. Kitty paused for a moment, but quickly followed Matron when it became clear she wasn't going to stop. They turned the corner and headed towards the end of the hallway, stopping at the last room. It was smaller than the others, with only two beds pushed up against the walls. In between them was a tiny side table that was bare. In fact, the whole room was bare. No curtains or anything decorative. The walls were drab and grey, and the metal beds were short and narrow. Kitty was sure her feet would dangle off the end. Not that she was about to complain – something about the way Matron was looking at her told her that she wouldn't care for Kitty's thoughts on the accommodation.

'Well, it's not as fancy as your hotels in San Diego, but it's a bed and it's your home for the next four months.'

'I grew up in Honolulu. My father and ... my brother were stationed in Pearl.'

'Well, good for them.' The words were spoken without any interest. 'I'll be back in an hour to deliver you to your first chores.'

'Chores?' Kitty said, and this caused the matron to launch into a fit of laughter.

'Yes, you stupid girl. Chores. Did you think this was going to be a holiday? This ain't a holiday. By the time I'm done with you, you're going to wish you'd never opened those legs of yours. This isn't paradise – this is penance for your sins. Don't you ever forget that.'

Matron walked away, and her footsteps echoing against the hard tiled floors were the only sounds around. Kitty sat tentatively on the bed and heard it creak under her weight. Yes, it was uncomfortable. Yes, she was accustomed to far more comfort than this. But she wasn't sorry she was away from her mother. That was the main thing.

'Oh.'

Kitty glanced up to see a girl who looked younger than her standing in the doorway. She seemed frightened. Her dark eyes were wide and her black hair was wild. Her skin was smooth and dark, darker than anyone Kitty had seen before, and even in her slightly dishevelled state, Kitty could see she was beautiful.

'Hello, I'm Kitty.' She smiled warmly, hoping to ease some of the girl's obvious anxiety. When she stood in the doorway not moving, Kitty continued, 'I'm new here. Just arrived about half an hour ago, actually. What's your name?'

'Gwen,' the girl said after a while. 'I wasn't expecting someone to come so soon.'

'So soon?'

'Yes.' She was waddling somewhat uncomfortably and slowly lowered herself on to the bed across from Kitty's. 'Phyllis, the girl that was in that bed, she went into labour yesterday. I keep asking about her, but no one will tell me how she is.'

'That must be scary, not knowing what happened to your friend.'

'We came here together. Her baby was always going to come before mine, but it was too early. Too early for her to have it.'

'And that's why you're so worried,' Kitty said quietly as she reached over and gave Gwen's hand a reassuring squeeze. She seemed a little shocked, and pulled back before relaxing and offering a tentative smile.

'Yes. I've been here long enough to see ... I know when things don't look good and they didn't with Phyllis.' Gwen looked at Kitty with tears brimming.

'Maybe ask Matron if she can let you see Phyllis and her baby. Just to make sure that they are okay.' In her heart Kitty suspected this wouldn't be allowed but it was so clear that this girl needed comfort and a little hope.

'Oh no, miss!' Gwen shook her head. 'They won't let me do that! Besides, the baby would be already gone.'

'Gone?' Kitty blinked.

'Yes, given to its family.'

'Was Phyllis giving her baby away?'

'Not that she wanted to. They made her.'

'They can't do that! If she wanted to keep her baby, she should keep it!'

Gwen cocked her head and looked at Kitty strangely. 'We all need to give our babies away. That's why we are here.'

Kitty's stomach dropped to her knees. 'But if you don't sign the form, they can't make you! Please don't tell me you signed the form, Gwen.'

'I wanted to. I don't want this baby, miss. The man who ... I wasn't wanting the man who made me ...'

Dread flooded her. 'Gwen, were you raped?'

Gwen dropped her head and nodded before she silently began sobbing. Kitty moved to sit next to her and pulled her close, allowing the girl to weep. Her heart ached for her. While Kitty carried a child from the man she loved, Gwen carried one from a monster. A man that should be thrown in jail, and yet it was Gwen who was being treated like a criminal.

'That's why my file has BFA. I'm not too good at reading, but that I know.'

'BFA?' Kitty asked in alarm. 'I saw that on my file too.'

'Yes, it means baby for adoption.'

Kitty felt her blood turn to ice. A giddy, sickly feeling consumed her. Even without her consent it seemed that her mother and the hospital thought that they could do as they pleased.

But Kitty wouldn't have it. She was never giving up her child. Never.

Twenty-one

Wai Momi

Pearl Waters

Sydney, 1942

March soon gave way to April. Time passed, and Kitty's baby grew inside her. They never found out what happened to Phyllis. When she finally did summon the courage to ask, Matron blatantly told her that she would discover in due course, that when her time came, she would know exactly what happened to Phyllis.

'I'm not letting you take my baby.'

Kitty lost track of the number of times she said those words. Each time the matron's response was the same. She wore an expression that showed she was bored and that the conversation was a nuisance. 'That's what they all say, in the beginning. But you all come around in the end. Your children are all illegitimate, you are all worthless, unreliable and of loose moral fibre. You have no rights, you are nothing, the lot of you.'

Their children may be illegitimate, but about everything else – Matron was wrong. The girls there all had their stories and not one of those stories came without pain, and not one of those

240

stories rendered them worthless or any other demeaning name that the matron and her nursing staff called them.

All the girls were young and vulnerable, and many were just plain scared. Kitty never heard the nurses place any blame on the men who got the girls pregnant. Rather, it was the young women who were constantly made to feel inadequate, immoral and unde-serving, and not able to raise their own child. One girl, Judith, had been working as a nanny for a well-to-do couple living in Sydney's Eastern Suburbs. They had three children, all under the age of five. Judith had been courted and seduced by the brother of the mother of the children she was caring for, but unbeknownst to Judith, he was already engaged to be married to a woman from Canberra, a politician's daughter. Within days of telling her lover that she was pregnant, he told her he was going to whisk her away. Instead she was brought to Crown Street where, ironically enough, the children she had been caring for had been born.

The more stories she heard, the angrier Kitty became and the more determined to keep her baby. There were some girls who were easily broken, brainwashed by the common line that if they loved their children they would relinquish them to a two-parent family who deserved them.

'We deserve our own children,' Kitty said to the matron one day. 'It is our basic human right that a child should not be removed from its natural mother. Even animals are not removed from their mother at birth.'

She had paid dearly for her outburst. Matron ordered her to be confined to working in the kitchen for two weeks straight. It was hot and hard work, and one of her tasks included scrubbing the floor. Her belly was growing and moving around was becoming more difficult. Mrs Brew, the cook, took pity on her one day and gave her a mop to use. Kitty had almost finished when Matron came in.

'What is she doing with a mop?'

'She was having trouble moving 'round, her stomach was scraping on the floor,' Mrs Brew explained.

'I don't care,' Matron boomed, wrenching the mop out of Kitty's hands. 'I want you down on your hands and knees before our precious Lord!'

Kitty slowly lowered herself to the floor and started scrubbing.

'That's better,' Matron said, 'on your hands and knees where you belong.'

Mrs Brew apologised to Kitty, but she didn't mind. Being in the kitchen was better than some of the chores she had been assigned to. She hated the job of erasing the names from the paper bags that were put over the feeding bottles for the babies in the nursery. Kitty would never forget the first time she was put on the paper-bag chore. The first baby to be born after she had arrived was Barbara's. She had come to Crown Street because she had read in a women's magazine that Crown Street Women's Hospital helped young women who were pregnant. She had assumed that she would be helped to keep her baby.

Poor Barbara laboured for two days before she had the baby, a little boy with a full head of hair and cherub lips. Kitty knew she was never meant to see the child, but when the nurse came in holding him she asked for the baby's bottle and instantly Kitty knew it was her friend's baby.

That night, she cried so hard knowing that the baby was never going to be held by his mother. She wondered if they let Barbara hold him after delivery. Surely, they wouldn't be that heartless? Gwen heard her sobbing and came over to comfort her.

'There, there, Kitty,' she said softly. 'It's a'right. They say that after a while you forget you even had a baby.'

Kitty wondered how that was even possible. How do you forget you grew another tiny human in you? How do you forget someone who you carried around for nine months as part of your own body? Every day her growing belly was a reminder of Charlie. She knew that Gwen's circumstances were vastly different from hers, but at the core of it their babies belonged to them.

By May, the cold had set in. Kitty could never remember being so cold in her life. Gwen's baby was due to come by the end of the month, but the date came and went with no sign of her labouring. Then on a rainy Sunday morning, Gwen woke screaming.

'What is it? Have your waters broken?' Kitty asked.

Gwen's eyes were wide with fear as she shook her head and peeled back the covers to reveal blood-stained sheets.

Nausea rolled through Kitty. A cold sweat prickled her skin. In the time that she had been at Crown Street, Kitty had learnt a thing or two about pregnancy. There were always tales about labour and birthing. Rumours really, some too shocking to believe, but the longer she was there, the more she became to believe them to be true. And as time passed, it became clear that none of the mothers left with their baby.

There were a few who were okay with giving up their baby. They had, like Gwen, signed the document relinquishing their child, but the majority, like Kitty, wanted to keep their baby. They wanted to be the mother they knew they could be. Kitty felt disheartened to see how easily they were broken.

'There's too much blood, miss.' Gwen's voice was threaded with fear and she was right, the amount of blood was alarming.

The little they had been told was that when their waters broke, there would be a small amount of blood, but nothing more than a few teaspoons; most of it would be clear. But that wasn't the case with Gwen. Blood had not only soaked through her nightclothes, sheets and bed covers, but it was trickling down her legs.

Kitty swallowed hard. Her throat was dry. She wanted to appear calm for Gwen. 'I'll go and get Matron. Everything will be all right.' Somehow, Kitty made it out of the room calmly, but as soon as she rounded the corner she was a mess. She knew that she was no use to Gwen if she fell apart, so she pulled herself together and sought help – fast.

'Matron!' She raced towards the nurses' station, yelling at the top of her lungs. It was still early, barely daybreak, and she could hear the wind howling outside. 'Matron!'

She was almost at the quarters when Matron appeared, looking somewhat unimpressed.

'Why are you making such a racket –' Matron stopped mid-sentence as Kitty approached. She had never seen the evil woman look so worried before. 'Is that your blood?'

Kitty looked down – her nightdress was completely covered. 'No, it's Gwen's. She is bleeding badly.'

Matron shot off, calling for one of the nurses to follow. Kitty was right behind her. When they returned, Gwen was sobbing in pain and shivering.

'My baby, my baby!'

Kitty's heart clenched – she had never heard Gwen refer to it as 'my baby'. Always as 'the child' or 'it'. Was she changing her mind about the child?

Matron said nothing, but the expression on her face said it all. It didn't look good.

'My baby! My baby!' Gwen's wailing became louder and Matron told her to hush.

'We are taking you to the labour ward, a doctor will look at you.' They lifted Gwen onto a gurney as another nurse came running into the room. 'Get Doctor Howard, prepare the team, the wicket keeper and midwife will have their work cut out with this one. Let's get her there on time so there is a baby to give today.'

'Kitty ...' Gwen called out to her and Kitty rushed to grab her hand. 'Don't let ... don't let them take your baby ... it's too late for me ... but you ... you ...'

'Shhh.' Kitty gently traced her fingers across Gwen's forehead, her brow was damp with sweat, causing her hair to stick together in clumps. 'They'll take care of you ... they'll –' Kitty never got to finish the sentence. Matron pushed her out of the way and Gwen was gone, behind the doors of the delivery room.

Kitty would discover that Gwen had given birth to a healthy baby girl at five past nine on the first Sunday in June. At a quarter past nine, barely ten minutes later, Gwen had died from massive haemorrhaging.

She had overheard a couple of the nurses talking about how easy the whole process was. Because Gwen was so sick, they concentrated on getting the baby out and that was that. 'There wasn't anything to be done. The bleeding was nothing like I've ever seen.'

Kitty didn't need it to be spelt out. They had left Gwen to bleed out. That night Kitty returned to her room to find no one had gone to the trouble of changing Gwen's sheets. Carefully she undid the bed, folding the now hard, blood-crusted sheets into a neat pile. On top she placed a flower that she had found in the garden. It was sodden from the rain, so she gently dabbed at it till it was dry. Then she did something that she hadn't done in a long time. She knelt down on her knees and prayed.

She prayed for Gwen, who probably never knew that she had a daughter. She prayed for Gwen's new little girl, who would never meet her mother, she prayed that whoever took her would love her and care for her the way she deserved, and lastly she prayed for her baby. She prayed that Charlie would be with her when she had their baby, that he could somehow protect her and protect their child.

'I want to keep her, Charlie. I want to keep our precious Pearl safe.'

That night she dreamt of the waters of Pearl Harbor as they were before the attack. The Hawaiians called it Wai Momi, meaning

'Waters of Pearl'. Years ago it was said that the water was filled with an abundance of pearls. In her dream, Kitty was swimming surrounded by oyster shells. She could see one that was open, so she swam deeper towards it, and she could see its beauty and brilliance. But when she went to pick it up, another hand claimed the oyster. She looked up and it was Charlie, smiling at her, holding the pearl in his hand. 'This is our pearl.'

Kitty kicked her feet, desperate to get to Charlie, but before she could reach him, she was jolted out of sleep.

Wrapping her hands around her belly, she was certain of two things. She was carrying a daughter and she needed to call her Pearl. Not only because she was precious, but also because the waters of Pearl Harbor had claimed her father. It would be her child's link to the father she would never meet, and one day, Kitty would tell her. When the time came, she would tell Pearl all about her father.

Four weeks later, her time came. She was finishing up cleaning in the kitchen when she felt a warm gush of fluid trickle down her legs.

'Oh, Mrs Brew! I'm so sorry!' While she immediately knew what was happening, her first instinct was to apologise.

'Don't worry about the mess, child.' Mrs Brew bustled over and helped her up. 'We need to get you to the ward. You're having the baby.'

'But it's too early!' She winced and a sharp pain flashed across her back and down the side of her leg. 'Aww!' The pain was excruciating, Kitty was sure it would never end, but when it did, sweet relief swept through her.

'That was a contraction.' Mrs Brew led her to a chair and helped her sit. 'I'll go and fetch Matron. They'll give you something for the pain when you're in the birthing room.'

But no relief was given. There was no interest in making the labour process any easier for her. Matron, Doctor Howard and two nurses were present. As soon as Doctor Howard walked into the room, the first thing he did was look at her file.

'The papers haven't been signed, Matron.'

Kitty may've been distracted by pain, but she knew full well what he was talking about – the papers to relinquish her baby.

'We will have them signed, Doctor. She's a stubborn one, but there hasn't been one that I haven't been able to break.' Later, Kitty would discover that because she was underage, her mother had signed the adoption papers.

'I'm not –' Kitty's protest was cut short by another wave of contractions, stronger and more powerful than the last. They seemed to be coming quicker now, faster and harder, and with more might. Her moans of pain were met with steely silence and without any attempt to comfort her. She could feel the doctor prodding inside her in a way that was callous and insensitive.

'The baby is posterior,' Kitty heard the doctor say and panic flared.

'What does that mean?' She lifted her head and looked for someone to answer, but no one looked at her. Instead, Doctor Howard glanced at one of the nurses and nodded towards Kitty. Within moments the nurse was by her side, speaking firmly to her, making sure that she was lying down.

'We need you to keep quiet now.' She pushed Kitty down so she was lying flat. 'The doctor cannot do his job if you don't do as you're told.' Her voice was firm, but there was a thread of hesitation.

When the next wave of contractions rushed through, Kitty was certain she was about to die. The pain was unbearable. She screamed, the sound of her own cries so raw and foreign, she was sure they were not from her.

'Nurse! Keep her quiet!' Matron bellowed.

'Now, I told you to be still and quiet.' The nurse bent her head, her face crowding Kitty's vision, and she could see something in the other woman's eyes that she hadn't seen in any of the hospital staff the whole time she'd been at Crown Street – she saw compassion, understanding and sympathy. Kitty felt around till she found the woman's hand and grasped it. The nurse squeezed it back and the small act gave Kitty the largest amount of comfort.

Each contraction was more powerful, more excruciating than the last. But as the minutes turned to hours, tension mounted. She could tell that something wasn't right.

'Can you spin the baby or do we need to prepare for surgery?' Matron asked.

Dread pooled in her stomach. 'What's happening?' Kitty squeezed the nurse's hand harder. She knew that if they took her into surgery, she wouldn't see or even hear her baby. They would take it away from her and keep her drugged. She made the move to sit up, but she was restrained.

'You need to lie down,' the nurse whispered.

'What's happening? There's something wrong, I know it!'

'You need to lie down,' she repeated.

'My baby, my baby ...' Panic mounted and Kitty was finding it hard to breathe.

'The baby is facing up, its head is resting on your back,' the nurse offered in a low, hurried tone. 'Doctor is trying to turn the baby.'

Grateful for the small act of mercy, but petrified, Kitty was beginning to lose hope. 'I know that it'll be a girl. I want her name to be Pearl. Please promise me you will call her Pearl.'

The nurse said nothing.

Another wave of pain and she became more and more fatigued. Kitty felt her energy fading fast.

Charlie, wherever you are, please help me!

If heaven was a place and her love with Charlie had been real, why wasn't he helping her?

Doctor Howard poked and prodded and then announced, 'It's time to push, young lady.'

It was the first time that Doctor Howard had addressed her.

'I can't,' Kitty whimpered.

'You can and you will,' Matron snapped. 'There is a baby that is ready to enter this world. It's been in you long enough.'

And that was the problem. Up till now, up till this point, the baby had been hers and only hers. It was a part of her. Never had Kitty allowed the thought of giving up her child to cross her mind because she held the power. But now, that was all changing. The power was slowly bleeding away from her. Kitty was not able to move without being forced to lie down.

'On my count,' Doctor Howard instructed, 'one, two, three, push!'

And once the baby was born, her own flesh and blood, Kitty knew what would happen.

'Push, push!'

She would fight.

'And again ... push!'

They would hold her down.

'Push ... push ... push ...'

She would scream.

'Almost there ... another couple of pushes!'

She would beg.

A cry echoed through the room. It ricocheted off the walls and like an arrow it flew straight into her heart.

'Here it is – nurse, cut the cord.'

A muffled weep lodged itself in her throat. Tears streamed down the side of her face as forceful arms pinned her down. 'I'm sorry,' the nurse uttered. The apology was not enough. Nowhere near enough.

It was too late.

They'd already taken her baby.

Twenty-two

Aloha On My Mind

Hawaii, December 2016

'I thought you were there for Charlie, not to fraternise with his grandson.'

Kit was starting to regret telling Ben that she was going to spend a day with Adam later that week. After her dinner with Penny and Adam, Kit had gone straight to her room and called her brother.

'And I thought you said he was egotistical and annoying,' Ben continued.

'Well, he is,' Kit said, rather unconvincingly.

'So why would you agree to spend the day with him?'

'Because he isn't convinced that we should look for the baby and maybe I can change his mind.'

'Okay, two things. One – you realise that you are not looking for a baby, you are looking for a seventy-four-year-old who may or may not be alive. And two – since when was this a "we" project? It was always your trip to find out what happened to Gran's first love. Hang on ...' Ben paused for a second and dropped an octave. 'Do you like this guy or something?'

'Ha! Are you *insane*?' Kit all but shrieked the last word down the phone. 'I told you. I need to convince him to look for the b–' Kit sighed and corrected herself, 'for Charlie and Gran's child, and before you say it – yes, I know we are looking for a senior citizen not an actual child. Anyway, I didn't call to get a lecture from you, I called to see if you've made any progress looking for the tin.'

A sigh on the other end of the line revealed the answer.

'Nothing?'

'It's like this box has completely disappeared.'

'It's a tin, a red Arnott's biscuit tin. Are you sure you're looking for the right thing?'

'Yes, I'm sure,' Ben replied tersely.

'Sorry.' Kit flopped back onto the bed and closed her eyes. 'It's been a long day.'

'It's okay, Kit. I get it – it's a lot to take in. I mean, you're the one that discovered Charlie, and now you're the one that discovered a secret baby.'

'I thought we weren't calling it a baby,' Kit said and Ben chuckled.

'What time is it over there?'

Kit pried open one eye and checked her watch. 'Almost midnight.' She groaned. 'I've been up since before the crack of dawn.'

'Go to bed.'

'Hmm.' Kit was already drifting off.

'Go to bed. Spend tomorrow by the pool or doing what you want to do. Go on your date –'

'It's not a date! We are sightseeing.'

'Okay. Whatever. Go spend the day sightseeing. Do what you need to do, then come home.'

'Just keep looking for it.'

'I will.'

Kit spent the next day by the pool. She tried and failed to read a book that she had bought at the airport before boarding the plane. It was a bestseller, highly recommended and decorated with no fewer than three literary awards. But how could this book of fiction compare to the story that was unfolding before her? The story of Charlie and Kitty. It couldn't. She was halfway through and she knew that the ending was going to be worth the wait. It had to be – this story was seventy-five years in the making. Snapping the book closed, she shoved it in her bag and walked down to the beach.

Two weeks and a bit out from Christmas, the beach was teeming with holidaymakers from around the globe. American accents mixed with Japanese, Australian and the occasional English. As she approached the Outrigger Beach Resort, the iconic yellow outrigger canoe pulled ashore and tourists climbed down onto the sand. In the distance, Diamond Head, a volcanic cone on a nearby beach, guarded Waikiki Beach like a fort. With the sun high, peeking in and out from between the clouds, Kitty wondered what life would have been like the day after the Pearl Harbor attack back in 1941.

Hawaii had gone into martial law hours after the attack. She'd seen pictures of deserted beaches and then later, barbed wire all down Waikiki. It was hard to imagine how people would have felt on that first day. The day America went to war and her grandmother's life changed – forever.

What would've happened to Charlie and Kit if Pearl Harbor hadn't happened? It was a pointless question, really. The attack had happened and it was very real. A chill shadowed her heart.

War had torn them apart. Kit knew why her grandmother had moved on, she thought Charlie was dead, but why had he? Why didn't he look for Kitty once the war was over?

Kit was deep in thought, then her phone buzzed. When she fished it out of her bag she saw it was a message from Adam.

Is 9 am still good for you tomorrow?

Kit replied back instantly.

9 am works well.

And then cringed at how quickly she had responded.

Good. Bring your appetite and an open mind.

Kit was intrigued and as much as she didn't want to admit it, she was totally looking forward to spending the day with Adam.

Sounds great!

She flicked back her reply and then cringed again, this time at the exclamation mark. Was it too much? It was too much. A simple: *That sounds good* would have sufficed.

'What the hell am I doing?' she muttered.

Kit made her way back to the Hilton, stopping when she came to The Royal Hawaiian, the 'Pink Palace', where Penny had told them her gran had her sixteenth birthday party, where Charlie and a young Kitty had first met. Walking through the grand hotel, the place that held, she believed, a special place in her gran's heart, she let her mind drift back in time. How would that first glance, that first spark that filled the heart with hope, and the tummy with butterflies, have felt? Falling in love was magical – Kit had been lucky to have felt it with Jeremy. She remembered how the fire of passion burnt bright, especially in the early days when they were young and full of heart and hope, full of plans for the future.

How quickly plans can unravel. Again the thought that she should've visited Jeremy when she was in Sydney invaded her mind, gnawed at her conscience as a dog might gnaw on a bone. One day she might make peace with her choice to stay and let

Jeremy go to Bali with Mick, but right now, Kit couldn't see it happening.

She thought of Ben's words back at the pub in Sydney, then his comment when she'd told him that she would be spending time with Adam. She told her brother she was doing so with the aim of convincing Adam that they needed to look for Charlie and Gran's child, and that was the truth, but there was also a part of her that wanted to spend the day with him because she knew in her bones it would make her feel good.

Leaving The Royal Hawaiian, Kit passed the Sheraton where the infinity pool teemed with patrons.

'Those people have it going on,' a guy walking in front of her said to his friend.

Kit glanced in and agreed. A couple floated on cushioned inflatables, each holding a cocktail of some sort in one hand. The guy held a selfie-stick as they tilted their heads expertly towards the Pacific and he took their shot. Even without seeing it, Kit knew it would be a perfect photo. How could it not be? The sun's brilliant rays broke through the clouds and bounced off the azure pool – the very tip of Waikiki, just metres away from the glimmering ocean. Her gaze fell on the waves crashing into the concrete wall of the walkway then drifting off towards the seemingly endless ocean, where the Maita'i catamaran drifted lazily, gently cresting the waves. Then further in the distance, a larger ship slowly navigated the waters. It seemed to be cruising so close to the edge of the horizon that it looked as if it might fall off the edge of the earth.

On the other side of that earth was another world – Australia. It was the same ocean, but a world away from the life her gran would have led as the daughter of a high-ranking naval official. By the time Catherine arrived in Sydney, Kit estimated it would have been 1942. By then, Australia had been in the war for three years already, and rationing and restrictions were a way of life.

Many homes had bomb shelters, and kids were drilled on what to do in the event of an attack. Kit had learnt all this years ago in school, but she was just starting to realise that she'd had no idea of the true impact of the war until today. Her gran was sixteen and pregnant, arriving in a foreign country in the depths of war. She would have been grieving the death of her brother and under the impression that the father of the child she was carrying was also dead.

Would she have been scared? Undoubtedly. Would she have been fearful of her future and that of her unborn child? Definitely. Would she have been pressured to give up her child? Kit could only assume so.

She wished she had known to ask all these questions before her gran passed. She wished she'd had the time to talk to Gran as she had hoped – to find out about Charlie, about their child – and most of all, she wished that her gran was still alive so Kit could give her the closure she had so desperately lacked. The thought of having a child out there in the world somewhere – a part of you and the man you loved – and not knowing where that child was. That would, without a shadow of a doubt, have weighed on her gran's mind each and every day.

Waves crashed along the shore, covering her toes, cooling her skin, intruding on her thoughts. It was imperative to convince Adam that they had to find the secret child. She needed to do it for her gran. Kit needed to find out what happened to her child. Tomorrow she would convince Adam that they must search for the child. Knowing all they did – that Charlie had a biological child he hadn't met – wouldn't it be the right thing to do? It was too late to reunite mother and child, but there was a chance to reunite Charlie with his child, and Kit firmly believed that chance was quickly slipping through their fingers, just like the sands of Waikiki Beach dragged from the shore, lost in the depths, forever.

Twenty-three

Memory Lane

Hawaii, Thursday morning

It shouldn't have surprised Kit when Adam arrived to pick her up in a red Mustang. After all, she already had pegged him as a beer and car guy. As she slid into the passenger seat he shot her a megawatt smile. 'Are you ready for a trip down memory lane?'

'Well, it's not really memory lane, more like getting-to-know-you lane.' Kitty was banking on finding out a little more today about her gran's life before she came to Australia. Maybe it would give her a better understanding of Catherine's relationship with Charlie too.

When she came to Hawaii, her goal was to find Charlie, but what she discovered was a whole lot more. The news that there may be a child was enormous. And there was still one big question playing on her mind.

Why hadn't Charlie followed through on his promise to find her?

Kitty suspected her gran thought Charlie had died at Pearl Harbor, and Penny had mentioned that she wasn't aware Charlie had survived till last year when she saw him at the commemoration ceremony. And it made her think.

'When did Charlie start attending commemoration ceremonies?' Kit's question elicited a sigh from Adam.

'I remember when I was a kid he went to one. I think it may have been for the 50th anniversary. I'd never seen Pop so wound up, so ... depressed. He was like that for days afterwards. I remember Nanna telling him that while she lived, she never wanted him to go again. She made him swear. He honoured that promise. Each year, as soon as that invitation came, it would go straight in the trash. Last year I was heading off to the mainland and I stopped in to see him. He asked me if I had any plans for December seventh. I was about to ask why, but then I noticed what he had in his hands.'

'The invitation,' Kit said softly.

Adam gave a brief nod. 'I knew there was no talking him out of it, but I also remembered how he was last time he'd gone. He was a ninety-three-year-old man who, for the most part of his life, had refused to talk about Pearl Harbor. There was no way I was going to let him go alone, so I went with him.'

'How was it?'

'Strange. It was sombre and uplifting at the same time, if that makes any sense. There was a decent crowd, nothing like the other day, though. The Hilton hosts a gala dinner the night before every year and Pop was able to mix with the other survivors. I remember a man walking up to Pop and literally crushing him. It was Commander Kerr. The first thing he said was, "Florio, I thought you were dead." It was the first time that he'd seen Jimmy Kerr since the day of the attack. The Kerrs had been coming on and off for years, but because Charlie hadn't, they had no idea he'd survived.'

Adam slowed the car as they took a turn. 'Later I stayed up drinking with Jimmy and Charlie as they reminisced. It was the first time that I heard about Kitty McGarrie, and as it turned out, it wouldn't be the last. I know it sounds insane, but after that day, I started noticing Charlie's symptoms. It was like remembering Kitty made him sick.'

'You're right,' Kitty agreed, as annoyance frizzled through her. 'That does sound insane.' Part of her could see how Adam would have made the leap, but the other part of her was irritated that he kept looping back to Gran.

Adam flicked her a smile. 'To be fair, the signs had been there for ages, I just didn't want to see them, and when Charlie was diagnosed it was easy to blame Kitty McGarrie.' The car slowed in front of a large, Gothic-style cathedral and Adam unbuckled his belt, nodding towards it. 'Right, this is our first stop.'

'You're taking me to church on a Thursday?'

'This ain't your usual, run-of-the-mill church. Come on,' he beckoned as they started up the path towards the grand entry.

'It's beautiful,' Kit marvelled as she took in the stonework. Her family wasn't overly religious, but from time to time, the splendour of a church drew Kit in, and St Andrew's did just that.

'That she is,' Adam agreed. 'St Andrew's is one of only three cathedrals on the Hawaiian Islands, but it's not the reason we're here.'

'It's not?'

'No. I'll take you inside, and then I have a surprise for you.' His smile was boyish, and the spark in his eyes unleashed butterflies in her tummy.

'What sort of surprise?'

'Hang tight and you'll see.' Adam's hand landed on her lower back as he gently ushered her in and the butterflies went ballistic.

'St Andrew's Cathedral was commissioned by King Kamehameha IV, but he died before ground was ever broken. Because he died on St Andrew's Day, the cathedral was named after him.'

'It's Gothic, right?' Kit asked and Adam was clearly impressed with her question.

'It's actually Gothic Revival. It was designed by two London architects and a lot of the pieces were prefabricated and shipped in from England. But the real pièce de résistance of this place is the stained-glass window, and as you have some architecture know-how, I think you might get a kick out of seeing it.'

The real reason for her knowledge was Jeremy. He was an architect and during their years together, Kit had picked up a thing or two. But this wasn't the time or place to be thinking about Jeremy and how he would've been in awe of St Andrew's, as a building that is. As far as she was aware, Jeremy had only been to church once.

As they walked down the nave, Adam pointed to the massive stained-glass window on the western wall that reached from floor to eaves. 'It's hand blown and the images depict European explorers that had visited the islands.'

Kit scanned the myriad of images that were fitted into the window between a mosaic of blue and violet glass. Sunlight shone through, illuminating the images, but one in particular caught her attention. 'Oh my God, is that ...' She tilted her head to get a better view. 'Jesus on a surfboard?' she asked in disbelief.

Next to her, Adam chuckled. 'I was going to point that one out to you, but thought it would be more fun for you to discover it on your own.'

'That wasn't your surprise, right?'

'Jesus on the surfboard is really cool and all, but no, it's not the surprise. One of the reasons I wanted to show you St Andrew's is because it was pretty likely that Kitty would've been in church that Sunday morning. This place,' he said, 'was considered prestigious back then. The Governor's mansion is also on Beretania, only a few doors down from here, and the Rear Admiral and Mrs McGarrie would've surely been guests of Poindexter, who was Governor at the time.'

'So you think because of this, my gran would've been here that Sunday?' While it seemed to make for a good story, Kit had to admit that it was a bit of a stretch.

'While I can't be certain, I do think there is a pretty decent chance she was.'

'How?' Kit was truly intrigued.

'The answer to that is next door.'

Next door ended up being a school, St Andrew's Priory School for Girls. Adam led her through the grounds; they passed beautiful old buildings surrounded by wonderful foliage, ironwood trees and breadfruit groves, and bright pink hibiscus basking in the mid-morning sun.

When he raced a few paces ahead of her to open a door, the action surprisingly made her blush. 'Thanks,' she said shyly, trying to recall the last time a man held open a door for her. Kit couldn't truly remember, which probably meant the answer was never.

'You're welcome.' Adam smiled, revealing a dimple in his right cheek and Kit wondered how it was possible this was the same man who'd almost stolen her ride barely a week ago.

'Hello, it's good to see you again, Adam.' A slender woman in her mid to late fifties greeted him before turning towards Kit. 'And you must be Miss Bennett?'

'Yes.' She extended her hand. 'Please call me Kit.'

'Hello, Kit. I'm Pamela Honeyfield, school librarian.' Kit's level of intrigue was rising. What were they doing in a school library?

'Pamela is the one who found your surprise,' Adam said, reading her mind, and Pamela gave a quiet laugh.

'All I did was a little digging around, this one did all the work.' Pamela gave a quiet modest chuckle as she hitched her thumb towards Adam.

Kit held up both hands. 'Okay, the suspense is killing me, what is the surprise?'

Without a word, Pamela led them upstairs to a mezzanine where there was a small room with a number of open books laid out on the table.

'Go on.' Pamela gave a small nod and Kit walked in.

The books seemed to be a collection of school yearbooks. Running her finger down the smooth page of the first one, she stopped at a photo and gasped. 'I think this is Gran!'

Pamela moved next to her. 'It most certainly is,' she said. 'That photo was taken in 1936, Catherine McGarrie's first year at St Andrew's.'

The photo was black and white, but there was no mistaking it – the young girl grinning back at her was her grandmother. As she moved through the photos, Kit felt as if she were watching her grandmother grow up before her eyes. She had never seen any photos of Catherine as a child, and even though she'd been told all her life how much she looked like her, Kit was astounded at the resemblance.

Kit looked at Adam standing quietly in the doorway, arms folded, watching her. 'I can't believe you did this.' She shook her head.

He shrugged, unfolded his arms and shoved his hands into his pockets. He suddenly seemed self-conscious. 'You wanted to get to know your gran, I thought this might be a good way to start.'

'It's more than a good way, it's a perfect way, thank you.' It was. Kit felt her eyes prick with tears and she swore she noticed Adam's face aflame.

'You're ah, welcome,' he mumbled. 'I think Pamela has made some copies that you can take with you.'

'Oh, yes.' Pamela retrieved a yellow envelope from the bench behind her. 'Copies of all the photos and clippings from yearbooks that I thought might be useful.'

'I appreciate this more than you know, Pamela,' Kit said as she held the envelope against her chest.

'My pleasure. It was good to meet you, Kit. Catherine may not be an alumni but she was a student at a very historical and significant period for Oahu. You're welcome to come back at any time.'

After bidding Pamela goodbye, they resumed their tour of Downtown. As they turned right onto Hotel Street, Adam explained the significance of the area. 'Originally, this was called "Palace Walk" because it was the road that led right to the front of the Palace doors, but after The Royal Hawaiian Hotel was built, the king changed it to Hotel Street. Later the hotel was torn down and a new one, the current Royal Hawaiian, was built in Waikiki. The YMCA was built on the site of the old hotel and in time, it became known as "Serviceman's Domain" because the bars and brothels and all the concessions catering to the military guys were all centred here. It started at the YMCA, just behind us here in Chinatown, and heads all the way down to River Street where the business district is. The bus from base was ten cents and it would drop the guys off at the Y. Most of the brothels were not even on Hotel Street, but the street became synonymous with the red-light district. There were more than just brothels here, but it's mostly what the men came for, and it gave the area its identity and its dark magic.'

Adam stopped from time to time, pointing out restaurants, cafes and bars from a very different time and place. Kit learnt that on the corner of Hotel and Fort streets there used to be the

Benson & Smith Soda Fountain and on the corner of Bishop and Hotel, currently known as Bishop Square, once stood the Alexander Young Hotel with its rooftop dancing and a bakery on the ground floor, famous for their doughnuts and lemon crunch cake.

'Did Charlie come here at all?' Kit asked, full of curiosity, and Adam chuckled.

'I think it's safe to say that Charlie was here a plenty, for both the women and the other fares the area offered. In fact,' Adam said as he stopped in front of a building on the corner of Hotel and Maunakea, 'this place used to be Wo Fat's.'

'Hang on, isn't Wo Fat –'

'The villain from *Hawaii Five-O*?' Adam nodded. 'The producers of the original series named the arch-villain as an insider joke and it was carried over into the new series. It was Hawaii's oldest restaurant till it closed in 2005. There was a tropical bar on the ground floor, restaurant upstairs and gambling on the third floor.'

'Okay, I'm a little astounded at the knowledge you have here.'

'Like I said, when Charlie became sick and started living in the past, this was one of the places he mentioned.'

'What did he say?'

'A lot of his stories jump all over the place, but this one was quite clear – maybe because it was from a couple of nights before the attack.'

'December fifth?' Kit's heart skipped a beat. That was the day before Charlie wrote Kitty the letter. Whatever happened the night before may be of significance.

'Yeah. He keeps talking about some guy called Ken Roberts playing the ukulele and singing off key, then how as they were leaving, Richie Walter wanted to go to a brothel, but Eddie McGarrie said no.'

'Eddie ... Gran's brother,' Kit mused.

Adam nodded. 'Apparently Walter kept pestering them to go and when Charlie put his two cents in, Richie told Eddie about Kitty and Charlie having a secret affair.'

Kit sucked her breath in. 'They were found out.'

'Two days later, the attack happened and we both know how things played out after that.'

'Eddie died, Kitty was pregnant and Charlie was presumed dead,' Kit said. 'But what I don't understand is why Charlie never looked for Kitty after the war?'

Adam's eyes narrowed slightly. 'Charlie met my Nanna Rose not long after the attack.' The mood between them shifted instantly.

'Adam, look, I'm not saying that Charlie didn't love your nanna –' Adam held up his hand to halt her.

'Kit, I know that you want to get to know your gran, and I get the need to understand her world before the attack, really I do. But I think there's no point in trying to change the past.'

'I'm not trying to change anything, I'm trying to understand what happened, Adam.' She didn't care how nice Adam had been today, she wasn't going to give up trying to piece together the whole story just because he didn't like it.

He looked poised to say something, but changed his mind. Instead, he shook his head. 'Are you hungry?'

Realising it was a peace offering of sorts, Kit smiled. 'Starving.'

'I know this tiki bar that may not have been around when your gran lived here, but it'll give you a feel for restaurants of the era.'

Leaving Downtown Honolulu, they headed up Vineyard Boulevard, past Shafter Flats and hit an industrial area before making their way to Ke'ehi Harbor. The Le Marina Sailing Club was nestled along the Ke'ehi Lagoon, but one step inside the restaurant and Kit was transported back in time.

'Wow, I feel like I'm in a cross between an episode of *Columbo* and an Elvis movie,' Kit marvelled as she scanned the oddly charming watering hole.

'Charlie loves *Columbo*. I swear I could recite every one of those episodes off by heart.'

'Me too,' Kit said.

'You like *Columbo*?'

'My dad,' Kit said. 'He's obsessed. Although, on second thoughts this place would never make the cut – the restaurants in *Columbo* are all underground or don't have windows.'

Adam chuckled. 'This place is like stepping into a Hawaii that no longer exists. It's perhaps one of Honolulu's last remaining authentic tiki bars. La Mariana is quite literally where tiki bars go to die.'

'You're not wrong there.'

The bar boasted furniture and décor from a bygone era, complete with murky aquariums and the watchful eyes of tiki totems. The menu complemented the feel of the place with rum cocktails with names such as Zombie, Tropical Itch and, of course, the king of the tiki cocktails, the mai tai. When she spotted a familiar name on the beer list, Kit smiled. 'So I know the real reason we're here.'

'What's that?'

'Your beers are on the menu. I've found you out, right?'

'My beers are on most menus across the island,' he replied cockily.

'Have you always had a passion for beer?' Kit asked after they had ordered their meals.

'Believe it or not, I have a Commerce degree. I'm a marketing major. I worked in media for a while in Los Angeles but when my parents died, I moved back here ...' The tone of his voice darkened some, and out of the corner of her eye, Kit could see him scowling. It was as if violent black clouds had rolled in and the promise of a heavy storm was imminent. Kit wanted to ask how his parents had died. It was evident that the impact of losing both parents at the same time was enough for him to uproot whatever life he had on the mainland. Kit knew instinctively that he'd done it for another reason as well.

'You came back for Charlie, didn't you?' she asked quietly, her hand suddenly itching to reach over and comfort him.

He nodded, silent for a while before answering. 'I was all he had left. How could I not?'

'I'm sure that meant the world to him.'

'He tried to fight me on it at first – tried to tell me that he had his work and his house, and that was enough for an old man like him.'

'Stubborn.' Kit could imagine her gran doing the same.

'You've got that right, stubborn as a mule. I won out in the end, moved here – started working for a marketing company and one of my clients was the Maui Brewing Company. I spent a lot of time on site and watched them grow. When I saw that they were bursting at the seams and struggling to keep up with the demand, my mind started ticking over. Pop had given my mom and dad a parcel of land on the outskirts of Kailua and my dad always said that once he retired, he would turn it into a micro-brewery. He even had a list of brews and a handful of pals roped in to help him. When they died, the land came to me. I sat down with Charlie one day and pitched him the plan. I already had a list of who I wanted to hit up at the Maui Brewing Company to help me set it up. I was even willing to pay them to produce the beer for me. Charlie was keen on the idea, gave me his blessing and demanded I make him a stakeholder and appoint him head of recruitment.'

'Stubborn and a taskmaster.'

'Believe it or not, before he got ... well, before the Alzheimer's got a hold of him, he was one of the savviest business men I knew.'

'I don't think it's that hard to believe,' Kit said truthfully.

'I watched him take his humble taxi service and turn it into one of the most successful hire car and transfer businesses on the island. He had a knack for turning the ordinary into extraordinary. And now ...'

The hurt, the rawness in his voice made her wish more than ever that Charlie wasn't unwell, not for her own reasons, but for Charlie himself and the obvious pain that Adam was dealing with. She wanted to ask about the prognosis, about how long the doctors estimated Charlie had left, but it seemed too cruel, as if she were rubbing salt into the wound.

Once lunch was done, Adam told her there was only one thing that they needed to do to complete their step back in time, actually two – a trip to Leonard's Bakery for *malasadas*, Portuguese doughnuts, and then to Waiola Street for shave ice.

'Shaved ice?' she repeated and watched as he shook his head.

'No, no, no, no. It's *shave* ice, without the d.'

'Right. *Shave* ice.'

'Have you ever had it?'

'Nope.'

'Well then, that's about to change.'

Leonard's was not far from the La Marina and as Kit bit into the doughy goodness of her very first *malasada*, she knew it wouldn't be her last. 'God, this is heaven!' she exclaimed, wondering if there was any way she could take some home with her.

'I know,' Adam said. 'Whenever I come back after being away from home for a while, one of the first things I do is grab a *malasada*, but they have to be from Leonard's.'

When Kit was done, licking the last of the sugar off her fingers, Adam turned and looked at her. 'Ready for our last stop?'

'I seriously don't think I can fit anything else in.' She groaned, patting her stomach.

Twenty minutes later they were at the original Waiola Shave Ice that was around in the 1940s. Not having any idea how to order, Kit let Adam take the lead and he came back with two rainbow cones and they took them to the nearby benches.

'You know, you really are lucky.' Adam broke the companionable silence after the longest of whiles.

'How so?' Kit asked, taking a mouthful of the ice and syrup concoction and savouring the contrast between the tart and sweetness of the flavours.

'Before you arrived on the island, and I know exactly when that was,' he said with a smile, 'it rained for almost twelve days straight. Rain isn't unusual this time of year, even a few days in a row, but almost two weeks is just rotten luck. While you've been here, it's been nothing but blue skies.'

Kit grinned. 'I'm flattered to be considered some sort of anti-rain goddess, but the truth is, I left Melbourne under the same dismal, grey conditions you're describing.'

'Then I hope that you take back to Melbourne the sunshine you brought to our island.'

'Actually, I'm heading to Sydney after here. I'm going to spend a few days with the family ... you know, being Christmas and all.' The thought of Sydney and her family made her think of her last conversation with Ben and what she said her aim was for today – to convince Adam. So far she had done very little of that. 'Are you spending Christmas with Charlie?'

'Christmas has always been a hard time for Pop ... we lost my mom and dad a week before and Nanna Rose a few days after the holidays. I try not to make a big deal of it if I can.'

'Oh, that's totally understandable,' Kit said, but the thought of how hard the day would be for Adam didn't escape her. While

Adam was trying to spare Charlie any more heartbreak by not highlighting the festive season, how hard it must be for him when the whole world around him would be focusing on it.

'Besides, I'm heading to New Zealand, then Sydney to meet with some potential distributors.'

Hearing this, Kit's mind started working overtime. It seemed perfect timing, fate almost. She bit her lip, carefully choosing her next words.

'Adam, I have to be honest, finding out about my gran's life before Pearl Harbor wasn't the only reason I came today. I wanted to let you know that I am going to start looking for Charlie and Gran's child.'

He shook his head and swore quietly under his breath. 'I thought I made my position about that subject clear.'

Annoyance rankled. 'Crystal clear,' Kit replied with the same lack of warmth. 'And my position is still the same.'

'Why, Kit? What good can come from it? Your gran is gone –'

'But Charlie is still here. You're his only family. Imagine if you could give him the joy of meeting the child that he and Kitty created.'

Adam's face darkened. 'You think that bringing a long-lost child into whatever time he has left will make up for all the heartbreak he's suffered? Losing his wife, losing his son?'

'No, it's just –'

'You think I'm not enough.'

'I didn't say that, Adam.' Her annoyance was building. She could understand that he may be defensive to some degree, but the level of hostility was getting a little out of hand.

'You didn't have to,' Adam said grimly, scrunching his napkin into an angry ball and throwing it into a nearby bin. 'Come on.' He stood and turned away, the heels of his shoes scraped violently against the bitumen. 'It is time I took you back.'

The drive to Waikiki was silent. Adam's mood had rubbed off on her, and not even the bright, cloudless sky could lift it. Despite Adam's views, she wasn't wavering. Kit meant what she said. As soon as she returned to Australia, she would start looking for the lost child. What she would do when she found him or her, she had no idea. The only thing she knew was that she needed to do this – with or without Adam's blessing.

Twenty-four

Joy

Sydney, July 1942

The days immediately after the birth were a blur. She was drugged, she knew that much, and she had a vague recollection of Doctor Howard instructing a nurse to administer another dose. She had no idea what it was, only how it made her feel. What followed were days of lethargy and grogginess, where her eyes could not open more than half-mast, if at all. In the rare moments when she felt lucid, even in the briefest moment of time, an overwhelming sadness consumed her, as if a string was wound tightly around her heart and someone was slowly, slowly pulling it tighter and tighter. The pain was so excruciating that she almost welcomed the haziness, the jumbled dreams.

Flashes of Charlie's handsome face on the beach in Kailua, a clear blue sky, the soft frangipani-kissed breeze, and dappled sunlight flitting through the coconut palms, causing mottled shadows to dance on their skin. Charlie reaches out, lazily trailing his fingers down her arm. Kitty sighs with contentment. One perfect day that she would cherish forever. Then, in a blink of an eye, angry charcoal-grey clouds stream in, darkening the sky, blanketing the day with a thousand shades of night. A chill whips through her. Kitty frantically and fruitlessly grasps the sand around her. Dread, the giddy sickening kind, sets in.

Charlie. Where was Charlie? She can't find Charlie.

'Charlie? Charlie!' Her voice is drowned out by the sound of planes, their violent buzzing screaming in her ears. She can see they are Japanese – the sky is brimming with them, their blood-red suns marking their arrival. The clouds droop lower to earth as if the sky is falling, mist and fog shroud the beach. Her vision is clouded.

'Charlie!' she yells again, and this time, her screams are swallowed by rain. Thick, heavy droplets, slow and steady, before a ferocious downpour drenches her skin, seeping through into her marrow, chilling her to the bone.

In the distance she can see a flash – an image in the water.

Charlie! her mind tells her, although there is no way she can be sure. Blindly she runs into the water; the rain is torrential, the flash of the vision disappearing in the choppy silver sea. The waves are angry, six feet, eight feet swells that swallow her in an instant.

'Charlie!' she manages to cry out before the sea consumes her, the waves tossing her this way and that as if she were a ragdoll. Water is filling her lungs – she is struggling to breathe. Her hands move frantically. She knows she must swim to the surface, but no matter how hard she tries, she cannot reach it. The water is murky in the depths, darkness reigns, and the smell of the end, of death, is overwhelming. She closes her eyes, waits for it to take her. She is tired ... so tired. Every part of her body is limp as if preparing her for eventual peace.

'Kitty.' The sound of her name sends a shot of hope through her.

Charlie!

She opens her eyes and sees his face framed by a halo of sunlight. He looks like an angel.

He takes her hand, threading his fingers through hers, and in an instant she feels safe, loved, protected.

'Look for our lost pearl, Kitty.'

He starts to draw away, losing his grip. Kitty grapples in the water, trying to hold on to him.

'Wait, I'm coming with you!' she tells him, but he is quickly slipping away.

'Find her, Kitty. Find our lost pearl.'

With a jerk, Kitty woke, breath ragged, skin flushed, head pounding. She blinked, taking a moment to comprehend where she was, and when reality set in, it crawled all over her like poison ivy. Her breasts were heavy, full and ripe with milk that had leaked, forming dark patches on her nightclothes. A nurse walked in; Kitty remembered that it was the same nurse who was in the theatre when she gave birth. She took one look at Kitty's gown and a sad expression settled across her face.

'Your milk has come in,' she said simply, before turning on her heels and heading back out of the room.

'Wait!' Kitty yelled, not expecting her to do so, but the nurse stopped in her tracks, looked around at her expectantly, waiting for her to speak.

Kitty opened her mouth, then closed it again, the words suddenly jarred in her throat. The other woman waited, but her eyes told Kit to hurry, her gaze flitting towards the door as if she sensed time was of the essence.

'My baby,' Kitty managed to say, finally. 'I want to know, did I have a girl? How is she? Is she still ... here?'

Sympathy filled the nurse's eyes. She opened her mouth, poised to speak, only for the moment to be stolen by the whoosh of an opening door.

'Nurse, what's going on here?' Matron demanded.

'Miss McGarrie's milk has come in,' the nurse stammered.

'What are you waiting for then?' Matron boomed. 'You know what to do.'

Timidly, almost fearfully, the young nurse scurried out like a mouse only to return later to administer, somewhat reluctantly under the watchful eye of Matron, what Kitty would later discover to be drugs to dry out her milk. Kitty wasn't sure what was worse, the reminder of the milk, knowing that her child was out there without her, or the way her full ripe breasts suddenly became deflated, shrivelled by force.

Kitty knew she had to find a way to focus on the present. It was five days since she'd given birth, her mother and Aunt Iris would be arriving soon to collect her. The room was dim at the best of times, but thick grey clouds blanketed the city outside and the room turned to darkness. A fitting farewell.

Carefully, as if biding time, she folded the blanket and standard-issue tunic that only days after birthing seemed like it had never fitted her at all. Kitty wrapped her hands around her belly. A void filled her, more than a mere physical reaction.

When her feet were steady enough to hold her weight, one of the nurses helped her shower. A shock of blood poured down her legs, pooling in a pink and crimson puddle around her ankles. Her gasp didn't alarm the nurse, who looked at the flow of blood and told her to expect another three or four weeks of it.

'After that, you'll be fine, back to normal, right as rain.'

Her words were spoken so flippantly that Kitty wouldn't realise the full weight of them until some time after. Would her life ever be the same? It was July, the depths of winter in Sydney. Not that she had seen much of the city, having spent most of her time at Crown Street. Many of the girls had compared it to a prison and in many ways they were right. They were treated like criminals, when the only crime they were guilty of was falling in love, or in some of the girls' cases, trusting those who they had loved to protect them, to help them keep their babies. Of course, Kitty now knew what a farce that all was. She had been a fool for thinking she was different, that somehow she wouldn't fall, wouldn't cave, that she would be one of the lucky few to leave Crown Street with her baby.

But now, harsh reality had set in. Kitty knew that the moment they had cut the cord, the child she had carried for a little over eight months, ceased to be hers. And there was no chance of her being whole again. No chance to be, as the nurse had put it, right as rain.

Emotion overwhelmed her. She perched on the end of the bed, letting the tears consume her. Tears that soon became a flood of sobs that racked her entire body.

A faint knocking sent a shock of alarm through her. Instinctively, she straightened, assuming it was Matron coming to let her know she was to leave, her hands flying to guiltily wipe away evidence of her tears. When she saw that it wasn't Matron, but the young nurse, she instantly felt the rigidness released from her body.

'I'm sorry to startle you.' Her voice was gentle, soothing almost, her smile warm, and Kitty relaxed a little.

'It's quite all right.' She sniffled involuntarily. 'I was lost in my own thoughts. I thought it was Matron arriving to give me my marching orders.'

The other woman's smile was sympathetic. 'I'm sorry I couldn't give you more comfort when you ...' her voice seemed to stumble over the words, as if guilt gnawed at her. Kitty knew that it was the nurse's job to toe the line, to ensure the 'us versus them' line was not blurred. Despite the outcome, Kitty knew that she would be eternally grateful for the small comfort that this young nurse had given her in a time that was both terrifying and bleak.

'I understand,' Kitty offered when she didn't finish the sentence. 'But thank you for your kind words, you gave me some comfort. Well, as much comfort as possible, under the circumstances.'

The nurse glanced behind her, as if checking the coast was clear. She closed the gap between them, stepping over quickly, with a sense of urgency that spiked Kitty's pulse.

'Here.' She thrust something into the palm of her hand, closing her fist over Kitty's tightly as if warning her to keep it hidden. Kitty had no idea what it was, but it felt both smooth and hard at the same time. As if sensing the question on Kitty's lips the nurse's eyes darkened with warning as they heard the harsh sound of footsteps in the hallway, heralding Matron's arrival. The nurse scurried away, before her presence could be questioned.

'Your mother is here to collect you.'

Kit sighed as she gathered her few belongings, slipping the object that was cutting her palm into her bag until she could inspect it properly.

Silently she glanced around, taking a last look at the room that had been her home throughout most of her pregnancy. Her gaze lingered on Gwen's empty bed.

'Come along now,' Matron said brusquely. 'Best not to keep your mother waiting.'

Her mother wouldn't be in any great hurry to see her again, Kitty was sure of it.

Walking out into the waiting room, she saw her aunt first, who at least showed a modicum of emotion, quickly gathering a tearful Kitty in the briefest of bear hugs while June McGarrie attended to the release paperwork. And as Kitty had suspected, she didn't display a single fragment of feeling for her daughter. She reminded Kitty of the Tin Man from *The Wizard of Oz*, except while at the end of the movie, the Tin Man had found his heart, Kitty was certain her mother would never find hers. By her own admission, it had been buried along with her brother. Instead, she acted as if she were collecting Kitty from the headmaster's office, as if she were in trouble for misbehaving, breaking the rules, or worse, having committed a crime. In reality, the only crime that had been committed was depriving a mother of her child and a child of her mother.

Half an hour later, as they drove to her aunt's, the rain dancing rhythmically on the roof of the automobile, Kitty stared out at the dull and dismal view before remembering the object the nurse had placed in her hands.

Carefully she searched her bag until her fingers closed over it. She slid it out and when she laid eyes on it, a gasp escaped her lips. From the front seat, her mother turned and threw her a quizzical look. Kitty quickly coughed, she didn't need her mother suspecting anything. June McGarrie scowled.

'I hope you are not full of cold. This winter has been dreary enough without the possibility of getting sick.'

'No, Mother,' she replied, her pulse hammering as she tightly clutched the object in her hands. Smooth and hard, it was cold against her sweaty palm. She waited, holding her breath till her chest hurt, waiting to be satisfied that her mother's attention was diverted before unfurling her hand. This time she schooled her reaction, the emotion clogging her throat, her breath trapped in her chest so tightly she was sure her heart would stop beating, cutting the supply of oxygen to her lungs.

Kitty regretted not finding out the nurse's name, but in her mind, she called her Joy, because ultimately, that's what she had given her. What she was holding in her hand was pure joy. A tiny bracelet with pressed glass beads encircling a number of slightly larger beads with letters on them. There were five larger beads in total, each letter spelling out a child's name, her child. Kitty stared at it for the longest while until her vision blurred, her eyes stinging with tears she dare not shed.

Closing her fingers, wrapping them tightly around the only link she had to her baby, she held the bracelet against her chest and breathed out slow and steady, allowing her heart to beat rhythmically. She closed her eyes, her mind flashing to the moment before her baby arrived, when she pleaded for her child, a daughter she was sure, to be called Pearl.

The nurse had listened. She had somehow named the child Pearl. The tiny bracelet she clutched against her gave her not only joy, but renewed hope. She had something of her baby, a link that would surely allow her to find her. Her lost Pearl.

When they arrived at the house in Rose Bay, Kitty was greeted by an almost bare home. It was cold and soulless, dim and dark from the thick velvet-like clouds that covered the sky. The house hadn't been fully furnished when she had last been there in March, but she knew her mother, war or not, wouldn't allow this amount of time to pass without filling the space, small as it was, with whatever she could to make her mark, make it feel like her own. The emptiness could only mean one thing.

'We're leaving?' Kitty asked, trying to temper her growing alarm.

Her mother sighed as she removed her hat and gloves. 'Moving,' she said. 'As much as I would like to return home, your father won't allow it. He would prefer we stay till the end of the war. God knows when that will be.'

Kitty wanted to ask where they were going, but a knock at the door captured June's attention. It was Aunt Iris.

'We're moving to Mosman,' her aunt offered, taking Kitty by the elbow and gently leading her to the solitary chair in the otherwise bare room. The tapping of their shoes against the hardwood floors echoed without the comfort of rugs or couches to cushion the sound. 'The house was your Uncle Michael's, we had planned to move there after ...' Iris's voice hitched before she expelled a staggered breath. It fogged against the frigidity of the air and Kitty shivered. Michael had been Aunt Iris's fiancé, the man who had never come home from the war to marry his bride. Kitty had always wondered why her aunt had never found someone else. After all, she was young when Michael was killed in action in France. Didn't she want to marry and have a family of her own? But now, knowing all she did about love and how cruel war could be in tearing lives apart, Kitty understood perfectly.

She thought of Penny, how close she and Eddie had come to getting engaged, and her heart tightened. So much had happened since those carefree times. Indeed, so much had happened since she had last seen her friend in San Francisco. Her thoughts flew to the scrap of paper Penny had slipped in her hand. A slip that held Penny's address. Would she still be there now? Kitty desperately wanted to write to her friend and tell her all about Pearl, her little girl.

'How are you feeling, dear?' Iris's voice pulled Kitty out of her thoughts. Her words were kind, her eyes filled with worry and it sent a dual pull of annoyance and gratitude. Her aunt wasn't strong enough to stand up against her sister. Iris had often reminded Kitty of a mouse. But her heart was kind, and Kitty knew that she would do whatever she could to help her.

'I'm feeling ... well, as best as can be expected under the circumstances.' She summoned a smile. It was a fake one and hurt her face to pretend. The truth was that Kitty was broken, irreparably, both physically and mentally, and she was certain she'd never be the same again.

'You were worried before, weren't you? Worried you were to be sent back.' Aunt Iris's eyes, searching her face, held an understanding that surprised Kitty. Her mother's lament in staying in Australia had been Kitty's relief. Her Pearl was here, somewhere in this foreign land, but if Kitty went back to America, how would she ever find her?

'It's just ...' she began, knowing her aunt could see through her. Would she disapprove of her thoughts? After all, she hadn't stood up for Kitty when her mother had taken her to Crown Street.

Her Aunt Iris grabbed her hands and held them tight. Hers were warm despite the frost of the room and thawed Kitty's chilled, white-knuckled fingers. 'You need a reason to stay, Kitty Cat.'

Kitty looked at her aunt. She was right. She needed a reason to remain in Australia after the war. No one knew when the end would come, but her mother already had voiced her intention to leave when it did. Kitty would need a reason, a very good one, to remain.

'What are you two doing, sitting around as if there is all the time in the world?' June McGarrie's voice rumbled like a thunderclap. It made Kitty jump, but to her surprise, Iris remained calm, a conspiring smile slowly spreading on her lips.

'I was telling Kitty about Queenwood,' Iris said, throwing Kitty a sly wink.

Queenwood? What the heck was Queenwood?

Iris sensed her questions and elaborated. 'It's a fine school for girls and it's not far from the house in Mosman. She could catch the bus, or even walk there. I think she could benefit from completing her education.'

School? The thought hadn't crossed her mind, but suddenly her spirits lifted a fraction. A flutter of excitement flitted in her belly. Kitty sent a nervous glance towards her mother, who seemed not to hate the idea. In fact, she seemed to be giving it considerable thought. 'Not the worst idea you've had, Iris.'

A few weeks later, on the very same day that her child was originally due to come into the world, Kitty started at Queenwood.
The gap in her schooling not even the slightest bit an issue.

'War is a terrible thing,' the headmistress, a tall but stout older
woman by the name of Mrs Noonan, commented as Kitty bid
farewell to her mother. June McGarrie was dressed top to toe
in black, in perpetual mourning for Eddie and at times, Kitty
thought, for the role of high society wife of a Rear Admiral whose
days of lunching with the likes of Mrs Walker and Mrs Ramsey
were well and truly over. Kitty didn't deny that her mother had
suffered considerable loss, but it seemed June had no room in her
shrivelled heart to see that her daughter was hurting.

'You lost your brother in the Pearl Harbor attack?'

'Yes, his name was Eddie. He was the best big brother a girl
could ask for.'

Mrs Noonan sighed heavily, obviously understanding such
loss. 'I lost my youngest boy, Simon, in Singapore in February.
My eldest, Charlie, is a doctor in Malaysia, although we haven't
heard from him in months and I fear ...' She shook her head and
cleared her throat. 'I apologise, dear. It's not often I let my guard
down, and in front of a new student.' The headmistress blinked
frantically, wiping an errant tear that had dared to escape. She
seemed genuinely remorseful for showing her emotions, and she
shouldn't have.

'Please don't apologise, Mrs Noonan. I ... my brother had a
friend named Charlie. When we left the island, we still hadn't
heard about him.' Kitty tempered her voice, daring not let emotion get the better of her. 'You're a mother, I cannot begin to
imagine the heaviness in your heart, knowing the loss of one that
you love and not knowing the fate or whereabouts of the other.'

Headmistress Noonan considered her thoughtfully. 'Your
mother was wrong, Catherine. You are not the foolish and flighty

girl that she painted you to be. I have been in this job for longer than I care to remember some days. I have seen many young women come through these doors. Many are wide-eyed, some are only here biding their time till they are married, some even engaged, promised to a man or, in some cases, a boy that may or may not come home. You seem more ... worldly somehow.'

'Perhaps it's because I've seen more than most girls my age. I mean – I appreciate that Australia has been in the war for years already, but when your home is invaded, when life as you know it is ripped at the seams, then I guess you become worldly. Whether you want to or not, ma'am.'

'I suppose you are right, young lady. And please, no need to refer to me as ma'am. While Queenwood prides itself on tradition, we don't stand on ceremony here. Headmistress Noonan or Mrs Noonan will suffice. Now come, I'll take you to your homeroom and introduce you to one of your classmates. There is a lovely young woman named Margaret Moore and I am sure you two will hit it off.'

Margaret Moore was a tall gangly girl with wildly curly hair the colour of a blazing summer sunset that looked as if, no matter how hard she tried to tame it, it would find a way to escape its ribbon prison. Unruly corkscrew tendrils swayed in the light breeze as blue–green eyes appraised her with slight apprehension.

'Margaret, this is Catherine McGarrie. She is a new student in the same form as you. Please be courteous and help her settle in.'

'Pleased to meet you, Margaret.' Kitty smiled warmly.

The apprehension fled from Margaret's eyes, instead, amusement and humour filled them. Kitty noticed a spray of freckles dancing on the bridge of her nose. 'Cor blimey!' she exclaimed, 'You're a Yank!'

'Miss Moore!' Headmistress Noonan admonished with a disapproving frown. 'Language, young lady.'

'Sorry, Headmistress,' Margaret said, before turning towards Kitty. 'Come on, Catherine, let me show you around.' She looped her arm through Kitty's and led her down the sunlit hallway. 'You best call me Maggie, all my friends do.' Maggie had a lively nature about her, the kind of energy that was contagious.

'Well then, you best call me Kitty. After all, it's what my friends do.'

Maggie sent her a megawatt smile. It was like a ray of light on a rainy day and as they walked arm in arm, Kitty knew deep down that she had just made a friend for life.

Twenty-five

What a Difference a Day Makes

Sydney, January 1944

The new year started with the world still in war, and for Kitty, it was another new year without her baby.

Heat settled on the city like a stifling blanket, so oppressively hot that Kitty felt as if she were constantly suffocating. Her heart ached, shrouded by a melancholy she knew could never, would never, be lifted.

Aunt Iris had convinced June to take a day trip up to Newcastle. Kitty was supposed to accompany them, but Maggie Moore had been over for dinner the night before and suggested that Kitty join her for a day at the beach instead. Surprisingly, her mother had agreed to the idea. June McGarrie had previously never warmed to any friend of Kitty's and she had certainly never liked Penny. But Maggie had a way of charming people like Kitty had never seen before. She was like a burst of sunshine that even on a cloudy day would find the smallest break, the most infinitesimal gap in the clouds, and spill her rays of light, and even June McGarrie was not immune to Maggie's infectious brightness.

'Don't worry, Mrs Mac.' Maggie flashed a smile while simul-
taneously serving her mother mashed potatoes. 'I'll make sure she
doesn't get into any mischief.'

Kitty almost choked on the water she was sipping. Her mother,
to her credit, managed to cover up her surprise with a well-timed
cough. Maggie's comment was made in jest – she wasn't to know
how close to the mark it was.

'I have full faith in your chaperoning skills, Miss Moore.'

Maggie beamed at the praise and Kitty couldn't help glower-
ing. Her mother's compliments were as rare as hen's teeth. Kitty
couldn't remember when she was last paid one and for Maggie to
score one so easily ... well it rankled.

'There's a dance on at the Troc tomorrow night. I was thinking
Kitty and I would go,' Maggie mentioned casually. Her attention
was not on Kitty, but her mother.

The Troc was short for the Trocadero, a well-known dance
hall on George Street in the city. While Kitty had never been, she
knew that Maggie had. Kitty also knew that American servicemen frequented the Troc and the last thing she wanted was to be
in the company of an American soldier.

'I'm not sure the Trocadero is a suitable place for young women,'
June said with her lips pulled tight into their trademark position.

'Oh no, Mrs Mac, it's not *that* kind of dance! The University
of Sydney, Faculty of Medicine, is holding it. All their graduating
young doctors will be there.'

Kitty had never seen the expression on her mother's face change
so quickly.

She was due to start teachers' college in a matter of weeks,
something she had fought hard for, but her mother was already
marrying her off to one, any one, of the would-be doctors that
would be there at the dance.

'That sounds like fun, doesn't it, June?' her Aunt Iris said, giving Kitty a secret wink.

'Well ...' Her mother was doing her best not to seem amenable to the whole idea, even though she clearly was. 'I'm sure that it would be fine for you girls to go ... as long as you are home by a decent hour.'

Kitty's stomach sank as Maggie practically bounced with excitement. She didn't want to go to a dance with medical students. She didn't particularly want to go to the beach either, but the alternative of spending the day with her mother was something that Kitty desired even less, so she chose the lesser of two evils.

The next morning, as she made her way to Maggie's house on the southern end of Bay Street, sweat beaded under her summer dress. It was just past nine and already the sun was heating her skin with the promise of more. Why they couldn't have just spent the day down at Beauty Point Baths was beyond her. This way they would need to walk a good mile to Military Road to catch the number 64 tram from Wynyard to Balmoral Beach.

'Morning!' Maggie bounded up her front path. Sunlight flittered through her flame coloured hair, making it look like ribbons of gold floating behind her. 'Ready for a day of fun in the sun?'

Kitty narrowed her eyes. 'Why are we going to Balmoral?'

Maggie closed the gate behind her and sent her a puzzled look. 'What do you mean? It's an absolute furnace out here! Of course we're going to the beach.'

'Yes, but we could easily go to Beauty Point like we normally do. Or even ... Pearl Bay.' It took a lot of strength to keep her voice even. When Kitty came to the Bay Street house and discovered the nearby Pearl Bay, she thought it quite serendipitous. Pearl Bay was beautiful. It was north facing, capturing the sun, and with the cliffs behind the bay and Beauty Point, it was sheltered from the westerlies.

Kitty would often walk along the beach, which was lined with houseboats that had originally been constructed during the Depression. She wondered what it was like to live on a house that was not quite a house and not quite a boat either.

Sometimes she imagined that she lived in one of the boats. In her daydream she lived there with Pearl, sometimes she even tried to put Charlie into the fantasy, but often it hurt too much to think of him. She imagined it would be a unique experience, living in your own home, the water underneath you, the fish and birds all around. She would look out the window and the view would be constantly moving. She would get to know the sea and all its moods. She would get to know the fishermen and the fish.

When she went to Pearl Bay she felt closer to her daughter, her lost Pearl, but every time she left it was like losing her all over again. Each time she wondered why she put herself through the torment, the torture, and yet, she went back again and again, especially now since school was out and would be for another couple of weeks.

'I thought it was time for something different.' As Maggie led the way down the street, a gust of hot wind blew around them, making Kitty feel like someone had lit a furnace. 'We go to Beauty Point *every* day,' her friend added with an air of boredom.

While that was true – they had been frequenting the baths regularly over the summer – there was a reason. It was spectacular and right on the harbour. If time and circumstances had been different, Kitty knew she could love this city without reservation. But while Sydney had beauty, it also had already caused her pain.

'Besides, the blokes that we'll be meeting tonight will be meeting us there.'

Maggie's revelation captured Kitty's attention. 'Blokes?' She narrowed her eyes, knowing there was more to the story and having an inkling that it spelt trouble.

'Blokes – you know, guys, or ...' Maggie wiggled her brows suggestively, which cemented her suspicions. 'I should say, men. We'll mingle. What's the harm?'

'I know what a *bloke* is,' Kitty sighed. 'It's just ...'

I don't want to mingle.

Kitty wasn't ready to be in the company of men. She wasn't sure if she would be ready for a very long time.

'What?' Maggie prompted when she stalled.

'I mean ... how old are these ... blokes? You said men? Maggie, we're barely eighteen.'

'Oh, stop being such a stick in the mud.' It didn't escape Kitty's notice that Maggie had dodged her question. Kitty sighed and decided not to push the issue for the time being.

An hour later, they alighted at the Esplanade. Balmoral Beach was crowded already, which was to be expected on a day like today. The sea was glittering blue, lapping against the golden sand, and for a blink of a moment she was transported to the other side of the ocean where, on another beach, there were golden sands and waves just like these.

'Kitty?' Maggie's voice snapped her out of her daydreaming.

'Sorry, what did you say?'

'I said let's claim a spot before there isn't an inch of space left.'

As they made their way onto the sand, they weaved through beachgoers on their towels. It seemed as if all of Sydney was intent on escaping the heat. As they found a vantage point, one that thankfully had some shade from a nearby tree, Kitty marvelled at the fun and frivolity of it all. Children frolicked in the water, as if they had not a care in the world. If it wasn't for the presence of American and Australian servicemen milling around the

Esplanade in their uniforms, you could be forgiven for forgetting that the country was still in the grips of war.

Most days, even Kitty forgot. Their house wasn't as extravagant as her home in Hawaii, but it was by no means modest either. She only had to look at some of her school friends to see how lucky she was.

Lucky.

Kitty almost scoffed. In a little over a year she had lost her brother, the father of her child, transplanted her life across the world and had her baby taken away from her. Kitty wasn't lucky – she was doomed to be cursed for the rest of her life. For the rest of her days, there would be a pit in her stomach that would never go away. The sound of a child's laughter caught her attention. A little girl, perhaps two years old or so, splashed in the shallows with her older brother. Her happiness was full of innocence and light and for some reason, it made Kitty smile, but at the same time, it made her sad. How many times had she looked at babies and thought of her own? At the very beginning it was hard to see mothers pushing prams along the street or seeing them when she was out shopping and not yelling at the top of her lungs, 'I am a mother too!' Of course, she never did. Instead, she would cry herself to sleep at night.

'Cute, isn't it?' Maggie nodded towards the children.

'Yes, how lovely it must be to be so carefree.' She forced a smile and blinked away her tears.

Maggie sighed her agreement as she peeled off her dress to reveal a stylish two-piece bathing ensemble. 'I would give a right leg to be like that, to escape the fact that we are at war even for just one day.'

'That would be nice,' Kitty said, meaning it more sincerely than Maggie could possibly comprehend.

'Holy moly!' Maggie exclaimed as Kitty folded up her dress.

'What is it?'

'Sweetie, why would you wear a one piece when you clearly need to be wearing something that shows off that tiny waist of yours.'

Kitty looked at her bathers, feeling her already hot face heat up even more. There was a very good reason why she was covering up her belly. She still had the dark line that ran from her rib cage to her pubic bone. It was faint, but still there, and a telltale sign that she had had a baby.

'It's too hot to expose more skin than I need to,' Kitty said and settled onto her towel.

'Well I for one want to get as much sun as I can.' Maggie slipped on her sunglasses and lay on her towel. Her whole body was exposed to the sun, not an inch of shade covering her fair freckled skin.

'Careful, you burn quick,' Kitty warned.

Maggie's response was to poke her tongue out. 'You sound like a mother, Kitty.'

It wasn't mean spirited, but Maggie's words hit her like a barb in the heart. She often wondered if she should confide in Maggie about Pearl. But every time she thought of doing so, she was unsure how to tell her. Telling Maggie about Pearl meant telling her about Charlie, and her grief was too raw on both accounts.

They lay in silence for a while. Kitty willed herself to enjoy the day but even with the shade, the heat was unbearable. Sweat pooled inside her swimsuit, she could feel it sticking to her skin. 'I'm going for a swim, are you coming?' Kitty asked.

'I think I'll sun my back for a moment. You go ahead. I'll join you later.'

Kitty braved the hot sand, making her way to the water. She didn't waste any time but dived in and let the waves pull her under. The surf was cold against her burning skin, but delicious too. Within moments of breaking to the surface, the sun's rays beat against her face. Kitty let the waves lull her, enjoying the contrast of the burning sun and cooling water.

A while later, when her fingers started pruning and it became obvious that Maggie wasn't going to join her, Kitty reluctantly left the water. The breeze had picked up and felt nice against her skin. As she made her way back to Maggie, she saw that her friend was not alone. Kitty now knew why Maggie had failed to join her in the water – two young men sat either side of her, looking amused as she told some tale. By the time Kitty came up to them, they were all laughing. The young man to the left of Maggie, sitting on her towel, was the first to spot her.

'G'day, you must be Kitty.' He smiled at her in a way that made her feel shy. When she noticed how his eyes roamed her body, she became acutely aware that her hair was wet and plastered all over her face.

'Hello,' she replied, her hands flying to her head. She combed her fingers through then twisted her hair into a loose bun at the nape of her neck.

'Oi! A Yank!' the guy on Maggie's right exclaimed.

'That's what I said when I first met her.' Maggie giggled and Kitty felt her brows rise. She knew that type of giggle. 'Bert, William,' Maggie introduced them right to left, 'this is my friend Kitty. Her name is Catherine, but everyone calls her Kitty.'

'Catherine.' William rose and extended his hand. 'How do you do?'

He was tall. Kitty had to crane her neck to look at him. She duly noted the broadness of his shoulders and his sun-kissed skin. He was still smiling at her, or was he laughing at her? She must look like a drowned rat and her hand felt rubbery against his soft palm.

'Um, fine thank you,' she said, clumsily trying to avoid the gaze of his grey eyes.

'We were about to grab some fish and chips,' Bert said. 'Would you girls care to join us?'

'Of course,' Maggie answered, not even bothering to confer with Kitty.

'Great!' Bert beamed at Maggie. 'William and I will go ahead and get a table at the milk bar then you girls can come when you've had enough sun.'

'Oh, we've had enough sun,' Maggie answered for the both of them once again, and Kitty felt a wave of annoyance flow through her. 'Let's go now.'

Maggie and Bert chatted as they packed up, and Kitty felt her annoyance at her friend reach fever pitch.

'Catherine?' William asked gently. 'Is that all right with you?'

'I'm sorry, what's all right?' she snapped, not looking at William. She was throwing daggers at her friend.

'That you join us,' William said. When her gaze returned to his, she could see his genuine concern and she felt a little foolish for being so rude to him.

'I'm sorry,' she apologised. 'It's completely all right, I'm just a little irritated at Maggie.'

'She didn't warn you that you were here as a third wheel?'

Kitty sighed. 'She did mention something earlier, but I failed to extract the full truth out of her.'

'Let me give you the full story – or at least the story that was fed to me. Bert likes your friend Maggie –'

'Somehow I suspect the feeling is mutual,' Kitty said and William laughed. Warmth flooded her and involuntarily, she laughed as well.

'Look, the short story is I was coerced here because Bert wanted to see Maggie, but since he's only seen her when he's delivered milk to her home, he wasn't sure he would like her enough to stay the whole day, so I was his escape plan, so to speak.'

'Maggie would be furious if she found out.'

'You're not going to tell her, are you?' William sounded panicked. 'Because I can tell you, he likes her an awful lot. I can see it,' he added in a rush.

'Your secret is safe with me,' she assured him. 'I can tell that Maggie likes Bert, too.'

'Thank you.' William breathed a sigh of relief, giving her a lopsided smile that made Kitty's heart beat a little faster.

'You're welcome.' Kitty felt shy. An awkward silence fell between them and she became aware, once again, of her state of disarray.

'Would you mind giving me a few minutes to gather myself? I'm sure I look like a mess.'

'Yes, ah, I mean no, ah, sorry – I mean not at all. I don't mind waiting for you ...' William fumbled over his words and it thawed Kitty's awkwardness.

'I should add, you don't look like a mess at all, in fact you look ... beautiful.'

Kitty felt her breathing hitch.

'And I'm also glad I was coerced in coming here today. I'm so glad that Bert twisted my arm,' he said.

Kitty was speechless. Was he saying what she thought he was saying?

'I'll wait for you at the top of the stairs.'

When William had gone, Kitty dressed and packed away her things with shaky hands, her mind replaying his words.

William liked her, but how did she feel about it? More importantly, how did she feel about him? She shook her head.

Get a grip.

She'd only just met the guy. Chances were she would never see him again. She knew nothing about him. He probably wasn't from around here anyway. He seemed nice and he certainly was easy on the eye. It wouldn't hurt to enjoy his company, but she would make sure she didn't grow attached to him. She had given away her heart once before and paid the ultimate price. Kitty needed to remember not to do that again.

Not that she was in any danger of doing so here – she just needed to remember how hard it was losing Charlie. A piece of her heart had died when she lost him, and then another when she lost her Pearl. While she could never get her Charlie back, she hadn't given up hope of finding her baby.

As she climbed the stairs that led to the Esplanade to meet William she vowed that she would never lose sight of what was important – finding her daughter.

'Ready?' William asked when he spotted her.

She nodded. 'Yes.'

'Well then, Catherine,' he offered her the crook of his arm and it only seemed polite to take it. 'Let's join the lovebirds.'

They made polite conversation as they walked to the milk bar. She discovered that William was a local – he lived on the other side of Military Road – and that he was a medical student at Sydney University.

'I just turned twenty-one, last week in fact.'

'Oh, happy belated birthday.'

'Thank you. The first thing I did was join the Army, much to my mother's disappointment.'

'My mother didn't like it when Eddie joined the Navy, but she had no say, since my father is a Commander.'

'Where are they serving?'

'Oh.' Kitty felt foolish for revealing a part of her life she hadn't meant to. 'I'm ... not sure where my father is at the moment ... they move him around a bit.'

It wasn't a lie, but the truth was she hadn't had any direct correspondence with her father since the day they left Honolulu. Any communication was funnelled through her mother.

'And your brother?'

Kitty stopped walking, tears pricked her eyes. She shouldn't have said anything about Eddie.

'Catherine?' William asked, concerned.

'Eddie ... we lost him at Pearl Harbor.'

'I'm so sorry, Catherine.' He gathered her hands in his. 'I have upset you,' he said when Kitty dropped her gaze to the footpath, willing the tears not to spill. When she failed to stop them, he placed a finger under her chin and tilted her face towards his. 'You miss him of course.'

Silently she nodded. Her tears were as much for Charlie as they were for Eddie.

'It still hurts after all this time.'

'I suspect it will hurt for a while longer.'

'I'm sorry – I've made such a mess of myself.' Kitty wiped her tears and gave a watery smile.

'Hungry?' William asked and as if on cue, her stomach rumbled and they both laughed. 'I'll take that as a yes.'

They found Maggie and Bert seated at a booth devouring a mountain of fish and chips laid out on newspaper.

'We waited as long as we could,' Maggie said sheepishly when she saw them. 'Honest,' she added when she noticed Kitty's doubtful look. 'Well, don't just stand there, sit down and help us eat it all.'

Kitty didn't have to be asked twice. As she slid into the booth, she knocked knees with William; the man was so tall that it was impossible not to. She tried to focus on the food, she was hungry after all and the fish and chips were just the thing to hit the spot.

'You girls should come to the Troc tonight,' Bert suggested as lunch was winding down.

'Oh we –' Kitty's sentence was cut short by Maggie's right foot coming down hard on her left.

'We'd love to.' Maggie beamed, and Kitty remembered their conversation with her mother and knew that Maggie had planned to go to the Troc even before Bert had asked them to come along.

'Great.' Bert beamed right back, leaving William and Kitty to exchange looks.

'Lovebirds,' he mouthed and Kitty bit her lip to stop her laughter. His grey eyes twinkled with amusement and Kitty felt her face flame. Suddenly her mind was ticking over, trying to mentally pick out a dress to wear.

A day ago when Maggie had talked her into a night at the Troc, it seemed as if it were the last thing she wanted to do. But yesterday she hadn't met William.

My, what a difference a day made.

Twenty-six
Chasing Ghosts

Trocadero, Sydney, 1944

As soon as she and Maggie walked through the Trocadero's art-deco doors, Kitty knew this was no medical faculty dance. American and Australian servicemen filled the auditorium. On the dance floor, the women's fluted skirts and dresses gave a pop of colour amongst the crowd of military uniforms.

She cast her eye around the room, soaking it all in, from the scarlet carpet covered with a pattern of fleur de lis in cream, gold and black, to the art-deco bas-relief murals depicting well-known dances from across the globe. The bandstand itself was amazing. Shell shaped with coloured lights that made it look like a constantly changing scene. For a moment it was hard to comprehend that she was in Sydney. She could be in Romano's in New York with all this grandeur.

The band launched into a jive number and the dance floor erupted into a frenzy. There must have been hundreds, if not more than a thousand people jiving to the cool tune.

'That's the Siren Band,' Maggie yelled over the music.

'They're all girls.'

'Yep, here most night too. Well probably not the night that Artie Shaw was here last year. Word is that night, a fight broke out between the Aussies and the Yanks and the band played "Stars and Stripes Forever" until the police arrived.'

Kitty felt a small smile play on her lips. 'Is that so?'

'Well, it's a rumour, so who knows?'

Kitty believed it.

'I see them.' Maggie took Kitty's hand and led them to where Bert and William were sitting.

'Ladies,' Bert greeted them as both boys stood up. They were dressed in their khaki army uniforms and Kitty's stomach filled with butterflies. As Bert and Maggie said hello, Kitty noted William's gaze linger on her – it was slow and appreciative and it set her skin alight.

'You look stunning.' He leaned over and placed a soft kiss on her cheek. Kitty's skin was positively on fire by now. 'Would you like to dance?' William offered his hand and Kitty smiled as she placed her hand in his.

For the next couple of hours, they jived and jitterbugged, waltzed and fox trotted to the rhythms of the band's tunes.

'I need a drink,' Maggie declared, her cheeks pink from exertion.

'I could do with one too,' Kitty admitted. 'And my feet could do with a rest as well.'

'Nothing alcoholic here, but the milk bar does sell specialty sundaes.'

'I have a bottle of whisky that I brought along.' Bert pulled out a bottle, seemingly from thin air. 'We can just add it to some soda.'

Although Kitty would've preferred a sundae, she drank the whisky and soda along with the others.

'Excuse us.' Maggie pulled her hand. 'We might visit the Ladies before we resume dancing up a storm.'

The whisky did little to cool Kitty's hot skin, and the stuffy air in the ladies powder room did even less to help.

'So, what do you think?' Maggie asked as they stood at the mirror, reapplying their lipstick.

'Bert's nice, and you seem to like him.'

Maggie sighed. 'I'm going to marry that man.'

'You seem certain of that.' Kitty didn't doubt her friend one bit.

'You betcha. But Bert wasn't who I was asking about.'

'Oh?'

'Don't you *oh* me. What do you think of William?'

'He's ... nice.'

'Nice?' Maggie's eyes caught hers in the mirror. 'That's all you have to say, nice?'

Kitty didn't have to say anything, her increasingly flamed cheeks were speaking volumes.

'I knew it!' Maggie whooped loudly, thumping her hand on the vanity and eliciting raised brows from nearby company. 'I knew you'd like him. And he likes you – I could see it the moment you both walked into the fish and chip shop at lunch.'

'You did not – you were too wrapped up in Bert to notice anything. Besides, what's the point? Aren't they shipping out soon?'

'Yes, but that's not stopping me from nabbing Bert before they do. Have a little fun. What's the worst that could happen?'

'I fall in love with him and he dies.'

Maggie paused and considered her soberly for a moment. 'Stop being such a worrywart. That's not going to happen. Lots of boys come home safe.'

Kitty didn't say anything, but in her mind she thought, *But some don't. The one that mattered to me didn't. I don't think my heart could deal with it again.*

Back at the table, Bert had poured them all another round of drinks. Maggie and Bert drank theirs speedily, but Kitty took her time, sipping and savouring, soaking in the atmosphere. When the music slowed to a waltz, William turned to her. 'Shall we?'

Kitty placed her glass down and nodded her reply. As they walked towards the dance floor, Kitty felt William's hand on her lower back and it sent a thrill through her. When the hand circled her waist she leaned into him, her cheek resting on his broad chest.

The band was playing Tommy Dorsey's 'You Taught Me To Love Again'. For a moment Kitty listened to the music, to the words, and they strangely rang true. But they shouldn't. She shouldn't be feeling this way.

'Are you always William? Or are you sometimes Bill or Billy?'

'My mother never allowed anyone to call me anything other than William,' he said, 'so that's who I am.'

'If my mother had it her way everyone would call me Catherine, not Kitty.'

'I quite like Catherine. Would you mind if I called you Catherine and not Kitty?' William's smile was luminous and she couldn't help but return it.

'Not at all.'

And then, something caught her attention. In the corner of her eye a flash of a blue and white navy uniform had her turning her head and inhaling sharply.

'Catherine, are you all right?'

'I ...' She turned, trying to follow the man who was heading towards the exit. Her mouth opened and closed with no words making it past the lump in her throat. The room was already hot, but at that moment she felt faint, as if she were about to pass out.

'You look like you've seen a ghost.'

'I ... need some air,' she mumbled as she tore out of William's arms and through the throng of dancers, following the man. She lost him once and then spotted him as he entered the marble and granite vestibule.

'Charlie!' she yelled. Her desperate voice bounced off the walls, ricocheting, echoing in her ears, but the man continued to walk, not yielding, not turning. She sprinted after him, running out onto George Street, but he was gone. She wasn't sure how long she stood there, scanning the crowd, willing him to appear. Only after a while did she slump on a tram-stop seat and start to cry. She knew it wasn't really Charlie, knew that her mind was play-ing cruel tricks on her. But the very fact she'd seen someone who so closely resembled him while she was dancing with William, developing feelings for William, said to her that she wasn't ready to love again. In her mind, in her heart, there would always be Charlie. Would there be any room for anyone else? Ever?

'Catherine, I found you.' William breathed in relief as he crouched down next to her.

She owed him an explanation. She owed him the truth.

'I'm sorry I ran,' she began between sobs. 'I saw a man that looked like ...'

'Your brother?' he offered when she failed to complete the sentence.

She stared at him for a moment – now was the time to cor-rect him, to tell William who she really thought she saw. But she didn't. Instead she nodded then sobbed even louder from the shame of her untruth.

'Shhh.' He wrapped his arm around her and pulled her close. 'It's all right.' He held her, letting her cry for a while before declar-ing, 'You've had quite a night. I think I will take you home.'

'But, Maggie –'

'Bert is gentleman enough to get her home safe. I promise. Now let me do the same for you.'

With a feeble nod, Kitty allowed William to pull her up and escort her home.

As William lifted her off the seat in front of the Trocadero and gently helped her into a taxi, an unfamiliar feeling came over her. Tenderness. Her heart had been shrouded in grief for so long she had forgotten how it felt.

By the time they arrived at her home, her tears had gone, but not the dread. William had been silent for most of the journey save for the occasional chat with the taxi driver.

As they pulled up, he got out first, telling her to wait. Then he ran around and opened the door for her.

'You're quite the gentleman, aren't you?'

'That I am. But something tells me, Catherine, that you're worth me being a gentleman.'

She wanted to tell him he was wrong, that she was damaged and he should run for the hills.

'May I call on you? Before I ship out?' he asked hopefully.

She should have said no, but instead she found herself saying, 'Yes, I would like that.'

She knew it was wrong. Knew it was worthless to pursue anything with William. For goodness sake, she had ruined their perfect day by chasing a ghost. So why did she say yes?

There was a reason, and years later she would remember it time and time again. And tonight, in the lowest of her lows, William had given her tenderness. And for that, she said yes.

Twenty-seven

Doubt

Hawaii, December 2016

'So the trip was for nothing.' Ben's voice taunted her from down the line.

Kit frowned as she haphazardly threw her clothes into her suitcase. 'Ben, it wasn't a *total* waste of time. I found Charlie, didn't I? And I unearthed a secret child. And I'm leaving here with a greater sense of who Gran was.'

'I think you knew Gran more than anyone else.'

'Ben, you and I know there was more to Gran than we realised. There was a whole part of her life that we never knew about.' As she spoke, her day with Adam replayed in her mind. Visiting St Andrew's, walking the streets of Downtown, the Marina, and finally the Waiola Street Shave Ice store where it all came to a frosty head.

'We knew about it, Kit, it was more that no one ever spoke about her life before Australia.'

Kit thought of all she had learnt about life in Honolulu before Pearl Harbor. Despite how the day had ended, Adam had given her a brief glimpse of what life was like some seventy-five odd years ago. It had filled her with awe and regret. She regretted all the years that her gran was alive and Kit didn't push harder to find out more about her childhood.

Through the opened doors leading to the balcony the strains of the Sultana and Matchbox Twenty duet 'Smooth' flittered into the room, heralding the arrival of yet another happy hour. Her packing was nowhere near done, but she had no urge to do any more now. Suddenly the appeal of a mai tai trumped cramming her suitcase.

'We should've tried harder.' Kit slumped on her bed, her mind made up. As soon as she'd finished the call with Ben she'd go down to the bar where maybe, just maybe, the combination of a cocktail and a killer Waikiki sunset could shake off some of her disappointment about the way she'd left things with Adam. 'Maybe then we would've found out about Charlie sooner, before he was sick. Maybe we could've found their child too.'

'Kit, listen to yourself. I get that you feel invested in this, but the reality is – when this all comes out, and it will – it will have massive ramifications for Dad and for all of Gran's kids. If this secret was revealed when Gran was alive ... well I don't know how the family would've dealt with it.'

Deep down, Kit knew that her brother had a point, but right now, she didn't want to listen. 'Any progress on finding the biscuit tin?' She changed direction slightly.

'Nada.'

'Keep looking, it's bound to be somewhere.'

'Kit, short of shelling the house, I don't know where it could be. Perhaps it's time to admit defeat. We might not find it.'

Annoyance filled her. 'But without it, we have nothing to go on.'

Ben paused for a moment – his silence spoke volumes. 'That might not be a bad thing.'

'How can you say that?' she said. 'You read those letters, you agreed that I should come here and look for Charlie.'

'And you did. By your own admission Charlie is not well and not likely to recover. And you said that you now know Gran's life in Hawaii better.'

'But the child –'

'Is seventy-five, possibly not even alive. Possibly with a life and family of their own. They've been a secret this long, what good can be gained from the search? Don't you think that if they wanted to find their birth mother, they would've done so by now?'

'You sound like Adam,' Kit grumbled.

'The man has a point.'

'Whose side are you on, Ben? Because right now, it doesn't seem like it's mine.' Kit knew that she was snappy but she didn't care. What Ben was alluding to was giving up. And that wasn't an option.

'Kit, what good can come from unearthing something that's been hidden for three quarters of a century? It's a long time and I bet there is a reason why. You have to ask yourself, why are you doing this?'

Kit had just about had enough of her brother. 'I don't have time for this – I've got to finish packing and you need to keep looking for that box.'

Ben sighed deeply. 'See you, Kit. Have a good flight back.'

Kit hung up without properly saying goodbye and by the time she was at the bar drinking her second mai tai, she regretted her outburst. As she listened to the band and stared out into the brilliant yellow and burnt-orange sunset, Kit wondered if her brother and, in fact, Adam had a point.

Why was she doing this? What was there to gain? Perhaps Ben was right – she risked opening Pandora's box, and Adam had made it clear that he wanted no part in it all.

By the time the band had wrapped up and her third mai tai was reduced to melted ice cubes and a pineapple chunk as garnish, Kit was ready to concede defeat. No one else apart from her wanted the secret uncovered.

Just as Ben said, she had come here to find Charlie and she had done just that. It wasn't the ending she had envisioned, but wasn't that always the case? Life rarely let you live it out according to plan. She and Jeremy were proof of that.

Maybe it was time to think about moving on, and Ben was right. But as soon as she thought of it, Kit dismissed the notion almost immediately, blaming her cocktail-addled brain. She knew that Ben was only trying to help but she wasn't ready to give up.

By the time she boarded her plane home the next day, Kit was regretting her third mai tai, but she was regretting the way she had spoken to Ben more.

Sorry, Benji.

Kit shot off a text knowing he would laugh at her for calling him that and be pleased with her apology. She was all set to turn her phone off when he surprised her by calling.

'I'm sorry about yesterday and you're right, I –'

'I found it.' With the mix of excitement and nerves in Ben's voice, Kit knew exactly what her brother was referring to.

She felt her heartbeat slow down. 'Where was it?' It wasn't the most pressing question, but it was the first one that tumbled off her tongue.

'You know how Gran had that potting shed?'

'Yes?' Her grandmother had a small garden shed in the back-yard; Kit had spent a fair share of her Saturdays there, helping her pot plants – Gran had favoured succulents.

'Her neighbour came round asking to borrow a trowel, so I took him out there and we were going through all her stuff and he was telling me how he's –'

'Get to the point, Ben.' Kit cut him off, impatient.

'It was there – on one of the higher shelves, kind of hidden. Boy, she must've used Grandpa's ladder to get it up there. Gran really wanted this thing hidden.'

Kit was poised to ask her next question. She wanted to know what was inside. But the flight attendant standing next to her had other ideas.

'Miss, you need to turn that off, *now*.'

'Hold on a sec, Ben.' She placed the phone on her chest and sent the woman whose nametag told Kit her name was Linda a pleading look. 'I'll be quick, just one minute, it's a really important call.'

Linda wasn't having any of it. 'End the call *now*.'

As much as it killed her, Kit knew she had no choice. She hastily ended the call then promptly spent the next ten hours on a knife's edge.

When she landed, she had a message from Ben. No words – just one image that spoke volumes.

The photo was of a baby bracelet – she had seen the type, they were once used as identification bands. She vaguely remembered seeing either her Uncle John or Robert's one years ago. They were made with tiny blue glass beads and lettered beads that spelt the baby's name.

This one was different. This one had pink beads, and she could see the name as clear as day.

Kitty and Charlie had a baby girl. And her name was Pearl.

Twenty-eight

Until We Meet Again

Sydney, September 1944

'When will this war end?' Maggie moaned as they sat on her bed painting their toenails. It seemed like such a normal thing for two eighteen-year-olds to do, but normal took on a different meaning these days. They had been enduring war for years – from rationing to preparing for raids. From what Kitty could gather from listening to news reports on the wireless, Australia was weathering the war with greater ease than countries such as Britain and France. Lately, she'd been listening to the reports on the battles with heightened interest. She knew that both William and Bert were stationed in New Guinea and every time it was mentioned, Kitty's ears pricked and she stopped what she was doing and took in every word. Of course, she really shouldn't be taking such an interest. Maggie had a right to be interested – her fiancé was away at war and William was just … well he wasn't anything but a friend.

'Doesn't the world know that I have a wedding to plan?' Maggie said as she examined her freshly painted shell-pink nails.

'You'll have your wedding.' Kitty gave her friend a reassuring smile. 'Bert will come home and you'll be married with a houseful of little ones before you know it.'

'Yes, you're right, but I'm just so impatient! Now I regret not listening to Bert when he asked me to marry him before he left.'

Kitty had been secretly glad they hadn't. She never voiced her true thoughts to Maggie, but Kitty lived with an overwhelming fear that Bert wouldn't come home. If they had married before he left and he didn't come back, Maggie would have become a widow at barely eighteen.

The loss would be the same, but greater in some ways.

'Hey, let's do something fun tomorrow.' Kitty deliberately steered the conversation away from Bert and war, not only because she wanted to take Maggie's mind off it, but her own too. She didn't like the way her heart was missing William more and more each day. At the beginning, when he first left, she told herself it was because of that night at the Trocadero when he showed her kindness and tenderness and had taken her home. She was sure that once he left, the feeling would subside. But as the days turned into weeks and the weeks turned into months, Kitty discovered she was wrong. The feelings didn't subside. She began to miss him, which was completely insane considering how little time they had spent together.

'I suppose so. Do you want to go to the Orpheum? We could take in a flick.'

'Great idea!' Kitty leapt off the bed. 'But let's not wait till tomorrow, let's go now.'

'Now?' Maggie blinked. 'But I was going to wash my hair.'

'Oh, come on – who are you going to impress? Your fiancé isn't even in the country. Besides, you know you always look beautiful.'

'Hmm.' Maggie tapped the side of her cheek with one finger thoughtfully. 'I guess you're right.'

Kitty laughed. 'You know I am, so let's get cracking.'

Later that evening as they left the Orpheum, there was a chill in the air. Spring had come, but the nights still held the frosty bite of winter. Light was fading and the pink sunset held a promise of a glorious day to come.

'I'm glad we did that,' Maggie said as they turned off Military Road and set course for home.

'I am too.' Kitty smiled and looped her arm through Maggie's.

'Of course, I didn't get to wash my hair.'

Kitty flicked a glance at Maggie's brilliant curls. 'There's always tomorrow.'

'True, and as you said –' Maggie faltered mid-sentence as she came to a screeching halt.

'What's the matter?' Kitty saw the look on Maggie's face before she saw what had caused it. She'd seen that look before and it filled her entire being with dread. When her eyes flickered forward, her worst fears were confirmed.

Standing in front of Maggie's front gate was a soldier dressed in all his uniformed glory. He held his hat in one hand and wore a solemn expression on his handsome face.

A look of grief, a look that told Kitty he had lost a mate, and now he was to be the bearer of tragic news. There was only one reason why William was here, only one reason why he would be standing in front of Maggie's house.

For a moment no one spoke. There wasn't a single sound save for a distant bark of a dog and a warble from a passing magpie.

'No!' Maggie's grief-stricken voice pierced the twilight. 'No, no, no, no, no!' The single word conveyed so much.

Instinctively, Kitty went to tighten her grip on her friend's arm, but she was a few seconds too late; Maggie's knees gave way and she slumped onto the footpath.

Within moments, William was by her side, helping Kitty to gently ease a now sobbing Maggie to her feet. Effortlessly, he gathered Maggie into his arms and silently they took her inside. As he lowered her onto the sofa where her mother was waiting to comfort her, Kitty briefly closed her eyes and was transported back to the moment they discovered Eddie was dead.

A rush of heartbeats, a giddy wave of nausea washed over her. She swayed slightly, her hands flying onto the wall to regain her balance. 'Catherine, are you all right?' William's strong hands were steadying her, his soothing voice calming her. His concern was touching, but this wasn't about her. Maggie needed her.

Two years ago, unbeknownst to Maggie, she had saved Kitty. If it wasn't for Maggie's friendship and humour, Kitty knew that she would have fallen into a deep dark hole and there would be a great chance she would still be there.

Now it was her turn to be there for her friend.

It wasn't the time for questions – Kitty knew that would all come later. Right now Maggie was hurting, and Kitty was going to do all she could to lessen the pain.

Later Kitty would learn that Bert had been killed on the fields of Saidor, New Guinea. He'd thrown himself in front of William to protect him from being shot. That last piece of information was something that Kitty chose not to disclose to Maggie. As William retold the story, she could sense the guilt he was carrying.

'You did a brave thing, William,' Kitty said as they sat on her back porch a couple of nights later.

'There was nothing brave about it.' His voice was heavy, weary. 'Bert paid the ultimate price. I am here, he isn't.'

Kitty was silent then. She wanted to say that such was the way in war. Some people made it, others didn't. Her mind drifted to the day of Eddie's funeral, how at his wake, she and Penny sat engulfed in grief as Jimmy and Richie stood wallowing in survivor's guilt. She still thought of Charlie every day. The hurt was still there, but it wasn't as raw as the days following the Pearl Harbor attack. Perhaps it was time, or perhaps it was the thought that she had her Pearl, her baby out there, her connection to Charlie that gave her some hope. She still wanted to look for her child. She had a plan. When she'd finished at teachers' college she would get a job, and once she'd saved enough, she would get her child back.

'Time will pass and the hurt lessens some,' she whispered into the night air.

'Was that how it was for you?'

'What?' Kitty blinked, momentarily confused.

'When you lost your brother,' William said. Even in the darkness, she could see the hurt in his grey eyes.

'Yes.' She breathed out, breaking their eye contact and swallowing the shame of her lie. 'Did I tell you that my brother was engaged at the time of his death?'

'Like Bert and Maggie.'

'Yes. Penny was a friend of mine. We left Honolulu on the same ship. I often wonder how she is doing.' Technically, Penny and Eddie hadn't been engaged, but had Eddie not died, it would've happened.

'Maybe you should write to her. It might give you some ideas how to help Maggie through this time.'

William had a point. She had been thinking of Penny a lot since learning of Bert's passing. If she was honest, Penny had been in her thoughts from the moment Maggie and Bert had announced their engagement. Kitty had hoped and prayed that their love story wouldn't be cut short like Eddie and Penny's, like hers and Charlie's.

'This war has taken so much,' Kitty said, her voice breaking as emotion clogged her throat. 'When will it all end?'

William expelled a long, drawn-out sigh, as if he'd been hold-ing his breath for hours. 'I wish I knew. I wish I could tell you that it will all be over tomorrow.' Slowly, his hand covered hers before he moved to entwine their fingers. 'Catherine, I want to say something ... well to ask you something really.'

'No, don't say it.' The words came out harsher than Kitty intended. She could see the surprise in his eyes. 'What I mean is ... please, don't ask me to promise anything,' she added hastily to soften the blow. 'We both know how fragile life is, how quickly circumstances can change. I just don't want either of us to say something now that –'

'We'll regret?'

'No.' Kitty quickly shook her head. 'Not regret. If we make promises now, it will only ...' her voice stammered as she realised how hard it was to say the words. But she had to say them; she had to protect herself from any future loss. 'It will only make it harder if you don't come home.'

William's eyes widened as he registered her words. Carefully, almost torturously he lifted their entwined hands and soft kissed each of her knuckles, his gaze unwavering as he did so. 'I know what I want, Catherine. It's you.'

There was a wistful catch in his voice that almost made her drop her guard. Almost.

'I've known it was you from the moment I saw you walk towards me on that beach all those months ago. I've spent every night away thinking of you, wondering how it would be to kiss you here ...' William dipped his head and placed a barely there kiss on the side of her neck.

Her breathing hitched. Her skin began to flush hot and cold.

'And how it would feel to kiss you ...' His words disappeared as his mouth found hers for a slow and tender kiss. When it ended,

Kitty ran her fingers across her swollen lips. It surprised her how much she wanted him to kiss her again.

Instead he stood up and placed his hat on his head. 'As per your request, I won't make any promises to you, but I can't leave here without you knowing that once I come home – and I have every intention of doing so – I'll be back and next time, there will be promises made.'

I don't deserve you.

'You're quite the gentleman, William.'

There was a mischievous twinkle in his eyes and a roguish smile that played on his lips. 'Believe me when I tell you, there's nothing gentlemanly about my thoughts right now.'

Kitty gasped at William's candour before they both burst out laughing.

'I'd better get going before your mother comes out here and tells me to bugger off.'

Kitty wasn't sure her mother would do that. She had an inkling her mother would approve of William.

'Goodbye, William. Safe travels.'

'No, not goodbye.' He dipped his head, planting a kiss on her forehead. 'Until we meet again.'

'Until we meet again,' Kitty echoed as she watched William walk down the street, and as he disappeared into the night, she wondered if she would see him again.

In May 1945, eight months later, the war was over.

Two months after that, Kitty had her answer.

Twenty-nine

Every Beginning Comes From Some Other Beginning's End

Sydney, July 1945

Kitty had never seen William be anything but cool, calm and collected. But that was before he had met her mother. June McGarrie didn't have the habit of making anyone feel at ease – ever – and despite knowing in the first five minutes that her mother did indeed like and approve of William, she didn't let him off lightly.

When William had returned home three weeks earlier, he made true on his promise to call on her. She already knew he had feelings for her – that much was clear from the last time she had seen him – but when he went away, Kitty refused to give her heart to him. She simply did not want her heart to leave with him because, as she knew, giving your heart away had dangerous implications. She vowed that if William were to return, she would deal with her feelings then. And now that he was back it seemed she had no choice.

'Do you plan to resume your studies now that you are home from the war?' June asked.

'I do indeed, ma'am,' William stammered, shifting slightly in his seat. Her mother had insisted that William be seated next to her and as far away from Kitty as possible. Her argument was that it made sense, since she was the hostess, but Kitty knew her mother wanted every opportunity to grill the poor boy.

'There are many things I plan to do now that I am back home.' William's gaze flickered towards Kitty, causing her to blush terribly. The look didn't escape her mother's attention.

'And you're studying medicine? At Sydney University?' Her mother continued with the questions until it seemed she knew everything there was to know about William – even things that Kitty herself wasn't aware of.

He was the middle of three children – an older brother who was also a doctor and a younger sister who the previous year had married and was expecting her first child. No, his brother didn't serve in the war – a congenital heart condition prevented him from doing so.

Yes, war was different from what he had anticipated, but he was proud to serve his country and king. Yes, his parents were happy that he was home safe and sound.

'They would love to meet Catherine,' he said as he sipped his drink. 'In fact, they are insisting to do so at the earliest convenience.'

June McGarrie paused and dabbed the corners of her mouth with her napkin. 'I am afraid that would depend on a number of factors.'

'And what would they be, Mrs McGarrie?'

'It would depend on your intentions towards Catherine, Mr Bennett.'

'I can assure you, I have plans in place for our future together.'

He did? As her mother reached for her champagne, Kitty tried, but failed, to catch William's attention.

'What sort of plans?' her mother grilled.

'Plans that involve marriage.'

Kitty felt a piece of meat become lodged in her throat, and as she reached for her drink she didn't think anything could make her more surprised. But she was wrong.

'I hope you don't mind, but I took the liberty of writing to Commander McGarrie, asking for his blessing.'

What? When had William done this? How had he even found out her father's address?

'And I gather that you have received a response?'

Kitty knew her mother. She knew every tiny facial expression, every poker face, every nuance, and right now, she could see that her mother knew all about William's letter, knew the nature of its contents, knew the response her father had given.

She chanced a look at Aunt Iris, who with the tiniest shrug of the shoulders had cemented Kitty's suspicions. Kitty was the only person at the table who was in the dark about her fate, her future. And she was not at all enthused about it.

Suddenly, she was numb with shock, but there was also something else. Betrayal.

She expected as much from her mother, and she wasn't surprised that her Aunt Iris had toed the line, but the fact that William had written to her father, and it seemed weeks ago, perhaps even before his return, that was the part in all of this that hurt.

William cleared his throat and it snapped Kitty's attention back to him. 'The Commander gave his blessing.' A wide smile graced his lips and a lick of colour settled on his cheeks, making him look almost boyish. He looked so deliriously happy that for a moment her anger somewhat abated.

'Well then, that settles it.' Her mother placed her fingers in a steeple and smiled. Kitty could guess what thoughts were behind her smile. She was finally able to breathe a sigh of relief – she was finally able to offload her hussy of a daughter. It was a look of triumph that settled on June McGarrie's hard features. As if she had somehow hand-picked William to be her ruined daughter's bridegroom. If anyone deserved credit for introducing William into her life it was Maggie.

Poor Maggie. It had been months since she had lost Bert, but she was struggling to keep going. It was only in the past few weeks that Kitty had seen a little of the old Maggie return. She had completed nursing studies and started working. It kept her busy, which Kitty thought could only be a good thing.

After dinner, her mother asked William to join her for a drink. The invitation clearly excluded Kitty and it only added to her irritation. Her mood was not lost on Aunt Iris.

'It's not a bad thing, Kitty Cat, is it?'

'No, but that's not the point.' Kitty drained the last of her champagne and refilled her glass, then went to do the same for her aunt. 'I would've liked a say in all of this. It is my life after all and I feel as if ... as if ...'

'All control and choice is out of your hands?'

Kitty ran her finger around the rim of her glass and met her aunt's gaze. 'Yes. It feels that ever since ... ever since we came here, that nothing to do with my future is in my control.'

'Ah, but that's where you're wrong.' Her aunt looked straight at her.

'With all due respect, Aunt Iris, I think you're the one that has it wrong.'

'Kitty, for the first time in a very long while, the odds are in your favour.'

'How? By having others plot and plan my life? What do you think Mother and William are talking about in there?' Kitty nodded towards the drawing room. I can assure you it's not the weather. They are planning my wedding. By the time William leaves tonight they will probably have a date set, the church booked and the guest list all sorted.'

'Consider the alternative, Kitty. Say that you don't marry William. What do you think will happen?'

Kitty was silent as she considered Aunt Iris's question. 'I'm not sure,' she answered honestly. It wasn't that she was opposed to marrying William, but she wasn't sure that she wanted to marry him *right now*. He'd only just returned from the war, and truthfully, they hadn't had a chance to get to know each other properly, not without the threat of war hanging over them. And William was about to resume his studies, shouldn't they wait till he graduated before they married?

'I'll tell you what will happen. If you refuse William, your mother will make you go back to the States. There she will have your father select a suitable husband for you, probably someone they feel may be strong enough to keep you in line.'

Kitty felt her eyes widen in shock, and when she went to open her mouth, her aunt held a hand up, halting her.

'You will marry their choice of husband and you will undoubtedly spend the rest of your life having someone make decisions about your future. And you will be miserable.'

It was the first time that her aunt had been so brutal with her. Normally her mild and meek Aunt Iris was not so opinionated.

'Or you can stay here, Kitty Cat. Stay here and marry William. You are very fond of him, I can tell.'

'You're ... you're not wrong there.'

'Nor am I wrong when I point out another benefit in marrying William.'

'What's that?' Kitty asked with interest.

Her Aunt Iris paused and took both of Kitty's hands in hers. 'It gives you a reason to stay.'

A reason to stay?

Puzzled, Kitty was about to ask her aunt what she meant when her mother and William walked back into the room.

'Catherine, you may say farewell to William.'

As she sighed, her Aunt Iris gave her hands a squeeze. Kitty walked William out into the winter night, wrapping her cardigan around her tightly.

'So are you free on Saturday?' William asked as he pulled on his coat.

'For what?'

'To meet my family, silly.' He laughed and placed a perfunctory kiss on her forehead. 'It's all so exciting, Catherine.'

'Yes.' Kitty drummed up the enthusiasm, or enough so as not to let on that she wasn't feeling quite so excited about it all. 'It is indeed.'

William seemed none the wiser about her mood, but after bidding farewell to him, Kitty found her mother waiting for her.

'You truly are an ungrateful child.' June's voice startled her. The room was dimly lit and her mother was sitting sipping a drink and smoking a cigarette. War had changed her mother. Gone was the luxury of staff and a big house to manage. Instead she seemed to be shackled with a wayward daughter and a spinster sister. At least, that's how it seemed to Kitty. Before the war her mother drank sporadically and she never smoked, often making a side comment to her father about the filthiness of the habit.

Some might say that war had dealt June McGarrie a cruel blow. The heartache of losing her only son, constant worries for a husband who was on active duty, and her unwanted relocation to a foreign land. Granted it was her birth land, but her return was not by choice but by a forced hand. On the surface, it seemed that June's cruelty was a cumulative result of her hardship. No wonder the drinking was heavier, the smoking now a formed habit.

But it only took a scratch beneath the surface to see past the façade.

June McGarrie may not have said it every day, but she made her daughter feel unworthy. Unworthy because she fell in love. Unworthy because she wasn't the child who'd died. It was because of Kitty's pregnancy that they ultimately ended up in Australia, and Kitty felt this was the one part of the trifecta her mother resented most.

'Pardon?' Kitty had heard her mother loud and clear, but it was the shock of it all that made her stop in her tracks.

'You heard me.' Her mother took in a long drag of her cigarette before slowly exhaling. The putrid smell of tobacco was suffocating. 'You have been given a second chance, one that you do not deserve, and yet you seem ungrateful. It puzzles me.'

'Puzzles you?' Kitty took a step towards her mother, folding her arms. 'You sat there tonight, planning my whole life without so much as consulting me.' She pointed to herself, thrusting her finger into her chest. 'And you wonder why I'm not grateful?'

'Did it perhaps occur to you that you do not deserve a choice?'

'I don't … I don't …' Anger was consuming Kitty. 'How do I not deserve a choice, Mother? Please enlighten me how *I* don't deserve a choice when it comes to *my* own life. God knows you've had a big hand in making my life choices. The pain and suffering you have caused me is irreparable.'

Silence followed, but the way in which June regarded her daughter was clear enough. She had seen that look in her mother's eyes many times, but the last time it had been this wild was the day they buried Eddie. 'You have no idea what you are talking about, Catherine. You are far better off than you realise.' Her voice was barely a whisper, but the words and their meaning were loud and clear. 'You came so close to ruin and you are extremely fortunate your father and I didn't disown you. I strongly suggest you marry William. God knows you don't deserve him, but he is besotted with you by some miracle. Bear him sons, daughters, and perhaps God shall grant you forgiveness.'

'My decision to marry William will be my own. If I choose to marry him, it will be because I want to, not to save myself or to redeem myself in the eyes of God. God knows that I deserve happiness just as much as the next man or woman. You never get over losing your first born, isn't that correct, Mother?'

As Kitty threw her mother's own words at her, the very same ones she had uttered the day they buried Eddie, June McGarrie looked as if she had been slapped in the face. For the first time Kitty could remember, her mother was speechless.

A look flickered across her mother's face, one that Kitty was sure she'd never seen before. It was equal parts regret and wistfulness and it took her by surprise.

June tapped her cigarette before inhaling deeply. 'It is an unfortunate pain that you will live with for the rest of your life, Catherine. Perhaps of all people I can best understand that. We have something in common after all, you and I.' She gave her daughter a sad smile.

'My pain has been caused by you,' Kitty bit out. She wanted to add that she was nothing like her mother, but June's next words stopped her.

'Sit down, Kitty.' Her mother nodded at the empty chair opposite her. Perhaps it was out of sheer shock of hearing June call her 'Kitty', or the pleading in her voice, whatever the reason, Kitty did as she was asked.

'I'm not sure how much you know about how your father and I met.' June's exhaled smoke billowed around her.

Kitty was stunned. It was the last thing that she had expected to come from her mother's mouth. Neither of her parents had been forthcoming about their courtship or any details prior to their marriage. All she knew was what Eddie had told her and she wasn't even sure how accurate that had all been either.

'Not much,' she stammered in reply.

'You know that your father was here briefly during the First World War, don't you?'

'Yes, I know that he arrived not long before Uncle Michael was killed.'

'Iris met him first, and I'll be truthful, your father was taken immediately with her. I don't blame him. Iris was always more ... vivacious than I.' Her mother paused as if talking so candidly was taking a toll on her. Stubbing her cigarette, she lifted her drink to her lips and sipped as if drawing courage to continue. 'But of course, Iris was engaged and when Conrad discovered she had a sister, he asked to meet me.' June drained her drink and went to pour another, then poured an equal measure into another glass and handed it over to Kitty.

'I didn't want to meet him.'

Kitty paused, her hand mid-air, and she almost dropped the crystal tumbler. 'What?' she asked, stunned. 'Why?'

'I know this may be hard for you to grasp, but I wasn't always so ... shall we say, a stickler for following the social expectation.'

Kitty remained silent. June was right – it was hard to imagine her mother doing anything other than what was expected of her. Instead she sipped her drink, the potent liquid burning as it slid down her throat.

'There was a boy in Melbourne,' June said wistfully, her eyes clouded as if transporting herself to another place and time. 'His name was Liam O'Brien. His mother, Mary, worked for us as a cook and he would come round after school and stay in the kitchen until she was done for the day. We became ... friends,' she said cautiously, but the small smile that ghosted her lips betrayed the innocence of their relationship.

'What happened to him?'

'He was drafted. Sent to Europe,' her mother said sadly. 'He was in the same battalion as your Uncle Michael.'

Kitty gasped. 'He was killed?' Was that why her mother was hesitant to meet her father, because her heart was broken?

A pained look settled on her mother's face. For a split second, Kitty thought she might crumple, but in true June McGarrie form, she tamed her emotions. The only sign of betrayal was the hint of a wobble in her voice.

'No, he didn't die. He returned home and married someone else.'

Kitty was stunned into silence. She hadn't expected that revelation. Staring at her mother, she tried to picture a younger June full of love and heartbroken from rejection. For the briefest of moments it made her view her mother in a different light.

'I told you this story, not to pity me.' Her mother seemed to be reading her thoughts. 'But to understand that when a second chance comes along, you take it.'

Kitty understood what her mother was trying to say. And as she walked out of the room, away from her mother, her conversation with Aunt Iris replayed in her mind.

It gives you a reason to stay.

The meaning was suddenly clear. Her aunt was pointing out that marrying William allowed her to stay so she could look for her child; Kitty remembered now that her aunt had talked to her about this when she came home from hospital. She had to find a reason to stay in Australia. But it couldn't be the only reason why she should marry him.

It was clear what she needed to do and she needed to do it straight away. Swapping her thin cardigan for her coat, she hastily wrapped a scarf around her neck and hurried out into the cold night. Halfway into the journey, her shoes began to pinch, but she didn't stop, not till she reached her destination and it was only as she rapped her knuckles on the front door did the nerves begin to fray. An older woman, who she assumed was William's mother, answered.

'May I help you?' she asked warily.

'Hello ... I'm William's ... I mean my name is Catherine McGarrie and I –'

'Catherine?' William appeared in the doorway, clearly puzzled.

'William, hello,' Kitty breathed out, her voice shaky.

'Mother, this is Catherine.'

'Yes, the young lady had kindly introduced herself already. We weren't expecting you until Saturday, nice to see that you are more than prompt.' Mrs Bennett smiled kindly and Catherine immediately liked her.

'Catherine, is everything all right? You seem anxious.'

'There is something on my mind, yes.' Catherine glanced at Mrs Bennett who thankfully could see that she needed to speak to William alone.

'It was nice to meet you, Catherine. William has told us so much about you. I hope that we'll see you for dinner on Saturday.'

'Yes, I hope so too,' she uttered not knowing how William would take what she was about to tell him.

'And for goodness sake, William, invite the poor girl inside, it's freezing out. She'll catch a chill. Take her in by the fire.'

When his mother disappeared back inside the house, William opened the door wider, his eyes full of questions. Only once he had led her inside where the warmth of a cosy fire crackled did she realise just how cold she was.

'Catherine!' William's voice carried alarm. 'You're shivering.'

Kitty looked at her bone-white hands and discovered William was right. She was shaking uncontrollably, not only from the cold but from the rush of nervous energy.

'I need to tell you something ...' she said shakily.

'Whatever you have to tell me, we can work through it. I promise.' William's voice was so tender, so full of love that she almost lost her nerve.

'I don't deserve you,' she blurted, her eyes stinging with tears.

'What?' He gently framed her face with his hands, thumbs brushing away the wayward tears. 'Why would you say that?'

Kitty closed her eyes briefly, then took a deep breath and started talking. 'In September 1941, the night of my sixteenth birthday, I met a man called Charlie ...'

Once the first sentence was out, the rest of the story poured out of her like a summer storm – slow drops of water quickly gathering momentum for a fast and furious drenching. Kitty cried as she divulged her darkest secret to the man who wanted to marry her. She told William everything – from that first night at The Royal Hawaiian, to the stolen day, then the confrontation with Eddie, and of course, the attack that claimed both Eddie and Charlie. The whole way through the story, William's gaze never left hers and not for a second did she see judgement or disgust or anything negative cloud his eyes.

'Oh, Catherine. You truly lost so much, and you were so young.'

Wordlessly she nodded. But there was more to tell.

'By the time we reached San Francisco, it was clear that I was pregnant.'

And that's when she felt William flinch. It was a small movement and it pinched at her heart, but it was too late now – it was out in the open and she needed to finish the story. She was all but certain that after hearing the rest of it, there was no way William would want to marry her.

'On July eleventh, 1942, I gave birth to a baby girl. She was taken from me moments after she was born. Her name is Pearl and one day I want to find her. You need to know all this, William. You need to know all there is to know about me before you decide if ... if you still want to marry me.'

With her soul bared, Kitty was exhausted. William's head was bent, his expression hidden. As much as she desperately wanted to know what he was thinking, how he was feeling, she knew that it was best to let him be for a moment or two. Slumping down on the chair behind her, she turned her face to the fire, watching the flames lick the sides of the chimney and wondering if she had just burnt her second chance at love. Her first was cruelly taken from her and she knew that as much as she loved William, there was no way she could enter a marriage with such a lie wedged between them. If there was anyone who deserved to know the truth, it was William.

'No one else knows this,' she whispered. 'Not even Maggie. Only my parents, Aunt Iris and ... and now you.'

William lifted his head then – the light from the fire flickered in his grey eyes and Kitty held her breath.

'I meant what I said earlier, Catherine, when I said that whatever you tell me we can work through. I love you, Catherine. I love who you are today, I love who you will be tomorrow – who you were and what happened in the past is just that, the past. I want to build a future with you, a family with you. The fact that you were honest and shared your secret with me tells me the most important thing about you.'

'What's that?' Kitty breathed out.

William smiled. 'You're the one for me, Catherine. The only one.'

And there in the living room of his childhood home, beside the warm winter fire, William Bennett dropped down on one knee and asked Catherine McGarrie to be his wife.

Sydney, September 1945

It was an overcast day when Admiral McGarrie walked his daughter down the aisle. Thick dark clouds that promised rain and lots of it had rolled in overnight and caused her mother endless anxiety.

'No bride wants rain on her wedding day,' June McGarrie muttered as she helped Kitty into her custom-made, imported silk and organza wedding dress.

Kitty wanted to tell her mother she didn't care about the weather, but the truth was, she had hoped for sun. The sun would at least calm her nerves some.

Catherine's tummy was aflutter with butterflies and nerves as they entered the church, but the moment William's gaze caught hers and he whispered 'I love you' in her ear, all her worries subsided.

As she pledged to love, cherish and obey William, tears welled. They were happy tears for the future she was about to share with him, but they were also bittersweet. Four years ago, she pictured a spring wedding of a different kind – in a different place, to a different man.

But that man was gone. And while a part of her would always carry a torch, she knew that the only way she could start a new beginning was if she let Charlie go, for once and for all.

Earlier that day, as dawn's first light broke through the disappearing night, Kitty went down to Pearl Bay where she felt closest to Charlie. There she closed her eyes and sent a prayer to the heavens above asking Charlie for his blessing.

And as she walked out of St Patrick's, her fingers interlocked with her new husband's, Catherine Bennett was greeted by a cloudless sky.

She smiled, knowing that someone was watching over her, and then she knew she was truly blessed.

October 1945, San Diego

With sweaty palms and a thumping heart, he walked through the pouring rain towards the house. He had waited almost four years for this day. All he had was the memory of the last time they were together and the promise he made to her.

How many nights had he dreamt of her? The image of her face burnt on his retina, etched in his heart, forever in his mind.

He was full of hope as he knocked on the door. Waiting.

Moments later, his heart shattered.

'Catherine was married five weeks ago.' June McGarrie delivered the blow with glee.

His grief and shock were palpable. How could that be? Did she not read the letter? Penny had promised to deliver it. Did she not believe his promise? He swore that no matter what happened he would find her, as soon as he could. It had taken him months to discover that the McGarries had returned to San Diego, and he had come as soon as he could. Did he really only miss this by a matter of weeks?

'She ... is Kitty in San Diego?' Nausea rolled through him.

'Here? Oh no, she's in Australia, the other side of the world. Her husband is a doctor.'

The message couldn't have been clearer – she is better off without you.

'This is the happy couple on their wedding day.' June McGarrie thrust a photo into Charlie's numb hands. 'Catherine looked rather beautiful, don't you think?'

He didn't want to look at it, but once he did, he couldn't look away. She was a little older than he remembered, more a woman, less a young lady, and if possible, she was even more beautiful. 'Yes, she does,' he mumbled.

But what shattered him most was the loving look she was giving the man that was holding her hand. Her husband. Anger and jealousy gripped him.

'Thank you for your time, Mrs McGarrie,' he said tersely as he handed back the photo.

'Oh, you can keep that.' She waved dismissively, already making the move to close the door. 'Think of it as a memento; you were friends with Catherine once, after all.'

Friends, Charlie thought bitterly as he turned towards the street. It was clear that Kitty had moved on, and it was time that he did too.

What a fool he'd been. In the days after the attack, Rose had been there, nursing him to health. She had been there, night after night, holding him, calming him when the nightmares came, when he woke drenched in sweat gasping for air. Some nights he dreamt he was drowning, others he relived the bomb blast that killed Eddie and almost killed him.

Night after night it had been Rose who had been by his side, and yet, all he could think about was Kitty.

It had been Rose who had risked life and limb after curfew to telegram his mamma to let her know he was alive. When he was well enough to fight again, it had been Rose who wrote every week. Her letters always cheered him up.

When the war ended he returned home. His mother was unwell and he spent three months with her before she passed. Rose convinced him to return to Hawaii, she promised she would help him find Kitty. And they thought they had.

Never once had she asked for anything from him, even as he bid her farewell to travel to San Diego. 'Travel safe, Charlie.' Rose hugged him, her chocolate-brown eyes welling with tears. 'Remember you always have a home here.'

She had loved him unconditionally, but Charlie had been too blind, too wrapped up in living in the past that he let his future slip away. Not anymore. Without looking at it again, he crumpled the photo with one hand and threw it in the gutter, letting the rain wash it away. He had a future and a home to build with a woman who deserved his love. There would be no more living in the past. Ever.

Thirty

The Search

Sydney, December 2016

'Take me to Gran's house. Now,' Kit demanded by way of greeting upon landing.

'I would've gone with "hello" or "thanks for picking me up, Ben" but hey, that's just me.' Ben screwed up his nose. 'On second thought, you stink so I *will* drive you to Gran's, which actually is your house, possibly soon to be mine, whereupon you will shower. Immediately.'

'Give me a break, there were twin toddlers sitting next to me,' Kit grumbled as she slid into the passenger seat. 'Both were sick as we were about to land and one decided to projectile it in my direction.' She lifted her t-shirt to smell it and instantly regretted the move. 'Oh, that's foul.'

'I told you.'

'So what else was in the tin? Why didn't you bring it with you?'

'Hold on a sec, one question at a time.'

'Ben, do you know how torturous that flight was? Normally I love the fact that a plane is the one place you cannot use the phone, but if it wasn't for that flight attendant who threatened me, I would've –'

'Committed a federal offence by using your phone when you're not supposed to? You do know they interfere with the plane's navigation systems? It's why they have those rules.'

Kit rolled her eyes. 'That's all a bunch of bullocks, Jeremy always said that ...'

'What did Jeremy always say?' Ben asked gently, taking his eyes off the road for a second to check on her. Even in that brief moment, she saw the pity. She hated that pity was still the go-to emotion displayed after all the time that had passed.

'Nothing.' Kit closed her eyes and pinched the bridge of her nose. 'We've gone off topic.' She steered the conversation well away from Jeremy and her past to someone else's past – her grandmother's – and asked, 'What was in the tin?'

'Besides the bracelet? Just a letter addressed to a woman named Penny Miller that came back return to sender.'

Kit felt the hairs on the back of her neck stand up. 'Penny Kerr,' she uttered. 'It must be Penny Kerr. She's the woman I met at the veterans' dinner. Penny was engaged to Eddie McGarrie, Gran's brother who died in the attack. She was also on the same ship from Honolulu to San Francisco. Penny was the one who told me about Gran's pregnancy. Apparently she was there when the doctor confirmed it. What was in the letter?'

'I don't know, I didn't read it.'

'What? Why?'

'I kind of thought you might like to be the one to open it.'

'Good call. Thanks.' She turned and smiled at her brother. Kit had been thinking about the tin the whole flight and now that she was home, and so close to finding out, her nerves were shifting into overdrive. She took a deep breath and made an effort to relax.

'We'd better hope that whatever this letter contains, it gives some clue,' Ben said. 'Otherwise all we have is a baby named Pearl, and chances are, they would've changed her name.'

'We? Does this mean that you've changed your mind and are willing to be part of the search?'

'I still don't think this is the best idea. All the evidence stacks up against our favour. You only have to think about where the tin was hidden to understand how much Gran wanted to keep this a secret.'

'But she never forgot the baby. I mean, she kept the bracelet, right? She kept Uncle John's, Uncle George's, Uncle Robert's and Dad's. Gran had a baby, a baby that was forcibly removed –'

'We don't know that,' Ben interjected. 'She could've willingly given the child up for adoption.'

'Why do you do that? Why do you have to throw a negative into the mix all the time?'

'Someone has to be the voice of reason. Look, the reality is, it was common practice that when a woman found herself in a compromising position, she gave the baby up.'

'She was probably coerced. I bet Gran's mother had a lot to do with it. Don't you remember the stories about forced adoptions from the 1940s all the way up to the 1980s? There was a Senate Inquiry into the whole thing. I remember the guy at work who covered the story. He was as tough as nails, but I clearly remember him saying it was one of the hardest assignments he'd ever worked on. Some of the stories were horrific. Mothers bullied into signing papers to give their kids up for adoption. A lot of these women were not even made aware of their rights. They were made to feel like they were the villains and these childless couples, they were the victims in it all. Apparently it was common practice for a woman to be told that if she loved her child, she would give them up.'

'Okay, now you're jumping the gun. One, we don't know for sure that Gran was forced to give her baby up and two, I've said it before, she never looked for the child. Ever. Doesn't that say something to you?'

'All it says to me is that there is more to this story than meets the eye. We *have* to find her.'

'Dad's not going to like this. None of the family is.' Ben shook his head as they turned into the driveway.

'Dad's not going to know.' Kit unbuckled her seatbelt, eager to go inside and read the letter her gran had written to Penny.

'Kit, that's not a good idea. We need to tell –'

'No!' she said. 'We tell no one, not until we have something concrete to tell.' And without waiting for her brother, Kit walked into the kitchen and made a beeline for the red tin and for the letter that she hoped held some answers.

17ᵗʰ December 1945

My Dearest Penny,

So much time has passed since we last saw each other. So much has changed that it seems a lifetime ago we were lying on the sand at Waikiki. Remember how the hardest decision back then was what movie we were going to see that weekend, or how hard it was to get an appointment at Miss Violett's? It's all so different now. We both know how much the war changed everything. I'm sure that wherever you are, you are feeling the same as I am – glad the war is all over.

I'm sorry I haven't written sooner. Truth was that I didn't think I could write, not before now. I often think of the very last time I saw you in that hotel room in San Francisco when you handed me the note with your address. I hope that you are still there, that this letter reaches you safely, because I have much to tell.

The journey from San Francisco to Melbourne was longer than the one we endured. As with our journey out of Hawaii, I took ill, spending most of my days below deck. I missed your friendship. You gave me so much comfort, even though you were suffering the grief of losing Eddie.

My mother was unbearable. The only emotion she displayed towards me was disdain. Thank goodness I have Aunt Iris, although she too seems to be under Mother's command most of the time.

My sickness subsided by the time we reached Australia. Oh, Penny, when I first arrived here, how strange I found it all! Strange accents that took me a long time to understand – you would hardly believe we spoke the same language! I saw little of Melbourne before we journeyed to Sydney, but my days in the city – or at least in the open – were numbered.

Soon after we arrived, Mother decided to take me to a doctor. It immediately became clear she wanted me to give my baby up for adoption. I was horrified! Even now, it makes my blood boil. We fought terribly – I stood up to her and told her I refused to go through with it. Penny, you know my mother well enough to understand how she didn't appreciate my view on this. The argument ended with Mother leaving me in the care of the hospital that had a home for unwed mothers. At first I thought this was the best thing for me. I could surely be in charge of my own destiny without my mother around to control me.

Penny, how wrong I was.

It soon became clear that not one girl that came to the hospital left with their baby. Not one. Girls came to the hospital terrified, frightened and alone. They came under the misguided impression they would be helped, that they would receive the assistance needed to keep their baby. But all they got – and I too – was suffering from bullying and intimidation that made us feel like dirty, worthless human beings. I won't go into too much detail, only to let you know that had I not experienced it myself, I would never have believed such a place existed.

Day after day we were told that if we loved our babies, we would give them up. We were told we did not have the means to support a child, but there were others who could. Every time they said it to me, I was strong. Until, that is, the very end.

My heart breaks each time I think of the day my beautiful Pearl was born. Yes, Penny, I had a daughter. Charlie and I had a daughter, her name is Pearl. Moments after she was born, she was barbarically taken from me, taken before I could hold her close to me, to soothe her cries. But I had no strength. The labour was long, the birth complex, and I am sure they sedated me to stop me from looking for my child. Days later, when I was lucid enough to realize what had happened, my baby was gone. I lost my Pearl.

I left hospital with an empty womb and a broken heart. I'm not sure how I survived those early days, and had it not been for my friend Maggie, I don't think I would have. Maggie is also the reason I met my husband. I'm married, Penny, to a wonderful man named William who knows all about Charlie and Pearl. We plan to look for her, once we settle into married life. William is completing his medical degree and I'm at teachers' college. I'm going to be a teacher!

That's enough about me. Please write me, Penny. I would love to hear all about your life. I hope you are well but most of all, I hope you are happy.

Yours fondly,

Kitty

Kit folded the pages and looked at Ben. 'Grandpa knew.'

'What?' He took the pages out of her hand and read the letter himself. 'Well I'll be damned, I would never have guessed that one.'

'It's a shame the letter never reached Penny,' she said. 'I wonder if things would've been any different had Penny known the details about Pearl –'

And then, a piece of the puzzle fell into place. It was as if she'd been trying to jam it against other pieces for so long, convinced it would fit there, only to realise she'd been holding it upside down all this time.

'Oh my God.' Kit felt her eyes widen as a rush of adrenaline flowed through her. She grabbed the letter out of Ben's hands. 'I lost my pearl. Pearl. Pearls.'

Ben sent her a worrying look. 'Ah, yes, I get it. The baby was called Pearl.'

'No.' Kit shook her head vigorously then calmed herself enough to collect her thoughts. 'Remember how Gran always gave me pearls for my big birthdays? Like my sixteenth, eighteenth and twenty-first?'

'Kit, I think you're reading too much into this.'

'No, I'm not,' she said firmly. 'While Gran was in hospital, she said something about losing her pearl that triggered a memory for me. An argument between Grandpa and Grandma.'

'I don't think I ever heard them fight,' Ben said doubtfully. 'Well, besides about what they were going to watch on telly.'

'I know, that's why this stuck. I was waiting for Gran, we were going out. I think it must've been my eighteenth because we'd planned to go to the pub and Grandpa was going off at her for buying me pearls again.'

'Are you sure?'

'Ben, I'm not making this shit up, trust me.'

'Okay, so what did he say?'

'Something like "Pearls again, Catherine?" And then he asked if she would ever let it go. Gran yelled that he couldn't possibly understand how it was for her. Grandpa accused her of pining over a ghost.'

'Charlie,' Ben murmured.

'Yep, and I then remember Gran getting really upset and yelling at Grandpa for breaking his promise and how every time she tried to start, he stopped her.'

'And you think Gran was referring to looking for Pearl? That he broke the promise he made to Gran?'

'I know now that's *exactly* what she was referring to.'

'We know that Grandpa knew about Pearl so that's all very possible.'

'But that's not all,' Kit said, almost breathless. 'The last thing I remember before Grandpa stormed off was how he accused Gran of not telling him everything.'

'What the hell is that supposed to mean? How much more is there?'

Kit shrugged. 'I don't know. But give me time, I will find out.'

Kit spent the better part of the next week doing as she promised. Her first step was to determine how she was going to get hold of Pearl's birth certificate. Initial research showed that as a relative, it was possible for Kit to obtain information about the adoption. But with so few details to go on, she realised she would have a better chance if she knew where the baby was born.

Gran's letter to Penny mentioned her seeing a doctor in a hospital and then staying in the home for unwed mothers that was attached to it. In her search to narrow down the possible places, Kit discovered that the now defunct Crown Street Women's Hospital was the subject of close attention several years ago when a Senate Inquiry was held into forced adoptions.

The hospital was established in the late 1800s and moved to Surry Hills just before the turn of the century. Kit's research uncovered that by the 1940s, Crown Street had become the largest maternity hospital in New South Wales, aiming to lift the standards of maternity care. But it was the other information Kit uncovered that was of greater interest. State records showed that Crown Street arranged a high percentage of adoptions in the state.

Did you have your baby at Crown Street, Gran? Kit mused. She could feel it in her bones that this could be the place.

When Crown Street closed its doors in 1983, the hospital records were sent to the Royal Hospital for Women, which was now Prince of Wales Hospital.

Kit needed those records. She needed to confirm what she suspected – that her gran had a baby either in July or August in 1942 at Crown Street and that the child had been adopted, illegally perhaps, from the hospital.

When an internet search led to a dead end, and the only way she could access the records was if she were a birth parent or an adoptee, Kit emailed her former colleague who had worked on the forced adoption story to see if he had any contacts. Gavin called her five minutes later wanting to know why, and Kit filled him in.

'Shit, are you sure?'

'That the baby was adopted? Yes, I am. But since all I have is my gran's name, I'm not sure how successful I'll be in gaining information about the adoption. I'm hoping if I can get confirmation that my gran had a baby at that hospital, it'll give me leverage.'

'I'll see what I can do, but we're four days out from Christmas. A lot of these departments close till well into the new year. You might be waiting a couple of weeks till we can get anything.'

'Bloody hell,' Kit cursed, rubbing the back of her neck that was stiff from sitting in front of the computer. 'I forgot about Christmas.'

Gavin laughed. 'Why am I not surprised? You were never into celebrating the festive season.'

'I wasn't?' Gavin's observation surprised her.

'You seemed resentful about travelling to Sydney to spend it with your family. I'm a little surprised you're there now.'

'It's more to do with this search than anything else, trust me.'

Gavin chuckled down the line. 'Family driving you crazy already, huh?'

They weren't. For the first time in as long as she could remember, being in Sydney ... well it felt right. 'Yeah, something like that.' Kit felt bad for lying to him.

'Hey, let's catch up for a drink sometime.'

'Umm, yeah, sure.' Kit tried not to sound nonchalant.

'Great, text when you're back home and we'll tee something up.'

'Will do,' she replied, knowing that the chance she would text him was probably close to zero. It wasn't that she disliked Gavin, he was a nice enough guy, but she never harboured any romantic feelings towards him.

As she disconnected the call she mulled it over for a while. Was it Gavin or just every guy that showed interest in her? The last time this happened Ben had told her that she needed to consider moving on. He didn't understand. He had never lost the love of his life or faced the need to start life over again, alone. It was scary. But maybe she needed to dip her toe in and test the waters, not necessarily just jump in feet first, and see what happened. After all, it was just a drink.

A knock at the front door dragged her out of her thoughts.

'Bloody hell, Ben!' She'd cut him a set of keys and thrown them to him before he headed off to the airport to pick Ness up. 'When I said here are your keys, I meant for you to –' The words were lodged in her throat as she saw who was standing on the other side.

It wasn't Ben. It was the last person she'd expected.

'Adam,' she said when she finally found her voice.

'Hello, Kit.' He gave her a nervous smile that created all sorts of chaos within her.

'How did you find ... I mean, what are you doing here?'

'Ben.'

'Ben?' Kit repeated. 'What has Ben got to do with it?'

'He answered your phone, yesterday. He told me where I could find you.'

'You were looking for me?' She willed her voice to sound steady. Nonchalant. 'Why?'

'Because I realised something.'

Kit felt her pulse hammering unsteadily. 'What ... what did you realise?'

'That you were right. I owe it to Charlie to look for his ... child.'

'You came to help me search?'

'Actually, I'm here on business. I had some meetings lined up with investors.'

'Oh, yes, I remember now.' Disappointment flooded her. For a moment she thought that Adam had made the trip especially for the search, and if she were honest, she also thought ...

Shaking her head, she didn't let her mind wander where it shouldn't.

'Come in.' She unlocked the screen door and stood back to let him through. 'There have been a few developments since I saw you last.' She led him into the kitchen and motioned for him to take a seat.

'Can I get you something to drink? Tea? Coffee? Wine?'

'Is what you're about to tell me worthy of wine just after noon on a Tuesday?'

'Ah, yes.' She took two wine glasses down from a shelf and a bottle of wine from the fridge, and then joined him at the table. She filled the glasses, sliding one across the table.

'Let's start with this.' She placed the red Arnott's tin in front of Adam.

'What is it?'

'Open it and see. Once you have taken in the contents, we'll talk. And trust me – we have a lot to talk about.'

Thirty-one

The Christmas Present

Sydney, 2016

'It's only fair that because you showed me some of Hawaii, I should show you my hometown,' Kit said as she and Adam stepped out of a taxi on Bridge Street in the city. Since his surprise arrival a couple of days ago, Adam had spent most of his free time helping her with the search for Pearl. Gavin hadn't called her back about the hospital records as yet, but Kit and Adam had forged on, pulling together an application to apply for the adoption records. They had also placed Catherine's name on a find and connect register. She was thankful for his assistance, but she was also conscious she was taking nearly all his downtime, when he wasn't in meetings, with the search, so she suggested a night on the town, visiting some of Sydney's best.

'Hey, I'm all yours. Wherever you want to take me tonight, I'm game.' He gave her a grin that made her insides flutter, and it surprised her to admit that his words thrilled her.

'Well, ah …' Kit felt her face flame as she stumbled for words and when his grin widened the heat intensified. 'We'd better get a wriggle on if we have any hope of getting a table anytime soon,' she said, motioning to the alleyway that led off Bridge Street.

'So our first stop in my Best in Sydney,' Kit used her tour-guide voice as they walked down the lane, 'is home to the best kung pao chicken outside of China.'

Adam shook his head as he digested her words. 'Now that's a big call.'

Kit shrugged. 'I stand by it one hundred per cent, and after tonight you'll agree.'

He narrowed his eyes. 'Did you have the chance to visit PF Chang's while you were in Hawaii?'

Kit knew that PF Chang's was a popular Chinese restaurant chain on the main stretch in Waikiki. She also knew that kung pao chicken was a mainstay on their menu. 'I can't say I had the pleasure. But trust me when I say, even without trying the PF Chang's version, that Mr Wong's is far, far superior.'

Adam didn't look convinced.

'Come on.' Kit dragged him into the fast-growing queue. 'Just give it a go; at the very least you'll be well fed by the end of it.'

The wait for a table was half an hour, so they were seated at the bar in the interim.

'Okay, so it's fancy Chinese,' Adam said as he took in the colonial-style furnishings and bamboo chairs. Above them a slow-turning ceiling fan completed the East Asian feel.

'It's contemporary Cantonese.'

'Hmm.' Adam perused the menu, rubbing his chin as he pored over what Kitty assumed was the beer list. 'Interesting selection here.'

Kit bit down a smile. 'Do you see anything you'd like to try?'

He lifted his gaze then, and even in the dimly lit surrounds she could see the intent in his blue eyes. 'There is one thing in particular,' Adam replied with certain daring and Kit felt her face flame once more.

She opened her mouth to reply, but was so surprised by his response that the words did not come. When her brain finally was able to form a sentence, they were interrupted by the bartender asking if they were ready to order. The moment was lost and the energy shifted from suggestive to playful, and by the time they were seated for dinner, they had moved on to debating which country was superior when it came to wine.

'Look, all I'm saying is that Aussie wines are underestimated,' Kit argued. 'There's a certain amount of arrogance that Americans have and you look down on us as if we're a backward little country and assume that everyone has a pet crocodile and kangaroo.'

Adam smiled. 'I've never thought that people had pet crocs. Kangaroos, yes, but not the crocs.'

Kit gave an exaggerated sigh. 'I rest my case.'

'There is a dominance of one certain brand of Aussie wine and I just don't get the appeal.'

Kit knew exactly the brand Adam was referring to and for once she wholeheartedly agreed with him. 'Me either, I wouldn't be caught dead drinking *that* wine.'

Adam looked at her in surprise.

'Don't look so shocked.' She laughed. 'I don't go out of my way to be disagreeable. I'm just opinionated.'

'So I've noticed,' he said with a low voice that shifted the mood once again.

'Are you willing to trust me to choose a wine that I think will blow your mind?' She hadn't planned on her words being so laden, but they elicited a slow smile from Adam that made her lips tingle.

'First we had the promise of the best kung pao chicken and now mind-blowing wine? What other promises do you have in store for me, Bennett, Kit?'

She tried to will a quick and clever comeback, but was distracted by the feel of his fingers entwining with hers. 'I ah ...' was all she managed before their food arrived and the mood was broken once again.

Kit watched as Adam sampled the dish she had talked up, her own hunger dissipating from nerves. He ate with a poker face, not giving her any indication of his displeasure or enjoyment. Kit sipped her wine and mentally scolded herself. Did it really matter what Adam thought of the food? They were having a great night, enjoying each other's company. After her mental pep talk Kit relaxed some, but was still eager to hear Adam's verdict.

'Well?' she prodded as the empty plates were whisked away and the bill placed smack bang between them. They both went for it as if they were playing a game of Snap.

Kit was the victor, but Adam wasn't going to let her win easily.

'You want me to give you my thoughts on the food, you hand over that cheque right this instant.'

'Uh ah.' Kit shook her head as if it were no big deal. 'My city, my shout.'

'You Aussies and your shouting business.' Adam shook his head and chuckled. 'Fine, but wherever we're going next, it's on me.'

A warm glow danced on her skin. She didn't want the night to end, not just yet, but she hadn't wanted to get her hopes up. 'I can live with that,' she replied, already planning their next destination.

The night was warm with no hint of a breeze, but Kit knew as soon as they hit the Quay, the breeze from the harbour would whip up. She was keeping their destination mum, but as they rounded the bend that led towards the iconic white sails, Adam got the drift.

'We're off to the opera?'

'Something better. We're heading to the Opera Bar. That way you can say you've been to the Opera House and you can take in a killer view of the famous coat hanger,' Kit said, nodding towards the Harbour Bridge. 'You know the fireworks that are lit off the Bridge on New Year's are something special.'

'Is that so?' Adam murmured as he reached for her hand and lifted it to his lips. 'You're full of big claims tonight, Kit.'

Her breath hitched and she couldn't help but shudder with delight. 'It's not a claim, they're world famous. I'm sure you've seen them on TV.'

He stopped walking and under the light of the full moon, she could see his smile. 'I have indeed, but I just might have to stick around and see it for myself. You know, just to make sure. Don't you think?'

'You should —' Her reply was cut short by Adam's lips moving to claim hers. The kiss was soft and light as a feather, but it had enough punch that it made her knees turn to jelly. He pulled her close, cradled the nape of her neck with each of his hands and deepened the kiss, making her drunk with the taste and smell of him. She wasn't sure who pulled away first, but she was sure she wanted to kiss him again, and it both excited and terrified her.

'Come on,' Adam said, breaking the silence they'd fallen into. 'Show me what's so damn special about this joint.'

The bar was noisy and as eager as Kit had been to take Adam to see the Bridge from the Opera House, after that kiss, she craved somewhere with more privacy.

They somehow nabbed a table right out front and by the look on Adam's face he was impressed. 'Okay, even I have to admit this view is something else.' The lights of the Bridge danced against the ink-black night.

'Sunset here rivals a Waikiki Beach one.'

'Don't push it,' Adam warned and Kit chuckled.

The drinks and conversation flowed with ease and by the end of the night, Kit had to admit that as much as Adam had annoyed her when they first met, the more time she spent with him, the more she liked him.

When he hailed a cab for her, she was torn between relief and disappointment that he hadn't asked her to go back to his hotel. Part of her wanted to, but another part knew she wasn't ready. Tonight had been as close as she had come to going on a date in years. She told herself that was a big enough step for now.

'I enjoyed playing tourist with you,' Adam said, leaning against the open taxi door. 'Thank you for a memorable night.'

'It was my pleasure.' She smiled, waiting, hoping that he would kiss her goodnight.

'Hey, are you getting in or what?' the impatient taxi driver barked.

'Guess that's my cue to leave,' he said as he stepped away. 'Goodnight, Kit.'

'Bye, Adam.' She smiled, burying her disappointment.

But as the taxi made a move to pull out of the curb, there was a thump on the roof that made the driver screech to a stop.

'What now?' he growled, but Kit's heart soared.

As she wound down the window Adam leaned in, cupped her face and kissed her fiercely.

'I'll see you tomorrow,' he whispered when they finally pulled apart. Kit could only nod and not even the driver's grumbling could wipe the smile off her face.

It was only when she was home and drifting off to sleep that regret hit her hard.

She woke the next morning with a feeling of unease. Her dreams were plagued with guilt and twisted memories.

Too soon.

What had she been thinking? She needed to put a stop to this, before it got too far. She had got carried away playing tour guide.

Even though they had arranged to meet up later in the day, Kit sighed with relief when Adam messaged telling her he would be tied up in meetings until late.

No worries, I'll see you tomorrow.

She sent the text without thinking it through. It was only when Adam's reply came that Kit realised her mistake.

Yes, Christmas Day. I'll bring breakfast. See you then.

Dammit. Christmas Day. How had she lost track of time? There was no way she could get out of seeing him. Ben and Ness were coming over in the morning, so at least they wouldn't be alone. She just needed to get through the morning then she'd be at her parents' the rest of the day. She could do it. She was sure she could.

'You should've seen her in high school.' Ben laughed as if it were the funniest thing on earth. 'She went through a stage where she thought she was Sporty Spice.'

Kit glared at her brother. Ben was very fortunate he was sitting a safe distance away from her, otherwise she would've happily clobbered him. Or at least, stomped on his foot.

'Is that so?' Adam cocked his head, amusement twinkling in his eyes as he considered her. 'I would've pegged you more of a Posh Spice or even Ginger Spice.'

'To be fair, I was Posh Spice,' Ness said. 'And we went to school with a girl called Geri who claimed dibs on being Ginger Spice because of her name. Kit didn't have blonde hair, nor was it curly, so by default, she was Sporty.'

Kit shook her head. She was disappointed that Ness of all people could betray her by revealing one of the most embarrassing periods of her adolescent life.

'And were you sporty at all?' It was clear that Adam thought it was hilarious.

'Hell, no!' Ben answered for her. 'She was awkward, a bit of a klutz and still is. Actually, I think it was Jeremy that –' Ben realised his mistake just in time.

'Who's Jeremy?' Adam asked, and the table fell silent.

'Thank you for a wonderful trip down memory lane, Ben.' Kit scraped back her chair and collected the empty plates. 'But it's getting late and we need to start getting ready for the BBQ at Mum and Dad's.'

'I guess that's my cue to leave.' Adam made a move to get up and Kit breathed a sigh of relief.

'Hey, Adam, you should come with us.'

Kit dropped the breakfast dishes into the sink with a thud. She could really kill her brother right about now.

'I'm sure Adam is busy, he's here on business after all.'

'But it's Christmas Day,' Ness helpfully pointed out. 'Surely you don't have anything planned.'

Adam shrugged. 'I don't have any plans, so yeah – that'd be nice. That is, if it's okay with you, Kit?'

Kit willed a smile. 'Of course, why wouldn't it be?'

An hour later, Kit watched through the kitchen window as her niece Piper, Cameron and Julia's daughter, explained to Adam the intricacies of backyard cricket. She smiled as the older boys tried to butt in – convinced they knew more than their younger sister – but to his credit, Adam's attention stayed squarely on Piper.

'He's something to look at, huh?' Julia sidled up next to her and bumped her hip.

'I don't know what you're talking about,' Kit lied, her face flaming from the untruth.

As if on cue, Adam whipped off his t-shirt and Julia whistled. 'Like hell you don't. Honey, if you weren't standing here waiting for that to happen, then you have rocks in your head.'

Kit chuckled. Julia had a point. It was hot out and the midday sun was about to strike the backyard. 'He's just a friend, Julia. Besides, nothing can actually happen.' Even though the truth was, *something* had already happened, the reality was it couldn't go any further.

'Why not? I thought you were both single, aren't you?' Julia asked.

'Well, yes, we're both single, but it's not as simple as that.'

'Why?' her sister-in-law asked.

'Because ...' Kit began and then realised she was grasping for words. 'We live in different countries for starters.' She hoped Julia didn't ask for more reasons, because at this point, Kit was finding it hard to come up with another plausible reason, even though there were many. There had to be many.

'Um, hello, you're a freelance journalist. How bad can it be to commit to being in one place for a while? Gosh, I'm not telling you to marry the guy.'

The mention of marriage was like a punch in the guts and it must've shown on her face because Julia's tone softened considerably.

'Honey, just allow yourself to give the guy a chance, okay? You obviously like him and it's crystal clear the feeling is mutual.'

And like a schoolgirl, Kit felt the butterflies unleash in her tummy.

'You think so?' Her gaze involuntarily returned to the back-yard where her nephews were trying to teach Adam how to hold a cricket bat. The way the sunlight reflected off his hair made her breath hitch.

'I know so,' Julia said. 'Take a chance, Kit. Jeremy may have been your love once, but maybe he won't be the only love of your life. If you don't let anyone in, how will you know?'

Julia's words were still milling in Kit's mind as they sat on the porch for the Christmas BBQ lunch.

'This wouldn't be too dissimilar to what you're used to, Adam,' Kit's father said as he handed him a beer. 'I mean coming from Hawaii and all, you'd have a hot Christmas too.'

'True, although my mom's folks are from Washington State. When I was little we went there every holiday season.'

'Is that where your parents are for Christmas?' Kit's mother asked.

'My parents were both killed in a car accident years ago,' Adam said softly.

'Oh, I'm so sorry, Adam!'

'It's fine, Mrs Bennett. I have my pop, Charlie, for now at least. He's the reason why I moved back to Hawaii.'

Julia, her mother and Ness all sighed in unison. Kit could almost hear their silent plotting. It wouldn't surprise her if by the end of the day they hadn't all banded together to plan Kit's wedding.

After lunch, her mother shooed away any attempts to help clean up and sent them all outside. Kit sat on the porch swing with her glass of wine as Piper sat next to her, giving her a detailed description of all her Christmas presents before heading off to join the boys in the pool. Moments after Piper vacated the seat, it was taken again, this time by Adam.

'Your family is –'

Whatever Adam was about to say was swallowed up by a ruckus that had erupted in the pool. Piper had declared a noodle war with her eldest brother Josh, who was easily twice her size. This didn't seem to deter the pocket rocket. Moments later, Cameron was in the pool, and Piper set her sights on her dad. Kit had to admire Piper's lack of fear.

'I believe "crazy" is the word you're searching for,' she said with a smile.

'Yeah, crazy would be one way of putting it.' Adam chuckled as he sipped his beer. 'But a good kind of crazy. Must've been interesting, growing up with two older brothers.' There was a wistful edge in his voice that wasn't hard to miss.

'You could say that. I was the first girl, not just in my immediate family but in the whole Bennett clan. My dad is the youngest of four boys and each of my uncles had sons, so when I was born ... well it was kind of special for the family and especially for my gran. It was why we were so close.'

'In some ways you were the girl she lost.'

'Yes, when I discovered that Gran and Charlie's baby had been a girl, a lot of things made sense.'

'Like how you thought your grandfather resented your grandmother giving you pearls.'

'I keep thinking about that – how he knew all about Charlie and Pearl, and I wonder how much it played on his mind.'

'It's only natural – his wife had a child with another man.'

'A man that Gran thought died at Pearl Harbor. Can you imagine if she knew Charlie survived?'

'It would've changed the course of her life,' Adam said.

'More than just her life; it would've changed Charlie's too and quite possibly you and I wouldn't be sitting here right now ...'

'Musing about what could've been,' Adam said, finishing the thought for her.

How many times had she done that after Jeremy? How many times had she questioned her actions, wondering what if things hadn't happened the way they had? Too often to remember. In the early days, she tortured herself daily. She went to bed pretending he was there next to her. It was the only way she could get to sleep some nights. In the morning, for a few brief moments, Jeremy was right there, until she rolled over and ran her hand over the cold, empty space that he used to occupy.

'I'm glad everything worked out as it did.' Adam's voice pulled Kit back into the present.

'I guess it's probably for the best. I know that despite everything I've uncovered, my gran and grandpa had a good life.'

'And Charlie did too. Losing Grandma Rose was hard, as was losing my dad, but Pop is made of stern stuff. And if Kitty ever found out Charlie survived, then I would never have met you.' Kit felt his hand thread through hers as he caught her gaze, powerful and intense, and at that moment all the noise around them, the whole world, ceased to exist. The thrill of his touch was electrifying.

'I –' The moment was shattered by the shrill of her phone. Never had the noise sounded more annoying. For a second or two she stared at the screen, knowing that she should answer but frustrated that the call had ruined the atmosphere.

'You should probably answer it.' He untwined his fingers from hers and stood up. 'I'll give you some privacy.'

Kit sighed as she watched Adam walk away. 'Gavin, hi, happy Christmas. Do you have any news for me?' She had been expecting his call for a few days, but was somewhat taken aback by the timing now.

His contact had come through, Gavin explained, and was willing to hand over her gran's medical records. As soon as she was off the phone, Kit pulled Adam aside.

'It looks like that phone call made you very happy,' he said coolly.

Kit cocked her head. Was he jealous? 'It was Gavin, the colleague I was telling you about – the one with the contact at the hospital.'

'He came through?' Adam asked, clearly surprised. 'On Christmas Day?'

'Yep.' Kit nodded. At first, she was just as surprised but Gavin had explained the timing of his call. 'There's a catch. Apparently they won't hand over the file, but we can see it for ourselves. Today.'

'Today?'

'It's not an essential service so the department is technically closed and Gavin made it clear that the person I'm meeting with is risking a lot to help. Apparently the hospital is pretty quiet. If I want to meet her, I need to leave as soon as possible.'

'What are we waiting for then?'

The eerie silence in this wing of the hospital was a contrast to the buzzing in Kit's mind. As the lift climbed up towards the top floor where answers awaited, so did her hopes. It was only after the doors open and they stepped out that she expelled a breath.

'Are you okay?' Adam gave her shoulder a supportive squeeze.

'Yeah, I'm just nervous. I know this isn't going to give us all the answers, but it's a start and having the information will give us more clout in the application for the adoption papers.'

'Just remember that no matter what you find, you don't have to deal with it alone, I'm here with you.'

Kit had spent years doing things alone and didn't mind, but today for the first time in a long time, she was glad she wasn't by herself.

'Kit Bennett?' An older, dark woman appeared out of nowhere.

'Harriett Smith?' Kit wasn't even sure that was her real name, but right now, she didn't care. All she needed was five minutes with the papers.

'Follow me,' she said, before turning and heading down the hallway. 'In there.'

Harriett stopped short in front of a closed door. 'I'll give you five minutes, that's all the time I can give you, I'm afraid.' Her eyes darted left and right, highlighting her unease. 'I'm sure Gavin explained that due to the delicate nature of it all, you cannot take a copy of the file.'

Kit knew Harriett was going out on a limb for them. If anyone found out she'd given them access to the files, she could lose her job, or worse, be legally liable for her actions. 'Yes, I'm – we're grateful that you are allowing us to see the file. I'll just write down the important information that will help me with my case for gaining access to the adoption papers.'

'Ready?' Adam asked, poised to open the door.

Kit drew in a breath. 'As ready as I'll ever be.'

The room was airless. Within moments sweat beaded at the back of Kit's neck, but the second she opened the aged file and took in the musty smell of the timeworn pages, her skin was covered in goose bumps.

Her eyes skittered over the pages, drinking in as much as she could. The first thing that jumped out at her were three letters stamped in the top right-hand corner of the file.

'BFA,' she said, a sickly feeling settling in her stomach.

'Wonder what that stands for,' Adam mused.

Kit had done enough reading on forced adoptions to know exactly what it meant. 'Baby for adoption,' she told him. 'The doctor, or a matron or someone, decided the fate of Kitty and Charlie's baby early on. And I'm pretty sure Kitty had very little say to the contrary.'

'Five minutes is not going to be enough,' Adam said.

'That's why I'm about to do this.' Kit pulled out her phone and hastily started taking photos. 'Harriett didn't say anything about no photos.'

'Good plan.' Adam started turning the pages to speed up the process.

A quick knock made Kit jump. 'One minute left,' Harriett's muffled voice came through the closed door.

'Shit.' Kit panicked, rushing through the remainder of the file. It was only as she took the last of the snaps that something else caught her eye.

'Bloody hell.' She put the phone down and stared at the page in her hand.

'What is it?'

'The baby was born five weeks early. The due date was estimated the last week of August, but the baby was born the eleventh of July, 1942.'

'And that's important?'

'Because it's the same date that I was born.'

Oh, Gran, Kit thought. *All those years we spent celebrating my birthday. That date was as special to you as it was to me.*

'Wow. What are the chances?'

A second later, Harriett opened the door. 'I'm sorry, but time is up. I wish I could give you longer, but I can't. It's risky enough that I've allowed this in the first place.'

'I totally understand.' Kit closed the file and handed it over.

'I hope that you got what you needed,' Harriett said, tucking the file under her arm and escorting them back towards the lift.

'I did, thank you.'

Harriett nodded and turned to leave.

'Wait, Ms Smith!'

Harriett halted. 'Yes?'

'Can I ask, why did you let us see the file?'

She took the file from under her arm and looked at it a while before answering. 'Because I also have one of these files. I was born a couple of months before the child in this file. Chances are my birth mother was at Crown Street at the same time your grandmother was.'

'Did you ever look for her? Your birth mother?'

'I did.'

'And?' Kit asked hopefully, her heart wishing for a happy ending. 'Did you find her?'

Harriett shook her head solemnly. 'No, she died not long after I was born.'

Kit felt a sharp intake of breath. 'I'm so sorry.'

Harriett shrugged. 'It is what it is. I was adopted into a good home, but it still never stopped me from wondering about the woman who had given birth to me. I'm part Aboriginal, I've always known that, and I'd hoped by finding my birth mother I would find a piece of myself.'

'I think that would be natural for any child who has been adopted,' Kit said, wondering if Pearl had ever had similar thoughts. 'What was your mother's name?' Kit knew it was an odd question to ask; she wasn't even sure why knowing would matter. Maybe it was because if there was a chance Harriett's mother had been at Crown Street at the same time as Gran, then maybe they knew each other. Perhaps they'd even been friends. It gave her a small sense of comfort knowing that Gran may have had a friend during what would surely have been a lonely and heart-wrenching time.

'Gwen.' Harriett gave a sad smile, as if the mere act of uttering the name of a woman she would never know was enough to break her heart every single time. 'Her name was Gwen.'

Kit would probably never see Harriett again, but she'd given Kit the greatest Christmas present she'd ever received, and for that she would forever be grateful.

As Adam ordered an Uber, Kit studied the photos.

'I have a printer in my hotel room. If you want, we can upload the photos and print them out.'

'Adam Florio, did you just invite me to your room?'

Adam gave a nonchalant shrug, but there was a smile on his lips. 'If you want to see it that way, hey, that's up to you. Do you have a printer?'

'No, but my parents do.'

'And you would prefer to go back there?'

Kit shook her head and sighed dramatically. 'Let's do it your way. If I take you to my parents' place again, questions will be asked. Boys don't have a habit of coming home with me.'

'So I've been told,' Adam said before instructing the driver to head to the city.

Kit groaned. 'Which one of my lovely family members was gossiping about me? Come on, spill.'

'Your mother.'

'Figures.' Kit laughed.

'She said the only guy you've ever brought home was Jeremy.'

Kit felt her stomach drop. 'She told you about Jeremy? What did she say?'

'Just that he's the only guy you ever took home.'

Kit looked out the window. 'My mother had no business telling you about Jeremy.'

'Hey.' Adam reached over and took her hand. 'I've upset you. I'm sorry.'

Kit sighed. 'No, it's not you. It's just that the thing with Jeremy ...'

'Sounds like it was a bad break up. You don't have to talk about it, it's okay.'

'It was worse than a bad break up.' Kit blinked back tears that stung her eyes.

'Kit, I mean it, you don't have to tell me.'

As they pulled up to the hotel, Kit looked at Adam. 'Do you have any wine in your room?'

'I'm sure there's a bottle or two.'

'Good, because I'm going to need it to make it through this story.' It was time for her to share her story of Jeremy with Adam.

Kit almost chickened out. To his credit, Adam didn't push her. He gave her time to gather the courage she needed, which turned out to be two glasses of wine later.

'Jeremy was my fiancé.' She took another gulp of her wine. 'He died five years ago and I ... I could've stopped it.'

'How?' There was no judgement, only concern in his eyes, his voice.

'He died while riding a scooter in Bali. I wasn't with him. But I should've been.'

'I don't understand. If you weren't with him, how could you have stopped the accident?'

Kit told him how days before they were due to leave, she decided to stay in Sydney instead, to work on a breaking news story. Jeremy's friend Mick ended up going in her place and three days before they were due to come home, Kit decided to surprise Jeremy.

'I didn't tell him I was coming, by the time I arrived ...' Kit closed her eyes as the image of a bruised and bleary-eyed Mick flashed in her mind and how one look at his face and she knew ... 'It was too late.' Kit breathed the words out like the heavy burden they were. She took a sip of her wine and composed herself before continuing. 'The road was wet and windy and according to the toxicology report they'd been drinking. If I had been there, I would've stopped it. I never would've allowed him to get on a scooter drunk. If I hadn't stayed behind, if I had got a flight out the night before instead of waiting for one the next day, it would have been so different.'

'Kit, are you listening to yourself?' Adam sounded angry, the patience he'd shown earlier was long gone. 'Have you been feeling like this for five years?' When her response was a wordless nod, he swore under his breath before softening his tone. 'Honey, you've been living with one foot in the past. His death was an accident, one that was brought on by his careless actions. You had nothing to do with it, are you listening to me?' He moved closer to her and rubbed her shoulder, and all she wanted to do was crawl into his arms.

The tears were flowing now and Kit felt helpless to stop them. She had been carrying the guilt about Jeremy's death like a chain around her neck and, it seemed, her heart, and she could pinpoint the exact moment that chain had shackled her.

At Jeremy's funeral, as they lowered the coffin into the cold, damp earth, Jeremy's mother, Lenore, had gripped Kit's forearm, her long nails digging into her skin like claws. At first, Kit thought she was collapsing and needed help, but the moment she looked into the older woman's red-rimmed eyes and saw the anger radiating from them, she knew she was mistaken.

'You let him go alone. You should've been there to stop him,' said the woman who was to be her mother-in-law.

Kit remembered how her skin began to flush hot and cold. Her already ingrained grief was compounded by Lenore's blaming words. They seeped into her, chilling her to the very core. It was as if at that point, all responsibility had shifted to Kit. The burden of blame lay squarely with her.

In Lenore's eyes Jeremy's careless actions that had resulted in his death could have all been prevented if only Kit had been with him.

If only ...

Kit had spent the last five years saying those words over and over again, bending her mind backwards about how she should've gone with Jeremy in the first instance, questioning why she didn't simply catch the earlier flight.

'Kit, you know that you're allowed to move on, don't you? You've been grief stricken for far too long.'

'I know it's just ... I don't know how.'

Adam tilted her chin and he leaned towards her. 'Sometimes it helps if you don't have to do it alone.'

Thirty-two

When Hope Turns To Dust

Sydney, 2016

Kit woke with a start. Sleep had been fitful and unsettling and for a moment, before remembering where she was, panic hit her. The realisation she was in Adam's hotel room, in his bed, calmed her some, but not enough. Dreams often plagued her slumber. Her memory of them was always murky, and more often than not, she couldn't remember a single detail, only that they were of Jeremy and they left her with a sense of dread. But this time, the dream had been vivid, crystal clear, as if she were there.

Even now as she lay in bed and briefly closed her eyes, the sound of her own scream chilled her to her marrow. In her dream, she had replayed the events one by one, as if she was on stage performing a play.

The plane trip to Bali, arriving at the hotel and seeing Mick, the sick feeling that washed over her as he looked up and uttered those two words that changed her life.

'Jeremy's dead.'

Kit walked back slowly, her head hitting the door as she let her body slump down, curling into a ball, sobbing. Mick had left her there for a while, consumed in his own grief, before her anger surfaced. Anger that Jeremy had gone and died on her. Anger that Mick was here and Jeremy wasn't. Anger that she'd stayed – for work.

'I want to see him,' Kit hiccupped between her sobs.

Mick gave a solemn nod and arranged for a cab. They sat in silence. Outside, the day was as any other in this part of the world. The sky was slowly giving way to dusk; soon brilliant hues of yellow, orange and pink would dominate. Holiday goers were perusing the street-market stalls, haggling over a bargain and then making their way towards the Kuta bars and clubs. Men loitering on the streets offering illegal fares, enticing foreigners with illicit substances. Outside, the world was typical, a normal day in Kuta. Inside, Kit's life was falling apart.

Tears streamed as she rested her head against the window, not caring how the pain jarred at her temple every time they went over a pothole. She tried not to think how barely an hour before she had been in a cab, heading down the same road as the driver chatted animatedly about the beauty of the island. There was no beauty for her now, only terror.

By the time they arrived at the hospital, darkness was fast approaching. Kit shivered as she stepped out of the cab. A pebble had made its way into her sandal, the tiny rock causing immense discomfort with every step, but Kit couldn't be bothered to stop and remove it. She needed to get inside. She needed to see Jeremy.

A young doctor led them towards the morgue. Mick stopped short of the two plastic doors, his hand resting on her forearm, halting her.

'I need to warn you ... You need to know ... It's not pretty.'

She shook his hand off and pushed through the double doors; the sight that greeted her on the other side made her stomach churn.

Jeremy's body was on a gurney draped with a white sheet.

Kit remembered how her legs had turned to lead, how it felt like it took forever to walk to the centre of the room. Slowly, with shaking hands, she took the edges of the sheet. She remembered the first thing she said to Jeremy's lifeless body. She remembered because she had been saying the same words for the past five years. But in her dream, it wasn't her who spoke.

As she peeled back the white sheet, revealing Jeremy's extensive injuries – head injuries compatible with blunt force trauma – his eyes flickered open and his lips moved. Words slurred at first, but then she heard him loud and clear.

'If only ...'

A strangled moan escaped her lips and in a flash, she covered her mouth to stop it. Adam stirred next to her and Kit watched him, her heart beating frantically as she prayed she hadn't woken him. When a moment later his breathing deepened, Kit expelled a shaky breath.

Adam's back was exposed, the sheet barely covered his butt, and the reminder that they were both naked had Kit pulling the covers to her chin. Memories of last night flooded in and she buried her face in her hands. Whether they were fuelled by wine, an accumulation of the days' events, revealing her story about Jeremy, or all three, as wondrous as the night had been, it had also been a mistake.

She was attracted to Adam – that wasn't the issue. The issue was that despite his insistence she needed to move on, Kit knew she wasn't ready. She needed more time and the dream had been a case in point.

She needed to go home. A glance at the alarm clock announced that morning wasn't long off, but it was still essentially night. Fumbling for her phone to use as a torch, she cursed when she discovered the battery was close to flat. It seemed charging it hadn't been a high priority last night. If she hurried, she might have enough power to find her clothes and call a cab.

Fossicking around the room in near darkness wasn't the easiest of endeavours but she eventually managed to collect her clothes and shoes without waking Adam, slipping away like a thief in the night. As she hurried down the hallway, her heart thumped and when the elevator flew towards the lobby, Kit ignored the voice in her head berating her for doing the wrong thing. Yes, it was cowardly, sneaking away, but in her defence what was she going to do? Wake Adam and tell him she was leaving because she'd just had a dream that Jeremy was there with her and it was enough to make her blame herself for his death all over again. Out of the two options, being a coward or a crazy, she would take the former.

Even so, her guilt only surged as she walked through the lobby, but before she could second-guess her decision, she jumped into a taxi and headed home. Outside, the morning sun glimmered over the horizon, shafts of light caressing the clouds, turning them to gold. By the time the cab pulled into the driveway of her gran's house, the sun was climbing and her phone battery finally died.

As Kit climbed the porch stairs, she debated whether she should deliberately leave it uncharged. She knew it was gutless. Adam would surely be calling her as soon as he discovered she was gone, but it was still early. She suspected she had a couple of hours, at least, before he would start calling her. She would charge it, but first she needed a shower and the strongest pot of tea she could stomach.

She ended up drawing a bath. Gran had loved her baths. Over the years, her grandparents had renovated the house a number of times and with each renovation came a grander bathroom. A long, wide claw-foot bath took pride of place in the middle of the room. Her grandfather had been a tall man, but it was mainly used by her grandmother, who was also above average height. Kit had inherited the Bennett gene for height, just as it seemed Adam had inherited the Florio gene for piercing light blue eyes.

Sinking into the water, Kit groaned. She would need to face the music when it came to Adam, but right now she was going to soak as much of her anxiety away as she could. Forty minutes later and suitably pruned, she stepped out from the bath, wrapped a robe around her and padded into the kitchen to make her tea. As she poured the first cup, she plugged her phone into the charger and by the time the tea had cooled enough to take a sip, she had three missed calls and two messages – all from Adam.

Shit.

She closed her eyes, wondering if she should read them now or after her tea. Figuring Adam's wrath could wait a few more minutes she took the tea outside and sat on the love swing; tucking one foot under her bum she dangled the other, using the leverage for motion. The sun was strong, the clouds that had lingered at dawn had disappeared, and Sydney was gearing up for another scorcher of a day. She had promised her niece and nephews that she would accompany them to the beach. Julia texted her at some point yesterday afternoon telling her they'd collect her bright and early to avoid the crowds and get a decent spot. Her sister-in-law also mentioned she'd message when they were on their way.

Inside, her phone pinged and Kit guessed it would either be Adam, again, or Julia heralding their impending arrival. When it pinged once more, Kit decided it was time she checked her texts. Sighing, she pushed off the swing and went inside, but a knock at the door stopped her from checking her messages.

It was barely eight o'clock, her family was sure keen to hit the beach. They hadn't given her much warning. Kit thought she'd have a good quarter of an hour before they arrived. The knock came again.

'Hold your horses, I didn't think you'd get here so soon,' she yelled as she approached the front door. 'You're going to need to –' As she swung the door open, the rest of the sentence became lodged in her throat. It wasn't Julia.

'Adam.' She breathed out his name. The sight of him caught her unaware and suddenly guilt consumed her.

'You were expecting someone else,' he said in a matter-of-fact kind of way.

'Umm, no, I mean yes ... Cam and Julia and the kids have invited me to the beach today.'

'I know, they invited me too.'

'They did?' Her response elicited a raised brow. 'Well, you should totally come,' Kit said, sounding keener on the plan than she felt. She didn't mind if Adam came along, did she? It would give her a chance to apologise. She should apologise. If he did come he would need to change into more appropriate gear. Right now he looked as if he was about to chair a board meeting.

Adam shook his head. 'I can't. I'm on my way to the airport. I only came by to give you this.' It was then Kit saw the manila folder in his hands. When she stared blankly, Adam said, 'It's the prints of the photos of the hospital records.'

'Oh.' In her haste to leave this morning, she had forgotten to take it with her. 'You're going?' She hated how disappointed she felt.

Adam nodded. 'I got a call a couple of hours ago. Not long after you left, I assume.'

Kit winced. 'Charlie?'

Adam ran his hand over his stubbled chin. 'He's not so great. It seems in the week that I've been away, he's deteriorated.'

'So you're leaving right now?' Kit heard a hint of desperation in her voice. Of course he was leaving right now. There was a cab waiting outside.

'Direct flights to Honolulu don't leave until late tonight, but I managed to find one that will take me via Auckland that gets me home sooner. I need to get back to him as fast as I can.'

'Of course.'

'Kit, listen, we need to talk about last night.'

'There's nothing to talk about.' Adam was trying to catch her gaze and she was deliberately avoiding any eye contact.

'I beg to differ. We spent the night together ... hell, Kit, I saw you fall apart and then I woke up only to discover you'd run away.' He was pissed off, that much was clear.

'Look, Adam. It was nice and all and I'm sorry I left but –'

'Nice?' he scoffed and ran his hand through his hair. 'I've had dentist visits that could be described in a more glowing fashion.'

'Adam, we both know that last night was a one-off, so I'm making it easy for you.'

'You're doing it again.'

'Doing what?'

'Pulling away. Retreating into the past.'

'Hey.' She pointed an accusatory finger at him. 'Those were your words, not mine. For your information, I *am* living in the present and by ending this now I'm ensuring less heartbreak for both of us because we both know that it was never going to work.'

'You seem mighty sure of that.'

'How could it, Adam? We live in different countries.'

'You're writing this off before we've had a chance to see if it's anything real.'

'Because ... because I just ...' Kit grappled to find a good reason, even though deep down she knew there had to be one. 'Because I just know.'

He was quiet for a moment. He simply stood on the porch watching her. 'How do you know that I'm not going to come back?'

'I doubt that's going to happen.'

'How do you know that one day you are not going to wake up and think, if only. If only I had given Adam a chance instead of walking away.' Kit fiddled with the belt on her robe. When she didn't answer, he continued. 'I know that part of the reason you are searching for Pearl is that you keep thinking, if only Gran didn't have to give up her baby.'

Irritation filled her. 'That's not true, I'm looking for Pearl because it's the right thing to do.'

'Is it? If you truly believed that you wouldn't be keeping it a secret. People keep secrets when they are afraid of the truth.'

'What the hell is that supposed to mean?'

Adam shrugged. 'You're a smart girl, I'm sure you'll figure it out, Bennett, Kit.'

At that moment, he reminded her of the Adam she first met – arrogant, cocky, so sure of himself, a regular know-it-all.

Anger and hurt surged through her as she reached over to snatch the file out of his hands, determined to have the last word. 'You're wrong about me. I know why I'm doing this, and as for keeping it a secret, it's only until I have something to tell.'

'You keep telling yourself that, Kit.'

Boy, did he know just how to rile her. 'God, you really are an infuriating man.' Kit shook her head.

'It's a good thing I'm leaving then.'

'Yes, it is. In fact, your driver looks quite impatient. You should probably get going.' The words tumbled out before she could stop them. 'Goodbye, Adam.'

'See you, Bennett, Kit. I hope you find what you're looking for. I hope that one day you can let go of your if onlys.'

Kit closed the door, moving to the window to watch as Adam walked down the garden path and climbed into the waiting cab. As it drove away, his words swirled in her mind, leaving an unsettling feeling in her stomach.

She wasn't living in the past and as for moving on, who said he had the right to tell her when she needed to do so? He was wrong – and now she was more determined than ever to find Pearl.

Three weeks later, Kit received a letter explaining that her application for the inheritance of the adoption papers had been successful. Pearl's full name was Pearl Russ and she lived in Melbourne, not far from where Kit's apartment was.

The joy that surrounded this was short-lived. Hours later Kit was informed by the reunion register that Pearl had requested no contact.

'What?' she asked in disbelief, blindsided by the news. 'Can you tell me why?'

'I'm sorry, all I can tell you is that she has requested no contact from her birth family.'

When the call ended, Kit contacted the only person she could vent to.

'Maybe it's probably for the best,' Ben said.

'But why doesn't she want anything to do with us?' Kit was miffed at her brother's calm reaction.

'Kit, it's really none of our business. I'm sure she has her reasons. Maybe it's time to move on.'

'I'm not giving up.'

'Have you told Adam about this?'

Kit chewed her bottom lip. 'I'm sure he's busy with Charlie.'

'Have you at least called him to see how Charlie is going?'

'No.' Kit closed her eyes and expelled a breath. 'I mean I've thought about texting him and asking but ...'

'But what?'

'I may have downplayed the way things ended when Adam left.'

'What did you do?' Ben's voice was threaded with accusation, and it bothered her that he assumed it was her fault.

'We argued, then he implied that I was only searching for Pearl because of some romantic notion I have about what life could've been for Gran.'

Ben was silent and Kit was taken aback. 'Oh, Ben, come on!'

'He has a point, Kit.'

'No, he doesn't,' she argued, annoyed that Ben seemed to be siding with Adam.

'Then why are you doing it, Kit?'

'Because it's the right thing to do.' The reasoning seemed hollow, even to her, and she hated it.

'I'm glad you called,' Ben said, changing the subject. 'I was about to ring to ask if you wanted help cleaning out the rest of Gran's place.'

'Dad offered to help, mainly because Grandad's study has been virtually untouched since he died, but I guess I could use an extra pair of hands.'

'Ness and I can both help. It's the least we can do since you're letting us stay there.'

'Technically, you will be paying rent.'

'Yes, but I still feel bad rushing you to leave. We never expected that our stuff from Singapore would arrive so soon.'

'At least you'll be settled before you guys start your new jobs. And it is time for me to head back to Melbourne.'

'Huh. Interesting.'

'What's interesting?'

'It's the first time in years that I've heard you refer to it as "Melbourne" and not "home".'

'That's ridiculous,' Kit said. 'I'm sure it's not the first time.'

'Hmm, I'm pretty sure it is. Normally when you're in Sydney you're always in a hurry to rush home, but you have spent more time here in the last couple of months than you have in total since Jeremy's ...'

'Death? You can say it, Ben, you don't have to tiptoe around it. It's been five years. I'm not going to burst into tears or anything.'

'I know that it's taken you a while to get to this point. I'm glad that Adam could make you see you could do it.'

'Wait, what? How did you ... what does Jeremy have to do with Adam?'

'Adam called me before he left, he told me you told him about Jeremy.'

'Son of a ... guess he told you I slept with him too.' Kit was fuming. He had no right.

'No, he didn't. That part I gathered. Look, Kit, the guy cares for you. He called me because he was concerned. After hearing about Jeremy, he didn't like having to leave you so soon.'

'He was pretty peeved when he left me. I'm sure the care factor is zero by now.'

'There is one way of finding out. Call him.'

'Is Saturday morning good for you?' Kit asked, deliberately skirting around Ben's comment. 'That way we can have the house cleared out before your stuff arrives on Monday.'

'Yeah, sure, see you then.'

Dammit, talking to Ben was supposed to make her feel better not worse. He was wrong – it wasn't time to move on. All she had to do was find a reason, something that would convince Pearl to change her mind. Everything else had turned to dust, but not this. She wasn't giving up hope. Not when the lost Pearl was within her grasp.

Thirty-three
Keeping Promises

Sydney, December 1949

Catherine knew the signs. After all, she had gone through this before, and yet for some reason, she chose to downplay what was happening. It was only when the nausea hit did the reality finally become too hard to ignore. William walked into the bathroom and found her slumped on the floor. It was the third day Catherine had woken up feeling sick.

'Catherine?' He bent down, his forehead creased with concern. 'What's wrong?'

Tears pricked her eyes. She wasn't ready for this. She wasn't ready to tell him. Not when she'd barely had time to acknowledge it herself, to come to terms with it.

'Darling, what's wrong?' he repeated.

'I think, actually I'm quite sure that I'm pregnant.'

The worry on his face turned to joy, which only made her burst into tears.

'Darling, oh my darling.' He gathered her into his arms, holding her against his warm chest. 'Don't cry. This is happy news. It's what we've been praying for all this time.'

Three years earlier, as a newlywed bride, Catherine had entered married life full of hope, and William had made it no secret that he wanted to start a family straight away.

'War made me see that time is precious. Let's not waste it,' he had said then.

Catherine agreed. Time was precious. 'I want a family too, but I want my family to be complete.' A look of fear mixed with irritation flashed across her husband's face. It was brief, gone in the blink of an eye, which made her wonder if she had imagined it.

'My love, when the time is right our family will be complete. But we've just got married. Shouldn't we enjoy our first few months as husband and wife?'

Catherine didn't push it any further. William was right – they were newlyweds. But as their first anniversary came and went, Catherine felt tension form between them. She could tell that William was wondering why she wasn't falling pregnant, and the truth was, she had wondered the same.

Almost a year and a half after their wedding, William insisted they see a doctor. William was a general practitioner, but he thought they needed someone with greater expertise on the matter.

'He's at Crown Street, one of the best fertility specialists in the city.'

'No!' The word had come out harsher than intended.

'Catherine, we need to find out if there is a problem,' William said tersely.

'I'll see a doctor, William. But I will never go back to that ... place. Never.'

'Fine,' William said curtly. 'I'll try to find someone else.'

He did – Doctor Dunlop – who confirmed that both William and Catherine were of perfect health. 'Young women are sometimes anxious about their first pregnancy. I'm sure you'll be pregnant in no time.'

Catherine had been poised to tell the doctor that she had already been a first-time mother, but William's hand covered hers at just that moment and a firm look discouraged her from saying anything.

Catherine had hoped the visit would alleviate the tension, but it didn't.

'It'll happen, William. You heard Doctor Dunlop. Besides, I've done this before, I'm sure my body can remember to do it again.'

'Yes,' he grumbled. 'I know.'

She had seen that look on his face before, and the hope that William would help her look for Pearl as he had promised began to wane.

Despite the vast difference between how her life had been before, her second pregnancy was very much like the first.

'Wait till you get towards the end,' Maggie had warned. 'Your feet are bound to swell and your back, oh – the aching. Mine hurts just thinking about it.' Maggie had met and married a nice man she worked with. Ten months later, they had their first baby – a boy named James. Then just over a year later came little Albert. 'The second pregnancy is harder because you already have a baby. Enjoy the peace that comes with your first. In fact, enjoy the peace now, full stop!'

Catherine said nothing, lifting the cup of tea that Maggie had placed in front of her. It was hot. She blew on it and took a hazardous sip and burnt her tongue.

'You'll learn to drink that in record time.' Maggie tipped her head towards the tea. 'Trust me, once you're a mother, there is nothing that's your own. But you love them,' Maggie said and her voice became wistful. 'From the moment you hear that baby cry and they place them in your arms ... there's nothing like it. You remember that moment for the rest of your life.'

Catherine's heart squeezed. So many times she had come close to telling Maggie about Pearl, but each and every time she stopped. She wasn't sure why, but in each instance it just hadn't seemed right.

'Oh, look at what I've done!' Maggie clasped her hand and gave her a sympathetic smile, and it was only then Catherine registered the tears on her wet cheeks.

Quickly, she wiped them away, slightly embarrassed she'd let her emotions get the better of her. 'I'm so sorry,' she apologised. 'The truth is ...' Her heart skipped a beat as she considered, pondered, wondered. 'This baby ... this baby.' Catherine placed her hands tentatively on her bump, willing her love to grow as the tiny life inside of her did. 'The truth is that we've been waiting on this baby for so long.' She swallowed, willing the tears to stay at bay. 'And William, well, he's been wonderful and so looking forward to being a father.'

And then Maggie, as perceptive as ever, tilted her head and considered her carefully. 'And you, Kitty?' she asked quietly, gently. 'Are you looking forward to being a mother?'

'Of course I am!' Catherine replied a little too enthusiastically, even though it was a lie. Catherine was anything but ready.

She told herself that by the time the baby was born, she would be ready. How could she not? With Pearl she had loved her as soon as she realised a life was forming inside of her, a life created with love.

She loved William and this child had been borne out of love, and yet, when she felt the flutters of the first movement and then the first kick, it all felt a little strange.

Her belly grew faster this time, the baby took up too much room, and Catherine found herself resenting how her body felt it was no longer her own. William treated her like a goddess, as if she were carrying the heir to the throne of England. She should have revelled in all the attention – the loving, the joy he was feeling – but it only served to highlight all that she was lacking. To make matters worse, the baby was due the week of her birthday.

'The ninth is Catherine's birthday,' William said. 'Wouldn't that be a nice present, darling?'

'Certainly,' the doctor said, not bothering to wait for Catherine's response. 'Your first baby born on your birthday! You'll be able to share the celebration every year.'

Neither man seemed to notice how horrified Catherine was at the prospect. Catherine willed the child to come before the ninth and in the end, her prayers were answered.

From the moment her waters broke and she went through the first contraction, Catherine felt as if she were transported back to that July day some eight years ago. Memories flooded her mind, nausea rolled through her. Her body wanted to give up before the fight.

'I can't do this.' She clutched William's hand as they wheeled her into the delivery room.

'Of course you can.' His words were meant to soothe, but all they did was kick up her alarm.

'We'll take care of you, Mrs Bennett.' The nurse smiled reassuringly. 'First-time mothers are always a little anxious, but don't fret, we'll have a baby in your arms before you know it.'

Catherine blinked. There was something oddly familiar about the nurse. Her voice was muffled slightly by the mask but it was her eyes ...

It couldn't be.

She was imagining things.

Another wave of pain washed over her, pulling her attention to the tightening of her belly as the next round of contractions rolled through.

'We're ready to go now, Doctor Bennett,' the nurse informed her husband. 'You can go into the waiting area.'

When William made the move to leave, Catherine tightened her vice grip on his hand, her knuckles white. 'No,' she whispered. 'Please.'

William looked at her for a moment before answering. 'I'm not leaving.'

'But Doctor Dunlop –'

'I said, I'm not leaving,' he said firmly. 'Doctor Dunlop will be fine with it.'

Four hours later, their son John Edward Bennett was born on 8 October 1950.

As the nurse placed the screaming baby in her arms, Catherine felt the dual tugs of joy and heartbreak battling in her heart.

'He's perfect,' she murmured, mesmerised by the sudden love she felt for this tiny human.

'He certainly is,' William said proudly, blinking furiously, doing all he could not to shed a tear.

'Thank you.' She smiled. 'Thank you for being there with me.'

William pressed his lips to her head.

Catherine held onto her baby even when the nurse came to take him to the nursery.

'Don't worry, Mrs Bennett. You'll get him back soon enough. Rest now, you're exhausted.'

But Catherine didn't rest. Nor did she sleep properly that night, for every time she closed her eyes, the sound of a crying baby shook her from her slumber. When the confines of her bed became too much, she pulled off the covers and went to the window, gazing out to the luminous moon shining in the dead of night. Somewhere under its glow slept her daughter, a child she'd never had the chance to hold and yet, Catherine loved her as much as her son.

Time may have dulled the ache, but today old wounds had opened up and the pain was as raw and fresh as the day Pearl was taken from her.

William had his child. He had the family he wanted. Now Catherine would ask for the same. Somehow, some way she would make him see how important it was to have all her children together.

Time and time again Catherine had asked William to help her look for Pearl and he'd gone back on his word. It was time to make him keep his promise.

Thirty-four

Skeletons In The Closet

Melbourne, January 1960

The church seemed airless. Outside the summer sun was high in the cloudless sky and Pearl knew that once the service was over and they left to go to the burial, the searing heat would be unbearable. Sweat pooled in her bra, and her skirt stuck to the wooden pew she was sitting on. To her right, her father stood ramrod straight, his gazed fixed on the walnut-brown coffin at the foot of the altar.

What's he thinking? Pearl mused.

Is he wondering how he will live without her? Is his heart broken? Or is he angry?

Pearl concluded with a heavy sigh that while her father may in fact be feeling every bit heartbroken, he most probably would be wondering what the hell he was going to do with Pearl.

He needn't worry. Even before her mother's death, she'd been planning on leaving. She was almost eighteen, after all, and the fights between her and her father were getting more frequent and, if she were completely honest, more bitter. Her resentment towards him was growing.

As an only child, her parents had been doting on her. It wasn't often that she went without or didn't get exactly what she wanted. She was often the envy of her classmates with the newest and best clothes and toys. While they coveted her material possessions, Pearl wished she had brothers and sisters like most of them had. Large families to share, play and laugh with.

In grade three, Martha Moss had asked why she had no brothers or sisters and Pearl had shrugged. 'I dunno.'

That night she asked her mother why. 'You are our precious Pearl and we want to give you all we can. If you had brothers and sisters you would need to share. Would you really want that? And you would fight – all the time.'

Pearl didn't think sharing would've been so bad and as for having someone to fight with, her father filled that role neatly.

'What's he doing here?' Her father's clipped tone snapped her out of her thoughts. Pearl turned her head to follow his gaze and found herself sucking in a breath.

Donald.

'He's here for me,' she replied, feeling a hint of a smile playing on her lips.

Donald's eyes met hers and the grief that gripped her heart like a vice lessened some. He had a habit of doing that – making the worst things in her life feel even the tiniest bit better. Pearl was the first to admit her relationship with Donald wasn't a conventional one. They'd met only weeks after her seventeenth birthday at a party held by Pam Withers, a colleague from secretarial college. Pam was twenty-one, recently married and as far as Pearl was concerned, the most stylish woman she'd ever met. Donald worked with Pam's husband Garry.

'That's Donald,' Pam had told her the moment Donald walked into the room. 'He's *divorced*.' Pam had whispered the word 'divorce' as if it were a curse.

Although Pearl didn't know anyone who was actually divorced, the innuendo surrounding Pam's words irked her. 'I wonder what happened,' Pearl said, musing out loud. Donald was tall and breathtakingly good looking. Truth be told, he was the most handsome man she'd ever seen.

'His wife left him,' Pam dutifully informed her. 'Lucky they didn't have any children, otherwise it would've been even *more* tragic.'

By the end of that night, Pearl would discover that while Pam had given her some facts, there was more to Donald's story than met the eye.

He was recently separated from his wife, Meredith. They'd been married for six years and it was true that she'd left him for someone else. But what struck Pearl most about Donald and perhaps what had initially attracted her to him, besides his tall, dark and handsome looks, was how humble he was. He didn't resent his wife for leaving him, not because he felt he was to blame for the marriage breakdown, it was more that it gave them both the freedom they needed.

'We obviously weren't the loves of each other's lives,' Donald said, as he reached out and wound a finger around one of her corkscrew curls. In the background someone had put an Elvis album on the record player. 'I mean, how else would I be able to find my true love, you know what I mean?'

Pearl's mouth was dry. 'I've never been in love.' Her head was spinning. Donald's gaze was intense, mesmerising. He made her body feel hot and cold all at once.

'How old are you, Pearl?' He cocked his head to one side.

Her heart skipped a beat. She knew Donald was older. He'd been married for six years, so she'd presumed he was in his late twenties and Pearl was sure when she told him her age, he would lose interest. At least she assumed he was interested. He'd brought her over a drink – whisky. She'd never really drunk alcohol before, unless she counted the few sips of champagne she'd had at her cousin's wedding last year. The amber-coloured liquid burnt at first, but she soon discovered taking small, measured sips worked better and now, as she was drinking her second drink, she could feel her body relaxing.

'I'm seventeen,' she stammered, watching the surprise in Donald's eyes. 'But I'm not at school. I'm at secretarial college with Pam,' she added hastily.

The rhythm and blues number 'Jailhouse Rock' blasted through the room and Donald smiled. 'You're jailbait, Pearl.'

Pearl took a sip of her drink and felt her cheeks flush. She waited for him to tell her she was too young, that she was a child, but he didn't. He leaned close and whispered in her ear, 'I really want to kiss you, Pearl.'

His breath was warm, voice so smooth and her body was jelly. Words wouldn't come, so she had resorted to nodding. And then, as Elvis sang about drummer boys from Illinois, Pearl's own heart went *crash, boom, bang*, as Donald's lips crushed hers.

She was smitten from that moment on. Her mother initially had been wary of her relationship. Oddly enough, it was more the age difference than Donald's marital status that had bothered her, but it didn't take long for her mother to see how madly in love she and Donald were.

'I want you to be careful, my precious Pearl. Donald is more ... experienced than you.'

Her mother's face had gone bright red and Pearl had hugged her tight. They were close, always had been, but sex was never something they had spoken about. 'Aww, don't worry, Mamma, I wouldn't do anything, not until we're married. I promise.'

While she had meant it at the time, weeks later she had broken the promise she'd made to her mother. It would be months before

Donald was allowed to be divorced and even though he was not pressuring her, Pearl wanted to be with him in every possible way.

Guilt ate at her for lying to her mother – even more so now that she was so suddenly taken away.

'He's not welcome. She wouldn't have wanted him here.' Her father's voice was loaded with bitterness. Pearl bit her tongue and gripped the pew in front of her, her hand digging tightly till her knuckles whitened. She wanted to tell her father that he was the last person to profess knowing what his late wife would have wanted. He spent more time at the pub than he did at home. In fact, he had insisted on the wake being held at their local pub, a place her mother had frequented only once or twice. It was a wake fit for his funeral, not hers. And right now, Pearl wished that were the case.

Her relationship with her father had never been easy. Even as a child she recalled his aloofness, a stark contrast to her mother's warm love. It was as if he had never wanted her. As she grew older, she concluded that being an only child, her suspicions had merit. It wasn't that he ever abused her, not physically anyway, but there were times she would catch her father staring at her as if she were some sort of alien.

Their relationship grew more strained over the years, and now, with Donald in her life, it seemed to have reached fever pitch. To be fair, Pearl was fairly certain that no matter who she was with, her father would disapprove. But Donald was eleven years her senior and he was still married to someone else. Her father took these two facts and used them as ammunition. He would pick fights with Pearl, usually when her mother wasn't around. Coward. He was scared that she would put him in his place, as she so often did when he and Pearl fought. It wasn't often her mother didn't side with her. Last week, Pearl had come home late one night. Donald had parked in front of her parents' house and he had leaned in for a kiss. One thing had led to another, and they ended up having a steamy session in the back seat.

'Your parents ...' Donald had protested when she reached for the button of his trousers.

'They're asleep,' Pearl had assured him, but some time later as she let herself inside the house, she discovered her father was awake.

'You were outside a while.' His tone was accusatory.

'We were talking.'

He pursed his lips, not buying a word of it. Pearl waited, braced for his wrath. They were alone, he had the perfect opportunity, but instead he remained silent. When it was clear he wasn't going to say anything, Pearl turned and as she headed towards her room, she swore she heard him mutter, 'Like mother, like daughter.' But it was late and her ears were still ringing from the band Donald had taken her to see.

The funeral service concluded and Pearl was able to move away from standing next to her father. Her mother's sisters – her aunts Rosa and Stella – walked over to her side as they followed the coffin out of the church. 'You were the light of her life,' Rosa said, her eyes shining with unshed tears. 'She'd wanted a child for so long.'

'And then she found you,' Stella said, taking Pearl's hand.

Found me?

Pearl felt her brow furrow.

'Pearl,' her father called and as if on cue, her aunts dropped their arms from around her waist and stepped away.

'I'll see you both later,' she said quietly, making a mental note to ask what Stella had meant.

In the car on the way to the cemetery, she wound down the window, desperate for fresh air. Gathering her thick curly hair from the nape of her neck, she willed the breeze to cool her some, but there was nothing but hot air blowing in. She fixed her gaze on the passing scene, watching the world whiz by as the city began to disappear.

The burial was short. Pearl wondered if Father Evans had purposely skipped a page or two, and in some ways she couldn't blame him. The poor man was as red as a lobster and struggling in the heat. Her father showed no signs of offence at the shortened ceremony, promptly grabbing a handful of earth and throwing it in the grave without a word. Pearl couldn't be so cut and dry. Tears had evaded her, but the moment she picked up the soil in her hand, they flowed thick and fast. Hot air hit her face, quickly drying her streaked cheeks as she clutched her closed hand to her heart and bid her mother a final farewell.

When she moved away from the foot of the grave, she felt a hand rest lightly on her back. 'Donald.' Her throat clogged with emotion.

'Here.' He offered her a handkerchief and a concerned smile.

'Thanks.' She sniffed, dabbing her eyes before blowing her nose.

'Your father told me not to bother with the wake.'

'Don't listen to him,' Pearl said firmly.

'He doesn't want me there.'

'*I* want you there.'

'I don't want to cause any problems for you,' he said, gently running his hands up and down her arms. Despite the heat, the action gave her goose bumps.

'You won't.' She shook her head. 'Besides, Mum liked you. She would've been touched you were here today.'

'She was something else. I'm sorry you lost her so young.'

'Me too.' Pearl swallowed the lump in her throat.

'I'll see you there. Maybe we can go to the Savoy later? I have some news.' His smile made her heart flutter with excitement.

'Is it what I think it is?' Pearl asked in breathless anticipation.

'I'm not saying. I didn't want to burden you with it today —'

'If it's what I think it is, I don't care. Burden me.'

Donald smiled. 'I'll see you later.'

By the time Pearl arrived at the Wellington Hotel, her grief was palpable. The loss of her mother was sudden and had it not been for her aunts and Donald, she wouldn't have made it through the day. In fact, she wouldn't have bothered to turn up to the wake. And then her father would have been furious — he would've called her selfish and ungrateful. Pearl often wondered what she had done to deserve his scorn. He treated her as a liability, a burden, and not the long-awaited child her mother had touted her to be.

When did it all start? Her recollections were sketchy, but it was roughly when she was twelve or thirteen. They were at Aunt Rosa's, making pasta, something she did often with her mother, aunts, cousins and their neighbours. Aunt Rosa lived in the biggest house Pearl had ever seen; her backyard was so big and long, it provided endless hours of entertainment for her and her cousins when they were growing up. The laundry was at the end of the property; Aunt Rosa liked it that way because it was closer to the washing line. With everyone else inside washing up, Pearl and her cousins Tina and Silvia headed out to the yard. The boys were playing soccer, as they usually did, and her little cousin Dario kicked the ball to her.

'I'm all messy and I need to wash my hands. They're covered in flour.'

'Oh, come on, Pearl! You don't need your hands,' Dario yelled back.

The kid had a point so she kicked the ball around with the boys for a while, then caught up to Tina and Silvia and told them she would see them back inside.

Pearl was scrubbing her fingers with soap to soften the dried flour on them when a shadow appeared behind her. When she turned, her cousin Paulo was standing in the laundry doorway.

Assuming he wanted to use the water to cool off after running around outside, Pearl turned off the tap and reached for the towel. 'I'm finished,' she told him as she dried her hands and moved aside from the basin. To her astonishment, Paulo didn't go to the basin but headed straight for her and kissed her.

In shock, Pearl pushed him away. Her heart thumping, her lips stinging, her head spinning. 'Paulo!' she yelled when her voice finally returned. 'Why would you do that?'

Paulo turned bright red, his eyes as wide as saucers. 'Pearl, I'm so sorry ... I thought that because ...'

'Because what? Because I kicked the ball to you I wanted you to come and kiss me? You're my cousin!'

'Pearl, please forgive me, I –' He took a step towards her, but Pearl moved past him and headed straight for the house.

It took Paulo a long time to look her in the eye after that day. Last year at her cousin Tina's wedding he finally broached the subject. 'You really don't know, do you?'

'Know what?'

Paulo shook his head. 'Nothing. Not my place to say.'

Pearl hadn't pressed him on the matter any further. But today for some reason, it played on her mind. She told herself that losing her mother, the harsh reality that now it was just her father and her left, made her think of it.

'Your mother would've hated this.' Her Aunt Stella's voice snapped her back to the present. Pearl looked around the room at the crowd that had gathered to honour her mother's life, and while the company didn't seem to be a problem, the location her husband had insisted on was. Cigarette smoke billowed from the cluster of poker machines where her father and his friends had gathered.

'You're not wrong there,' Pearl said with a heavy heart.

'I offered my house, we would've had everyone pitch in and make the food, but ...' Her aunt stopped mid-sentence to blow her nose. 'You know your father.'

'I know.' Pearl wrapped a loving arm around Stella's shoulders. 'Maybe I could come over during the week after work. We can make all of Mamma's favourite foods and have our own private wake. Something that she would've wanted.'

Stella leaned against her. 'That would be wonderful.'

'We could invite Aunt Rosa, Tina, Silvia too, if she's not busy with the baby. Just the Moretti girls.'

'Oh, Pearl,' her aunt sobbed. 'I can't believe she died without telling you.'

Pearl froze. 'Telling me what? What didn't Mamma tell me, Aunt Stella?'

In an instant, her aunt sobered. 'It's nothing.' She dried her eyes, but when Stella avoided looking Pearl in the eye, she could tell it was something. A big something.

'Has this got to do with what you said earlier today? About Mamma finding me?'

'Forget I said anything.' Stella waved her hand around dismissively. 'I'm all emotional and gibbering nonsense.'

'No,' Pearl said firmly, her mind connecting all the dots at lightning speed.

The reason why Paulo thought it was okay to kiss her, and his words, 'You really don't know, do you?'

Her father's remark, 'Like mother, like daughter.'

Her aunt's comment, 'And then she found you.'

And the final nail in the coffin – 'I can't believe she died without telling you.'

There was only one explanation. A secret. A secret about her that everyone seemed to know – except her.

She wasn't who she thought she was. The realisation – the cold hard truth – hit Pearl like a slap in the face. The sting was numbing.

'Aunt Stella, tell me again where I got my blue eyes from?'

It was a question she had asked before. Many times. And each and every time she had been told the same answer.

'Pearl, please.' There was a sense of urgency in her aunt's voice, almost begging her not to ask, not to pry.

'Answer the question, Stella.' Her tone was cold. She had never spoken to her aunt with such directness, and never had she disrespected her by not calling her 'Aunt'.

Stella didn't answer. Instead she slumped her shoulders and shook her head. It was all the confession Pearl needed.

'I didn't inherit them from Nonna Ilaria, did I?' She had never seen a photo that clearly showed her grandmother's eyes. It was something she'd been told and had never questioned it. Until now.

'No.' It was a whisper, but it was as if her aunt had shouted the word from the rooftop.

Her skin began to flush hot and cold. Dread filled her stomach.

Her whole life had been a lie. Everything about her, everything she knew was a falsehood. Pearl knew that every family had skeletons hidden in the closet; what she never expected was that she would be one.

Thirty-five

The Choice

Sydney, July 1960

The sound of a loud crash, followed by wailing, had Catherine hastily wiping her hands on her apron and following the noise. There on the living-room floor was the vase her Aunt Iris had given her as a wedding present, now in tiny pieces strewn this way and that. Catherine felt the pit of her stomach drop.

She adored the vase in more ways than one, but mostly because it had come from Aunt Iris, who for the past few months had been battling lung cancer. After spending some time in a hospice, she was home now, but Catherine knew it was only a matter of time.

In the years since her mother returned to the States, Catherine's relationship with her aunt had grown stronger. As the only person, besides William, to know about Pearl, her Aunt Iris had been a source of comfort over the years, a shoulder to cry on when yet another attempt to convince her husband to look for her child had failed. She was losing a confidant, but more than that, she was losing her beloved Iris.

'Boys!' At the sound of her voice four pairs of eyes turned towards her, followed by a brief moment of silence before the finger pointing began.

'It was Matty!' Robbie declared, his blue eyes darting from between his two older brothers to Matthew, who at just shy of turning two wasn't able to defend himself like his three older brothers.

'Robert,' she said sternly as John and George, who at ten and nine should've known better, suddenly avoided eye contact. 'Was it really Matty?' She tried to keep her voice level and not convey the anger she was feeling.

Today was a hard day as it was; she didn't need to make it any harder by flying off the handle at her children.

'Yes,' six-year-old Robbie muttered, eyes glued to the floor as he kicked a piece of the broken vase with his shoe.

Catherine stooped, scooping Matthew up in her arms before he could step on a shard of the broken vase. Out of the corner of her eye she spotted John leaning over to whisper something in George's ear. It was then she noticed that George was holding something behind his back.

'George, what are you hiding?'

'Nothing!' George said guiltily.

'Hand it over, George.'

Slowly George produced a leather football and with great hesitation, and, it seemed, shame, placed it in his mother's out-stretched hand.

A heavy sigh escaped her lips. 'How many times have I asked you boys not to play football inside?'

John and George both answered with wordless shrugs while Robbie's tiny voice broke the silence, 'Lots.'

'Exactly.' Catherine glared.

'But it's raining out,' John protested.

'And we were being careful!' George piped up, obviously buoyed by his brother's defiance.

'Obviously not careful enough.' Catherine nodded to the mess around them.

'As punishment, you three boys are to go to your rooms – separately. Find a book or a toy there to occupy you before I call you for dinner.'

When no one moved, she added sternly, 'Now.'

'Yes, Mum,' three young boys muttered in unison before shuffling off.

Returning to the kitchen, Catherine placed Matthew in his highchair, only to discover the water her potatoes were boiling in had evaporated and all that was left was a pile of burnt mush. Without thinking, she grabbed the saucepan handle, only to drop it a second later, causing the pot and its contents to splatter all over the floor.

'Oh, for God's sake!' she yelled. Her hand throbbed, the agony excruciating despite letting the handle go so quickly. Catherine ran her hand under cold water for as long as she could to alleviate the pain.

'Oh no, mess!' little Matty exclaimed, his eyes wide as saucers.

'It sure is, my little man.' Catherine pressed a kiss on her baby's cheek, his pudgy hands coming out to capture her face.

'Atty kiss, Mama?' All her boys were special to her. Each one filled her heart in a different way. Maybe it was because he was her baby and gut instinct told her she wouldn't have any more children, or maybe it was because his green eyes reminded her of Eddie, but Matthew was special to Catherine.

John had been the long-awaited child.

George had been the pleasant surprise.

When Robert came along a few years later, William was convinced they were having a girl, but Catherine wasn't so sure. As different as each pregnancy had been, when she touched and spoke to her growing belly she always called it Buster. Maggie once laughed that she would never have a girl if she kept referring to her unborn child by a boy's name. She duly informed her friend that by the time the child had been conceived, the sex had already been determined. 'Well, I know that, silly. It's more that you're putting it out there – telling the universe that all you want is boys. Wouldn't you want a girl?'

'A girl would be nice,' Catherine said, but deep down she knew that if she had a girl, she would still not take Pearl's place. It was almost a relief when Matthew was born and they'd had another boy.

'Kiss?' Matty's voice broke through her reverie and a stab of guilt hit her. The poor baby had been waiting for her answer.

'Yes, Matty, kiss Mama.'

Catherine smiled as Matty's wet kisses tickled her cheek. Sometimes she felt guilty being happy with her boys when there was always a piece of her heart that she felt was missing. And that missing piece ached more on one particular day – Pearl's birthday.

Eighteen years ago today she lost her Pearl.

Eighteen years ...

Catherine had always thought by now she would have found her daughter. Anger surged through her as she recalled the day she had told William about Charlie and Pearl. He had promised, and time after time, he had broken his promise to her. When he found her crying this morning, he said nothing at first and then he sighed.

'When are you going to move past it all, Catherine? When are you going to put the past in the past and let us be a family?'

'When my family is complete.' It was her answer each and every time and normally William would walk away. He would let it be, let her grieve in peace.

But not today.

'Sometimes I wonder if you love me at all.' There was hardness in his voice, a brittleness that made her stop and look at her husband of fifteen years as if he were a stranger.

'What are you talking about? Of course I love you. You're my husband. I stood in a church and declared to love, honour and cherish you. I'm not the one breaking promises, William, you are. Remember the promise you made to me? The promise you made to help me look for my child?'

'I remember,' he said tersely. His back was to her as he looped his tie, but in the reflection of the vanity mirror, Catherine clearly saw his frosty expression. 'My promise was to look for the child when the time was right. But from the moment we were married, you've been breaking every single vow you made. You haven't loved, honoured or cherished our children and me. Not the way you do your ghost and the other child.'

The other child.

Catherine's heart began to boil. Swallowing tears, she balled her hands into fists, knuckles white as she gripped the side of the bed. 'I told you – my heart isn't complete, it won't be unless –'

'I can't compete anymore.' He cut her off coldly without a sign of apology. 'Correction. I *won't* compete. If you insist on going against my wishes and pressing on with this ... ludicrous fantasy, then ...'

'Then what?' she spat out. 'Tell me, William. What will you do if I insist on looking for *my* child?'

His eyes softened slightly. 'Have you thought for a second that perhaps it's better this way? That God had a plan for that child and she is exactly where she ought to be?'

'Without her mother?'

'With two parents who love her. Two people who have spent the last eighteen years raising her, who undoubtedly were childless before she came into their lives. That child gave them joy. The way our children give us joy, or at least, they give me joy.'

'How dare you! How dare you insinuate that I don't love my children? They are my life!'

William blinked, straightened his tie and adjusted his cuff links. 'Then it's time you started acting as if that were the truth.'

He walked off then. Walked away without kissing her goodbye and telling her he loved her and that he'd see her tonight. He'd never done that before and it stung, but it wouldn't be until much later that the full blow would hit her like a punch in the guts.

Thirty-six

Letting Go

Melbourne, July 1960

'I found her.' They were more a breath than words. She had run up the three flights of stairs to the flat she shared with Donald. Her lips were chapped from the cold, harsh winter wind. Her hair and clothes drenched from the rain, but she didn't care. The letter, the all-important letter, was tucked snuggly in the pocket of her coat. Warm, dry and safe.

'What?' Donald's hair was still rumpled from sleep, his eyes barely open as he nursed his cup of tea.

'I found my mother.' Her heart soared as she spoke, thumping wildly as if she were a thoroughbred coming down the line in the Melbourne Cup.

'What?' Donald repeated, his eyes wide awake now. 'Where?'

Slowly, with trembling hands she reached into her pocket and retrieved the letter. Handing it over so Donald could read it.

Ever since the day of her mamma's funeral earlier in the year – the day Pearl had discovered her whole life was a lie, the family she thought was hers wasn't, the mother she had just buried in the ground wasn't really her mother – Donald had been there.

She had fled the pub, unable to look at her Aunt Stella, or face the man she had called Father for almost eighteen years. It was only luck that Donald was walking in as she was walking out, and after taking one look at her face he knew there was something wrong.

He took her away, drove her to his house where she told him all she had just discovered. Then she made him drive her home where she tore up her parents' room till she found what she was after. Her birth certificate.

Catherine McGarrie. Her mother's name was Catherine and she'd been just sixteen years old when Pearl had been born.

After the shock of learning she'd been adopted, Pearl didn't think anything else would surprise her, until she discovered this.

Her mother had been sixteen, still a child herself and younger than Pearl was now when she'd given birth. She'd been born in Crown Street Women's Hospital in Sydney but what astounded her even more was that under the section where her father's name should've been listed was the word 'Unknown'.

She grabbed her birth certificate, as well as the papers pertaining to her adoption, and fled the house with only the clothes on her back. By the time she returned the next day, her father had changed the locks, but Donald helped her break in to gather what she could of her things.

'What are you going to do?' Donald asked her as she walked in and peeled off her sodden coat.

'I don't know.' The cold had finally hit her and her teeth were chattering. Her fingers were numb, making it hard to remove her soaked dress.

'Tell you what,' Donald said as he helped her out of her clothes. 'You go have a shower and warm up and I'll make us some hot tea and toast.'

'Sounds good.'

As she slowly defrosted under the scalding water, Pearl closed her eyes and imagined meeting her mother. From the moment she had seen her name, Pearl was convinced her mother had a good reason for giving her up. Perhaps because she was so young Catherine had nowhere to go. She was all but convinced her father, whoever he was, would've abandoned her when she told him she was pregnant, leaving her with more than tears and heartache to carry.

Walking into the tiny kitchen, she knew what her next step was going to be.

'I want to go to Sydney,' she announced.

Donald placed two steaming mugs on the table and looked up. 'Are you sure that's what you want?' He didn't ask the question by way of dissuading her. He had been nothing but supportive to her throughout the process.

'It is,' Pearl said with unwavering certainty as she sat down and wrapped her hands around her mug.

'Okay then.'

'Would you come with me?'

'I will,' he said. 'On one condition.'

'What's that?'

'The day of your mother's funeral, my divorce came through.'

'I know that already. It was a red letter day for us both.'

'What you don't know is, on that day I was also going to ask you to marry me.'

'What?'

'I know, it's kind of morbid. I was going to ask you to marry me after your mother's wake –'

'No. I think it's beautiful.' She reached over and grabbed his hand, tears stinging her eyes.

'But after you discovered you were adopted, I thought I would wait. Wait till you got some certainty in your life before I threw in a question that could change it all for you again.'

'Donald, *you* have been my certainty. You've been my rock. I couldn't have managed these past six months without you.'

He gave her a smile. 'Does that mean you will marry me?'

'What do you think?'

'But you're barely eighteen and I'm almost thirty. I'm an old man.'

'Hardly,' she said.

'But I've been married before. I don't think I can get married in a church again.'

'Are you trying to talk me out of this? I don't care if we're married in a church. I just want to marry you.'

'Okay, then. I guess we're going to Sydney and getting married.'

Pearl scraped back her chair and deposited herself on Donald's lap. 'You need to ask me first.'

'You're sitting on my lap. I think you need to get up so I can follow tradition.'

Pearl gave him a coy smile. 'We've been living in sin for months now. I think we're past tradition.'

His eyes danced with mischief as he played with the ties on her robe. 'You're right. Perhaps it's time for a different approach.'

Pearl walked her hands up the side of his torso and interlocked them on the nape of his neck. 'Yes, I agree.'

'Pearl, will you marry me?' Donald's smile was wide and it filled her with hope.

She dipped her head, leaning in and kissing him before answering. 'Yes.'

'I think you were supposed to answer before we kissed.'

She shrugged. 'We're done with tradition, remember?'

'There's one tradition that I do like, though.'

'What's that?' Pearl asked.

'This.' Donald moved fast. He stood up with Pearl in his arms and carried her over the threshold of the bedroom.

'We're supposed to do that after we're married!' Pearl said between her shrieks of laughter. She had never been so happy in her whole life. She was going to Sydney to marry Donald and meet her mother.

Three days later, Pearl and Donald began their journey to Sydney. The long drive was made even more arduous by the relentless rain. By the time they reached the outskirts of Sydney, the rain had eased and they were greeted by a cloudless sky.

Donald had booked them a room at a pub in St Peters. He'd been to Sydney once before and knew a little about the city.

The lady at the front desk made a point of mentioning how she noticed the absence of wedding rings. Apparently she wasn't comfortable renting a room to an unwed couple. 'Don't you worry about that,' Donald said enthusiastically, not the least bit put off by her judgemental tone. 'We're getting married tomorrow so this is our last night of sinning.'

The woman, who wasn't that much older than Donald, said nothing, pulling her lips into a thin line to convey her disapproval. Her judgement irked Pearl, she itched to say something about being a nosy parker and how she should mind her own beeswax, but Donald simply smiled and winked at the woman as she handed over the room keys.

'You have a nice day, ma'am,' he said, sliding his arm around Pearl's waist, and as they walked out of the reception area he gave her bottom a purposeful squeeze. An audible gasp was the last thing they heard.

Pearl held her laughter till they were out of earshot, her belly still aching by the time they reached their room. Donald had a habit of making her laugh, and right now it felt good. Her stomach had been a bundle of nerves ever since receiving the letter with her birth mother's details, but now it was at fever pitch. This morning when they'd stopped at a service station just outside of Goulburn, the realisation of what she was about to do had hit her and she'd thrown up. She was too nervous to eat or drink anything.

'What do you want to do first?' Donald asked, his lanky frame sprawled on the bed, a boyish smile on his lips. In an instant, the nerves were gone and excitement took its place. Her heart was bursting with love for this man – a man that come tomorrow, would be her husband.

'I don't know,' Pearl said as she shrugged out of her coat and draped it over the back of a chair. 'I should be tired after that drive, but I'm not. I have all this ...'

'Energy?' Donald offered.

'Yes, I mean, I'm going to meet my mother.' She hiccupped nervously. 'What if I'm wrong about her and she doesn't want to see me, Donald? I mean she gave me away, after all?' Suddenly a giant ball of fear wrapped itself around her heart and tightened itself like a stronghold. The room felt airless; she clutched at her chest, struggling to draw oxygen into her lungs as her mind whirled with a thousand thoughts.

'Hey, my darling, don't think like that.' Donald propped himself up on his elbows and patted the bed. 'Come 'ere.'

She climbed onto the bed, removing her shoes and letting them drop to the floor, and snuggled close against his broad chest.

'Relax,' he murmured softly as he eased them back onto the pillows. 'Close your eyes and take a deep breath in ... then out ...' Pearl listened to the gentle sound of Donald's calming voice, losing herself in the rhythm of breathing, letting it lull her to relaxation.

'Just breathe.' He stroked her brow, then her forehead with feather-like touches. 'Whatever happens when you meet your mother, remember that you have me. You will always have me by your side, Pearl. I love you. Tomorrow we're getting married and after that we've got our whole lives ahead of us. If that includes your mother, great, but if that doesn't, then that's fine too, because I'm here and I'm not going anywhere. We've got each other.'

Pearl felt the tightening around her heart give way. With Donald next to her she felt safe, warm, loved. All her anxiety – her fears about how the meeting with her mother would play out – disappeared.

'We've got each other,' she mumbled sleepily; her body felt heavy and she could feel herself slipping into slumber.

Donald was right, no matter what the outcome, she would still have him, and for now, that's what mattered the most.

On her wedding day, Pearl didn't wear white. It wasn't because she was a staunch traditionalist and forwent the customary colour for brides. It was simply because she had a lovely ivory dress with a full skirt. The fabric was a little light for July, but she had figured that with Sydney's climate being milder and more forgiving than Melbourne's harsh winters, she could get away with it. And certainly by the clear day that graced them when they stepped outside, she would have. But ten minutes before they were to leave, Pearl was sitting on the bed, her tummy aflutter with nerves. Nerves that quickly escalated to waves of nausea and before she had a chance to register what was about to happen, she was wearing her breakfast.

Donald rushed from the bathroom, half shaven, and cleaned her up.

'I've ruined our wedding day!' Tears pricked her eyes, shame and anger eating at her.

'You've done no such thing,' Donald soothed as he helped her out of the ruined dress. 'You could be wearing a potato sack and I would still think you look beautiful.'

'Hardly,' Pearl sniffled.

'Hey.' Donald hooked a finger under her chin and tilted her face till she met his gaze. 'I mean it. I love you, Pearl. I don't care what you wear. I just want to marry you.' His eyes were full of love and honesty, and Pearl could hardly believe that this man who loved her so much was soon to be her husband.

'I just want to marry you too,' she whispered. 'I can't wait to be your wife.'

'Well then, let's get you into your wedding dress, Mrs Peterson.' His smile was luminous, infectious.

'Pearl Peterson.' She rolled her soon-to-be married name off her tongue, a shiver of excitement flowing through her. 'I like the sound of that.'

She changed into a navy dress with a cream sash, the dress that she had bought to meet her mother in. Donald had registered their intent to marry the day before, so all they needed to do was turn up and let someone marry them. He told her that he had somewhere special in mind for lunch afterwards. Then tomorrow, they would visit her mother as husband and wife. She knew it was crazy, but she wanted to show her mother that she was happy, that her life was a good one.

'Ready?' Donald asked as he fiddled with his suit jacket.

'Who's nervous now?' Pearl smiled.

'Not nervous, I'm excited, impatient to make you mine.'

'I *am* yours,' she whispered, standing on tiptoes and planting a soft kiss on his lips. 'Always.'

'Right then, your chariot awaits.' He offered her his arm, and together they headed towards Donald's Holden that was still covered with morning dew. When he opened the door for her, she saw the posy of flowers on her seat.

'Donald!' she gasped.

He reached around her and picked up the lovely combination of carnations and tuberoses. Bright and cheerful, they were perfect.

'Every bride deserves a bouquet on her wedding day.'

Plucking a tiny carnation out of the bunch she slipped it into his buttonhole. 'I love you, now let's go and get ourselves hitched.'

The ceremony was simple. No frills, just her and Donald, the celebrant and a witness who was a ring-in from a nearby office. Her voice was shaky as she said her vows, but with Donald's strong hands holding hers, the nerves quickly faded. It was, as far as Pearl was concerned, the most perfect wedding.

That evening they sat watching the sunset on Bondi Beach. Dusk was quickly disappearing and soon the inky night would take over, but right now, Pearl wanted to soak in every moment, every second of their wedding day. 'It's beautiful here,' she murmured, cocooned by Donald's warmth. 'It makes me wonder what my life would've been like if I grew up here.'

'But then you wouldn't have met me.' He pressed a kiss on top of her head.

'Yes, that's true.'

'How about we see how tomorrow goes, and if you want to move closer to get to know your mother, we can move here.'

'Move here?' She turned to see his face, to see if he was mucking around with her, but even in the fading light she could see how serious he was.

'Sure.' He shrugged as if it wasn't a big deal. 'I can get a teaching job here and you can find a secretarial job, or you can stay home. Whatever you want to do is fine with me.'

Pearl squealed in delight and hugged her new husband tight.

'Pearl, your fingers are freezing!' He took her hands in his and rubbed warmth into them.

'I know.' She shivered. 'But I want to stay here. I don't want this day to end.'

'It doesn't have to.' Donald stood, scooping her up with him. 'Let's go back to the hotel and enjoy the rest of our wedding day, Mrs Peterson.'

Pearl smiled, her head resting against the warmth of his chest, lulled by the sound of his beating heart.

At that moment she was drunk on love, so high with happiness. For years later she would look back on this moment, on the exact moment, and remember the last time her life was blissful.

William was late. Often if he had a function on after work, or if he planned to catch up with a colleague for dinner, he would call and let her know. Sometimes he would call during a lull between patients or in the three-hour break when the surgery was closed, but he hadn't called today.

After their fight in the morning, Catherine didn't expect a call, nor did she expect a lunchtime visit, but she was disappointed when he wasn't home for dinner. She waited as long as she could before sitting the older boys down.

'Dad's not here,' John said as they all sat down around the kitchen table. On the days that Maisey, their housekeeper, worked, they ate dinner in the living room, but the two days she had off, Catherine made them eat in the kitchen. It was something her mother would've baulked at if she knew. Her mother would have baulked at the fact that Catherine insisted their housekeeper have two days off each week, too.

'He had something come up after work.'

'But he normally tells us when he won't be home for dinner,' John said.

'It just came up.'

'Will he be home to tuck us into bed?' Robert asked. Of all her sons, Robert idolised William the most. They all adored him. Often the first question when they woke in the morning was, 'Where's Dad?' In the afternoon when she picked the older boys up from school it would be, 'When's Dad going to be home?'

Three pairs of grey–blue eyes awaited her response. How could she answer when she didn't know where her husband was?

'He's going to try to be home soon,' Catherine said as she seated herself at the table. When no one made a move to eat, she looked at her sons. 'Well, come on, the food will be cold in a minute.'

They ate in relative silence. The boys sulking, Catherine forcing her food down, the anxious feeling in her stomach killing the little appetite she had. When William wasn't home by bedtime, her temper grew. It was one thing to be angry with her and to punish her, but to miss the boys' bedtime without any notice was cruel. Robert was tearful, and even Matty, her normally happy and placid baby, was irritable.

'Boys, bed now!' she bellowed when their whining pushed her patience to the limits.

Later, when the house was deathly quiet and her ears started to ring, Catherine regretted how cross she'd been with the boys. If she were honest, it didn't take much for them to make her raise her voice. She often felt like a bad mother when she screamed. William never raised his voice. But then again, William was rarely home.

The last thought left a bitter taste in her mouth. She lit a fire in the living room and poured a generous glass of William's finest single malt scotch. Swirling the amber drink in the crystal glass, she watched as the light from the flames seemed to dance with the liquid. The grandfather clock chimed nine times and Catherine sighed. At this point, she expected William was out drinking to drown his frustration with her and wasn't coming home anytime soon. She placed her glass on the side table and went into her bedroom. Opening the wardrobe, she then pulled the chair from her vanity and carefully removed the red Arnott's tin from the top shelf. Tucking it under her arm, she went back into the sitting room and placed the box on her lap. She took a sip of her drink, then another, then another, building the courage to open the box.

When her tumbler was empty, she refilled it and with shaking hands, she slowly pried opened the tin, her Pandora's box. Her secrets. A part of her life that seemed to belong to someone else. It had been years since she opened it. Years since she allowed herself the memory of her lost life, her lost loves.

First she picked up Pearl's baby bracelet, running her fingers over the tiny smooth beads. Carefully she placed it back in the box as if it were a fragile piece of glass and picked up Charlie's letter.

She sucked in a breath and held it there, trapped in her lungs, as she removed the pages from the envelope, and then for the first time in so many years, she allowed herself to remember him. She imagined his voice as she read his words of love and promise and the undying passion he felt for her. She was weeping by the time she came to the end of the letter. She cried for their lost love, cruelly taken away by war, and finally she cried for their lost Pearl, a child taken from her without her consent. She downed her second drink and was halfway through her third when a knock at the door startled her. Glancing at the clock, she could see it was past ten. Whoever could it be? She stood, her balance slightly unsteady, her mind addled by alcohol. With trepidation, she opened the door and gasped.

Two policemen stood looking at her with matching grim expressions.

'Mrs Bennett?' The taller, slightly older of the two spoke first.

'Yes.' Catherine breathed out but already her chest was tight. 'Is something wrong? Has something happened to William?' Her voice was a panicked shrill. She didn't need to wait for their response, their exchanged glances spoke volumes.

'I'm afraid we have some bad news, Mrs Bennett. Can we come in, please?'

In an instant she was stone cold sober, and in a blink of an eye, her life changed.

She wasn't sure how long it had been, only that when she woke up, she was in a hospital and her head was killing her. Confusion set in before she remembered.

The car. The screeching tyres. The crash. Then ... nothing.

It happened so fast; one minute they were laughing, the next thing Pearl remembered were the blood-curdling screams ringing in her ears. The memory of the sound sent a shiver through her, intensifying when she realised the screams had been hers.

'Donald?' Her throat was dry; it hurt to breathe. She tried to move but her body ached everywhere.

'Donald?' she said again, this time louder, with more urgency. A few moments later, a nurse was in her room.

'You're awake.' She smiled then proceeded to check the drip that was attached to her. 'How are you feeling?'

'Where's Donald?' Pearl asked.

'Donald? I'm sorry, dear, I don't know who that is. Was he in the car with you when you had the accident?'

'Yes. He was driving.'

'I just came on shift. A doctor will be by shortly to see you. Maybe he knows what happened to your friend.'

'He's my husband,' Pearl said as fatigue engulfed her and she felt herself slipping into the darkness again. 'Donald is my husband.'

Time was a funny thing when you were waiting for something to happen. For the past week, Catherine had been by William's bedside waiting. Waiting to see if he would wake up, waiting to see if he was going to be all right. The problem was that while she waited, life and the world didn't stop. There were children to look after, to feed, to get ready for school, a baby to attend to. By the third day, Catherine knew she was struggling, so Maisey and Maggie stepped in and took over at home so she could spend more time with William.

When the policemen told her about the accident, how William's car collided with another, how they were not sure about her husband's state, only that he had been rushed into surgery with internal bleeding, guilt consumed her.

The doctors told her that they'd discovered William had suffered a heart attack just as he was leaving the pub. Catherine's first thought was why would William get in the car after having a heart attack.

It was a small heart attack, they explained; the accident had caused the more serious damage.

'But he's only thirty-eight,' Catherine had uttered to one of the doctors. 'He's fit and healthy. How could he possibly have had a heart attack?'

'Stress,' was the doctor's response.

As she paced the linoleum floors of the hospital corridor, anxiously waiting to hear how the surgery went, waiting to hear if her husband was still alive, guilt snaked its way through to her heart. Catherine had no doubt that she'd contributed to William's stress. She suddenly understood his frustration. Her refusal to let go of Charlie, living one foot in the past, was driving a wedge between them. She knew that if William survived and if she had any chance of ensuring her marriage was a happy one, she needed to let Charlie go – once and for all. But letting Charlie go meant giving up on Pearl, and that broke her heart.

Days later, as she sat by William's bedside waiting to learn his fate, her remorse still wasn't assuaged. If anything, she knew that if William didn't make it, she would never forgive herself. The same way that she would never forgive herself for letting Charlie and Pearl go. It was a no-win situation.

'Catherine?' Maggie's voice broke her thoughts and it was then she realised she was crying. 'Has the doctor been in? Is there any news?' Her tone was anxious and Catherine could tell Maggie was concerned her tears were a result of bad news.

Catherine glanced at William and her heart squeezed when she saw how helpless he appeared as he lay motionless. She unfurled her legs from beneath her and stood up. Every muscle in her body ached from sleeping on the hard hospital armchair. She hadn't been this sleep deprived since Matty was a newborn. 'No,' she said, wiping her wet cheeks with the back of her hand. 'No news yet.'

Maggie walked over and enveloped her in a tight hug. 'You need to be strong. Dry those tears now, Kitty.'

Hearing her childhood name only made her sob more. 'Oh, Maggie! I've been such an awful wife.'

'Hush now,' Maggie chided. 'Don't talk silly things.'

'It's true. The morning of the accident, William and I had a terrible fight. It's all my fault.'

'Catherine, you didn't cause William to have a heart attack.'

'But he was so angry with me. I've never seen him so *angry*. And it was all my fault ... all my fault.'

'Whatever the fight was about, I'm sure that once William wakes up, it will all be forgotten. Then you can concentrate on getting him better and home to your boys.'

'But it'll never be forgotten, Maggie. Not if I don't make some changes.'

'Catherine?' Maggie eyed her with suspicion. 'What are you talking about? Have you ...' She lowered her voice to a whisper despite the fact they were alone. 'Have you been having an affair?'

Catherine let out a half-sob, half-strangled laugh. 'If only it were that simple. This is far worse.'

'I don't understand.' Maggie furrowed her brow. 'What could be worse than an affair?'

For years she'd been keeping Pearl a secret and now it was time to tell her friend. She sucked in a deep breath, and slowly let it out before meeting Maggie's gaze. 'On July eleventh, 1942, I gave birth to a baby girl. A baby girl that I have kept a secret from everyone apart from William.'

And then she told Maggie the whole story. About Charlie, how she lost him at Pearl Harbor, how she discovered she was with child when they arrived in San Francisco, and how her parents made the decision to send her and her mother to Australia.

'They took her away from me, Maggie. They took my precious girl away before I could hold her, before I could see her ...'

'But you were sixteen,' Maggie said softly. 'You were just a child yourself.'

'I know. That's why I told William about her. I told him that he needed to know before he asked me to marry him. I wanted him to have the chance to walk away.'

'Catherine, William was mad about you, he still is. He was never going to walk away.'

'I made him promise to help me look for my baby girl, and he agreed. He said that once the time was right, we would do it. But it never was, Maggie. There was always something, some reason, and then the morning of the accident, it all came to a head. I accused him of making an empty promise, one that he never intended to honour, and he accused me of not being committed to our marriage, to our children.'

He was right, Catherine thought.

'Remember the Dorseys who lived next to my parents?'

Catherine strained her memory. She remembered a kindly older widow who had the most fragrant roses growing in her front yard. 'Yes, vaguely. Why?'

'She and her husband couldn't have any children, and years later they adopted a little boy, Morris. Morris was about five or six, but he was so tiny he looked about three. I remember the first day I saw him. He was dirty and scruffy and the skinniest little thing you ever did see. Within months Morris started filling out; in fact, he became rather plump. But the biggest change I saw was in Mr and Mrs Dorsey. Morris had brought out a light in them that I never knew existed. Truth be told, before that little boy, I thought them a pair of old cranks.'

Catherine was silent for a moment. She knew why Maggie was telling her the story about the Dorseys. 'You think Pearl is better off where she is, don't you?'

Maggie nodded. 'I think that deep down you know this, too. I think when William made you the promise he meant it. I know you, Catherine. I know that when you put your mind to something, nothing and no one can stop you. If you really thought it was the right thing to look for Pearl, you would've done so, even on your own.'

Catherine opened her mouth to argue, then closed it again when she realised Maggie was right. 'It's time to let go, isn't it?'

'Only you can know that for sure, Catherine.'

And she did. Catherine knew that she needed William to pull through so they could finally be a family, and she knew that while Charlie and Pearl would always be in her heart, she needed to let them go.

Thirty-seven

The Letter

Melbourne, August 1965

Pearl grabbed the wad of letters sticking out from the tiny letterbox and trudged up the flight of stairs. Shoving the envelopes under one arm, she fished around in her handbag in search of her keys. When she finally found them, she jiggled one into the lock and turned the handle. It wouldn't budge. She knew what she needed to do to get the door open, there was only one thing she could do to open the damn thing. Sucking in a deep breath, she used her shoulder to give it an all-mighty nudge. The door opened, the nudge worked every time, but it also always aggravated the pain. Rubbing her shoulder, she walked in, deposited what were likely all bills on the kitchen table, and then went to have a hot shower. Heat seemed to alleviate the dull ache that, even five years after the accident, was yet to fully disappear.

Five years. She could hardly believe it had been half a decade since the accident that had shattered her life.

Donald had died. She found out later that he was pronounced dead at the scene. Pearl had been in a coma for three days. The broken collarbone was the first thing she discovered. Then she was told she had lost the baby. Donald's baby. A baby she didn't even know she had been carrying.

And then, as if to rub salt on the open wound that was her bleeding heart, came the biggest blow. The internal injuries had been so severe that they needed to perform a hysterectomy. At barely eighteen she had lost her husband, her child, her future.

'It was that or let you die,' she had been told. The latter seemed the better option at the time. Even now, there were days she wished she had died with Donald.

The only small mercy had been the money she had been given as compensation. It would never be enough to make up for losing Donald, but it was enough that she could keep living in his flat. Returning home alone had been hard. Donald had been her compass. With him she always had a sense of who she was, and now all she felt was lost. She was still struggling to find her way, and some days she wondered if she ever would.

Her father had been the one who came to Sydney. She knew the moment she saw him that the situation wasn't great. He wouldn't have come otherwise. When they told her about Donald, the nurse asked if there was anyone to call. But there was no one. Her husband was dead.

'What about your parents? Your mother and father, wouldn't they want to know that you are okay?'

Pearl had closed her eyes. It wasn't an easy question to answer.

The woman she thought was her mother was dead; the other mother didn't even know she was in Sydney. A phone call from a hospital wasn't the way she envisaged having first contact with her birth mother.

As for her father ... Pearl wasn't even sure her birth father knew she existed, and she had no idea who he was. She was pretty sure that the only father she knew of, wanted nothing to do with her. 'You can call my ... Aunt Stella,' she had told the nurse. But it was her father who had come, looking gaunt and unshaven. For a moment Pearl thought him to be drunk. She was about to hurl abuse at him but one look in his eyes and she could see he was stone cold sober.

'I'm sorry about Donald,' he said by way of greeting. He removed his hat and Pearl was further taken aback by his appearance. It had been a little over six months since they had buried her mother and in that time, he seemed to have aged a lifetime. When he stepped closer into the light, she could see that his white shirt looked murky grey, and despite all the resentment she had built up towards him, she felt pity, but more than that, she felt sad.

'You should've told me,' Pearl whispered. Her vision blurred, she blinked, letting the tears flow softly.

His face softened, his eyes flashed with guilt and grief before he took her hand. She felt it tremble and wondered if it came from his nervousness or if there was a more sinister reason behind it. 'We always said we would. That was the plan. But then ...' He shook his head and sighed. 'I'm not proud of many things, and maybe if we had the courage to tell you then things may've been different between us. But your mother ... she was scared of losing you.'

'I would've understood. It would've explained a lot of things. I felt so lost, so confused a lot of the time and it was only when I met Donald that I –' Her voice was muffled by a sob and for the first time in years, for the first time since she was a little girl, her father held her. He smoothed her hair and told her it would all be right. But unlike when she was a child, she didn't believe him. Maybe because her loss had been so great she couldn't imagine feeling anything but forlorn for the foreseeable future, or maybe it was because he was crying too.

It wasn't until they were halfway to Melbourne that her father asked why she and Donald had come to Sydney.

Upon discharge, they had given Pearl her belongings, an enormous bag that held only three items – her purse and their wedding rings, Donald's and hers. She had retrieved a necklace she had in her purse and looped the rings through it. Slipping her hand between the buttons of her shirt she found the rings, warm from her skin, and drew strength from them before she answered. 'We came to get married.'

Her father gave a silent nod. 'I thought as much. When the nurse told me that your husband had died – well, I put two and two together. But there is more, isn't there?'

'I found her,' Pearl said, knowing her father would understand exactly who she was talking about.

'We never told you, but your mother and I used to live in Sydney. We moved when you were given to us. At first we told ourselves it was because all our family was in Melbourne. Your aunts, uncles, even your grandmother, who loved you from the moment she saw you. She called you her *Bella Bambina*.'

'I don't remember her.'

'You were quite young, maybe three or four when she passed away. Anyway, we were always going to tell you, we only thought it was fair to do so, but your grandmother said something to us once that maybe put doubts in our minds.'

'What did she say?'

'She said that if we really intended to tell you, we would never have left Sydney where we knew your birth mother was. I think that was the turning point. We knew the right thing to do by you was to tell you, but ...'

'You thought if you did, that I would leave,' Pearl finished her father's sentence.

His response was a solitary nod.

'I –' Pearl was poised to say that it wouldn't have been like that, that she wouldn't have looked for her birth mother if they had told her, but she stopped when she realised she would've been lying. 'I would never have done anything to hurt you both. You gave me a home and a family.'

'Your mother gave you all that. I'm ashamed to admit that I could've been a better father. You have to understand. It was just your mother and me for so long ... when you came along, you brought out a light in her that I had never seen before. Here was the woman I loved, and I had never made her happy the way you did. I'm not proud to admit it, but I was jealous. I resented how happy you made her.'

It explained a lot, a whole damn lot.

'I really do love you, Pearl,' he said tearfully. 'Can you forgive me?' His face was old and weary, older than his barely sixty years, and Pearl knew that this man had lost a wife, but there was no reason to lose his daughter.

'There's nothing to forgive, Dad,' she said softly.

'My darling girl, there is much to forgive, but you were always selfless. I think that may be a credit to your mamma's rearing.'

For the first time in a long time a semblance of a smile came to her. 'I think you may be right.'

'And if ... if you want to see your ... birth mother, I want you to know that I won't stop you. I will drive you back to Sydney, if you like.'

Pearl thought about this, thought long and hard before she replied. 'I'm not ready to see her. Not now. I think it may be a while before I will be.'

A while ended up being five years, and then, a month ago, on the fifth anniversary of the accident, Pearl felt it was time. She wrote her mother a letter, and today, clustered amongst the bills and her *Reader's Digest* subscription was an envelope addressed to Pearl Russ and on the back was the sender's name: Catherine McGarrie. Her mother.

Sydney, September 1965

There had only been one occasion in his life that William had blatantly lied to his wife. He didn't count the little white lies, like telling Catherine her meatloaf was every bit as good as Maisey's. Or telling her that no, he didn't allow John to have a sip of his beer. This was larger than that. Much larger.

The first time he lied to Catherine was the night he proposed to her. The same night she had told him about Charlie and about Pearl and asked him to promise to help her look for the child. If he were consulting his solicitor on the matter, he knew the advice he would be given: he hadn't verbalised an answer to Catherine's question so it could be argued that technically he had made no promise and therefore no lie had been told. But deep down, he knew the inference had been made. Over the following years, Catherine had accused him time and time again of breaking his promise, lying to her when he pledged to help her look for Pearl.

Pearl. That damn name haunted him from the moment he bloody well heard it. It drove a wedge between Catherine and him for years – until his heart attack. The morning after the fight, as he drove to the surgery, he resolved to head to the pub straight after work. When he started to feel nauseous after his second beer, he thought it was because he'd downed them in quick succession. The next thing he remembered was waking up in hospital. Catherine was asleep, her head resting on his bed, her hand firmly holding his.

William was a good man. He worked hard to provide for his family. He was a good doctor and he had a good reputation. But even good people were capable of doing bad things, and a month ago, he did the worst thing he could.

He arrived home one night and found the mail still in the letterbox. Normally Catherine collected it earlier in the day, but Matthew was poorly with chicken pox and she hadn't had a chance. Flipping through the envelopes, there was one that stood out. It was addressed to Catherine McGarrie, but that wasn't what caught his attention; it was when he flipped it over to see the sender's name:

Pearl Russ Peterson.

His skin had broken out in a cold sweat. He knew without a shadow of a doubt who she was.

William had two choices. He could give Catherine the letter and give her something that she had wanted for the past twenty-five years, to be reunited with the daughter she was forced to give away, or he could keep the family together, and keep together a marriage that had gone from strength to strength.

When he looked at the timing of it all, it certainly was as good a time as ever for Catherine to meet Pearl. Their boys were growing. John was almost old enough to get his driver's permit. Maybe they would be old enough to understand. But this wasn't any ordinary circumstance. Of all of them, William had the most to lose.

After the heart attack Catherine had vowed to stop asking him to look for Pearl. She told him she was committed to him and to their boys, and to date she had been true to her word. If he gave Catherine the letter and they let Pearl into their lives, so much would unravel. William really only had one choice, he decided. He shoved the letter into his pocket and vowed to end this once and for all. And God have mercy on his soul, he knew exactly how he was going to do it.

Melbourne, September 1965

Her stomach full of nerves, Pearl checked her reflection in the window for what seemed like the hundredth time. Every time the restaurant door opened, her head shot up, each time her pulse would accelerate in anticipation, only for it to drop in disappointment soon after.

Glancing at the wall clock, she could see that it wasn't quite quarter to, and they had agreed to meet at noon.

She'll be here, Pearl silently chanted.

It's what we agreed to, wasn't it? A wave of panic hit her and frantically, she drew the letter out from her handbag to double-check she hadn't misread the details.

She hadn't. There it was in black and white – the agreed time, date and location. It even had the suggestion that they both wear red coats to help them recognise each other. Pearl wanted to think that she would know her mother the moment she walked through the door. She had questions, questions that had been rolling through her mind these past few weeks. Did she have any brothers or sisters? Could she meet them? Did Catherine know who her father was? Where did she meet him? Did she ever love him? She was aware that she might not have the chance to ask these questions all at once. After all, it was only their first meeting.

The first of many, I hope.

Outside, it began to rain. Soft drops hit the glass and soon the windows began to fog, making it hard to see out. A flurry of people rushed inside the busy city cafe. It was almost lunchtime, soon the whole dining area would be abuzz with office workers, mothers on a day trip into town with their babes, and her mother.

As the clock ticked closer to the midday hour, Pearl's palms became slick with sweat. Her legs stuck to the vinyl-upholstered booths. It may've been cold out, but it was warming up inside. Still she couldn't remove her coat, not until Catherine arrived.

'Pearl?'

She looked up at the sound of a man's voice. In his mid to late forties he was well groomed, impeccably dressed with an almost statesman-like look about him, like a lawyer or politician.

'Yes?' she asked. 'I'm sorry, do I know you?'

'No. Not really. I'm Catherine's husband, William.'

Alarm bells were going off in her head, and yet, Pearl refused to accept what her gut was telling her. 'Is Catherine running late?'

'No. Catherine is not here.'

It felt like a punch in the stomach. Immediately it was clear that Catherine wasn't coming.

'May I sit down? I can explain a few things.'

She blinked. He was polite and, after all, he had travelled all the way from Sydney. 'I guess so. You must be tired from your drive.'

'Thank you.' He removed his hat and placed it on the seat, then removed his jacket. 'But I didn't drive, I flew in.'

Annoyance filled her. Who travelled by plane? She didn't know anyone who had been on a commercial jet. Pearl's instincts were right. This man had 'politician' written all over him. 'I'm just very pleased this weather didn't hit till after we landed. Would've made for a bumpy ride.' He gave a nervous laugh.

He was making small talk. Pearl didn't want small talk. All she wanted was to know why Catherine said she was going to meet her and then failed to show up.

'I'm guessing you would like to know why Catherine didn't come?'

Pearl clasped her hands together and squeezed them tight. 'That would be nice,' she said in a calm voice, but inside her blood was boiling.

'She wanted to, she really did, but in the end she changed her mind.'

'Changed her mind?' Pearl's voice went up a considerable number of decibels, enough that a few patrons at surrounding tables turned their heads towards them.

'I'm sorry, Pearl. But you won't be meeting Catherine today.'

Pearl gave a derisive laugh. 'By today you really mean *never*, am I right?'

For the first time since his arrival, William looked slightly taken aback and if Pearl was right, relieved. 'Yes, I'm afraid so.'

'Tell me, Mr ... I'm sorry, what did you say your name was?'

William shifted slightly in his seat and dropped his gaze. 'Bennett, my name is William Bennett.'

'Well, Mr Bennett, you can tell Catherine that's fine. I never want anything to do with her ever again.' Pearl made the move to leave, there was no need to stay any longer, but William reached over and placed his hand on her forearm to stop her.

'We can offer you some money, something to help you, if you'd like.'

Shaking off his hand she stood up, enraged. 'Keep your filthy money and shove it.'

Without another thought, she walked out of the restaurant and into the rain. She was better off without Catherine Bennett or any of her family in her life, and she vowed to remember that for as long as she lived.

As William watched Pearl storm off he should have felt content. It seemed that from now on, Pearl wouldn't want anything to do with Catherine or their family.

Ever since intercepting her letter, William had been harbouring a large amount of guilt. What he was effectively doing was cutting off all ties between mother and child. He knew the chance of Pearl wanting anything to do with Catherine after she failed to show up would be slim. And it all had gone to plan. He couldn't have asked for a better outcome. He was leaving Melbourne with exactly what he came for. Except, there was one thing that he hadn't bargained for. One element in this whole master plan that had blindsided him and told him that despite thinking Catherine had told him every-thing about Charlie, there was still one thing, one very important thing, that she had been keeping from him for twenty years, a secret that was revealed the moment he laid eyes on Pearl. She bore little resemblance to his wife; with her curly dark hair and olive skin it was unlikely that Charlie had been the typical all-American boy William had envisioned. There had to be mixed race or European heritage. Greek or Italian perhaps? William hadn't considered him-self a racist or bigot, but at that moment, knowing that Catherine had kept something so important from him irked.

He felt vindicated. He had done the right thing. He told him-self it wasn't Charlie's heritage that bothered him; it was that his wife hadn't bothered to share a crucial detail. When Catherine had spoken about Charlie, she had eluded they'd been from the same social circles. But now, meeting the child that had been a wedge between them for so long, he knew enough about race and navy ranks to know this not to be true.

William had always thought his mother-in-law was a little harsh with his wife. He didn't mind her, and certainly he respected the Rear Admiral, but now he could see why June McGarrie was the way she was. She knew all about Charlie, and her actions were warranted – she had saved her daughter from social disgrace. If anything, Catherine should've been grateful.

On the way home he debated whether or not he would con-front Catherine about his discovery. He weighed up the pros and cons. In the end he decided against acting on it – for now. Instead, he sat in his study and slipped Pearl's letter in between the pages of a book and closed the lid on the matter.

Thirty-eight

The Past Rears Its Ugly Head

Sydney, January 2017

'You've been a little quiet lately, Kit,' her father said as they drove towards her gran's house to help Ben and Ness with the last of the clean up. 'Is everything okay?'

Kit was staring out the car window. It seemed that every second person they passed was dressed for the beach and not surprisingly so. Sydney was heading into its ninth straight day of heatwave conditions. It was barely after eight am and already the mercury was nudging the mid-thirties.

'Kit?'

'Hmm?'

'I asked if you're okay?' he repeated.

'I'm fine, just in dire need of coffee.' She was fully aware that she had dodged her father's question. He wasn't simply enquiring about her mood this morning, but over the past few weeks. 'Can we make a pit stop?'

'In this heat?' He looked at her as if she were trying to sell ice to an Eskimo.

'I'm going to need a caffeine hit to deal with Ben's plan of attack for today,' she said. 'I bet he'll have a schedule whipped up and jobs allocated to each of us.' Even though Kit was the one who had started the clean up, Ben had taken over, literally. Kit may be mocking her brother, but deep down she loved his bossiness.

'He's organised,' her father said in Ben's defence. 'I guess some of that comes from being a teacher.'

Or from Mum, Kit thought.

'I'll get you an iced coffee if you like, complete with the ice-cream and whipped cream,' she said sweetly.

Her father sighed. 'All right,' he said. 'But your mother can *never* find out.'

Kit made the silent motion of zipping her lips. 'Not a word.'

'She would kill me,' he said wryly. 'Apparently I need to watch my sugar levels so I don't become a diabetic.' He shook his head. 'Sometimes that woman drives me crazy.'

'She loves you. She wants to keep you around for as long as she can.' Kit and her brothers all made fun of their mother for her fussing and her sometime bossiness, but the truth was that by spending more time with her parents recently Kit was starting to realise how much she wanted what they had – someone to drive her crazy.

When she lost Jeremy, Kit thought she had lost all hope of finding anyone who she could grow old with. She thought that Jeremy had been her one and only chance, and then she met Adam ...

'Right.' Her father slowed the car and pulled into a spot outside a cafe around the corner from the house. 'Find out if Ben and Ness want anything.'

Unclipping her seatbelt, Kit grabbed her phone and messaged her brother. 'I'm on it.'

'If they have any of their fresh muffins get me one of those too.'

'Got it.'

She was halfway out the door before her father added, 'And not a word to your mother.'

Kit smiled and gave her father a wink before walking into the cafe.

Ben's message came in the nick of time and as she placed the order, an item on the menu caught her attention. Shaved ice.

'*It's shave ice, never shaved ice.*' She could almost hear Adam's voice.

Kit frowned. It was the second time in a matter of minutes that she had thought of him. This really had to stop. She shook her head as if that were the solution and reached for her latte while she waited for her father's iced coffee. What she needed was caffeine and just to make it through today. Then she could go back to Melbourne and get on with her life. Melbourne had nothing to do with Adam so the likelihood that she'd –

'Kit? Kit Bennett, is that you?'

The sound of a man's voice snapped Kit out of her thoughts.

'Mick?' she asked in disbelief before she felt all blood drain from her face. She hadn't seen Mick Toohey since the day of Jeremy's funeral. In an instant she felt winded and dizzy at the same time.

'Yes, how are you?' He came closer to give her a peck on the cheek and Kit grasped a nearby chair to steady herself.

'I'm fine,' she said, her response sounding wooden and forced. 'How are you? You look well.'

He was slightly more rounded about the midsection and had considerably less hair, but Mick looked well. He looked ... happy.

'I am.' His grin was so wide it stretched from ear to ear. 'And there's the reason why.' Mick nodded to a petite blonde woman sitting at a table nearby. Even from where she was standing, Kit could see her bulging belly.

'You're going to be a dad?' She hadn't meant for the words to come out with such amazement, but Mick didn't notice or if he did, he didn't seem offended.

'I know, right?' He chuckled. 'Did you ever think I would be a dad?' he asked in wonderment.

'Never,' Kit murmured.

'Come over, let me introduce you to Sarah.'

Kit followed Mick and met Sarah. The baby was due the first week of March. They were having a girl. They had a name picked out but were keeping mum on it. Kit smiled and nodded and said that keeping the name a secret was a wise choice.

'Don't be a stranger,' Mick said as he kissed her goodbye. His overt pleasantness took her aback. He was a completely different person to when she had seen him last. Unsure how to respond, Kit smiled and wished them all the best with the baby.

'Kit, you look like you've seen a ghost!' her father exclaimed as he helped with the trays of coffees and muffins as she slid back in the car.

'I just saw Mick Toohey.'

'Mick Toohey? Mick who was with Jeremy when –'

'You can say it, Dad. Yes, the same Mick who was with Jeremy when he died.'

'It still makes you so sad, talking about Jeremy.'

'It will always make me sad,' she said truthfully. 'But I'd like to think that enough time has passed that I can talk about him without feeling ...'

Guilty.

'Like you are going to fall apart?' her father offered when she didn't finish the sentence.

'Yeah,' she lied.

'So how's Mick?'

'He seems to be doing really well. He's going to have a baby.' It wasn't until she said the words that Kit realised how envious she felt, and if she were completely honest, angry too. It seemed that Mick's guilt had faded with time, so why was it so hard for her?

'Fair dinkum?'

'Yeah. I never pictured him as the fatherly type.' Her words were more abrasive than she intended them to be.

'Time changes people, Kit. Circumstances and fate change paths. I know you must have carried some resentment towards Mick after Jeremy's accident, but I think he would've had his fair share of guilt. I reckon if Mick's able to forgive himself, then maybe you can too.'

'I never blamed Mick, Dad.' It was the truth. Seeing him had been unnerving but she knew Mick wasn't to blame for Jeremy's death.

'I know,' her father said, his eyes darting off the road to give her a perceptive look. 'You blamed yourself.'

'It's not as easy as it sounds.'

'Maybe you need to find something or someone that'll help you.'

Kit was grateful they had pulled into the driveway and even more grateful that Ben was waiting for them, holding a clipboard. 'Told you he'd have a schedule.' She nodded in her brother's direction. 'Come on, let's get this over with.'

For the next three hours they worked through the list Ben had prepared. They would have kept going through lunch if Ben had his way, but thankfully Bev Bennett arrived armed with enough food to feed an army and demanded they all take a break.

'I think I've inhaled about a kilo of dust,' Kit said, wiping her brow with the back of her hand.

'I know what you mean,' Ness wheezed next to her. 'But we've made good progress and with the furniture arriving sooner than we thought it's perfect timing.' Their footsteps echoed as they walked through the almost empty house. 'Have I told you how grateful we are that you're letting us stay here?'

'Ness, honey,' Ben said behind them, 'we *are* paying rent, it's not like Kit's allowing us to live in the house for nothing.'

Kit was about to tell Ben off for being a smart arse but was distracted by the heavenly scent drifting from the kitchen. Immediately her taste buds stood to attention. 'Mum, you made bolognaise!' Her mum's spaghetti sauce was Kit's favourite food ever. She never ordered it when she went out because she knew it wouldn't hold a candle to her mother's. Even Pino's, but not that she would ever say it to his face.

'In this heat?' Ben complained.

'It's Kit's favourite,' Bev said as she tipped steaming pasta into the colander. 'I thought it would be nice to make it for her since she doesn't have it that often.'

'That's because she insists on living in Melbourne.' Ben's words sent a wave of irritation through Kit.

'What's with you today?' she snapped. Her brother had been a little on the cold side since the whole Adam incident. At first she thought she was imagining things but it seemed, judging from his current attitude towards her, she wasn't.

'Nothing.' He sat without looking at her. 'It's hot and I just want the place ready by tomorrow.'

'Jeezus, you spent a handful of years in Singapore and yet you can't handle summer in Sydney.'

'Now, cut it out, children,' Ness chided them with her best school-teacher tone. 'I don't want to put one of you in the naughty corner.'

'Where is your father?' Bev asked.

'He was finishing up in the study. That room hasn't been touched since Grandpa died.'

'I told Catherine a hundred times I would help her clean it up. We all did, but she insisted she would do it when she was ready. That was William's sanctuary, I think it reminded her of him and maybe it was hard to let it go.'

'She had a hard time letting a lot of things go,' Ben muttered and it caught their mother's attention.

'Like what?' she asked, clearly puzzled.

Kit glared at her brother, and Ben darted a look at her before turning back to their mother. 'Like that ...'

Kit held her breath and prayed her brother was smart enough to come up with some quick-witted reply.

'Like that Arnott's tin she kept for all those years.'

Kit gripped her fork. She couldn't believe her brother. Thank goodness Ness was more on the ball and tried to defuse the situation. 'Since we're all set, how about I go and see what's keeping Matthew.'

But it did little to throw her mother off the scent. Once she got a whiff of something, Kit knew that her mother could be like a dog with a bone. 'How did you know about ...' Brows furrowed in concentration, Bev pondered for a moment before her face lit up. 'You found it!'

Kit groaned and shook her head.

Ben, you idiot!

'What was in it? I've always wanted to know. I bet it was something secretive.'

Kit felt her face pale.

Say no. For the love of God, Ben, say no!

'Umm.' Ben was clearly floundering for an answer.

All he had to say was that it was full of old recipes or something that like and they would be home free.

'Whatever it was,' Bev said, 'Catherine guarded it like she was hiding some vital secret.'

In the end it wouldn't have mattered what Ben said, because ten seconds later, her father walked in and the gig was up.

'She was.' Matt Bennett looked like he'd seen a ghost.

He was holding a letter, and instantly Kit's heart stopped beating.

He knows.

But how could he? Kit had the box, it was in her bag – she carried it everywhere she went. She knew it wasn't safe in the room at her parents' house. So, the question was, how?

'What are you talking about?' Bev asked.

'My mother ... had a daughter ...' Her father was saying the words as if he could scarcely believe it.

'Matthew, you are making no sense! What's that you're holding?'

'It's a letter to Mother from a woman claiming to be her daughter.'

Ben and Kit exchanged wide-eyed looks. 'Pearl wrote to Gran?' The words flew out of Kit's mouth before she had a chance to properly think.

'Yes, she ...' Her father paused, realisation dawning. 'How did you know her name was Pearl?'

Kit sucked in a deep breath, her pulse reverberating in her ears.

'Kit?' her father said when she didn't answer.

'Kit, it's time,' Ben said gently and she knew what she had to do.

Sighing, she scraped back her chair.

'Where are you going?' her father demanded.

'I'm going to get the answer to your question. But before I do, I need to see that letter.' She put out her hand but her father eyed her suspiciously and folded the letter, drawing it away from her.

'Not till you tell me everything you know.'

'Then you may want to take a seat. It's a long story.'

Kit watched her father's face as she took him through everything she knew – from finding Charlie's letter after her gran's funeral, to her visit to Hawaii for the commemoration, about meeting Charlie and Penny Kerr, and the discovery that Kitty and Charlie had a child, Pearl, and how the search for Pearl came to an abrupt end.

When she had finished, Kit's head hurt. Her mother, who was not one to remain silent often, was rendered speechless. It was her father who spoke.

'What you are telling me is that for the past three or four months, you knew about all of this. You not only kept it from us, but you led us to believe that your trip to Hawaii was for work.'

Her father's words stung like a slap in the face.

'Dad, no, it wasn't like that. I mean yes, I knew there was something when I found the letter in Gran's room but –'

'You decided to hide this, Kit.' The disappointment in his eyes was palpable and it broke her heart to have him looking at her like that.

'It wasn't intentional –'

'Yes, it was. You knew exactly what you were doing, Kit.'

'Okay, besides the fact that I kept this from you, which I had a perfectly valid reason for doing –'

'And why is that, Kit? Why didn't you tell us, or at least me about it?'

'You wouldn't have approved of me going to Hawaii.'

'And you would be correct there. There was a reason why your gran never spoke about her life before she came to Australia. She didn't want to remember it. Kit, 1941 was a very different time and place. She was an unmarried mother, of course she was going to give up the child.'

'Dad, I know that this is a shock to you, and I know that it may be hard for you to believe that Gran would've wanted us to find Pearl, but I really think she would.'

Her father silently considered her argument for what seemed the longest time. 'Why are you doing this? For all we know this woman doesn't want anything to do with us.'

'She doesn't,' Ben said and Kit gave him a death look. 'What? It's the truth.'

'No. She doesn't.' Kit sighed. 'And I think it might have something to do with that letter. I just don't know why she wouldn't.'

'It seems pretty straightforward to me,' her father said. 'Your gran wrote her back telling her she didn't want contact.'

'But in the letter she wrote to Penny, Gran said that she wanted to look for Pearl.'

'That was before she had us. She probably changed her mind.'

'But what if she didn't? What if it wasn't Gran who wrote back?'

Her father narrowed his eyes. 'What are you saying, Kit?'

Kit knew her father wasn't going to like what she was about to say. 'I think it was Grandpa who replied to that letter. And I think whatever he said in it is the reason why Pearl cut all ties.'

Her mother gasped. 'Kit, that's ridiculous!'

'That's a big accusation to make,' her father said.

'Think about it, Dad. Everything that Gran had to do with Charlie and Pearl was in the tin. This letter was in Grandpa's study. We all knew that was Grandpa's space, even Gran didn't go in there, and in the letter she wrote Penny, we know she told Grandpa about the baby. So really, it's not that big of a stretch.'

'Why is this so important to you, Kit? Why do you need to find this woman?'

'I've thought of that a lot. Adam said I was doing it to redeem Gran's past somehow, but he was wrong. It was something that you said this morning that now makes a lot of sense.'

'Something I said?'

'You said that I couldn't stop Jeremy's accident because I wasn't there. I didn't know it was going to happen. That it was out of my control, and you're right. But *this*, Pearl, Charlie, this is all in my control. I'm the one who knows about Pearl. I'm the one who has the potential to reunite a daughter with her father before it's too late. This I can control. And that's why I think it's important, and I guess, that's why I'm doing it.'

Silence descended in the room. Eventually her father said, 'I'm not saying I condone this and in no way do I want anything to do with Pearl, but if this is something you feel that you need to do, then do it.'

'It is, Dad.' Kit smiled, knowing for the first time the full purpose of the search for Pearl. 'It's something I *have* to do.'

All this time she thought the search had been for her gran, and in a lot of ways, it had been, but it was so much more.

Adam had been right when he said that she had been living with one foot in the past. He had been right when he said her guilt about Jeremy's death was unfounded. It was logical, Kit knew this and yet, she didn't believe it, or at least, she wouldn't allow herself to believe it. Even this morning when her father had said virtually the same thing to her, she was still in a state of denial.

But then, the letter from Pearl changed everything.

The whole search had been a series of letters, each providing clues and cues that led her to the next part of the journey. From Charlie's letter to Kitty, Kitty's letter to Charlie written the day before their lives would change forever, a letter that never reached him. Then the letter to Penny, and now, finally, Pearl's letter.

A week later, after a very intensive search, Kit flew back to Melbourne. When the taxi driver asked where she was headed, she didn't give him her address. There was somewhere more important she needed to go first, someone she needed to see, the person she'd been looking for who held the missing piece of the puzzle, who could complete the mystery and draw it all together.

She went to see Pearl.

Thirty-nine

Pearl

Melbourne, 2017

Pearl was finishing washing up the last of the breakfast dishes when there was a knock at her door. Figuring it was one of the kids who had forgotten their keys, she wiped her hands dry on a tea towel and took out a spare key from the drawer, then made her way to the door.

'How many times have I said not to forget –' Pearl stopped mid-sentence when she realised she didn't know the woman standing on the other side.

'Oh, are you lost?' It was the first question that came to mind, mainly because the building's numbering system had never been straightforward, and it wasn't unusual for someone to make their way to the top floor and realise they were completely lost. She had brought it up numerous times at strata meetings, but with the turnover of residents these days, no one seemed to care. Pearl was sure they thought her a silly old woman living on the top floor with her gaggle of misfit kids and hordes of cats. She may have been heading into her mid-seventies, but her kids were not

438

misfits. Every child she'd fostered over the past forty years had purpose and they fitted into society just fine. All they needed was for someone to believe in them and show them they were wanted.

When they came to her they were lost, they didn't believe they had a purpose in life. And every single one of them reminded Pearl of herself, how lost she had been, how Donald made her feel loved and safe, and how all that was taken away from her when she lost him.

Pearl thought finding her mother would fill the void, but all it did was show her that she would be better off without her. The day she walked out of the restaurant after meeting William Bennett, she realised that.

She spent the next few years studying to become a nurse and in her first week of work she met Graham, a young boy who had been to three foster homes in two years, and in the past six months had been to the emergency department of the hospital four times.

When his foster parents failed to show and pick him up after he was discharged, Pearl applied to become his foster mum. She didn't think it would happen. She was a single woman with no history of looking after children, but by some stroke of luck she was approved. It wasn't always easy, Graham had come with a lot of anger and anxiety, but Pearl had been patient and gradually they bonded. Over four decades, Pearl had cared for ten children. Each one of them came to her a little lost, some more broken than others, but every one of them left knowing their worth. The kids didn't live with her anymore – in fact, they were all adults now, some with children of their own – but her door, like her heart, was always open to them. She was the family they never had, and Pearl felt exactly the same about them.

'I hope not,' the young woman answered. She was in her mid to late twenties. 'I'm looking for Pearl Russ.'

'And who, may I ask, are you?' Pearl said cautiously, not missing the moment the younger woman's expression went from hopeful to nervous.

'My name is Kit Bennett.'

The realisation hit Pearl like a freight train. Her blood turned to ice in her veins.

'I'm Catherine's –'

'I know who you are,' she said frostily, her hand poised on the door to end the conversation. 'And I want nothing to do with you or your grandmother.' Pearl made the move to slam the door but Kit stopped her, not with physical action, but with two simple words.

'Catherine's dead.'

Pearl froze for a second. She had to admit, the news her birth mother had passed affected her more than she would've liked. Sensing her hesitation, the younger woman seized on the opportunity and splayed her hand on the door frame. If Pearl let the door swing, it would surely crush her fingers.

'She died a few months ago.'

'Is that why you're here? To tell me she's dead?' Pearl could feel a tremor pulsing through her body, making her voice wobble. 'It makes no difference to me because, honestly, I imagined she had died years ago.' It was the truth, she'd just assumed that Catherine was already dead – or at least, she had hoped. With her mind still processing the news, Pearl grappled with the many emotions surfacing within her, but the one that was the strongest, was anger.

How dare Catherine live to a ripe old age!

All her life, Pearl had lost people way before their time – her mother, Donald, and even her father. By the time she was thirty, only her Aunt Stella was left, and she lost contact with her a few years later. When she attended Stella's funeral in the early seventies, the cousins she'd been so close to and grown up with were like strangers. Graham and her other foster kids were the only family she had, the only family that mattered.

'I'm not here because – well, yes, I guess I am here to tell you she passed, but that's not the only reason I came.'

For the first time since Kit's arrival, Pearl noticed a suitcase behind her. 'Were you looking for somewhere to stay? Because you can't stay here.' Perhaps after discovering about her grandmother's little secret, young Kit decided to track down the lost half-aunt and had some romantic notion that they would have some kind of family reunion.

Nope. Not happening.

'What?' Kit looked puzzled for a second before she followed Pearl's gaze. 'Oh. Oh, no. I'm not looking to stay with you. I actually live in Melbourne. I've just flown in from Sydney and I came straight here to meet you.'

'You live in Melbourne?'

'In Elwood. I've been here for five years.'

'Huh.' Elwood was less than ten minutes away. Pearl wasn't sure how she felt about Catherine and William's granddaughter living so close to her. One of the reasons it was easy to push Catherine out of her mind was because the Bennetts lived in Sydney, over a thousand kilometres away. 'Why are you here, Miss Bennett?' Pearl got back on track. She already could see herself making a pot of strong tea and taking some time to decompress as soon as she could get rid of her. 'And I should also ask how you found me?'

'I was granted access to your adoption papers.'

Pearl felt her hackles rise. The thought of a stranger having access to her files was unnerving. She didn't care that this woman was Catherine's granddaughter and probably had some sort of legal right. It was personal, it was her life. 'And with that you should also have been informed that I requested no contact. In fact,' she said tersely, 'I'm going to need to call the department and –'

'Please, don't do that,' Kit pleaded. 'The department didn't give me your address, I did that on my own, through my own contacts. I really think that once we've had a chance to talk you will see the reason I'm here and you won't want to slam the door in my face.'

There was something about the look in the young woman's voice – hope mixed with desperation – that stopped Pearl and made her reconsider. 'All right.' She sighed heavily. 'Come in. I'll give you five minutes.' Kit's face beamed, her blue eyes lit up. They were sapphire blue, Pearl realised, the same shade as her own. 'But if after five minutes I don't think you should be here, you will leave and never bother me again, do you understand?'

'Yes, of course, absolutely.' Kit rushed the words and Pearl could feel her excitement.

She moved aside to allow her to enter. 'I'll make us some tea.'

The young woman followed her into the kitchen. 'Sit,' Pearl instructed as she placed the kettle on the stovetop. As she moved around the kitchen gathering the mugs, sugar bowl and milk, Pearl could feel Kit's eyes on her. When the shrill of the kettle filled the room, Pearl filled the pot and poured it into the mugs. Sliding one across the table in front of Kit, she then sat down opposite her. 'Okay, talk,' she said, scooping up a teaspoon of sugar and stirring it into her tea.

'I know about the letter you wrote to your ... to Catherine.'

Pearl paused stirring and looked at Kit in bewilderment. 'She kept the letter?'

Kit hesitated. 'The letter was kept ... and I'm assuming you received a reply.'

'You're correct about that.'

'I also think that whatever was in that letter prompted you to request no contact.'

Pearl shook her head and resumed stirring her tea so violently that it spilt over the edge of the mug, burning her skin. 'You're wrong there.'

'What?'

Pearl winced from the pain of the scorch and the memory she was about to recall, one that she'd locked in the corner of her mind and vowed to forget. It didn't work though; as soon as she closed her eyes she could visualise it all as if it were yesterday.

Receiving the letter, the joy she had that day as she sat in the very same room that she and Kit were in now, the nerves, the excitement, the anticipation she felt the day she was to meet Catherine, and the crushing heartbreak she felt when it all fell to pieces.

'The letter your grandmother wrote me said how she'd *love* to meet me, how she couldn't *wait* to meet me ... how she hoped that *I* would find *her* one day ...' A corrosive laugh escaped her lips. Across from her, Kit watched her with interest.

'So you met?' she asked hopefully. They both knew the story didn't end well, and she could see that young Kit was trying to keep the denial at bay.

'We agreed to meet, but she never showed up.' Pearl took a sip of her tea and watched the shock on Kit's face.

'What do you mean, she never showed up?'

'I'm not sure I can be any clearer. Catherine didn't show up at the place we were scheduled to meet.'

Kit furrowed her brow as if she couldn't fathom her grand-mother's behaviour. 'Did she at least contact you to explain why?'

'No. But she sent someone in her place to tell me she wanted nothing to do with me.'

'Who?'

'William. She was too cowardly to come and tell me herself so she sent her husband to do the dirty work for her.'

Kit's expression and demeanour changed in an instant. 'No, that's wrong. She didn't send him.'

'Yes, she did. Which one of us was there, Kit?' Pearl glanced at the wall clock. Surely she had given this girl more than enough of her time. She was a fool to have done so – all it was doing was making her upset. 'You obviously worshipped your grandmother, but all she was to me was the woman that abandoned me not once, but twice. Now I think we've had enough of a catch up. It's time for you to leave.'

'She didn't want to give you away. She wanted to keep you.'

'If that was the case, we wouldn't be here discussing it, would we?'

'Pearl, please,' Kit said. 'There's so much about this that you don't know. So much that I need to tell you.'

Pearl shook her head and stood up. She was sure there was nothing this Kit Bennett could say that would make her listen to another word about her mother. 'I appreciate your passion, but I think we're done here, and I would like for you to leave.'

Pearl waited for her to stand too, but she didn't and just as she was about to repeat her request, Kit played her trump card.

'I know who your father is.'

'What did you say?' Pearl whispered. She wasn't sure if she heard correctly. Surely she said she knew who her father *was*.

'His name is Charlie Florio and he's still alive, but not for long. He's sick.'

Of course he was. Pearl narrowed her eyes. At this stage Kit would say anything to get her to listen. 'Don't tell me he lives in Melbourne too,' she said sarcastically. 'Is he my neighbour? Maybe he's one of those old men that live in the retirement village across the road.'

Kit shook her head, unperturbed by her mocking. 'No, he lives in Hawaii. You have Gran's eyes and her nose too, but everything else, it's all from Charlie.'

Pearl stood rooted to the spot. Since discovering she was adopted it was only natural for her to wonder which one of her parents she looked like. For over fifty years not knowing her parentage had played on her, no matter how many times she'd told herself it didn't matter. And now, sitting in front of her was a girl who had known her mother and knew of her father. Charlie Florio. *Florio.* Pearl knew it was a Sicilian surname. How strangely coincidental that her father was of Italian heritage and hailed from Southern Italy no doubt, as did her adoptive mother.

Slowly Pearl sat down and wrapped her hands around her mug. It was empty but it didn't matter, she just needed something to hold on to to stop them from shaking.

'I would like to tell you about your mother and father,' Kit said quietly. 'But only if you want to know.'

'Yes,' she said finally. 'Yes, I do.'

Kit sucked in a breath and refilled their mugs before starting. She took Pearl through everything she knew – right up to the point where her father found her letter. 'The letter was in my grandfather's study. My grandmother rarely went in there. I knew instantly that he was the one who read your letter and that Gran never knew anything about it.'

Pearl was silent, head bent with her fingertips on her temple. It was a lot to take in. Kit had been uncovering it all for months – and it seemed frustratingly slow, not knowing the full story. But now, putting it together as she relayed it all to Pearl, she could only imagine how overwhelming it all must be for her.

Pearl drained her tea and went to pour another. 'If it weren't so damn early, I would break out something harder for us.' When she held the pot up, Kit shook her head.

'I'm fine, thanks.'

Pearl sighed. 'My poor old brain is having a hard time processing all of what you've told me.'

'You must have a lot of questions.'

'I have ... so many that I cannot pull my thoughts together to form a proper sentence. But there are a few that stick out.'

'Ask away, I'm here to help.'

'How sure are you that it would've been William that wrote to me?'

'I've thought a lot about that. There's something that can help me prove it. Do you still have the letter you received?'

Pearl blinked. 'Yes, I do.' She stood up and moved to the cupboard above the fridge and pulled out a red Arnott's tin that looked identical to the one in Kit's bag.

'What's so funny?' Pearl asked as she made her way back to the table and saw Kit smiling.

'The tin. It's virtually the same one as this one.' Kit retrieved the tin from her bag. 'It seems that you and Gran had similar ideas when it came to where you stored your memories.'

'It was a pretty common tin. I'm sure that virtually every household back in the day used it for storing something or other.' Pearl brushed away the similarity. 'Now why do you think seeing the letter will prove it wasn't Catherine that wrote it?'

'Because,' Kit said as she opened the box and pulled out the letter her gran had written to Charlie, 'I have this. It's a letter that Kitty wrote to Charlie. When I said earlier that I knew your parents loved each other, it's because I found these.' Kit handed the letters to Pearl so she could read them herself. Kit watched as Pearl looked at the letter she had received and then Kitty's letter to Charlie.

'Well, the writing is surely different,' she said and Kit could tell she was becoming convinced that her gran hadn't written the letter to her.

'When I went to Hawaii in December, I wanted to give Charlie the letter that never reached him.'

'Why didn't you?'

'At first I thought that perhaps the shock of discovering Charlie was unwell had stopped me. Adam, his grandson, was so protective of him and I didn't want to do anything to upset him or confuse him even more. But now, I think I know why I never did it. I wasn't the right person to give Charlie the letter. I think it needs to come from someone else. Someone that links Charlie and Kitty.'

Pearl's eyes widened. 'You think that I should be the one?'

Kit nodded.

'But ... Hawaii?' Pearl spluttered. 'And you said Charlie wasn't well when you saw him a couple of months ago. How is he doing now?'

Kit knew the right thing to do was to be honest and tell Pearl that she didn't know. She hadn't had any contact with Adam since he left, but she could tell that Pearl was seriously considering going to Hawaii and there was no way she was about to let that slip through her fingers.

'There's only one way to find out,' Kit said.

'Hawaii.' Pearl shook her head. 'How soon do you think we can leave?'

Kit felt her heart skip a beat. It was really happening, she was about to take Pearl to meet Charlie – father and daughter meeting for the first time. She had found Gran's lost Pearl. 'How's tomorrow for you?'

Her only fear was that they would be too late.

Forty

Leimomi

My Pearl Child

Honolulu, 2017

Kit's nerves kicked into top gear as the plane touched down in Honolulu. Her fingers trembled as she switched the phone on and waited. She had messaged Adam the moment their tickets were booked, but she hadn't heard from him by the time their plane left Melbourne. Her pulse quickened as her email and texts starting to load, only to be flooded by disappointment. None of them was from Adam.

'Damn it,' she muttered.

'Is everything okay?' Pearl asked. She looked exhausted. Kit was sure that neither of them had slept a wink on the way over. Pearl was nervous, that was a given, and there was no way that Kit was going to add to her anxiety by admitting she hadn't heard from Adam.

'Umm, yes, all good.' Kit stood up from her seat and retrieved their hand luggage from the overhead locker.

'Thank you, but I'm more than capable of getting my own bag,' Pearl said as Kit handed over her bag. 'I may be older than you, but I'm not that old. Not yet anyway.'

Kit smiled. 'That's something Gran would've said.' The plane ride had given them plenty of time to get to know one another. Pearl hadn't had an easy life, but there was a lot about her that reminded Kit so much of her gran. The more she discovered about the woman, who was really her aunt, the more she knew that her father and the rest of the family needed to meet her.

She had called her father, right after she'd seen Pearl, not to tell him that her suspicions about what her grandpa had done were right, but to tell him that when he felt ready to meet her, Kit was confident that he would love Pearl. Her father, as she'd suspected, told her that he wasn't sure when or if he would ever be ready, but Kit knew that all he needed was time.

'I am sorry I never got to meet her,' Pearl said. 'Knowing what I do now, it seems a shame.' Her regret was palpable.

'Yes, it is. But you're here and you're going to meet your father today, and no matter what happens, at least you can say you have no regrets.' Maybe that last bit of advice was every bit as much for her own sake as it was for Pearl. The trip was for Pearl to meet Charlie, but it was also for Kit to make amends with Adam. She owed him an apology. It was a hell of a long way to come to say sorry, but considering she had yet to hear from him, Kit wondered if she'd get a chance.

She spotted Clint and as they approached she could see him holding up a sign that read, 'Aloha Leimomi.' After she'd texted Adam, Kit had then called Clint and arranged for him to meet them at the airport. She told him everything about Pearl knowing that Adam wouldn't be too thrilled about it, but she trusted Clint not to divulge Pearl's parentage.

'Leimomi?' Kit said by way of greeting. Kit had spoken to Clint only hours before boarding their flight, so it felt as if she'd just said goodbye to him, and certainly returning so soon after the commemoration felt somewhat surreal.

'It means "My Pearl Child".'

'It's beautiful,' Pearl said.

'Clint, Pearl; Pearl, Clint.' Kit made the introductions and as Clint began to load their luggage in the trunk, Pearl's attempts to help him were waved away.

He made small talk while they drove away from Honolulu and towards the windward side of the island. Kit watched Pearl as she keenly observed the passing scenery. She was thankful for Clint's running commentary to pass the time, but as they inched closer to their destination and the conversation slowed down, Kit's palms were slick with sweat.

'How's Charlie today?' They had spoken at length on the phone about Charlie's condition. She knew that for a while after Christmas and into the New Year, he'd been declining, but that for the past couple of weeks he seemed better – even having days where he was himself. It had been a relief to hear.

'I called in on my way over to collect you both and the nurse said that he'd had an uneventful night and was eating breakfast.'

'That's a good sign, right?' Kit knew that one of the difficulties that they'd been having was getting Charlie to eat.

'It's an excellent sign,' Clint replied and Kit expelled a breath. Her next question had her stomach all jittery, but it needed to be asked. She wiped her hands on her jeans and cleared her throat.

'What about Adam? How's he been ... lately?' Her question came as a surprise to both Clint and Pearl. Out of the corner of her eye she caught a glimpse of Pearl's shock. Clint took a second longer to react, probably because he was concentrating on driving.

Clint's gaze momentarily left the road and met Kit's in the rear-view mirror. 'You haven't spoken to him?' There was no mistaking the consternation in his voice.

'No, not since ... well not since he left Australia.' Kit came clean.

'So how ...' Next to her, Pearl seemed to be grappling for words as she processed Kit's deception and for that, Kit was truly sorry.

'Adam has no idea you're here, does he?' Pearl said.

When she'd called Clint, she'd made no mention of Adam, but instead went along with it when Clint mentioned that Adam was in LA, that he was due to return the day before Kit and Pearl arrived. Kit was hoping that she would have heard from him before they landed. Even if Adam was still harbouring ill feelings towards her, Kit thought that explaining she'd found Pearl and they were coming to Hawaii would have warranted a response, but it seemed that wasn't the case. 'I'm not sure,' Kit conceded. 'I mean I did send him a text ...' It sounded lame even as she said it, and by the sighs she heard from both Clint and Pearl, she gathered they thought the same.

'Kids these days,' Clint tutted and shook his head.

'If Adam doesn't know we are here, then why would we come?' There was more than just a mild hint of panic in Pearl's voice.

'Look, I'm sure he does know, it's just that I haven't heard from him, and Clint did mention that he was only getting in last night from LA so maybe he hasn't seen my text yet.'

Or maybe he just doesn't want anything to do with you and not even bothering to reply.

'Still, I just feel that showing up unannounced ... it's not right,' Pearl said.

'I'd suggest calling Adam but we're almost at Charlie's so there's no point in that. Chances are that Adam will be there anyway, he tends to visit after he's been to the office,' Clint explained.

Before Kit could reply, they pulled up in front of a beautiful beach cottage and there was Adam's red Mustang parked right out front. Clint slowed the car and turned into the driveway, and Kit reached out and took Pearl's hand. 'I'm sorry that I wasn't forthcoming about my communication with Adam, so if you don't want to do this we can –'

'No,' Pearl said with conviction. 'I'm here and I'm going to meet my father today.' She turned to face Kit, her eyes filled with unshed tears. 'I came here to deliver a letter to him and no one is going to stop me.'

'All right then.' Kit unclipped her seatbelt. 'What are we waiting for?'

'I'll stay here,' Clint told them. 'When you're ready for the bags, you just let me know.'

Kit wasn't sure if they would get that far. For Pearl's sake, she hoped that Adam wouldn't slam the door in their face.

They climbed the porch stairs together, matching each other's footfalls. Kit was about to lean in and grab Pearl's hand for solidarity, but Pearl beat her to it. Kit was unsure which one of them was shaking more. When they reached the top, they stood in front of the wooden door for what seemed like forever. The only sound Kit could hear was that of her thundering pulse. Behind them the call of a bird cut through the silence, the sound startling Kit.

'Are you going to knock or should I?' It was Pearl who spoke first.

'How about we do it together?'

'Good idea,' Pearl said.

They rapped their knuckles, the sound vibrating against Kit's ears. Then they waited.

Kit heard footsteps. It was hard to tell if they were male or female, but as the door unclicked open, Kit sucked in a breath and held it. The door swung open and there he was. 'Adam.' His name came rushing out along with all the oxygen in her lungs.

'Kit?' He blinked as if it was a complete and utter shock to see her. As if he had no idea she would be here.

Kit was taken aback, his reaction knocking her slightly off kilter. 'I ...' she was lost for words. He looked tired, the tiny creases that lined his eyes more pronounced, he was unshaven and his hair scruffier than when she last saw him, and yet he made her stomach flutter in an instant.

'Hello, I'm Pearl.'

Adam's gaze flickered towards Pearl. 'Pearl,' he said automatically before his eyes widened and the realisation kicked in. 'Pearl,' he repeated then moved aside and motioned them to come in.

'Charlie's upstairs,' he said as they made their way through the house to an open-plan area at the back. The space was larger than it seemed from the outside, and even though it was distinctively Hawaiian, the house had a touch of The Hamptons here and there. Light spilled through the floor-to-ceiling windows and as they moved to the back of the house, the ocean greeted them like the scene on a postcard. 'I can take you up if you want to meet him.'

Pearl's eyes widened, surprised that Adam was being so accommodating, and Kit had to admit, she was too.

'You do want to meet him, don't you?' Adam asked when Pearl remained silent.

'Yes! Yes, of course.'

'All right, then, follow me.' Adam and Pearl disappeared, leaving Kit on her own. She was nervous and excited for Pearl. Hell, Kit was nervous and excited for *herself*. She walked over to the large windows and watched as the waves crashed against the sparkling golden sand. Here she was, back on the other side of the Pacific, where the story had first begun. And that's when it hit her. She had finally done what she had set out to do – she had found Kitty and Charlie's lost child. And while her gran wasn't here to meet her daughter, Charlie was. A fresh breeze fluttered through an open door causing goose bumps to rise on her bare arms. The sweet smell of frangipanis enveloped her and in an instant, Kit felt the energy in the room shift. It was barely there, a whisper of a feeling, but Kit knew she wasn't alone. She wasn't one for ghosts and spirits. She had never felt Jeremy's presence after he passed, and never before today had she considered that her gran was around. But the feeling was overwhelming.

Tears pricked her eyes. 'I did it, Gran,' she said quietly. 'I found your lost Pearl.' It was a bittersweet victory. Kitty had thought her story with Charlie had ended years ago, and in some ways, Kit knew her gran had never been able to move on. How could she? There was a part of her out there – her child. Kit hoped that she had, in some ways, righted the wrong by bringing Charlie and Pearl together.

And now, there was only one thing that needed to be done. Catherine Bennett needed to move on.

Upstairs, a door slammed shut, then the sound of footsteps on stairs, footsteps that were coming closer.

'I can't believe you're here.' Kit turned at the sound of Adam's voice. It was filled with surprise.

'You didn't know we were coming? I sent you a message before we left.'

'I didn't,' he said and Kit believed him. 'I dropped my phone on the way to the airport yesterday. Smashed it to smithereens. Got in pretty late and this morning decided that a new phone could wait until after I checked in on Charlie.'

'Oh. Well that would explain it.'

'You thought I wasn't replying because I didn't want you to come.' It wasn't a question, and yet, Kit felt compelled to answer.

Kit shrugged, suddenly feeling shy. 'Something along those lines.'

'I never doubted that you would find Pearl. It wasn't a matter of if, but when. I would've let it go, but you didn't. You set out to find Pearl and you did. You were right to keep looking. I'm sorry I didn't help more.'

It took Kit a moment to compose her thoughts. She came expecting to be the one doing the apologising. 'It was something that I had to do, for myself.'

'I know. And it was only natural that you came with Pearl.'

'Yes. Yes, it was ... only natural that I came with Pearl. For Charlie, I mean, so she could meet Charlie.' She stumbled through the sentence, her tongue struggling to form words, her brain addled by his intense gaze.

'Is that the only reason you're here? For Pearl and Charlie?' Adam walked over, stopping at arm's length from her, and for the first time since she arrived, Kit could read his expression clearly and it made her legs turn to jelly. The intensity of his stare was disarming. It was as if he were looking into her soul. Outside waves crashed, birds chirped, life was carefree, passing time almost lazily, but inside, at this point, Kit knew that every moment that ticked by was time wasted.

'I'm sorry that I pushed you away that day. I'm sorry that I ran away.' She apologised. She held her breath and waited.

'Is that all you have to say?' A slight tilt of his head, a hint of a smile played on his lips matching the taunt of his words. Adam wasn't letting her off easily.

'You were right. I was living in the past. I was chained to my guilt and it took me a long time to see that what happened to Jeremy wasn't my fault. And now ...'

His eyes softened, his hands coming out of his pockets and lightly skittering down her arms. Barely there, feather-like touches that heightened every nerve in her body.

'And now?' he repeated.

'I'm ready to move on, Adam.'

'Moving on can be hard,' he murmured.

'Someone once told me that it's easier if you don't do it alone.'

'Smart man.' Adam's smile widened.

'I'm not sure if he is, but I'm willing to find out. It's just that ...'
She paused for a moment before saying the words that needed to
be said. 'I don't know how to do this; I mean, we live in different
countries.'

'It took me a long time, but I finally know why Charlie never
wanted to leave this house.'

'Why?' Kit asked, unsure what this had to do with their geo-
graphical problem.

'I thought it had something to do with Grandma Rose, but I
should've known better. This is where Charlie and Kitty spent
their last day together. He may've loved my gran, but it didn't
hold a candle to what he had with Kitty.' Exhaling, he took her
hands in his, the smile gone. 'Kit, I'm not going to stand here and
tell you that I have all the answers, because I don't.'

Disappointment flooded her. 'Oh.'

'But I know this ...' Adam crooked a finger under her chin,
tilting her face upwards, giving her no choice but to look straight
into his eyes. 'I know that if I let you walk away, I will regret it
for the rest of my life. And chances are, you will too. If there is
one thing I have learnt from Charlie, from all this, is that I don't
want to get to the end of my life and wish that I was living back
in the past.'

'I don't want that either. I'm done living in the past.' Kit had
said it before, but never had she meant it more than right here,
right now. 'I want to move on, with you, Adam.'

'I like the sound of that,' Adam whispered moments before his
lips captured hers.

There was something bittersweet in the fact that their story began in the same house where Kitty and Charlie's story had come to an end. But perhaps every new beginning came with something ending.

A little while earlier, in the same house, another new beginning had taken place. A father was meeting his daughter for the very first time.

The knock at the door startled Charlie.

'Pops, are you awake?' Adam gingerly pushed the door open and waited for his reply. It was a fair question. He did a lot of sleeping these days.

'Adam, come in.' Charlie smiled at his grandson and watched as relief washed over his face. Adam was glad he'd recognised him. It indicated that Charlie was himself and for a moment, he let his guilt get the better of him. He hated being a burden on his grandson. With any luck, he wouldn't be a burden for much longer.

'I have someone to see you, Pops. Someone special.' Adam wasn't one to exaggerate, so Charlie sat up straight in his chair and paid keen attention.

'Who is it, son?'

Adam stepped aside and a woman appeared. 'Hello, Charlie,' she said quietly, apprehensively.

Charlie was puzzled. Who was she? By the sound of her voice, she was Australian. Nervously she took a step forward, her mannerisms slightly familiar.

'Do I know you?' Automatically he feared his mind was failing him as it did so many times. Charlie racked his brain trying to place her. There was something about her ... he was sure he knew her ... but how?

'No.' The woman shook her head. 'You know nothing about me, and in fact until a couple of days ago, I knew nothing of you. I mean, I knew that you existed, of course, but not that it was *you*.' She was nervous, rambling, and truth be told, she was talking in riddles. His confusion must've been clear as day.

'My name is Pearl Russ. I've come here to give you this.' She held out an envelope and, tentatively, Charlie took it. It was old and worn and bore his name.

'It's a letter,' she explained. 'One that was written a long time ago, but was never delivered to you.'

Running his fingers over the neat cursive writing, he looked at the woman standing before him. Her eyes were like beautiful sapphires. He knew a girl with the very same eyes once. Of course, it wasn't her, and yet there was something about this woman ...

'Who is it from?' he asked, already suspecting the answer, but he asked all the same.

'The letter is from Kitty, my mother. I'm your daughter, Charlie.'

Charlie felt the breath rush out of his lungs. Suddenly, his eyes blurred. Furiously he blinked until he could see her clearly again. He held his arms out and she fell into them. He held her tight, with no words, only the sound of whispering tears and the beating of hearts.

My daughter.

My leimomi.

My pearl child.

Epilogue

He'd read enough about it when he first got sick to know what was happening to him right now. He'd seen enough to recognise the signs. Terminal lucidity: the unexpected return of mental clarity that occurs in the time preceding one's death, allowing them a few final moments of clarity before passing.

He ran his hands over the envelopes Pearl had delivered to him, and he marvelled at the years and miles they had travelled. From Hawaii to San Francisco to Sydney, and now back to Hawaii. With trembling hands he freed the letter he'd written to Kitty, and for the first time in a long time, he wasn't fearful to let his mind, his body and soul drift back in time. He remembered every word by heart, as if he'd penned it only yesterday ...

My Darling Kitty,

Even though my worst fears have been realized and I regret the irreparable damage it has caused to my friendship with Eddie, I cannot and will not, regret my love for you. How could I? These past few months have been the most memorable of my life.

Kitty, I didn't think I could love you more, but that day at Kailua was heaven on earth. When we made love for the first time, I felt my soul entwine with yours. I will replay that day in my mind till I can have you once again.

The feel of your skin intoxicates me. The touch of your lips to mine does unspeakable things to my body. Just thinking of you makes my heart beat like a drum.

You are my true love. My one and only love. We may have obstacles in our path – I am not sure how our worlds can exist as one. Certainly on the mainland we would not have permission to marry, but here in our beautiful paradise, we could build a life together. I want a life with you, Kitty. A home. A family. I want to grow old together, and I shall love you with every part of me for the rest of my days.

I will never forget that night at The Royal Hawaiian. The first time I saw you, you took my breath away. When I held you in my arms as we danced, I never wanted to let you go. My love for you is like an old Hawaiian proverb – No keia la, no keia po, a mau loa – From this day, from this night, forever more.

No matter what the future may hold, I will find you Kitty. I will make sure we are together. I will not let war, anything or anyone come between us.

With all my love, always,

Charlie

Then he moved to the timeworn envelope bearing his name and as he read a letter written for a much younger man, his heart squeezed.

My Charlie,

My heart is torn in two as I write this. I've never fought with Eddie before, and I never thought there would be anything worth fighting for, but for you, for our love, for us, I will stand my ground.

I will forever cherish our time together, especially our one lovely day. I don't regret a single thing, Charlie. Not a single thing. I love that you were my first. You were so gentle with our lovemaking. Your touch brings my body to life, lights a fire deep within, a fire that will burn bright until the day I die. A fire that burns only for you.

I hate that my father is making me go to Australia. Hate that I will be so far from you. I will wait for you, my love. Wait till the threat of war is over and then we will be together. I dream of the day I will be your wife, to have you as my husband, to bear your children. Nothing would give me greater joy.

I pray that all this talk of war is nonsense and that you will be safe in my arms soon once again. Until that day, know that I love you with all that I am.

Yours in love,

Kitty

Carefully, he folded Kitty's letter and held it to his chest. Emotion engulfed him. How different his life might have been had he received the letter. How different it might have been if Kitty hadn't thought he'd died as Eddie did on that terrible day.

He shouldn't be ungrateful. His Rose had given him much love and joy. She had given him a son, and they had many years of happiness, but the words he wrote to Kitty all those years ago still rang true. It was Kitty who had been his one true love. A rogue tear slid down his cheek, landing on the old envelope, seeping into the C of his name, making the ink bleed into the porous paper.

Charlie was thankful for the past three months and the time he'd had with Adam and Kit, and of course, his Pearl. But now as he saw the tunnel filled with blinding light he knew she would be there, that after all these years, they would finally be together.

'There you are.' Her sparkling eyes as blue as the Pacific, her smile as bright as the sun. 'I've been waiting for you.' She was wearing the summer dress she wore on their day together at Kailua, her long hair spilling down her back like soft waves. 'Come,' Kitty said and held out her hand, and Charlie took it without hesitation. 'I have so much to tell you.'

Reader Letter

Aloha!

There are places in the world that you visit and have an instant connection with. Hawaii has held a special place in my heart for many years, so when I had a seed of an idea for a story that spanned not only multiple generations but islands in the Pacific Ocean it was a no-brainer – I *had* to go to Hawaii, for, you know, research.

I loved writing Kitty and Charlie's story. I loved imagining their lives way back in 1941 when Hawaii and indeed the whole world was a very different place. Without launching into a history lesson, before Pearl Harbor the US was not in World War II. The Japanese invasion changed all that and overnight all but one member of the US Congress passed a motion to join the war.

In the blink of an eye, life changed – not only for those fighting, but also for those left behind. Some of the hardest scenes to write were those around the Pearl Harbor attack and the aftermath. While this book is not based on anyone's actual life, the battle scenes are as close to reality as possible.

I hope you enjoy the journey not only into the past, but also to Hawaii.

Mahalo and Happy Reading,

Emily x

Acknowledgments

It is often stated that writing is a solitary profession. But much like it takes a village to raise a child, it takes a lot of people to bring a story together and give it life.

To the Harlequin/HarperCollins team – thank you! To Sue Brockhoff and Jo Mackay for believing in the story. To Johanna Baker for all your enthusiasm and thoroughness (Goombare is a real word, I promise I didn't make it up!).

Thank you also to my editor Bernadette Foley – your attention to detail and love of the story made for a much better book.

To my agent Selwa Anthony: I'm indebted to you for all your guidance, support and encouragement. Saying thank you doesn't seem enough. You truly are remarkable.

When writing a book that is part set overseas and in the past, there's a lot of research involved. While the internet and books are wonderful, nothing beats a research trip and talking to people face to face.

To Jean Navarra – your insights and understanding of 1940s Honolulu were invaluable. Mahalo for taking the time to meet and for providing the resource information on the US Navy. The way Honolulu is represented in *The Lost Pearl* is more authentic because of you. Any mistakes or misinterpretations of the era and island are mine.

Special thanks goes to Joe at The Royal Hawaiian who saw me loitering and didn't bat an eyelid when I told him I was doing research for a story. Thank you for giving me the book about The Pink Palace's history.

To the Pearl Harbor survivors, you will probably never read this, but thank you for sharing your stories.

To Liz Kemmler, my fellow bubbles and bestie and first reader. I cannot thank you enough for all your support and suggestions. You're a gem!

To Susan Wilson, my wonderful Scottish friend – I love that you read my draft three times. I can't wait to see you in New York and have a cocktail or two.

To my writer's camp crew: Beck Nicholas, Amanda Knight, Lisa Ireland and Rachael Johns. Writing without you all would suck. Thanks for the sprints, for listening to my woes, for just being there!

To my mum, dad, sisters, mother-in-law, father-in-law, sister- and brothers-in-law and all my wonderful nieces and nephews – I love you all and if I happen to use your name in one of my books, don't worry, I won't make you a serial killer.

To my girls – you are my world and I love you so, so much. Keep being the wonderful humans you are. You make me proud. Maybe one day I can make you proud too.

And last but certainly not least, an extra special thanks to Trajan. I know you thought I was trying to swindle a holiday when I said I needed to go to Hawaii for 'research'. Maybe I was, but look how it turned out! It's an actual book! It wasn't all about the mai tais (although they didn't hurt). As promised, the next book isn't set in an exotic location (not really), but stay tuned for 2019 when I tell you about my idea that's set in New York and Las Vegas. I promise I'll let you tag along (if you're good!).

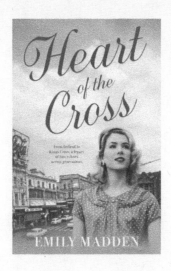

Turn over for a sneak peek.

Heart
of the
Cross

by

EMILY MADDEN

Available September 2018

One

Rosie

Tinahely, Ireland, March 1955

'I need to be at work early tomorrow, Mrs O'Brien is relying on me,' Rosie Hart duly informed her friend Sinead, steadfast in her resolve not to be swayed. But Sinead Colleen Murphy had a way with swaying. Her ma had once commented that Sinead could sell ice to an Eskimo, and Rosie had not a doubt in the world she could.

'But *I'm* relying on you, Rosaleen.' Sinead pouted. 'I may be meeting my future husband after all, and I promise, if it all goes to plan, you're sure to be my head bridesmaid.'

Rosie sighed. She hadn't been able to say no to Sinead since they were six years old when she had convinced Rosie that her mother wouldn't mind if she chopped off her long blonde ringlets. Sinead was wrong; Aoife Hart had minded very much. Rosie had spent the better part of the next six months looking like a mop, until her hair was long enough for her mother to even it out.

'Apparently, he's quite a ladies' man,' Sinead continued, her voice full of awe, eyes full of stars. 'A bad boy,' she added wistfully.

'Well, I want nothing to do with no Englishman, or any other man for that matter. As I said, I have a job to be at tomorrow.' Rosie was aware how prim she sounded, but she meant every word. She'd not long started working with Mrs O'Brien as an apprentice dressmaker, and she was told she showed promise. Rosie had plans. One day she would design her own clothes and she'd have someone else make them, and she'd be damned if she would let some man ruin all that.

'Aww, Rosaleen, just one drink. Come on, do it for me.' Sinead was the only person in the world to call her by her full name.

'One drink,' Rosie said firmly, but knew already her threat was a lost cause.

'Sure, just the one.' Sinead sagely nodded her flame-coloured head, but it was the mischievous twinkle in her hazel eyes that revealed her true intentions.

Rosie sighed once more and Sinead cheered victoriously, looping her arm through Rosie's and leading them into the frostbitten late-March afternoon. The day was waning, night slowly creeping in, and soon darkness would throw its thick velvet cloak over the streets of Tinahely and the faint glow of the streetlights would cast their amber shadows.

Rosie shivered against her thick coat and automatically Sinead pulled her closer, warming her. She may be annoying at times, but Sinead knew Rosie better than anyone. She was more than her best friend, she was the sister Rosie never had, and Rosie knew the feeling was mutual. Sinead was the youngest of seven and the only girl.

Rosie could hear O'Malley's before they rounded the corner, and as the doors of the pub swung open, the acrid scent of tobacco assaulted her. Gasping for air, Rosie placed her hand on her chest and wheezed. Sinead grabbed her free hand and pulled her through the throng of those already drunk and those not far off, and forcefully squeezed them both between two burly men at the bar. The moment Sinead let go of her wrist, Rosie's hands automatically landed on the bar countertop. The pungent smell of stale beer blended with nicotine filled the air, and Rosie screwed up her nose, having a hard time determining which offensive smell was worse.

'We will never get any male attention with you pulling faces like so.' Sinead scowled.

'I don't fancy the perfume of nicotine and whiskey.'

'Come on, it's not that bad. Half the time I know where to find my da by following the smell of his pipe and *uisce beatha*. I'm sure every house in all of Tinahely has the same sorta scent.'

Not every house, Rosie thought. And certainly not her house as it was just Rosie and her ma. Her da had left years before, when Rosie was a small child. She couldn't remember exactly when. Aoife Hart had made a hard-and-fast rule when her husband had walked out on her—never would she utter his name again. To this day, Rosie was sure her mother had abided unwaveringly by the rule.

'Tell ye what, you get another round while I head to the jacks,' boomed the voice of a man to her right, presumably to his mate, before turning towards Rosie and near trampling her. Rosie yelped and the man let out an almighty holler. 'Jaysis, you put the heart crossway in me. I didn't see you there at all!'

'She's as thin as a stick, this one,' Sinead quipped, her voice threaded with more than a modicum of envy.

'Aye, that she is. *Gabh mo leithscéal.*' His apology was heartfelt.

'Come on,' Sinead said as they braved the rambunctious crowd, drinks firmly in hand.

'Where are we going?' Rosie yelled over the cacophony that seemed to be getting louder and louder.

'I spotted Michael in the corner. I'm sure the Englishman's with him.' Sinead threw a smile over her shoulder and Rosie shook her head.

One drink, she promised herself. *One drink then I'm feigning a headache and going home.* It wouldn't be a stretch; she was sure she felt the niggling of one—

Her thoughts were interrupted by a scuffle erupting nearby, followed by a loud crash, and in the next instance Rosie found herself propelled backwards, drink and all. It was sudden, but she still had time enough to realise she was about to hit the ground as her feet quickly moved from underneath her and the liquid from her beer slapped against her face and blurred her vision. She held her breath, bracing for the fall. Except she didn't. The next thing she knew there was a pair of hands grabbing her torso from behind. So shocked was Rosie that she hadn't connected with O'Malley's floor that it took her a good while to process it. Beer trickled down her cheek as her saviour righted her.

'Are you alright, Miss?' he asked, his accent sticking out like a sore thumb.

'I …' She turned to face him, then blinked, seemingly losing the power of speech. He was looking at her from lofty heights, piercing blue eyes marked with concern, or perhaps, it slowly dawned, as a bead of liquid pooled at her lips, that it was because she resembled a wet rat.

Self-consciously, she straightened her back, jutted her chin and ran a hand through her gat-soaked curls. 'I'm fine,' she managed, even though her voice said otherwise. Her saviour's eyes sparked with entertainment and he gave her a doubtful nod but didn't press the matter. Instead, he reached inside the pocket of his trousers and produced a handkerchief. When all Rosie did was stare at his outstretched hand, his lips formed an amused smile and one brow cocked. 'It's clean, if that's what you're thinking.'

English. You're English. That's what I'm thinking.

'Thank you.' She took the hanky from his proffered hand, the brief brush of fingertips setting her face aflame. Even with her eyes cast down, Rosie could tell he was watching her with those blue eyes setting every nerve in her body alight and making her heart thump uncontrollably in her chest.

It's the adrenaline, she told herself. It must be.

'Rosaleen!' Sinead crashed into her like a hurricane. 'Are you alright? You had me worried there for a second.'

'I ...'

'I think we managed to avoid disaster,' the Englishman said smoothly.

'You're a right knight in shining armour,' Sinead added. Something in her friend's voice made Rosie flick her gaze towards her. Sinead's face looked somewhere between annoyance and resentment and it sent a frizzle of alarm through her. Where was this coming from?

'I'm Sinead, by the way, Michael's sister.' Sinead placed herself between Rosie and the Englishman, and not so subtly, her hand extended for him to take and kiss. Rosie watched as he gave a nod, ignoring the implied intention, and took Sinead's hand in a brief, friendly shake.

'Nice to meet you, Sinead. I'm Tom.'

No wonder Sinead had pushed in front of her. This was the man she had dragged Rosie for here tonight.

Tom's gaze skimmed over Sinead's head. 'And who's the damsel I rescued?' There was no mistaking the change in tone— from polite to playful—and there was no doubt of the extremely annoyed look on Sinead's face as she spun around to glare at Rosie.

'That's just Rosaleen,' Sinead said dismissively, flipping her hair over her shoulder. 'She's only staying for one drink.'

Irritation bloomed. After begging Rosie to come with her, she now was eager for her to leave? Was it because Tom was paying her attention? Attention that Sinead was banking on coming her way?

'One drink?' Tom cocked a brow and smiled in a way that released a thousand butterflies in her stomach. 'We'd better make it count.' Tom stepped around Sinead and crooked his arm. Rosie paused, unsure of what she should do. On one hand, Sinead was her friend and Rosie was only here for her, but on the other, this man was quite fetching and seemed more interested in her than Sinead. It was, Rosie had to admit, flattering. And so, she threaded her arm through his, leaving Sinead astounded and fuming.

Her friend sat silently across the table. Part of Rosie was disappointed in herself, but Sinead never lacked male attention. In fact, as soon as they took their seats, scores of admirers began vying to get noticed and her sulkiness eased slightly.

Rosie did only stay for one drink. Tom insisted on walking her home, much to Sinead's obvious chagrin. The conversation was easy and Rosie had to confess she was captivated. When they arrived at her doorstep, he kissed her with passion and abandon. The kiss blew Rosie away, leaving her lips tingling long after it was over, her body yearning for more. She lay awake for hours after, her fingers tracing the outline of her mouth.

The next morning, Mrs O'Brien chided her for being preoccupied. 'Your head's in the clouds, child.'

'I'm sorry, Mrs O'Brien. I didn't sleep well.' It wasn't a lie. Not entirely.

'Just as long as some boy isn't pulling your attention away from your dreams.'

'No. Nothing like that, Mrs O'Brien.' Rosie cast her eyes downwards, the shame of her untruth blooming.

'You've got talent, Rosie Hart. Don't let it go to waste.'

It would take Rosie some years before she would fully understand just how veracious Mrs O'Brien's words were.

LET'S TALK
ABOUT BOOKS!

JOIN THE CONVERSATION

HARLEQUIN
AUSTRALIA

@HARLEQUINAUS

@HARLEQUINAUS